12/11

PIER
52

Don Gregory

Chapter 1

Pike Place Market begins to stir around 6 AM. The flower sellers are just arriving, the sky still dark and the streets still wet from a passing November shower. I stood and watched for a few seconds as they emptied their cars and vans with a smoothness and grace that seemed to be a well choreographed ballet, the explosions of color carried in their arms a stark contrast to the grey pre-dawn light just starting to creep across the Seattle sky.

I suppose it was fortunate that I was already awake when the phone rang about a half hour ago, so I didn't have to wake up out of a sound sleep and drag my ass down here at this ungodly hour. I wake up every morning at 6AM. Unfortunately, it's 6AM east coast time. Don't bother to do the math. That's 3AM west coast time. At first I thought it was some kind of jet lag. But I've been here a year and I still wake up at 3AM. My son's been here for two years and he says eventually you adjust. But he's 30 years younger than I am and I think adjusting is something much better done at a younger age. So far, I see no signs of it happening.

I parked the car down on Pike Place across the street from the Market and away from the flower sellers and the fruit vendors who are also starting to arrive. I figure they have a job to do, too, and they don't need a cop car parked in their way. I could have driven straight to the scene, but I thought that maybe a little walk in the fresh Seattle air might do me some good just before my day is completely ruined with another dead body.

I'm John Elliott and I'm a detective in the Homicide Unit

of the Seattle PD.

I parked near the corner of Pike Place and Stewart and started the climb up the hill toward Post Alley. That's always a challenge. People think of San Francisco as a hilly city, but Seattle can match them breath for wheezing breath. Apparently that's where the body was found (not San Francisco – Post Alley) by a couple of night workers. Post Alley crosses Stewart about half way up the hill between Pike Place and First Avenue.

Post Alley gives this part of downtown a little bit of a European flavor. Hand painted signs hanging from black iron brackets are like an outdoor art gallery. It's a somewhat predictable but pleasant mix of restaurants with outdoor tables, book stores, cheese shops, galleries and...well, you get the idea. Most of the merchants have planters with some combination of flowers and trees which still look pretty lush even though it's November. One of the perks of the Seattle climate. Every time it drizzles for three weeks in a row I have to keep saying to myself: "Yeah, but it sure is green!"

During the daytime, delivery trucks can drive through but otherwise it's pretty much pedestrian traffic only. Oh, and early morning trash trucks.

Somebody on one of those trucks discovered the body about 6:00 AM just as I was finishing my mid-morning snack.

I turned into the Alley and made my way toward a small group of uniforms and suits about a hundred yards away standing in the headlights of two cars, one Seattle PD patrol car with lights flashing and one Ford Crown Vic. I always wonder if we think we're fooling anybody with these unmarked Fords. I mean, does anything scream unmarked police car like a dark blue Crown Vic without a speck of chrome and no wheel covers? You'd think somebody would try an Outback once in a while, especially here in Seattle.

As I walked up to the group I could see a foot between two small, blue dumpsters in an alcove. The foot was wearing some kind of black shiny patent leather shoe with a high heel, a fishnet stocking and an ankle bracelet - the sparkly kind not the home confinement kind.

"Morning, guys. You'd think they'd at least wait until daylight before they start phoning in the bodies."

"Hey, John. You'd think you'd at least wait until daylight before you start being cynical."

That's Al (short for Alfonso) Russo. Detective Al Russo. Capital 'D'. Al and I have worked a few cases together and seem to get along reasonably well. He's hard working and clever and, more importantly, has lived in Seattle most of his life and has, as they say, "connections." More importantly, he doesn't take anything I say personally. Al is more of an east coast kind of cop. I don't know exactly what that means but, as Justice Potter Stewart said about pornography, I know it when I see it.

They obviously hadn't been there long. The CSI guys were just arriving from the opposite side of the alley along with the guys from the Medical Examiner's office with the body bag and the gurney.

"What have we got, Russo?"

"911 call about 5:30AM saying there was a body here in the Alley between Stewart and Virginia. 911 Operator says 'stay where you are, we'll send a patrol car'. Officers Russell and Lynch, these two gentlemen right here, were in the area and showed up about 3 minutes after the call came in. Appears to be a young woman maybe about 25 or 30 years old dressed kind of like one of those French dance hall girls you see in the movies."

"Hooker of some kind?"

"I don't know. This is a strange place for a hooker."

"What do you guys know?"

"Not much, Sergeant." Lynch spoke up first. I knew it was Lynch because he was wearing his name sewn to his chest. Pretty good detective work, huh? Well, actually, sewn to his shirt not his actual chest. At least that I knew of. "When we got here, the trash truck was parked right here, motor running, two guys standing next to the truck on the side away from the dumpsters. They pointed out the body to us, we got their IDs, but other than that we didn't really question them."

Camera flashes were starting to go off and latex gloves were being snapped on. I turned to Lynch and Russell. "Who's the Watch Commander tonight?"

"That would be Lieutenant Gonzales," replied Russell. "He's on his way here."

"Ok. Until he gets here, I want one of you at each end of the Alley. Nobody in or out without my say-so until Lieutenant Gonzales arrives. Got it?"

"Got it, Sergeant."

I turned back and tried to get a better look at the little I could see. At this point I couldn't really tell whether or not we had a homicide or maybe just a drug OD and this poor unfortunate woman just happened to fall between two dumpsters. For the time being, we'd treat this like a crime scene and keep movement in and around the body to an absolute minimum until we knew for sure one way or the other.

The night shift CSI guys were actually a guy and a woman. The guy I didn't really know. I've seen him around but never worked with him on a case. His name is Craig-something. I don't think I ever really knew his last name. Young guy, about 30.

The woman, I really didn't know either, although I've slept with her a dozen or so times. Marianne Robinson. She was one of the first people I met when I came to Seattle a year ago. I was introduced to her during the obligatory walk-through of the Department on my first day. You know: "John, this is so-and-so. John's here from the east coast to straighten us all out. Ha, ha." I don't remember anybody from that first day. Except for Marianne.

I don't know if it's ever happened to you. I've always assumed it happens to everybody now and again, but maybe not. You see somebody for the first time and they look at you and there's an immediate chemistry or connection or whatever you choose to call it. That's the way it was with Marianne, at least for me and, I think, for her, too. So I said something dumb or awkward like "Wow, what a great set of hooters!" (No, I didn't really say that.) I said something more like: "How can you stand these guys? I've only been here 45 minutes and I can't stand them already." And she said: "Nice to meet you, too."

Marianne, it turns out, got a degree in Criminal Justice from Salve Regina University in Newport, Rhode Island, which was about 20 minutes and two bridges away from my police chief's job. So, over the next few weeks, we chatted about the 5th ward and the Brick Alley Pub and the Jazz Festival out at Fort Adams until I finally got up my nerve to ask her out for coffee. See, in most places you'd ask a woman out for a drink to kind of test the waters. But in Seattle, the entire city ebbs and flows to coffee cups being filled then drunk then filled again. For some reason, going for coffee with someone in Seattle seems a lot less intimidating than going out for a drink.

In any event, she was so unintimidated by me that at some point I asked her out to dinner and she said 'Yes'. One of the things I liked about Marianne was I found her so easy to talk to about almost anything. I tend to have a lot of opinions about a lot of things, especially politics, even if I don't know crap about what I'm talking about. It's probably one of the things that made me a good lawyer. But she would listen attentively to my wild theories about just about anything, then proceed to take me apart, piece by piece with the proverbial red velvet knife. For some reason it would make me positively horny.

But as much time as we spent together, both dressed and undressed, I began to notice it was always about me or about stuff. We could talk or argue for hours about anything I could bring up, but it was never about her, never personal. I mean, I know I have a huge ego, but I truly was interested in getting to know her a little more intimately. Outside of the statistical stuff (she's 38 years old, born in some little town in New Jersey, the Salve Regina thing), I really didn't know much about her. She never talked about her family. Anytime I would ask a direct question (lawyer, cop, remember?), she would deflect it with some kind of off-handed comment or sarcastic remark but not really answer the question. Even though I used to be an FBI agent, even I can recognize when someone's being evasive.

At first I thought, well, give her a chance to get to know you a little. But we got past the 'getting to know you' stage a while ago. Sometimes I think she must be in the Witness Protection Program. I know, or think I know, how she feels about things but not how she feels about herself or stuff that really matters. Or about me.

Anyway, it's kind of put a damper on things for me and I find myself spending less and less time with her. Too bad, because I really like her and I think she really likes me. But my first marriage was characterized, in the words of those 60's poets and philosophers, Simon and Garfunkle, by dangling conversations and superficial sighs, and I am determined never to go back to that.

So, anyway, here we are at O-dark-30, as my son would say, doing our jobs.

Lieutenant Gonzales arrived with 3 or 4 uniforms.

"Morning, Sergeant."

"Morning, Mike. I don't know exactly what we've got yet, so if you could seal off this section of the alley for the time being, I'd appreciate it. Anybody says they have to get in here except for our guys, the answer is 'no' until further notice. And I think we should cordon off the immediate area around these dumpsters. People who live upstairs in these buildings are gonna wake up pretty soon and start wondering why they're suddenly getting so much protection from the Seattle PD."

I walked over to Marianne and Craig. "Morning, kids."

"Good morning, John," answered Marianne. "Have you met Chris?"

Ah, shit. Well, I was close.

"This is Chris Hopkins. Chris, this is John Elliott."

"Hi, Chris. I've seen you around. Nice to finally meet you. Anything yet?"

"We haven't moved anything yet," said Marianne, "but it appears you probably have a homicide. The body is face down with some pretty serious damage to the back of the head. I haven't seen the front yet but I'd be willing to bet there's a hole in it, probably around the forehead."

"How long before we get a good look?"

"We've photographed just about everything we can without moving anything. We'll be done with a physical scan of the immediate area in about 20 minutes. Then we can move those dumpsters. Maybe you could get a couple of the uniformed guys to begin a search of the area for anything that looks like a weapon, probably a gun. The damage to the back of the head is outward so it's probably not some type of brute force instrument like a pipe or a baseball bat."

"Ok, I'll see if I can get Gonzales working on it. Let me know as soon as we can get in close."

I had Gonzales and his guys start an area search for anything that either didn't look right, like a weapon or something that could have been used as a weapon. I also had them start knocking on doors and ringing door buzzers to start questioning anyone who might have seen or heard anything. By now there were uniforms everywhere and lights were starting to come on in some of the upstairs apartments.

True to her word, in about 20 minutes Marianne came over to me and said we could
start to move things, including the body. "Looks like a single gun shot to the head. Entered through the front. The damage in the back was an exit wound. You're definitely not looking for a blunt instrument."

The first thing I wanted to do was roll the dumpsters out to get a better look at the body and to have the guys go through the dumpster in case anything significant, like a gun covered with fingerprints, got thrown in there, although I wasn't really expecting anything that simple.

A couple of Gonzales's men rolled out the dumpsters and started looking through them.
And I thought my job was revolting. I'm sure they never told them at the Police Academy that there'd be days like this.

With a better look at the poor, unfortunate corpse, I could see she was probably in her mid to late 20's, dark brown curly hair cut short and had been quire pretty before somebody spoiled it with a single shot. She was wearing a considerable amount of make-up with some

especially red lipstick and heavy eye make-up, although not in a cheap
street walker kind of way, but more in a theatrical kind of way. Don't ask me how I know the difference. I don't need to get that close to my feminine side at 7:00AM.

Anyway, the make-up and the clothing seemed to say 'theater' more than 'hooker'.

Over her shoulder was a pocketbook, a fairly large leather bag and not at all in keeping with the rest of the outfit. I turned and asked Marianne if anyone had gone through the bag and she said "no," which was a bit curious since the contents were half in and half out of the bag. Even though the strap was still over her shoulder, it was sitting upright on the pavement. The stuff on the ground didn't really look like it had fallen out, more like it had been pulled out then dropped. Somebody probably looking for money. It's amazing how little some of these druggies will shoot you for.

"John," she said. "If you're going to touch anything, don't forget the gloves. We're not done yet."

"Right. I knew that." Damn, I hate it when she does that. She knows sometimes I get so focused on something I tend to forget the simplest things.

There was nothing in sight that looked like a wallet or something with an ID. That was probably long gone. I opened the top of the pocketbook a little wider and looked for something that might have an ID in it. I don't know why, but I hate poking around in women's purses. It makes me feel like a Peeping Tom. You would think a detective wouldn't think twice about searching for stuff and normally I don't. But pocketbooks? Whole different story. I mean have you ever had a woman say to you: "John, would you look for my glasses? I think they're in my bag." I don't know about you, but I always just pick up the whole bag and say: "Here, you look for them." I almost think I would have rather been searching the dumpsters.

Anyway, after looking through the contents of the bag trying not to look, I found an alligator purse with a leather strap and a snap holding it shut, the kind women carry their money and their credit cards in. I opened it up and found everything I would expect to find, including cash and credit cards. So much for robbery as a motive. Nothing is ever simple.

 I found a Washington State driver's license. The picture was not very flattering (surprise, surprise) but it was definitely our victim. The license identified her as Anna Noble, age 32. If the address was current, she lived on 8th Avenue NE up in the Northgate section of the city.

I also found something I wasn't expecting to find. A U.S. government issued ID card.
Seems Ms. Noble was an employee of the U.S. Justice Department.

Chapter 2

The crime scene investigation would probably take up
the better part of the morning
and was in good hands, so I decided to take a ride and
check out the Northgate address.

The Northgate address was a large, fairly anonymous
looking apartment building about a block in from the
commercial strip of drug stores, dry cleaners, restaurants
and a myriad of other establishments that is Northgate
Way. Three stories tall with a plain cement exterior
painted a kind of light green. When I was a kid, they
used to paint school rooms that color. I don't think they
do any more – I think the Supreme Court ruled it was
cruel and unusual punishment and was having a
negative effect on the number of interior decorators our
public schools were turning out.

The main entrance wasn't all that obvious but after a bit
of investigative work I found an entrance with an outer
door that was open, a small lobby with mailboxes,
buzzers and a plastic tree, and a fairly sturdy looking
inner door that was locked. I checked the buzzers and
found one that said "NOBLE – CAREY" with the number
312 next to it. I told you I was good at this stuff.

I pushed the button and after the second push a male
voice said: "Yeah?"

I took a chance and said "Mr. Carey?"

After a pause the voice said "Who is this?"

"John Elliott, Seattle Police. May I come in?"

Another pause. But not very long. The door buzzed and I made my way inside. The inner lobby was small and plain, well-lit with a small set of elevator doors just to my right as I came in the door. There was a slight smell of Lysol.

I got off at the third floor and headed down the carpeted hallway to 312. Before I could knock, the door opened and a young, white male about 30, with long brown hair (not 60's long, but long, nonetheless) and wearing khaki colored cargo pants and a University of Washington sweatshirt said: "This isn't good is it?"

I said: "May I come in?"

"Oh. Yeah, sure."

I stepped inside. The apartment was I want to say cluttered, but not really cluttered in a disorderly sense. There was a lot of – stuff. The more I looked around, the more I became aware that most of the things were purposely placed, but there was a lot of it.
The walls were covered with posters – some framed, some unframed. They all had a theatrical theme, mostly circuses and carnivals and it appeared most of the "stuff" was theatrical as well. Costumes, parts of costumes, hats. And color. Color everywhere.
Even the furniture. Nothing matched but there was a lot gold fringe. And photographs.
A lot of photographs. Mostly snapshot-looking pictures of people in costumes. Even the lap-top over in the corner on a small desk had circus picture as a screen saver.

"I'm Sergeant John Elliott", I said.

"This is about Anna, isn't it?" he said, with a note of foreboding in his voice.

"Yes, I'm afraid it is. Anna Noble was found dead this morning downtown."

"Oh, shit," he said quietly, sat down heavily on the couch and put his head down on his knees. I still wasn't sure who he was or what his relationship was to Anna Noble but decided to go slowly and just wait a little. Sometimes you can learn more by just keeping your mouth shut and not feeling like you have to fill every silence. My sense was this was genuine shock and the beginning of grief, but I always adopt a wait and see attitude, especially when there's a murder involved.

"What happened?" As he looked up I could see tears glistening in his eyes and the color
seemed to have drained from his face. He looked like he had suddenly gotten very old.

"We're still investigating but she was shot. Her body was found by some early morning workers in Post Alley."

"Oh, shit," he said again, quietly. He was staring at the floor.

"I'd like to ask you a couple of questions, if you don't mind."

No response, but I decided to go ahead anyway.

"Are you Mr. Carey?"

He raised his head slowly and nodded.

"What's your first name?"

"Anthony."

"What was your relationship to Anna Noble?"

"We've been living together for about a year and a half. I met her at a gym near here and we started going out together. We got along really well and decided to move in together."

"When was the last time you saw her?"

"Last night around dinnertime. She left for work around 6:30. I got in around 5:00 last night and made dinner for both of us. I usually make dinner on the nights Anna goes out to work."

"Did Anna work nights a lot?"

"Every Friday, Saturday and Sunday."

Ok, now I was getting a little confused. I know the Feds work strange hours sometimes, but every Friday, Saturday and Sunday night? I decided to play dumb, which wasn't very hard at this point.

"What kind of work did she do?"

"She works in a restaurant downtown."

"As a waitress?"

"No. As a performer."

"What kind of performer?"

"Anna's a gymnast. Well, kind of a gymnast. I guess more of an aerialist. This restaurant, the one she works at, has a circus theme and Anna does a routine that involves a trapeze. Anna really loves the circus. All this stuff is hers. She's been collecting it since way before I met her. I think if she thought she could have made any money at it, she would have tried to join a real circus. You know, like a Cirque d'Soleil kind of thing."

"And when she left here last night, that's where she was headed? To the restaurant?"

"Yeah. Place called 'The Center Ring'. It's actually on Post Alley." Ok, that explains that.

"How did she get to and from the restaurant?"

"She usually took the bus. The last bus out here from the city leaves 3rd Avenue around 1:00 and she'd usually get home between 1:30 and 2:00."

"She call you anytime last night from the restaurant?"

"No. Anna was pretty independent. She didn't check-in or anything like that. She came and went pretty much on her own. I mean I got to know her general schedule, but she was never, like, you know, 'I'll be home at such-and-such a time'."

"But you were worried about her last night."

"Yeah. Well actually this morning. It's just not like her to not come home at all. Early this morning I started calling around to some of her friends to see if they had seen her or talked to her. Nobody had. That's when I started to get worried."

"She have any family you know of?"

"Her parents live over on Bainbridge Island and she has a sister on the east coast. Somewhere near DC, I think. Other than that, I don't know of anyone."

"We'll need to contact her family. Do you have a name or a phone number for her parents?"

"Yeah, around here somewhere. Her father is Ed Noble, some kind of builder or developer I think. I don't know that much about him. Anna never said much, never saw them very much. He's the one who got her her day job."

"What exactly was her day job?"

"She worked for the Justice Department. Anna had a law degree from U Dub. I think that was more to please her father than anything else. She always had this circus thing which, as far as I could tell, didn't go over real big with her parents. But at least she made some money with the law thing."

"Any idea what she did for them?"

"None. I know it had something to do with Homeland Security or something like that, but that was something else she didn't talk much about and, frankly, I wasn't really all that interested in it. Kind of a joke as far as I'm concerned. Not her, but the whole Homeland Security thing." He put his head back down and his body began to shake almost imperceptibly. "What can I do, Sergeant? I mean, we're not married or anything, but we're pretty close."

"We've got to notify the family," I said. "It's really more up to them than it is to me. Maybe you might want to wait until we've talked to them then give them a call. Listen, just one or two more questions. Do you have any idea who might have done this or why?"

"My God! No! I mean, I was just assuming this was some kind of street crime or something. Are you telling me it's not?"

"No, I'm not telling you anything of the sort. It's just at this early stage we don't rule out anything or anybody.

"One more question: In hind sight, did Anna ever mention anything that, looking back, would indicate she had been threatened or felt threatened in any way?"

"No," he said, slowly shaking his head. "I can't think of anything."

"Well, as they say on TV, here's my card. If you think of anything no matter how insignificant you think it might be, will you call me?"

"Yeah. Sure."

As I was getting up to leave I noticed his eyes were still glistening. I don't think he was faking it.

Then again, I never thought my first wife was faking it either.

Chapter 3

The dashboard clock said it was just a little after 9:00 o'clock. There was cold November drizzle in the air. I remember when I lived in New England they always used to say: "Don't like the weather? Wait a minute." But, man, is that really true out here. It can be 47 degrees and raining and ten minutes later the sky can be sapphire blue with big white puffy clouds and 60 degrees. I couldn't wait for the sapphire blue part.

I suppose the next step would be to try to locate the Noble family and break the bad news to them. I hate this part of the job. I called the office and asked them to get me an address for an Ed or Edgar or Edward or E. Noble on Bainbridge Island and headed back downtown to the ferry terminal at Pier 52 to catch the ferry over to Bainbridge.

Seattle is a special place, almost impossible to define. But one of the things I (and a lot of other people, I guess) like about the whole Seattle experience is the ferry system. It makes things faster and slower at the same time. Faster in the sense that if you want to do anything on the west side of the Sound, you can either drive south on the 5 through Tacoma and that whole mess then north again up 16, which, depending on the time of day, which could be anywhere from, oh, I don't know, say, 6 AM to midnight, will take hours, or you can take one of a couple of different ferries from downtown to Bainbridge Island or Bremerton which will probably take you no more than 35 or 40 minutes.

But slower in the sense that for 35 or 40 minutes of your day, there is nothing to do but sit or stand quietly and feel the gentle rocking of the boat and the almost imperceptible vibration of the engines.

I have to say I am not a big believer in government running anything. I have seen very few things the government can't find a way to screw up. But this Seattle ferry system is an exception. I mean, I don't know what it costs the taxpayers, but these suckers run on time, they get the cars and people on and off like you wouldn't believe. And the tickets are relatively cheap. Cheap and quiet. An unbeatable combination in ferries and women.

While I was waiting in line watching the bomb-sniffing dogs go up and down the lines of cars, my cell phone rang. I love caller ID. I never had it on my phone until I got the cell phone. Man, am I picky about who I talk to now. In this case it was my son.

"Hey, Ben, what's up?"

"Hi, Dad. Not much. Just wondering if we're still going hiking today."

"Ah, crap. I forgot all about that. I'm on a new case. We had a homicide in Post Alley last night and I'm just starting to make the rounds. In fact, I'm sitting in line down at the pier waiting to get on the ferry over to Bainbridge."

"No big deal."

"Look, I need to stay on top of this thing. You be around this week?"

"I might have to go down to Portland for a couple of days. I won't know until Monday."

"Ok. Well, if this thing opens up a little bit, I'll give you a call. See if we can do something."

"Sure, that's fine. Or just come over for dinner. Just call up and say you're coming.
No big deal. Besides, I want to get your take on this election. I don't know if Obama can take the country in the right direction or not. I mean, I'm thinking about voting for him because I can't stand the thought of another four years of the crap we've been through, but I'm not 100 per cent sold either."

"Ok. Sounds good. Maybe tonight if you guys are going to be around.. I'll give you a call."

Ok, Dad. I'll talk to you later. I love you."

"Yeah, I love you too, Ben."

As I hit the "End" button, the cars started to move. In about 5 minutes flat, all the cars and trucks were on board in a double row, two by two, like some kind of mechanical Noah's Ark, all the walking passengers were loaded on and the ferry slipped easily away from the pier. You know, you watch these ferries gliding over Puget Sound and you don't realize how big the system is. I read an article in the PI recently that the Washington State Ferry system moves 24,000,000 people and 11,000,000 cars every year. No wonder it's near the top of everyone's list of potential terrorist targets.

I made my way up from the car deck to the top deck,

stepped outside and walked over to the rail.

On each side of the ferry there was a small Coast Guard boat buzzing along, racing along side, making wide circles then coming back but never getting very far from the side of the ferry, looking very much like big life rafts with an ugly little wheelhouse about two thirds of the way back. Except these life rafts had 50mm cannons, one in the bow and one in the stern.

And fast. Every so often, they'd open it up and, man, do they fly. Reminded me of Marianne's Mini. Kind of pudgy and not looking like much of anything, but knock-you-back-in-your-seat fast and corner like it was on rails. Of course, Marianne's Mini doesn't have a 50mm cannon.

Anyway, I guess these little boats are all part of the phony Homeland Security scam. Or maybe not so phony, I don't know. I mean, don't get me wrong, the World Trade Center disaster was just that: a disaster. But isn't the point of terrorism to terrorize people. So if we allow ourselves to be terrorized by one incident, no matter how horrible, don't the terrorists win?

After about a quarter of a mile of making donuts in the water (you hot rod fans will know what I'm talking about), the annoying little mosquitoes peeled off and headed back toward the pier. I guess terrorists only have boats that go a quarter of a mile off-shore, so apparently we were safe for now.

Thirty minutes of peace and quiet later, the ferry bumped gently against the pier on Bainbridge and the cars and passengers began an urgent but orderly departure. I had shut my phone off for the trip across and when I turned it back on, there was a voicemail message from the office with the address of a James Edward Noble. I cranked it into my Garmin (best invention ever for a guy who works in a big city but really hasn't learned his way around yet), turned. Left. In. 50. Feet. and headed, apparently, toward the west side of the island. (Note to the Garmin people: Men hate taking directions from women. I said it was a great invention, I didn't say it wasn't annoying.)

After about 20 minutes I found myself on a heavily wooded rural road. I followed the purple line on the Garmin until Miss Know-It-All informed me I had reached my destination. The Noble house was a kind of low and rambling, unprepossessing log-style building nestled into a gently sloping hillside and looking out over Port Orchard Sound. Pulling into the driveway, the house didn't look all that big, but it soon became obvious that was an optical illusion mostly created by the gigantic evergreens dotting the grounds which made the house look small by comparison. The design was classic northwest, with a honey-brown log exterior and the green tin roof. There were a couple of smaller outbuildings partially hidden by the surrounding woods and three cars parked in the gravel circular drive – a black Land Rover, an even blacker Mercedes and a Subaru Outback. The Subaru and the Land Rover both had roof racks. The Mercedes didn't.

I rang the bell and waited.

I don't like peeking through windows, but there were large clear glass panels on either side of the door and there wasn't much else to look at. I mean I wasn't exactly peeking. If you don't want me looking into your house, don't put windows next to the front door.

23

Eventually, a smallish man with slightly disheveled but neatly cut gray hair came down the hallway toward the door. I watched him smooth his hair just before he opened the door and it was pretty obvious I had woken him up. He opened the door about three feet but kept one hand on it. Clearly he had no idea his day and his life were about to change.

"Hi. Can I help you?" he said, in a friendly but controlled way.

"I'm sorry to disturb you. I'm looking for Ed Noble," I said.

"I'm Ed Noble. What can I do for you?" he answered, with more of a note of curiosity in his voice than anything else.

"I'm Sergeant John Elliott of the Seattle Police Department. May I come in?"

"Sure, Sergeant."

He stepped aside, I stepped inside about three steps and turned back towards him. He closed the door and turned to face me. He was about 5'8" or 5"9" with an athletic build. Looked like a runner.

"Do you have daughter named Anna?"

"Yes, I do. What is this about Sergeant? Is Anna in some kind of trouble?"

"Can we go in and sit down?"

"Oh, sure." He stepped past me and I followed him down a hallway with shiny dark wood floors to a large, high ceilinged room with a large field stone fireplace and a magnificent view out of floor to ceiling windows of Port Orchard Sound and the Olympic Mountains on the horizon just over the tree tops on the opposite shore. I don't know much about real estate, but I know well-off when I see it and the Nobles were definitely well-off.

On the mantel over the fireplace were a number of framed photographs, mostly of smiling family-looking folks including, I noticed, Anna Noble. There were also a couple of photos of Ed Noble standing and smiling with people I recognized. In one he was standing with our illustrious Democratic Senator from the great State of Washington. In the other he was standing with the previous occupant of the Oval Office and a gentleman I recognized as being the Secretary of Something-or-Other that I couldn't quite remember from that Administration. Interestingly, the photo appeared to have been taken in the room in which I was standing.

We sat down opposite each other on matching couches across a polished coffee table that looked like a slice out of a giant redwood.

There's never an easy way to say this: "I'm sorry to have to tell you Anna died last night, Mr. Noble."

"Oh, no...," he whispered. "That can't be...are you sure?"

"Yes, sir. We're pretty sure."

"Oh, no," he said again to no one in particular. "What happened?" It was barely a whisper.

"She was found this morning in Post Alley downtown, apparently near the restaurant where she worked."

"Oh, my poor baby," he said, with tears starting to fill his eyes and his voice. "Do you have any idea how this happened?"

Like I said, there's never an easy way to do this. "She had been shot."

Ed Noble was clearly a man used to being in control and you could see him trying to make some sense out of all of this in an effort to gain some kind of control, without a lot of success.

"But why?" he asked.

What he was asking without asking was whether or not she had been mugged, robbed, beaten or, yes, raped, or any of the other horrible things that were going through his mind
making him think his head was going to explode.

"We don't know for sure yet, but robbery does not appear to have been a motive and, although we're going to wait for the Medical Examiner's report, there were no apparent signs of any kind of beating or any other kind of assault."

He just nodded silently. "What happens now, Sergeant?"

"Well, we are continuing to investigate the crime scene, we will be talking to the people who knew Anna trying to determine a motive and possible suspects, if there are any, and at some point, I suppose, we'll need you or some family member to make a positive identification."

"So you don't have any idea why this happened."

"No, sir, we don't. I'd like to talk to you more about Anna and anything that may have been going on in her life that might be helpful. I know this is a terrible shock to you but I have to ask you if you a couple of questions. If this is not the time, please say so."

"No, Sergeant, I'll try my best."

"When was the last time you saw her?"

"About a week ago. I had lunch with her in the city."

"Have you spoken to her since then?"

"Just once. She called Thursday night. Said she might be going to DC sometime soon. Asked me how she could get in touch with a friend of mine there. Guy by the name of Jeff Feinberg."

"She say why?"

"Why what? Why she was going to DC or why she wanted to get in touch with Jeff?"

"Either. Both."

"No. No, she didn't. I've learned not to ask. If Anna wants you to know something or share something with you, she let's you know. Although I did wonder about it. I've known Jeff for a number of years. He's been here to the house a couple of times. But he's not exactly an old friend of the family. I didn't think Anna knew him well enough to be looking him up on a trip to Washington."

"Did you tell her how to get in touch with him?"

"To tell you the truth, Sergeant, I don't have any current information on Jeff."

"I understand she may have worked for the FBI."

"Yes. Yes, she did. I spoke to a friend and he found a position for her in the Seattle office."

"Do you know what she did for them?" I asked.

"No," he said, "not really." And I saw his eyes shift down and to the left as he said it. I'm told that's a sign someone is not telling you the whole truth. But, then, why would he lie to me? His daughter's just been found dead in an alley and I'm here trying to put the pieces together and figure out why, so why would he lie to me?

"Did you also know she worked part-time in a restaurant in the city called 'The Center Ring?'"

"Yes, Sergeant, I'm afraid I did."

"You're 'afraid' you did? Why 'afraid', Mr. Noble?"

"It's just that I don't like this whole trapeze thing – you know what she does there, don't you?"

"Yes, I do." He kept talking about her in the present tense, not unusual when somebody close to you has just died. The brain hasn't had time to process the fact they're no longer living.

"That and this whole fixation she has with circuses. I just don't consider it any kind of life for people with Anna's upbringing. I think she's capable of more than just swinging over people's heads."

"Do you know of anything or anybody she knew either at the restaurant or any place else that might have led to this?"

"God only knows who she was hanging around with, Sergeant. That was part of my worry. I don't think circus people are the most upstanding citizens in the world."

"Mr. Noble, I've taken enough of your time. By the way, is there a Mrs. Noble?"

"Yes, there is. She's sleeping right now. We had a late night last night." He paused. "I don't know how I'm going to tell her this."

I stood up to leave. "Mr. Noble, I'm truly sorry about this."

"Thank you, Sergeant," he said, staring off into space. After about three heartbeats that seemed like an eternity he stood up and looked me in the eye, beginning to regain his composure. "Look, Sergeant, I'm a man with a few friends. I don't mean to interfere with your job, but if you need anything, and I mean anything, I want you to call me. I want to know who did this to my Anna and why. I have to say this is not making a lot of sense to me."

"I appreciate that Mr. Noble. Look, you'll probably be hearing from the Medical Examiner's office about Anna. They have a procedure they have to go through in situations like this. But if you think of anything she might have said to either you or Mrs. Noble that may not have seemed like anything at the time, I wonder if you would call me? Here's my card. Its got my contact information including my cell phone. Call me any time."

Just then, an older woman, probably in her 50's appeared from down a hallway in a bathrobe, her dark hair slightly mussed, with sleepy eyes. She was Anna Noble 25 years from now. Except there wouldn't be an Anna Noble 25 years from now.

"Ed?" she said. "I heard voices. What's going on?"

I introduced myself to Mrs. Noble, thanked Ed Noble, and told him I'd let myself out as he led his wife over to the couch. As much as I didn't like what I had to do, I didn't envy Ed Noble right about now. No parent should ever have to go through this.

As I got into the car and turned my cell phone back on, it made that stupid little chiming sound that tells you you have a voicemail message. It was Al Russo.

"John, it's Al. Just wanted to bring you up to date. Didn't get much more out of the trash guys but we did find three video surveillance cameras in the alley near the scene. We're working on trying to locate who owns them to see if they tell us anything. Oh, and the CSI people may have found the slug that killed her. Call me."

Time to head back to the city.

Chapter 4

While I was waiting for the cars to start moving off the ferry back in Seattle, I called Al.

"What's going on, Al?"

"Where've you been?"

I decided to treat that as a rhetorical question and just move on.

"Any luck on those video cams?"

"Maybe. It's tough trying to track down easy things, like who owns a building, on a Saturday. Nothing yet but we should have something soon."

The cars started to move. When they do, you'd better be ready.

"Listen Al, I'm just getting off the ferry. I'll be at the office in about 5 minutes."

"Oh, John, speaking of the ferry – we got an email from the JTTF earlier this morning. The Coast Guard is raising the threat level for the ferry system from MARSEC 1 to MARSEC 2 but it's not being released to the public for now, just law enforcement. I don't know what it's all about – probably nothing, as usual - just a bunch of Feds trying to justify their jobs."

Ah, yes. The Joint Terrorism Task Force. You want to screw something up really good, set up a committee with a bunch of people from every conceivable state and federal agency and call it a Task Force. Sounds more impressive than a committee. We have somebody on that, I think more of a courtesy than anything else. Talk about rearranging the deck chairs on the Titanic. I've seen this thing from both sides, first with the FBI and now with the Seattle PD and if 9/11 was any indication, we just better be ready to pick up the pieces. Us and the fire department. They can have all the task forces in the world, but when the balloon goes up, it's the cops and the firemen that are going to do the heavy lifting. My opinion? (Yeah, I know: 'John, you have an opinion? Alert the media.') Anyway, I think the whole terrorism thing is meant to scare the crap out of us. Not only by the terrorists but by our own government. I think it's like the war on drugs. They don't want to win it, they want to keep on fighting it. Too many jobs at stake. After all, nobody makes any money if we win. Not to mention how the government can keep taking away our rights as long as they can convince us it's making us safer. I can see how easy it would be to become one of those government conspiracy freaks. Hope nobody heard me think that.

It suddenly dawned on me Al was still talking.

"Anyway, the CSIs are still on the scene. The body's been taken to the morgue but they're trying to pin down all the physical evidence. I talked to Marianne about fifteen minutes ago. She thinks they have another hour or so to go."

"Ok, Al. I'm just pulling off the pier."

A few minute later, I pulled into the garage behind headquarters and took the ramp up to the seventh floor. There was an empty spot right next to the door and I took it. The door from the parking deck on seven leads right into Violent Crimes and the Homicide Unit. I went into my office, took off my coat and threw it across the back of the chair next to my desk and sat down to check my little pink phone message slips.

Nothing much. Call from my ex-wife. I must have missed some kind of payment. Call from some real estate agent down in Florida who I made the mistake of giving my real phone number to. (I told you the beach bum thing was looking better and better.) Call from my insurance agent. I definitely missed some kind of payment. And a call from a Danielle Noble. Says she's Anna Noble's sister and left a phone number with a 202 area code. Better return that one.

I picked up the phone and punched in the number Danielle Noble had left. Two rings.

"Hello?"

"Danielle Noble, please."

"This is Danielle. Is this Sergeant Elliott?"

"Yes, it is. I'm sorry about your sister."

"Thank you, Sergeant. And thanks for calling back so quickly. My father called me just after you left his house this morning. I hope you don't mind that he gave me your number. I'm in a cab on my way to the airport. I'm catching a flight to Seattle on Southwest. I should be landing at Seatac at around 5:00 this afternoon. I wonder if you could meet me there?"

"Well, I'm sure I could but wouldn't it be easier if you just took a taxi or rented a car? I don't know if I'm going to be available to take you over to Bainbridge."

"I don't need a ride, Sergeant. We need to talk and I would prefer not to do it on the phone."

It suddenly dawned on me there was something other than sadness or sorrow in her voice. Maybe a little anger, maybe a little fear? In any event, I decided not to press her.

"Ok, Ms. Noble. I think I can arrange that. Why don't you call me on my cell phone when your plane is on the ground here in Seattle?" I gave her my number.

"Sergeant, I'd appreciate it if you wouldn't tell anyone we spoke or that I'm coming out there."

"Not a problem. Call me when you get here."

She hung up and I sat back in my chair. Now what the hell was that all about? In my line of work you develop a sense of recognizing when something doesn't fit with its surroundings. Kind of like a grown-up version of "Where's Waldo?." Sometimes it's more difficult than others. This wasn't particularly difficult to spot. But figuring out what it meant was a whole different story. I stuck the message slip with her phone number on it into my pocket.

My phone rang. "Elliott."

"Sergeant, this is Dan Suzuki out of the North Precinct.

We've got what looks like a robbery-homicide up here in Northgate. I'm calling you because the victim had your business card in his pocket. Looks like the victim's a guy by the name of Anthony Carey."

Chapter 5

I walked out of my office and over to Al's desk. I
motioned to him to hang up the phone.

"I'll call you back," he said, hanging up. "What's up,
John?"

"You know how they teach you there's no such thing as a
coincidence?"

"Yeah," he said cautiously, kind of drawing out the "ah."

"Well, we have an interesting coincidence in the Noble
case. I haven't had time to catch you up, but this morning
after I left the scene I went up to Northgate to check out
the address on Anna Noble's ID. Seems she shares an
apartment with a young guy named Anthony Carey.
Well, it appears they've both moved to a better
neighborhood."

"Meaning?'

"Meaning I just got a call from a Dan Suzuki up in the
North Precinct saying they have a homicide with a victim
who appears to be Anthony Carey. I'm going to take a
ride back up to Northgate and check out the scene. Had
any luck with those security cameras?"

"Nothing yet. Two of the buildings are owned by
corporations. Those will take more time to track down an
actual person. One of them is owned by a guy with a
Mercer Island address. No phone number available, so I

sent a couple of uniforms over to see if we can locate him. When I'm done here I thought I'd go over to The Center Ring and try to talk to anyone who knew her or may have seen her last night."

"Yeah, fine. Hey, before you leave, see if you can find out something about exactly what she did for the Justice Department, maybe who she worked for or something like that?"

"I'll do my best, but it's Saturday. Why can't these people get killed on a week-day?"

"Yeah, I know. Damned inconsiderate. See what you can do. Oh, Al, one more thing. See if one of your guys can get a line on a Jeff Feinberg. Probably lives somewhere in the DC metro area."

I headed back to the garage. As I was getting into my car, my cell phone rang. It was Marianne.

"Hi. It's me."

"Great. For a minute there I thought it was someone else."

She's learned to ignore comments like that. "We're pretty much finished over here. Chris is wrapping it up. Didn't know if you had time for lunch."

"I'm just leaving my office and headed up to Northgate. You want to take a ride?"

"Sure, as long as it involves food at some point. I never got breakfast this morning."

It always amazes me how people like CSIs and MEs can hang around corpses and not want to miss a meal. I guess you can tune out anything if you're around it often enough.

"I'll pick you up on Virginia. And be ready. I don't want to get a ticket." Click.

Hmm. Not even a 'good-bye'.

Traffic was starting to pick up but I made it to Post and Virginia in about five minutes.
There she was standing on the corner. Considering she was rousted out of bed at 7:00 AM and had been picking over trash and blood-spattered who-knows-what for the last three or four hours, she still looked great. Her long dark hair was flipping in the cold breeze that had come up off of the Sound, and even though she was wearing jeans and a Red Sox sweatshirt, her tight little ass and those hooters I mentioned before were enough to make me momentarily forget whatever else it was I was thinking about.

As I pulled up alongside of her she threw her kit in the back seat and jumped in. "God, I hate this fucking job," she said.

"I love it when you talk dirty."

"Oh, shut up, John. Why does a beautiful young girl have to end up in an Alley next to a dumpster?"

"That, my dear, is the question of the day."

"That's not what I mean. Anyway, I'll have a report for you on Monday, but I thought I'd at least tell you what we found. Or didn't find."

"Ok. Anything helpful?"

"Not much. Based on the splatter pattern of the blood we found, it appears she was shot just inside the little alcove where the dumpsters were located but not between them where we found the body. It looks like she was facing outward toward the alley when she was shot. There were no signs of a struggle, although in a place like that it's sometimes hard to tell. The ME might be able to tell you better if there was any bruising or other marks on other parts of her body. But the condition of her clothing doesn't seem to suggest a struggle of any kind.

"We did find a slug that could have been from the murder weapon. We bagged it and we're going to have it tested for any kind of tissue residue to see if it matches. My guess is it's probably from the gun that killed her. Not likely there would be another bullet in that same area."

"Did you go through her handbag?"

"No, we didn't. I bagged that, too, and we'll go through it downtown in the lab. By the way, where are we going?"

"I told you: Northgate."

"Oh, I see. Such a nice day, you thought you'd take a ride."

So I told her about my morning, about Anthony Carey, about Ed Noble and about getting a call from Dan Suzuki. I also told her about the call I got from Danielle

Noble. I know I wasn't supposed to tell anyone, but Marianne wasn't anyone. No, wait, I didn't mean it like that. I meant…oh, forget it.

"God," she said. "What are you thinking?"

"I'm trying not to think. I'm trying to use all that Zen and meditation shit my daughter-in-law has been trying to get me into. You know, just let it flow over you and the answer will come clear. She says I'm too intense. She thinks it's why I'm not sleeping. She also says I'm not trusting enough."

"She's probably right, you know."

"Excuse me, would you be the pot or the kettle?"

"What's that supposed to mean?'

"You know damn well what it means."

"Jesus, John, let's not start that again. Can we stick to this case?" She slips another tackle and keeps on running.

I stared at her for a long second and decided this conversation, like so many before it, was going nowhere in a hurry.

We pulled up in front of the seasick green building that was now surrounded by flashing red and blue lights.

Anthony Carey's body was still lying on the floor, lying face up half way in and half way out of the door to 312 with his head, or what was left of it, in the hallway and his feet inside the apartment. Lying close to him on the floor was a white paper bag with a bagel and what looked like probably coffee of some kind spilled out and soaked into the carpet. Not only could people not live without their coffee in Seattle, now it was beginning to look like they couldn't die without it either.

I try to leave the forensics to others (try a little harder, John), but it appeared from the blood on the wall opposite Anthony Carey's door and the round hole where his left eye used to be he was shot in the head when he opened the door and started to walk into his apartment. My guess is he went out to get something for breakfast and when he came back, he surprised somebody inside the apartment. Or someone was waiting for him and he was the one who was surprised. Either way, the head shot had the markings of a professional.

Being careful not to step on anything, Marianne and I moved into the apartment. There was the usual crime scene activity. What was previously organized chaos was now just plain chaos. This place did not look like this a few hours ago. Having just seen this apartment a few hours ago, I would say this place had been thoroughly tossed.

There's a difference between trashing a place and tossing a place, and this place had been tossed not trashed. When someone trashes a place, or if there's been a fight of some kind,
stuff is still all thrown around like this, but things are broken. Not everything, but enough so you know there was anger or violence involved. This didn't have that same look. Everything was in a state of disarray but someone was apparently looking for something. Cushions were pulled out of the sofa, the closets were open and boxes were open and strewn around. Drawers

were pulled out and (always a dead give-away someone is looking for something) the freezer door was open. Here's a tip for everyone trying to hide something at home: don't hide it in the freezer. That's the first place everyone, including the bad guys, looks. Crooks watch TV, too. Somebody should have told that to the clown Congressman who hid $97,000.00 in cash in his freezer.

The other thing that was obvious was this was a rush job. I've seen crime scenes where only the owner would know somebody's been in the place. You know, one or two little things that are not quite where they ought to be. But this was just slash and burn without the burn.

In the middle of this chaotic tableau was a rather large Japanese American guy wearing a bright blue North Face windbreaker and an ID hanging around his neck, somewhere between 35 and 60 years old - with Japanese guys half the time you can't tell. I mean, these guys never show their age. Maybe my daughter-in-law is right about this ancient oriental philosophy shit. Is that racist? Probably. It's getting so I can't tell any more.

Anyway, he looked up as I walked across the room towards him.

"Suzuki?" I said.

"Elliott?" he replied, "Nice to meet you."

"What have you got?"

"Precinct got a call from a neighbor. Actually, we didn't get the call, 911 got the call and they called us. She heard some noise in the hallway, not too loud, no gunshot, but apparently this is a pretty quiet building so she went to her door and looked out one of those little fish-eye peepholes and saw two guys heading down the hallway away from her toward the stairwell and what looks like a guy, or part of a guy, laying in the hallway."

"How come we didn't get a call down at Homicide?"

"Well, actually you did. We just got a call there was a disturbance and I happened to be in the area. As soon as I discovered there was a homicide, I radioed back to the precinct to notify you guys. In the meantime, I found your card and called you. By the time our guys notified your office, they said you were already on the way. Sorry if there was any confusion."

"Have you interviewed the neighbor who made the call?"

"Yeah, we have. You can talk to her if you like."

"No, that's ok. Look, I'm sure you know the drill. I'll call downtown and get the CSIs out here. In the meantime, nobody touches anything, ok?"

"Sure, not a problem."

Like I said, I'm not a big believer in coincidences and there were things that were pretty quickly starting to bother me. My phone rang. The caller ID said it was the office. It wasn't Al.

Chapter 6

The call had been from Pete Gilbert (only he pronounces it 'Jeel-bear'). I'm always suspicious of guys who go out of their way to pronounce their names some other way than good ol' American. But Pete was Canadian at some point in his history before he became a US citizen (apparently he was a Mountie early in his career), and was actually a pretty good cop, for a Canadian. (Yeah, I know, I get in a lot of trouble for that, too.) So I cut him some slack. I'm sure that was a huge relief to him.

Anyway, I work for Pete. He's the Captain in charge of homicide as well as the other violent crimes units including CSI. He called me to tell me he needed me back in the office as soon as possible. I always take "as soon as possible" to mean "as soon as I can get around to it." I told him I wanted to stay until the CSIs arrived and he reminded me the CSIs, or one CSI anyway, was already there and I should leave her in charge and get my ass downtown. With Pete, "as soon as possible" means "drop everything and do it now." Just a slight nuance in interpretation.

I hung up the phone and wondered why he "needed" me downtown. I also wondered what he was doing downtown on a Saturday. I also wondered how he knew Marianne was with me since I didn't leave the office with her and I didn't even know I was going to pick her up until I got into my car. Zen, John, Zen. Just let the waves wash over you.

I found Marianne. "I just got a call from Pistol Pete. They

want me back downtown for some reason."

"There goes my lunch."

"Maybe you're pregnant."

"No, I didn't mean…" She just stared at me and shook her head.

"Anyway, I need you to do a couple of things. Call downtown and get another CSI out here. Then I need you to retrieve the bullet that killed this guy. If I'm not mistaken, it's stuck in the wall in the hallway opposite his front door. You probably already noticed it. Take it and go track down the one you guys recovered in Post Alley and hand carry them over to the Crime Lab. I want to know if they're from the same gun. And I want you to wait for the results and call me as soon as you get an answer."

Marianne wasn't the only one thinking about lunch. It suddenly dawned on me (with a gentle reminder from my stomach) I hadn't eaten yet today. Ah, well. Looks like that's not going to happen for a while.

Just because the hairs were beginning to stand up on the back of my neck about this whole business, I started checking my rear view mirror. Just for the hell of it I got off at 85th Street and headed over towards Greenlake. A couple of cars followed me off the exit ramp but that's not all that unusual. After a couple of blocks they disappeared and there was no one behind me until I got to the lake. That one disappeared after a couple more blocks and no one followed me when I made the left turn onto Aurora and headed into the city. My phone rang. It was Ben.

"Hi, Ben. What's up?"

"Hi, Dad. Hey, listen, Abby just reminded me there's a debate on CNN tonight. I guess one last chance for these two guys to try to swing some votes before Tuesday. Can I talk you into coming over to watch it with us? I guess they're carrying it live at 6:00 out here but they're going to replay the whole thing again at 9:00."

I thought about my 5:00 rendezvous with Danielle Noble. "I probably won't make it at 6:00, but I'll try to make it at 9:00. Don't hold dinner for me. I'll just raid your refrigerator if I'm still hungry. You know what they say: If we don't work ourselves to death, the terrorists win."

Long sigh. "Ok, Dad. Whatever. Hope you can make it tonight. I won't watch it at six so I won't know who wins."

I smiled. "Thanks, Ben." My phone made that little beeping sound that says another call is coming in.

"Ok, Dad. See you tonight."

"I love you, Ben."

"Yeah, I love you, too, Dad."

I hit the TALK button. "Elliott."

"Hey, John, it's Al."

"Hey, Al. What have you got?"

"I got a phone number for this Jeff Feinberg you asked

about. You somewhere where you can write it down?"

"Actually, I'm just getting off Aurora downtown. Hang on a second while I pull over."

I came to the top of the ramp, turned right and pulled over. "Ok," I said. "Go ahead."

Al gave me the number that started with a 202 area code. "And, John, just so you know. This was no 411 deal. I had to go into a couple of secure data bases to finally get this number. Who is this guy anyway and why do you need his number?"

"I'm not sure who he is. I got his name from Ed Noble. Said Anna asked him how to get in touch with him. See what else you can find out about him before I try to call him. And Al?"

"Yeah?"

"Keep this Feinberg thing between you and me for now, will you? Do the digging yourself and don't hand it off to anyone else, ok?"

"I'll see what I can do, John. I'm just headed back to the office."

"Any luck with the people over at The Center Ring?"

"I don't know. Maybe. I talked to few people over there. Most of them didn't work last night and mainly work the lunch shift. Didn't really know Anna Noble. I'm trying to get a hold of the manager. I spoke to his wife. She said he was at the gym working out but she'd have him call me as soon as he got home. I'll let you know as soon as I talk to him."

"Ok, Al. I'm just over on Denney Way. I'll be back in in a couple of minutes myself. Apparently Pete wants to talk to me."

"Pete? What's he doing in on a Saturday morning? Something to do with this case?"

"I don't know Al. I was kind of wondering about that myself. I guess we'll know in a few minutes."

I hung up, pulled back out into traffic and headed downtown. It was starting to rain. Again. Dashboard thermometer said it was 52 degrees. These are the days I really struggle with where my life is going. It's been different in a lot of ways since I moved out here, and in some ways it's been good. But in many ways it's been the same. I'm still a cop, I hate the cold, damp weather, I don't have any kind of serious relationship going on. I'm cold, lonely and bored. A dangerous combination.

I saw a piece on PBS the other night. Apparently we keep doing stuff as we get older that we really don't particularly like but do it because we already know how. It's easy.

That's where I'm at. I'm a pretty good cop and I know the drill. I don't have to work too hard to figure out what to do. But I don't particularly get excited about it. Especially on days like this. Beautiful young girl dead in an alley. Some probably innocent young guy dead in a hallway. I don't know. I don't do drugs and I don't drink a whole lot, but as Peggy Lee used to say: "Is that all there is?"

Chapter 7

Al and I arrived back at the office at about the same time. I spoke to him briefly and said "I'll catch up with you later." Like the good little foot soldier I am, I headed for the Captain's office

As I walked across the floor from the elevators and in front of the Captain's office, I could see through his plate glass window that Joe Nakamura, the Lieutenant in charge of the Homicide Unit and my immediate boss (at least I like to let him think he's my boss) was already there. Nakamura had his back to me talking to Captain Pete. There was also a third person in the office standing with Gilbert and Nakamura. I didn't recognize him but his haircut said "Fed" the same way a Crown Vic says "Cop."

The Captain was facing the window with its pretty magnificent view of the city and the Sound, but somehow I didn't think he was standing there enjoying the view. He must have said "Here comes that asshole, Elliott, now," because he made brief eye contact with me, said something to Nakamura, and Joe and the haircut suddenly turned and looked in my direction.

The Captain is a no-nonsense kind of guy. Very military. There's not one thing out of place in his office. He's got the American flag and the Washington State flag on either side of the wall behind his desk flanking two pictures exactly centered, one of the Mayor and one of the Chief. Not a piece of paper out of place anywhere on the top of his desk. A couple of pictures on his credenza, one of his family and one with him in a Mountie uniform with a couple of suits. Some police commendations framed on a side wall. He even has a picture of the President hanging on the wall. His whole office is very Republican. It must kill him to have a picture of the Mayor, an old fashioned "Scoop" Jackson Democrat, staring over his shoulder. But, see, that's the thing I can't help but like about Pete. Democrat or no Democrat, the Mayor is the top dog in city government and I think Pete would take a bullet for him.

But, like I said, he's a good cop, he's thorough and he's predictable. And patriotic. Almost too American. Especially for a guy who used to be Canadian. One thing I hate about converts is they're more Catholic than the Pope, if you know what I mean. If he hadn't been Canadian he probably would have been a Marine.

As I walked into his office he said "Thanks, Joe."

Nakamura said "Thank you, Captain," and turned to walk out, saying "Hey, John" as he walked by me.

I said: "Hey back, Joe" and watched him go.

"Close the door, will you, John?" the Captain asked me in a way that seemed like a polite request that I might or might not comply with but really means "Close the door, John, and do it now." With guys like Pete you know what sounds like a request is actually an order. I haven't forgotten everything I learned in the Navy.

"Have a seat."

I sat. The haircut sat. Then I waited. I didn't have to wait long.

He sat down behind his desk and said: "This is Special Agent Todd. Bring us up to speed on the Noble case."

So I did. The whole time I was talking I was wondering why he was in on a Saturday and why he had taken an interest in Anna Noble. And Anthony Carey. And, oh, by the way, what the fuck was the FBI doing here?

He asked me a couple of questions but pretty much didn't interrupt me. I told him everything that had transpired since I first got the call this morning. Everything, that is, except the part about Danielle Noble coming to Seattle and the part about Jeff Feinberg. Something about those two wasn't fitting together for me with the rest of it and I just decided to keep it to myself for a while.

"Any suspects or any idea of motive?" Pete asked me.

"No suspects yet and the motive thing is bothering me a little."

"All right, John. I realize it's a little soon to have a lot of answers. From now on, Agent Todd is going to work with us on this case." By "us" he meant me. "So as far as I'm concerned, this is our case. But they might be helpful if you need them. I'll let you decide."

Hmm. Let me think about that. Ok, I've decided. They can't be helpful. But, like I said, my mother didn't raise any stupid children and I knew I wasn't going to get rid of the Bureau that easily, especially if Pete had "suggested" we work together. I also knew Pete well enough to know he wouldn't voluntarily just let some FBI guy, or any other agency for that matter, just waltz in here and look over our shoulder. Somebody higher up had obviously "suggested" it to him, of that I was pretty sure. Besides, even though they're pretty much a bunch of dicks, they do have some resources that might be useful.

Agent Todd and I left the office together and as we stepped out into the hall, he said:
"Listen, Elliott, I'm not real comfortable with this either. But my boss says stay on top of this and that's what I plan to do. I hope we can work together."

So let me get this straight: We had two murders in less than eight hours (on a Saturday, I might add) and I've already got the Captain of Violent Crimes and the FBI watching my every move. All I can think of is a little kid: "Are we there yet? Are we? Huh, are we?"
The question is: Why?

I said: "Don't worry about it. Listen, I'm sure you have other things to do on a Saturday. Why don't you just give me your cell phone number and I'll call you if anything comes up."

"Yeah, sure, I'll give you my cell number." He handed me his card. "But if it's all the same with you, I'm just going to hang around for a while a see what develops."

"Listen, Todd, I don't mean to be nosey or anything, but, hey, I am a detective. So let me ask you something: I know Anna Noble worked for Justice, but we've had other federal employees involved in violent crimes. Why is the Bureau so interested in this case?"

"To tell you the truth," (Uh oh. Keep your hand on your wallet when an FBI agent says that) "I really don't know."

Yeah, right. Ok, let's take a different tack. "What, exactly, did Anna Noble do over at Justice?"

"I don't know that either. I've heard her name occasionally, but I don't think I've ever met her."

"Well, do you suppose you could find out for me? It might be helpful."

"I could try. Do you have a quiet place where I could make a couple of calls?"

"Sure. Actually (I pointed over to the other side of the office), there's some interview
rooms over there. Why don't you just use one of them?"

As soon as he turned his back, I headed quickly for the elevator. I had a distinct feeling he was not supposed to let me out of his sight, so I thought I'd make him earn his money. Let's see how good he is.

The elevator door opened and Al was coming out. I jumped in and said "Al, ride down with me."

He looked out the door then back at me as the door closed. "What's going on?" he said.

"The short answer is: I'm not sure. The long answer is the Captain wants me to buddy-up with an FBI agent named Todd and pal around together and I don't think he's trying to fix us up. I'm sure when Agent Todd discovers I'm gone, he'll try to find out from you where I've gone, so I'm not going to tell you. Just keep your cell phone on."

"Ok, John. Anyway, I was just coming to look for you. I went across the street to grab a coffee and a bagel and I got a call from the manager of The Center Ring. He said Anna seemed a little up-tight or more serious than usual last night, but he didn't think much of it. He said she was usually, how did he put it, 'charming'. He said she wasn't, y'know, 'buddy-buddy' with everyone, but was very conversational and pleasant. Smiled and laughed a lot. But last night she just seemed really quiet. Her last show was at 1:00 and she left right after it. Said she usually hung around for at least one drink at the end of the night since she didn't drink while she was working. But last night she just said good-night and took off.

"He knew she had a day job with the Feds but said he never pressed her on the details. Said he was more interested in her acrobatic skills anyway and wasn't that interested in her resume."

By that time we were down in the lobby and the doors opened. Al reached over and hit the "OFF" switch locking the doors open.

"So he also tells me that she told him she had to go away unexpectedly for a couple of days and wouldn't be in Saturday night or Sunday night, but would be back next week-end. He was a little upset, he said, with such short notice because her act was the big draw on the week-ends and it was going to be hard to find someone to fill in at the last minute."

"Good work, Al. Listen, keep working on the Feinberg thing, will you? I still want to try to get in touch with him, but I need to know a little more about him before I do."

Meanwhile, the elevator had been off long enough where an alarm bell started to ring. So I flipped the switch back again, stepped into the elevator and hit the '8'. We have doors that open into the parking deck on 7 and on 8. I figured if I hit 7 I'd likely run right into Todd. So I'd go to 8 and walk down one level.

Al got back in with me. "One more thing," he said. "The manager said that between two of her acts, he was sitting at the bar with her just shooting the breeze. He said he mentioned to her he was planning to take the ferry over to Bainbridge on Saturday with his wife to do a little shopping and to have lunch at Café Nola. And she says to him, 'I'd stay off the ferry for the next couple of days if I were you'.

Chapter 8

I pulled out of the garage onto 5th just as my phone rang. I flipped it open and saw it was not Agent Todd. So far, so good. It was Marianne. I hit TALK and said "Hi, ugly."

She said: "Hi, John. Listen, I'm just leaving the Crime Lab and I have the results you were looking for."

"Ok," I said. "Hold on. I'm just leaving the office. I'll swing down and pick you up." I hung up before she could answer me. My senses were starting to sharpen up. I find in my line of work, a little paranoia is actually a good thing. Adding the FBI into the mix when, as far as I could figure, we didn't ask for it and it wasn't obvious why they were there, notwithstanding all this bullshit about how she worked for them and they 'just want this thing solved', was as good a reason as any to raise my own personal Threat Level from yellow to orange.

So my first line of defense is always to use as little electronic communication as possible.
Besides, I still hadn't had anything to eat and I thought we might combine a little pleasure with business.

The Crime Lab is operated by the Washington State Patrol. Next to the SPD, the State Patrol guys are the guys you want in the foxhole with you. I've worked with them on a couple of cases. All business, very professional and very dependable. And, considering that they're a state agency, not all that responsive to political pressure.

The Crime Lab is over on Airport Way about a mile and a half from headquarters. I jumped onto 6th Avenue and headed south. My phone rang. I didn't recognize the number although it was a Seattle area code. The way this day has been going, I figured I'd better answer it. At this rate, a telemarketer would be a welcome relief.

It was a telemarketer, all right. Selling U.S. government law enforcement services.

"Very cute, Elliott. Where are you?"

"Y'know, Todd, I'm not really sure." Nice to know that he didn't know. "I haven't been in Seattle that long and it looks familiar but I don't know, exactly."

"Look, Elliott. Don't escalate this thing. I don't like it any more than you do. But I have a job to do and I plan to do it. All you have to do is your job and not take this as a personal challenge."

"Speaking of doing your job, did you find out any thing useful about Anna Noble?

"Possibly. I'd be happy to share it with you. Face to face."

Score one for Agent Todd. I said: "Ok. Why don't you meet me over in Pioneer Square in about 20 minutes. Meet me in front of the Elliott Bay Book Store." I hung up.

Marianne was waiting for me when I pulled up in front of the Crime Lab. She tossed her gear in the back and dropped into the passenger seat. This time she gave me a kiss on the cheek before she fastened her seat belt and I knew she was starting to wake up and feel a little better about a day that hadn't started off too well. Maybe it was because nobody had been killed in at least six hours or maybe it was the prospect of finally getting to eat something. In any event, she was in a much better humor than she was when I left her up in Northgate.

"What did you find out?"

"Well, you were right. The crime lab said the bullet we found in Post Alley and the one I dug out of the wall at the apartment house both came from the same gun. And something else that might be important. I got a call from Chris. We bagged a few things at the scene where Anna Noble got shot, including her handbag, then Chris took them back to the lab to go over them. He found an airline ticket print-out in her bag for an eticket on Southwest to BWI in DC for this morning at 7:05. One way."

"Ok. Listen, I'll give you the whole story later but right now I have to meet an FBI Agent named Todd in front of the Elliott Bay Bookstore in Pioneer Square. What I need you to do is to drop me off about a block away, drive around for about five minutes, not near the book store, then swing by the corner and pick me up. I'm just going to jump in, probably in a bit of a hurry, and you just keep going. Can you do that?"

"Yeah, sure. But why?"

"Let's just say I'm testing the waters."

"Then do I get to eat?" Ah. A woman after my own heart.

I pulled over and we switched seats. Marianne dropped

me off on South Washington Street about a block away from the book store. As I turned the corner and walked down 1st Avenue, I could see the front of the book store and Agent Todd standing with his hands in his pockets looking from side to side. I decided to watch him for just a minute or two to see if he was communicating with anyone else. As far as I could tell, he was just standing there looking for me. Then, just as I started to move and while he was not looking in my direction, I saw his lips move. These guys have all kinds of state of the art communications crap and I thought it might be safe to assume he was talking to someone other than an imaginary friend. Not a big surprise, but it appeared there was more than one of them. A good thing to know.

As I got to the corner across the street from the book store, he turned and looked in my direction. Then, just for a fraction of a second, he looked over his right shoulder back up South Main Street before looking back at me. I figure he wasn't concerned I might get hit crossing the street. I looked to my left, half checking the traffic, since I was concerned I might get hit crossing the street.

I stepped up onto the sidewalk and said "What've you got for me?"

"I don't have anything for you unless you've got something for me," he replied.

"Listen, Todd, I don't know anything you don't already know," I lied. "In fact, I'm getting the sneaky feeling you know more than I do."

"I'll let that one go, Elliott. But this is not a one-way street. If you expect me to help you, you've got to stop

trying to ditch me. I told you. I have a job to do and I'm going to do it.
One way or another."

I looked away from him then back squarely in the eye. "First of all, I don't make deals. Not for this kind of shit. Either you're going to give me the info on Anna Noble or not. But not for any reason other than you'd like to help me solve her murder. That is what you guys want, right?" I paused to let that sink in. He just kept staring at me. "Otherwise, no offense to my furry friends, but there's more than one way to skin a cat. See, I have a job to do, too, and I'm going to do it." Pause. More staring. "One way or another." I could see the wheels turning.

Finally he said: "Let's see what Captain Gilbert has to say about that."

"Suit yourself," I said, as Marianne came around the corner from 1st Avenue and pulled up beside me. I stepped off the curb and opened the passenger side door. "Call me if you change your mind. You have my number."

I jumped in and slammed the door. "Let's go," I said. She goosed it. "Go up and make a right on 2nd then head north on 4th." I looked back to see what Todd was doing but he wasn't there. "You hungry?" I asked.

Chapter 9

"All right," she said, "are you going to tell me what's going on?"

"The short answer," I said, "is I'm still not really sure. Pete Gilbert has given me a new partner. A Bureau guy named Todd who is apparently supposed to watch my every move. I don't really think it's Pete's idea – in fact, I'm sure it's not, but somebody higher up has told Pete it's a good idea and he's decided to go along with it, good soldier that he is.

"I'm assuming that was your new partner you just left standing in the street back there."

"Yeah. But I know I'm missing something. It's another one of those "Where's Waldo?" moments. I know it's right in front of me, I just have to sort it out from all the background noise. I keep trying to figure out what the Bureau's interest is in this case. They clearly want more than just status reports from the local gendarmes. I mean, otherwise they just call up Pete and say "Keep us posted, will you? And let us know if we can be of any help." But instead, they assign an agent to watch my every move and, apparently, there's more than one of them. I almost feel like I'm the one being investigated, you know what I mean?"

"Don't you think you're being a little paranoid?"

"No, I think I'm being a lot paranoid. Listen, I used to work for the Bureau. They always have an agenda.

Sometimes it's local and some times it comes from high up and I mean really high up. But there's always an agenda. I believe Todd when he says he's been given a job to do, I just haven't figured out yet what that job is or who might have set this particular agenda. I do know somebody thinks this is important enough to take at least one agent and probably more than one from an office that's already short-staffed and put them on this. I know the Special Agent in Charge here in Seattle from another life. I guarantee you whatever it is, it's something he thinks will get him closer to a big office in DC.

"Let's head up to Queen Anne and find some place for lunch. Only don't go straight there. Take a few random turns and run a couple of red lights without getting us killed. I just want to watch for a bit."

I watched out the back window and started thinking about what I knew. Something was ticking right at the edge of my consciousness. I tend to treat those feelings like a night blind spot – if you try to look right at it all you see is a black spot. But if you look away just a little, you can see it. So I decided to let it go for now and concentrate on something else. Like why Anna Noble had told her manager to stay away from the ferry. Not just 'stay away from the ferry', you know, in general, but 'stay off the ferry for the next day or two'. I didn't like the sound of that especially since Al had told me the Coast Guard had raised the threat level. So I decided to follow up on that.

The Homeland Security Division of the Coast Guard was down on Pier 36. I made a decision. "Take a left here and head over to Alaskan Way."

"Where are we going?"

"Over to the Coast Guard Station on Pier 36 I have a friend there I need to talk to."

"I don't suppose they have food there."

"No, probably not. Nothing you'd want to eat, anyway. Look, I promise as soon as I take care of this, we'll find some place for lunch."

Just then, my phone rang. I glanced at the caller ID. "What've you got, Al?"

"A little progress on the security camera thing. One of the cameras wasn't wired up – just a dummy, I guess to give the impression of security. One camera we haven't been able to track down yet. But one camera that's apparently wired right into the building and has it's own security system with a 24 hour play-back loop."

"And?"

"And, you can look at this when you get a minute, but what you see is a female figure walking down the alley away from the camera. Based on the time stamp and what comes next, it's definitely Anna Noble. Although these security cameras are pretty crappy on detail, especially at night. Anyway, as she comes into view in the bottom of the screen, there are two figures coming from the other direction. Neither seems to be concerned about the other. Then, as they get close to her, they step in front of her and all three of them stop. They look like they're talking. Nobody's moving much and, from her body language, she doesn't seem to be frightened or feeling threatened. This goes on for about thirty seconds, when suddenly one of these guys reaches for her handbag. She pulls it away from him and tries to walk away. Then it all happens really fast. These two guys, one on each side, pick her up under her arm pits and lift her off her feet and in about five steps they disappear into the alcove where we found her body. About 30 seconds later the two guys come out of the alcove and walk back in the same direction they came in not looking like they are particularly in a hurry."

"You thinking what I'm thinking?"

"Well, I don't know what you're thinking, but I think these three knew each other. Either that or they identified themselves in some way that she didn't initially feel threatened. I don't see Anna Noble as the kind of person who would stop and chat with two strangers at 1:30 in the morning in a deserted alley. I think it was probably something more like them giving her some plausible story and her not thinking she would be dead in the next minute."

"Based on what we found at the scene, it still doesn't sound or look like a robbery," I said. "It seems more like these guys are looking for something and want to look in her handbag to see if it's in there. After what happened at her apartment, my guess is they didn't find what they were looking for. But why did they have to kill her?"

"Maybe to keep her from IDing them?"

"Yeah, maybe. Any luck with that other thing?"

"Not yet. This guy's a ghost."

He hung up or whatever it is you do with cell phones.

"What are we doing over at the Coast Guard?"

"I need to talk to a sailing buddy of mine. Harry O'Connell."

"We going sailing?"

"No, fishing."

Chapter 10

My sailing friend, Harry O'Connell, is actually Captain
Harry O'Connell, United States Coast Guard. Harry is
stationed down at Pier 36 and although I never talked to
Harry about the details of his job, I know from comments
he's made it has something to do with Homeland
Security. But I still like Harry just the same. I figured
maybe Harry could tell me something that might shed
some light on Anna Noble's comment about staying
away from the ferry for "the next couple of days."

Harry's been working week-ends for the last month or so
and I was hoping to catch him in.

While we were sitting in a line of traffic at a red light,
Marianne said to me: "John, what's going on with you
today? You've been all business, which is definitely not
like you. Are you pissed at me about something?"

"No more than usual," I said, then turned and smiled.
Sometimes she's a little sensitive about my sarcasm, so I
figured I'd better let her know it wasn't her. This time.
"Nah. This case has just been nibbling at me right from
the beginning." Which was true. But there was that kind
of low level…what? Anger? Disappointment?
Inevitability?…that what started out so great between the
two of us was not living up to the rave reviews it got. I
just didn't think this was the time to get into it.

We went through gate security showing our badges, had
a brief conversation with the officer on duty about

checking my weapon - which was not about to happen - and indicated we were here to see Captain O'Connell, who was not expecting us. A quick phone call and we were informed that Captain O'Connell would be waiting for us at the main entrance.

I drove out onto the pier and pulled into one of the "Visitor" spaces in front of the building.

Harry was waiting for us in the lobby. "Hey, John, good to see you. What are you doing here on a Saturday?" He glanced at Marianne then back at me as if to say 'And who's this?' Harry's single same as me, and for the same reason. One disastrous brush with marriage and we both seemed to be cured, at least for now. I actually met him through my son. Ben's been crewing for a friend of his in a Tuesday night racing series on Lake Union and those sailing guys are always looking for crew, which is to say a warm body that can pull on a rope – excuse me, a line – and follow directions with a minimum of supervision. Ben asked me one week if I'd like to crew for this Coast Guard type on another boat and I said 'Is there drinking involved?' and he said 'Yes, there probably is', and I said 'Then I'm your man'.

So I met Harry at the beginning of the summer, crewed for him all summer and he's become one of my very few friends since I moved out here. We went to a few Mariners' games now and then during baseball season and still hang out together once in a while. Harry's a good shit. He's about 3 years away from retirement and he and I talk not too seriously about buying a 40 foot sail boat down in the Caribbean and running a little charter company. I've become a pretty good deck hand and I like to cook so when we talk about it, it all seems very doable. Did I mention sometimes I think I wouldn't mind adding

'Beach bum' to my resume? I did? Ok.

"Working on a case," I said. "What can you tell me about anything that might be going on with the ferries?"

"What do you mean?" he asked, looking again at Marianne. Only this time he wasn't good 'ol Harry checking out the broad. He was Captain Harry O'Connell, United States Coast Guard, not about to talk about the ferries in front of some bimbo I might have picked up last night and hadn't gotten around to taking home. You know, 'Hey, honey, let's take a ride while I do some cop stuff. Wanna see my gun again?'

"Oh, sorry," I said. "Harry, this is Marianne Robinson. She's a CSI with the Department. She's working on this case with me. Marianne, this is Captain Queeg."

"Nice to meet you," she said, sticking out her hand to shake Harry's.

"Ah, ha," he said. "That Marianne. Nice to finally meet you."

"Nice to finally meet you, too," she said, with a big smile, "even though I only heard about you five minutes ago."

"Ok," I said, "before you two start picking out wall paper together…"

"Curtains," she said. Harry held back a little smile.

"What ever," I said. "We know you guys raised the security level from MARSEC 1 to MARSEC2. Let's start with that."

Harry looked at me for a long moment then at Marianne for not quite so long then back at me. I could see some kind of wheels turning. "Why don't we go to my office?" he said.

Chapter 11

Harry's office was on the west side of the building with a couple of pretty good sized windows looking out over the bay. The view was pretty nice but the office was typical U.S. military. Black steel desk with wood grain Formica top, credenza off to one side with stacks of files on it, a couple of steel chairs with vinyl seat cushions in front of the desk, some kind of commercial carpeting probably built to last 150 years, a black vinyl covered couch against one wall and the obligatory picture of the President on the wall over the credenza. A second credenza behind Harry's desk had a few photos on it, mostly stuff from his Coast Guard career, as best as I could tell – a couple of boat pictures, some guys in military uniforms, but nothing that looked personal. His desk faced the door and I thought to myself that for a guy who loved the water as much as Harry did, I would have thought he would have set his desk up so he could look up and see the bay every once in a while.

"Have a seat," Harry said.

We sat.

"How much do you know about MARSEC?" he asked.

"Not much," I said. "I know it's pretty much limited to law enforcement and private security. I know you have to take an oath of secrecy before they let you see any of the memos. And I know you have to leave a testicle or a loved one on deposit with the government to insure your loyalty. Other than that, not much." Harry was used to me and just proceeded on as if he didn't hear that last crack. Most people who get to know me develop that same habit.

"MARSEC is a threat level system the Coast Guard maintains similar to the Homeland Security threat level system for terrorist activity. For some reason, we have three levels and they have five. Don't ask me why. Typical government. Anyway, we have different marine security procedures depending on what the MARSEC level is set at. Usually, it's Level 1 which pretty much means try not to go to sleep, the bad guys are out there plotting something or other. It more or less corresponds to the Homeland Security threat levels of Green, Blue and Yellow.

"Level 2 is obviously one step up from Level 1 and is used when we have information there might, and I emphasize might, be a more specific threat out there. See, it all starts to get a little hazy at this point because Washington tells us when to raise the threat level but they don't necessarily tell us why. So we start boosting up security both in the field and here in the office and we don't always know exactly what we should be looking out for. Sometimes I don't think our guys in Washington do either. Personally, I think it's a mystery where this stuff originates from then it just kind of spreads like a rumor. You know, 'the sky is falling' kind of stuff.

"Anyway, we raised the threat level to Level 2 just this morning."

"This may be a silly question, but any idea why?"

Once again Harry chose to ignore me, but this time I

suspect it was for a different reason.

"What's your interest in MARSEC on a Saturday afternoon?" he asked.

"I'm investigating a homicide that took place early this morning. Young woman who apparently worked for the US Justice Department was found dead in Post Alley. To make a long story short, she had a part time job in a restaurant near the scene of the murder. My partner interviewed the manager there and in the course of the interview the manager happened to mention a conversation he had with the victim not long before she died in which she said to him 'I'd stay off the ferry for the next couple of days if I were you'. I don't know if it's relevant or not but I thought since you guys also just raised the threat level, that there might be some connection."

"When did she have that conversation?"

"Sometime Friday night, I don't know exactly when. Why?"

Harry looked at me then at Marianne. "Would you excuse us for a few minutes," he said to her.

"Of course," she said. She looked at me as she got up and said: "I'll wait for you in the lobby."

When the door closed, Harry said: "What do you know about semi-submersibles?"

Uh, oh. Here we go. Keep your mouth shut, John. Good ol' Harry could be losing it or this might actually be going somewhere I care about although it isn't obvious yet where that might be.

"Well," I said, "I could probably sum it up in one sentence: What the hell is a semi-submersible?"

"A semi-submersible is a kind of boat. It's not really a submarine but it doesn't float on the surface like regular boat either. It looks kind of like a submarine that's just breaking the surface, or maybe like a whale floating on the surface where you can just see the top of it but most of it is underwater. Our guys along the Gulf coast and in parts of Florida have been seeing more and more of them lately."

"Drugs?"

"Yeah. Apparently these things are being made in the jungles of Columbia then being used to transport drugs to the US. Until recently they've been made out of fiberglass and pretty cheap construction. But I guess, as with most things, they've gotten better at building them. Now they're starting to be made of steel and they can carry upwards of 12 tons. They're a real pain in the ass for us because first of all, they're hard to detect because they don't show up on radar or sonar and second of all, once you find them they're hard to disable without actually sinking them, in which case, for our guys, that's a real problem because, once you sink them, there's no evidence."

"No offense, Harry, but what's this got to do with the price of beans?"

"Hold on, John. I'm getting to that. I need to share some information with you because something you said interests me. A lot. Before I do I need to get a couple of things understood between us. Over the past six months

I've gotten to know you and I think you're an honest and honorable guy. I'm about to tell you some things my people consider to be highly classified. Now I'm not going to go through a whole lot of security clearance bullshit because first of all I know you well enough to know you wouldn't stand for it. But, more importantly, I don't think I have time for it. So all I need is your word that anything we talk about here doesn't go any further. Agreed?"

"Harry, my job here is a murder investigation. All I can tell you is if you decide to share information with me, you'll have to trust me to decide how I use it."

Harry stared at me for a few seconds. "Ok, John, fair enough."

Harry got up and turned to look out the window. It was gray and drizzling. Again. Off to the right I could see two ferries, one coming and one going into the terminal at Pier 52, the Coast Guard inflatables right along side of them.

He turned to me. "This morning just after dawn, one of our patrol boats up in the San Juan Islands was doing a coastal patrol. We don't have anywhere near the activity up here that they have down in the Caribbean, but occasionally we have a little drug smuggling so we keep an active presence up there. They were doing a slow speed visual scanning of some of the little bays and inlets when one of the look-outs spotted something in the water near the shore line he actually thought was a couple of beached whales. It's pretty boring up there for the most part, so our guys headed in toward these particular whales. Only they weren't whales. They were semi-submersibles. Two of them. They were moored side by side on some type of underwater mooring with nobody around, at least that our guys could see."

I'm sure this is going somewhere I care about. All of a sudden it dawned on me I was really hungry. Focus, John, focus.

"We've spent the morning debriefing the crew of the patrol boat but it appears at first they thought these were drug runners and this was a whole new wrinkle for us up here in the northwest. They radioed it in and went through the usual drill in the event there was armed crew aboard, but when they finally boarded these two things, there was no one aboard.

"What was aboard was some pretty sophisticated remote control navigation equipment. And about a hundred pounds of Semtex in each one."

Chapter 12

See, now, I knew sooner or later Harry would get my attention. Semtex is something I know a little about. Back in my FBI days, and way before 9/11, we did some work on an IRA cell operating in the US. That's Irish Republican Army, by the way, not Individual Retirement Account. I didn't want you to think we were chasing a bunch of stockbrokers. Although, now I think about it, that might not have been a bad idea.

Anyway, back in the 1980's the IRA got a bunch of crap from the Libyan government for blowing up people and other stuff, including, we estimated, about a ton of Semtex. Nasty stuff. And pretty powerful. Three or four pounds of Semtex can level a two story building. Yeah, I know. Holy shit!

So, now, Harry's guys have just found two boats of some kind each with a hundred pounds of this stuff inside. I've heard of fishing with dynamite, but somehow I didn't think this stuff belonged to fisherman.

"Anyway," Harry continued, "we immediately notified our guys in Washington. About five minutes later we get the word to raise the MARSEC level. Then, about 30 minutes later, we get a second directive, this one marked 'TOP SECRET', telling us all information related to this incident is immediately and retroactively classified 'TOP SECRET' and we are to discontinue any search or investigation. Period."

"Did you change the MARSEC level after the second

directive?"

"No, that wasn't part of it."

"What about these two boats? What happened to them?"

"The short answer is: I have no idea. We were told to secure from the area and they were no longer our problem. You can imagine I wasn't entirely happy with that answer, so I contacted the guy in Washington who I answer to. He tells me, off the record, the first directive to raise the threat level came from our guys when they found out what we had up there. The second directive came from somewhere else, not the Coast Guard, after the information about what our guys found was passed up the chain of command.

"So we're doing what MARSEC2 requires us to do, but were operating pretty much in the blind. Since that second directive, it's pretty much gone black as far as we're concerned. But you can imagine I'm more than a little curious as to what's going on."

"Shouldn't you guys be up to your eyeballs in this thing?" I asked.

"Ordinarily, you'd be right. This is squarely within our jurisdiction. I mean we'd probably be dealing with some other agencies, but we should be in the thick of it. And at a high priority level. I mean this isn't just something somebody overheard and might or might not be something. This is 200 pounds of fucking Semtex loaded into two boats.

"I would have thought the Navy over in Bremerton might just be a little interested in this. But I made a kind of casual call to a guy at the base over there I sometimes work with on security drills here in the Sound and he clearly didn't know anything about any of this except for raising the MARSEC level. In fact, he thought it might be some kind of drill.

"Then you come along and mention your victim apparently warned off a friend about going near the ferry for the next couple of days. Tricky part is apparently she mentioned it about eight or nine hours before we discovered these floating bombs. Needless to say, you got my attention."

Well, well, Anna Noble. What were you into?

I said to Harry: "So what are you thinking? You think Anna Noble knew about some kind of plot to blow up a ferry? Or two?"

"I don't know what to think right at the moment, John. I'm still trying to put a few pieces together. It's not a casual comment like, oh, I don't know, 'I wouldn't go hiking tomorrow if I were you. It's supposed to rain', you know what I mean? You've got a murder victim who works for the Justice Department...."

"As far as I know."

"What do you mean 'As far as I know'?"

"I mean we found a Justice Department ID in her purse, clearly belonging to her, but nobody, including my brothers at the Bureau seems to want to tell me what she did for them. Although they also seem to be quite interested in what we find. I've been dodging them since this morning just because I don't like their attitude."

"Yeah, well, my guess is they probably don't much like yours either."

I looked at my watch. It was getting closer to the time when I was supposed to pick up Danielle Noble at the airport.

"Anyway," he continued, "I feel like I just can't let this thing go. I have to be really careful because I've received a direct order to mind my own business. Except I can't help thinking somehow this should be my business."

I stood up. "Listen, Harry, I appreciate you sharing this with me. Do me a favor, will you? I still have a few leads to track down. I have a feeling that whatever is going on, we don't have a lot of time. Just keep me posted if anything new turns up, ok?"

"Sure, John. I just hope you'll do the same for me." He came around his desk and opened the door for me.

"I'll do my best, Harry. I appreciate this little chat. Keep your cell phone on."

Speaking of phones – mine rang.

"Elliott."

"Can you come to the 14th floor over at 1110 Third Avenue?"

Ah. The old invitation ploy. Apparently they figured out the best way to get me not to do something was to tell me I had to do it. Fast learners. I knew this wasn't going to be easy. But I figured, what the hell, I clearly have no idea what's going on so why not? On the other hand, why just roll over? Might set a nasty precedent.

"Why would I want to do that?" I said.

"Because," the voice said, "I may have some information that could be useful to you."

"That's what your guy, Todd, said. I guess you know how that worked out."

"Todd doesn't work for me." There was a slight, almost imperceptible hesitation. "Anna Noble worked for me," he said.

That got my attention. I looked at my watch. I didn't want to lose track of the fact I was meeting Danielle Noble at the airport around 5:00. And I was wondering why they were suddenly dangling this carrot in front of me. Careful John. "Look," I said, "I've got a pretty full schedule today. I have to check my Blackberry, my laptop, my desk calendar, my voicemail, those little notes I scribble on the back of my hand… How about if my people call your people? Let's do lunch."

"Suit yourself," he said. This guy's a cool customer. The worst kind of pressure. No pressure. "Call Todd if you change your mind. He'll know how to get in touch with me.
By the way, the number on your Caller ID? It doesn't lead anywhere." He hung up.

Chapter 13

I dropped off Marianne at the office, mumbled an apology about not getting anything to eat and then headed toward the nearest on-ramp to the 5. Depending on the traffic, it's about a 20 to 30 minute ride south to Seatac and I wanted to be in the vicinity when Danielle Noble arrived.

Have you ever tried to remember something, like a name, and it seems the harder you try, the harder it gets? So you put it out of your mind and suddenly, maybe an hour later, maybe a day later, maybe at 3AM, it just pops into your head? Kind of like the little plastic capsule you stick your money in at the drive-up window at the bank. Put it in the little trap door, listen for that giant sucking sound, then sit back, listen to Kenny Chesney on your CD player and go away to the Caribbean for a few minutes. And then, magically, without even thinking about it, it comes back with your receipt. I have no idea what goes on in between except it seems to work pretty slick.

I do that a lot with my cases, especially the more difficult ones and it seems to work pretty slick, too. In this case there were a number of things I was waiting for to come back from the drive-in teller in my mind. One of them was what I had seen at Anna Noble's apartment the first time I went there and spoke to Anthony Carey and what I saw the second time I was there. At the time, the second time, I know there was a lot of chaos from the place being tossed, but something wasn't right. Between the attention everyone was paying to poor Anthony and everything else that goes on at a crime scene, not to mention the phone call from Pete Gilbert I wasn't able to process it. So I filed away the images.

And now, just when I didn't need it, there it was. It suddenly occurred to me that the first time I was in Anna Noble's apartment breaking the bad news to Anthony Carey there was a lap-top sitting on a little make-shift desk off to one side of that small living room. But the second time I don't remember seeing it. I also recall Marianne said they found a computer print-out of an eticket for Southwest in Anna's handbag. So, presumably, there was a computer there before Anthony's ticket got punched but perhaps not after.

Maybe it just got tossed and was there all along, just not where it was before. I was beginning to get the feeling somebody was looking for something, couldn't find it, and was hoping maybe we might come up with it. So I thought I'd try a different route and see if I could get lucky.

I was about to make a call when a little alarm bell went off in my head. Better stop making it so easy for them to track you. First, I shut off my cell phone and pulled out the battery. I reached into my glove compartment, threw my phone in, pulled out a prepaid phone I carry for emergencies and dropped it into my shirt pocket. Then I pulled off of Alaskan Way and looked for a pay phone. Somewhere in the International District, just over from Qwest Stadium and Safeco Field, I found a little Asian market and went inside. Just inside and next to the door I found what I was looking for. I dropped in two quarters, dialed the direct line for the CSI Unit and asked for Chris.

After a few seconds, a voice said "CSI. This is Chris."

"Chris, John Elliott. You didn't by any chance get called up to Northgate this morning, did you?"

"Yeah, John, as a matter of fact, I did." Bingo

"Did you go through the whole place top to bottom?"

"Pretty much. I brought in Kevin Moran to help me because the place was such a mess and I didn't want to miss anything. You looking for something in particular?"

"Did you guys find a computer?"

"I don't recall seeing one. I can tell you we didn't bag one. Hang on, let me ask Kevin."

As he turned away from the phone, I glanced out the door and what to my wondering eyes should appear but a dark blue Ford Explorer with two guys in it. The guy closest to me on the passenger side looked strangely like Agent Todd. Why was I not surprised.

Chris came back on the line. "John? Kevin doesn't remember seeing one, but then, again, we weren't looking for one. That place was a CSI's nightmare. It could very well have been there, just tossed to one side. The scene is still secure. You want me to go back up there and look for it?"

While he was talking, I watched the Explorer slow down and saw Todd look directly into the market. I don't think he saw me, but I'm pretty sure he saw my car and figured out where I was. This was really starting to annoy me.

"John? You there?"

"Oh, yeah, Chris, I'm here. Just thinking. Let's start with something easier. Did you guys take pictures at the scene?"

"Yes."

"How about if you email them to me? All of them. Let me look those over first, ok?"

"Yeah, sure, John. What's your email address?"

I thought for a minute. Then I gave him my son's email address. I'm not quite sure how this stuff works, but I'm assuming Big Brother can tap an email account just like they can tap a phone. I'm also assuming they're not checking everybody I know. Like I said, why make this easy?

"Thanks, Chris. And do me a favor, will you? Don't release that scene yet. I want a uniform there at all times. And I want to know who comes and who goes from that apartment. Tell him to get an ID on anybody who shows up and keep a list. Might not be anybody, but you never know. I'll check in with you later. I'm assuming you'll be working late tonight.

"Oh, and one more thing. I don't care if anybody finds out we've been talking, but if you could forget to mention any of this computer stuff, I'd appreciate it. Marianne seems to like you, so I assume I can trust you."

I hung up. All this time I'd been watching the Explorer.

They had pulled into a parking space down the street and steam was coming out of the tailpipe. I picked up the phone again, checked his card and dialed Agent Todd's number.

Two rings. "You can't stay in there forever."

"I don't know. There's plenty of food here. And a bathroom. How long can you hold it?"

"Listen, Elliott. Why are we playing this game? You must have figured out by now we're not going to have any trouble finding you." That sounded like a challenge. "Why don't you just let me ride shotgun and get on with your investigation?"

"See, Todd, as the old saying goes, my mother didn't raise any stupid children. So it's pretty obvious to me you guys are looking for something you're having trouble finding and you're hoping I'll find it for you. What I haven't figured out yet is why it's so important. Or maybe if I knew what it was you were looking for, then I'd know why it's so important. Either way, I just plain don't like being used. Especially by my old alma mater. So let's cut the 'we're here to help' bullshit. Unless, of course, you'd like to tell me what it is I should be looking for?"

Silence.

"Yeah, that's what I thought. And oh, by the way, I think I'm beginning to resent the fact you guys really don't give a shit about Anna Noble."

I hung up and pulled another card out of my wallet. I dialed the 800 number on the card.

"Good afternoon, this is Zipcar. How can I help you?"

"This is John Elliott. I need a car right now. I'm in the International District in Seattle.
Do you have anything close to me?"

"Let me check, Mr. Elliott. Yes, I have a car at the corner of 5th Avenue South and Dearborn. Does that help you?"

"Yes, it does. Thanks."

"I'll activate that car for you now."

"Thanks very much." I hung up.

I wondered how much time I'd have before Todd and company figured out I wasn't in the market anymore. In any event, I figured I'd better get a move on. I headed for the back of the market and made my way through a cold storage room with that damp produce smell and bare light bulbs hanging from the ceiling. I went out the back door, through a small alley and out onto a back street away from my minders. It took me just a second to get my bearings then I headed away from the market, out of sight of the Explorer, and over toward the corner of 5th and Dearborn.

Sure enough, parked in a space with a little sign next to it that said "Reserved for Zipcar" was a dark blue Toyota Corolla. I jumped in behind the wheel, turned the key which was already in the ignition and pulled out into traffic.

I checked my watch. I still had a little time before I had to be at the airport and I wanted to see those pictures Chris was supposed to send me. I pulled the phone out of my pocket and dialed my son.

Two rings. "Hello?"

"Ben, it's me. I need your user name and password for your email."

"What?"

"Long story. I need your user name and password for your email account. I'm expecting an email I didn't want coming to me. Don't ask."

Ben and I have developed an understanding over the years. It doesn't happen very often, but if one of us calls the other and says 'I need this or that' we can sense when it's not just 'Can I borrow your sleeping bag?' and we don't ask questions. So he gave me the info. "Thanks, Ben. I'll talk to you later. I'm still hoping to make it over tonight for the debate." I hung up.

The thought occurred to me that with my cell phone unplugged Danielle Noble would have a tough job getting in touch with me when she landed. Better call her and give her the number to this phone. I dialed the number on the message slip from this morning, got her voicemail, and left the new number. Now I just hope she's like the rest of us and turns on her phone as soon as the plane lands.

Chapter 14

Internet cafes are almost as common in Seattle as coffee
shops. In fact, they're usually the same place. I didn't
have much trouble finding one. I logged onto Ben's email
account and, bingo, there was an email from Chris.

The first thing I looked for were pictures in the area of
that little desk. Sure enough, there was the desk with a
printer, a power strip, some CDs, an iPod, a couple of
computer cables or cords of some type not connected to
anything and an empty space where there obviously
used to be a computer.

The rest of the pictures were not very helpful except by
what they didn't show. No computer. It would appear
our visitors may have taken Anna Noble's computer.
But some things were not adding up. The two bozos in
the alley on the surveillance video were apparently
trying to look in Anna Noble's purse. If she was carrying
a computer it would have been obvious. I mean, her bag
was big but it wasn't that big. And it seemed to me, with
the criminal mind I've developed over the years, if the
computer was what they were looking for, they would
have gone to the apartment first, assuming it was the
same two guys, and, if the computer wasn't there, then
they would have gone looking for Anna, not the other
way around.

As much as I hated to admit it, I needed to know more
about Anna Noble, especially what she did for my Uncle.
The voice on the other end of the phone seemed to be my
best (only?) option, but I hated to ignore my instinct that

going to the Federal Building wasn't such a great idea.

I looked at my watch and decided it was time to head out to Seatac. Traffic was heavy but moving. I speeded up a little bit and changed lanes a couple of times, checking my rear view mirror for anything that looked like a tail. Then I picked a random exit, got off, pulled into a gas station, sat for a couple of seconds, didn't see anything particularly suspicious and headed back to the highway.

In about 15 minutes I was on the access road to the airport. Seatac has a live parking area away from the terminal that's marked for people who are picking up passengers and are waiting for a cell phone call to say 'come get me'. I pulled in, shut off the engine and angled the car so I could watch the entrance driveway, just in case.

Time to check in, I guess. First call was to Al. I was still trying to get more on Jeff Feinberg and was hoping Al might have come up with something.

The phone rang once. "Russo."

"Al, it's me. Go find a clean phone and call me back." I hung up. I knew my number would register on his "Incoming Calls" list so there was no need to give it to him and wait for him to write it down. At this point I was less concerned with them knowing I was calling than I was with them being able to pinpoint where I was. I figured they'd catch up with me sooner or later but I wanted to keep them off my tail until I had a chance to talk to Danielle Noble.

About two minutes later my little prepaid phone started to play an annoying little tune. I don't use this thing very often and I always forget to change the ringer to something a little less obnoxious.

"Al. Where are you?"

"Jesus, John, where are you, for crissake? Pete's going bullshit looking for you."

"Just running down a couple of leads. Bring me up to date. How are you making out?"

"Not great. I keep running into dead ends. But I did manage to get something on your friend Feinberg. Or, at least, I think it's him. I spent some time Googling him and running some secure data bases I'm not supposed to be in and came up with a Jeffrey M. Feinberg that was connected to the State Department. His name shows up in a couple of old press releases. He apparently was in charge of embassy security in the Middle East up until about the time of the start of the Iraq war. Prior to that there was a Jeffrey Feinberg that was some sort of low-level liaison between the State Department and the Office of Naval Intelligence. Right after the start of the war, his name disappears off the list of State Department employees and, here's the interesting part, shows up on a list of employees in – are you ready for this?- the friggin' Agriculture Department!"

"The Agriculture Department? Are you sure it's the same guy?"

"Same as what? The same as the guy we're interested in or the same guy in Agriculture that was the guy in State? In any case, the answer to both is: no, I'm not. But I've got two Jeffery Feinbergs. One disappears from State and, at the same time, the other shows up at Agriculture.

I mean, I'm sure it's just a coincidence. Probably two different guys, right? Aren't you the guy who keeps telling me there's no such thing as a coincidence?"

"Yeah, I know. But Agriculture?"

"I'll call you if I come up with anything else." He hung up.

Agriculture. Why does a guy with a security background go to work for Agriculture? The answer is: he probably doesn't. I ran into this once with a case I was working on at the Bureau. Only it wasn't a person, it was a project. Apparently there are certain situations when people in our government want to hide a project but need a budget so they bury it in some obscure place, usually in a place like the Department of Agriculture budget where it's accounted for on the books, but no one would think to look for it there. I don't know a lot about how it works, but I know it does. And usually it's spooks who do it.

So, my guess is Feinberg is still in some kind of security operation, went to work on some secret project and they're paying him through Agriculture. Neat trick. I think they call it hiding in plain sight. So the question is: What is Jeffrey Feinberg up to and what is his connection to Anna Noble? Somehow I don't think it has anything to do with corn.

Chapter 15

At 5:22 my phone rang. I hit the TALK button on the first ring. "Elliott."

"Hi, Sergeant. This is Danielle Noble. My plane just landed and I got your message.
Are you nearby?"

"Hi, Danielle. Yeah, I'm in the cell phone parking lot over by the cargo area. Are you at the gate?"

"No, we're still taxiing. Sergeant, I have only my carry-on so I'm going to head straight for the 'Arrival' area. I'm on Southwest. I should be there in about 5 minutes."

"I'm driving a dark blue Toyota Corolla. What am I looking for?"

"You mean 'who' am I looking for?"

"Yeah. Sorry. I meant what are you wearing? What do you look like? What distinguishing marks do you have on your body? You know, helpful stuff like that."

"Well, it's a little soon to be talking about my distinguishing marks, but I'm wearing a black raincoat, no hat, blondish brown hair pulled back and I'll be pulling a pink duffel with white and black flowers."

"Stand close to the curb. I'll be looking for that duffel." I hung up.

The rain started coming down for real and the traffic slowed down accordingly. I pulled out onto the ring road and headed toward the terminal. I always get confused at airports and generally make at least three passes before I figure out which lane I'm supposed to be in. But I didn't want to keep Miss Noble waiting so I paid close attention and as soon as I saw the first 'Arrivals' sign I got into the correct lane.

The Seatac terminal is kind of a semi-circle with the ring road on the inside of the circle with the terminal on your right and a large parking deck on your left. So as you approach the 'Arrival' area, you can't see all of the doors for the various airlines and that includes Southwest which is maybe half to three quarters of the way around. With rain and my unfamiliarity I was almost on top of it when I saw the sign.

I slowed down and looked for the pink duffel.

It all happened pretty fast. I spotted a lone female figure grasping the handle of a flowered pink duffel standing on the edge of the sidewalk standing directly under the Southwest sign and looking in my direction. No more than 30 or 40 yards in front of me was a black SUV of some type going just a little too fast. Just as it got almost even with her, the stop lights came on and the SUV came to a quick stop right next to her. The passenger side door opened up and a guy wearing blue jeans, sneakers and a Seattle Mariners warm-up jacket jumped out and grabbed her arm. I heard somebody say "Ah, shit," and realized it was me.

I hit the gas and the little Corolla dropped down into some kind of passing gear that pushed me back in my seat. Just as I hit the gas pedal, I saw her drop the duffel handle and bring the heel of her left hand up under this guy's chin. His head snapped back, he let go of her and started to fall backward as I pulled along side the driver's side of the SUV and lost sight of both of them. I cut the wheel hard to the right and ran the right side of the Corolla into the left front fender of the SUV.

I jumped out of the car and ran around the front end of the Corolla and the SUV, pulled my gun out of my holster and yelled "Seattle police." I thought:'I'm too old for this shit'. As I came around the front of the SUV, I could see the guy picking himself up off the ground and trying to get back into the SUV. The driver already had the thing in reverse and as he backed up, the open passenger door knocked the poor bastard down again. He rolled over backwards and somehow managed to get to his feet. By that time, the SUV was moving forward again and pulling out around the Corolla, making a combination of tire squealing noises and metal scraping noises. As he passed the Corolla, he sideswiped it with the half open passenger side door which banged shut. He shot over into the high speed lane, somehow managing not to hit anybody and disappeared. I got a quick look at the plate and a partial number but was still trying to focus on the guy who got left behind.

Everyone on the sidewalk and around the cars loading up seemed to be frozen and just staring.

At that point in front of the terminal there are four lines of cars: one parked next to the curb with driver's just sitting and waiting, one picking people up and loading luggage into their trunks, one fairly slow moving line of cars looking for a spot to pull into, and an outside lane of traffic, including cabs, moving at a pretty good clip and not really interested in slowing down for anyone.

As I rushed past Danielle Noble, the guy on the ground got up and started running away from me and out toward the road. He ran past some people loading a bunch of luggage into the trunk of a car, knocked over the pile, just enough to slow me down, which, believe me, doesn't take much. He dodged a couple of cars in the third lane, but when he tried to cross the fourth lane without slowing down his already miserable luck got a little worse, and a cab, doing probably 50, smacked into him, lifted him off the ground kind of in slow motion, and dropped him on the hood of the cab, where he promptly rolled off the front, over the grille and under the front wheels as the cab driver hit the brakes trying to stop. By the time the cab stopped, the body was lying in the street next to the right rear wheel. Cars were swerving and stopping everywhere trying to avoid hitting the cab which was stopped in the middle of the high speed lane.

Now I'm no Medical Examiner, even though I did stay at a Holiday Inn Express one time, but even my untrained eye could see that this guy wasn't going to be answering any questions. As I ran toward him, or what was left of him, I holstered my gun and pulled out my shield waving it at the cab driver who was just starting to get out of his cab. "Stay in your vehicle," I yelled in my most authoritative cop voice. I wanted to do a quick check to see if this guy had any ID, which I didn't really expect to find. I wasn't disappointed. Clean as a whistle.

All of those frozen people started moving again and there was suddenly a lot of yelling and pretty much general chaos. I looked up and saw some uniforms coming my way moving quickly. I flashed my shield at the first guy to come close and said: "Seattle PD - better get this guy an ambulance," then I moved away and toward where Danielle had been standing when all of this started to hit the fan.

She was still standing about where she had been and I walked over to her. People were pushing past us and toward the cab. "You ok?"

"I take it you're Sergeant Elliott. Nice welcome."

Pretty cool customer for someone who just almost got kidnapped. "Yeah, well the Chamber of Commerce tries to make everybody's first visit to Seattle a memorable one. Come on, let's see if we can get out of here."

We walked quickly over to the Corolla and I gave it the once over. Other than some serious dents, it appeared to be drivable. I was glad it wasn't my car. The Zipcar folks were not going to be too happy about this one.

She tossed her pink duffel into the back seat and jumped into the passenger side. The door made a weird kind of grinding sound when she opened it. Oh, and she had to slam it three times to get it to close. Not bad. I was amazed it worked at all.

I popped it into Drive, maneuvered through a couple of lines of cars that were loading up and pulled into the far lane which was now completely devoid of traffic. I didn't even want to think about the back-up behind the cab.

"So," I said, "how was your day?"

Chapter 16

We drove around the parking deck and toward the highway. There was silence in the car while everybody's adrenaline levels returned to something near normal, whatever that might be.

"I thought I could trust you," she said. "My dad said he thought I could trust you."

"What are you talking about?" I said.

"I asked you not to tell anybody that I was coming out here."

"What makes you think I did?" I responded. This was not going well.

"You're kidding, right?" she said.

"No, I'm not kidding. In fact, I've violated about ten department rules going out of my way not to mention to anyone that you were coming out here or that I was picking you up. And I ditched my car down in the International District and picked up this rental car just to make sure nobody followed me."

"Well, somebody sure as hell did."

"I'm not so sure about that."

"What makes you say that?"

"First of all, they were there ahead of me. Second, even if they did follow me, there was no way for them to know why I was there and they clearly were looking for you. And as much as you may find this hard to believe, I never mentioned to a soul that you were coming."

Silence again. "Look," I said, "let's start over. Hi. I'm John Elliott. What's your name?"

She looked over at me and stared at me for about a count of five. Then she looked away out the side window and I could see a little smile flicker across her face. When she looked back, the smile was gone but her expression had softened.

"Ok," she said. "I'm sorry I jumped to conclusions, but being assaulted standing in front of an airport only happens to me once or twice a year so I'm just a little edgy. And thanks for rescuing me."

"Ah, that's all right. I only do rescues once or twice a year myself. You're lucky I've only done one so far this year. Any idea who those guys were or why they wanted you?"

She let out a long sigh and stared straight ahead through the windshield. "I really have no idea about either one of those things, but it may have something to do with why I asked you to meet me. Look, I know I said I didn't need a ride and I could have easily rented a car, but I thought if you could drive me out to my dad's house, we could talk about a couple of things that may be related to Anna's death. After what happened back there, I'm not sure I want to be alone anyway."

"Speaking of 'back there'," I said, "what was that little

move you put on that guy? You actually looked like you knew what you were doing."

"I decided when I moved to DC that I needed to be able to protect myself, so I took some self-defense classes. I never thought I'd actually have to use it, but it just made me feel more comfortable about walking down some of those DC streets."

"Ok," I said, beginning to lose my patience. "Now I could be dead wrong here, but I can usually tell the difference between somebody who's taken 'some self-defense classes' and somebody who's pretty well trained in martial arts. See, there's a huge difference between laying out your instructor who's being paid to take a fall and instinctively reacting in a split second to real danger. It's kind of like learning to shoot a gun. You can blast away at all of those black silhouettes you want and cluster your shots right in a tight little cluster, but when some bad guy is coming at you with evil in his eye and coke in his brain and a gun pointed straight at you, most people who are not thoroughly trained will freeze, even if it's just for a second. I mean, I was moving pretty fast, but your timing looked pretty professional to me.

"Look, lady, I've had a long day and I'm tired. And I may not be the smartest bear in the woods, but I'm sick of people who think I'm a candidate for the short bus. So let's cut the bullshit and why don't you tell me what this is all about?"

She let out another long sigh and looked out the side window. I waited.

She turned and looked at me and I could see that she was struggling with how much she wanted to tell me, how much she could tell me. I gave her a side ways glance and when I did, she looked straight into my eyes. I had to force myself to look back at the road. Even in the dim light inside the car, her eyes were the most incredible shade of blue I'd ever seen and seemed to be looking into my soul. Freaky. I don't like it when total strangers peek at my soul. It's an invasion of my privacy. I'd rather get caught with my pants down.

"All right," she said, "I'll tell you as much as I can. But there are certain things I can't tell you."

"Then let's just start with the things you can tell me," I said. "That all by itself would be refreshing."

"Anna and I were six years apart. Ordinarily, I guess, that's far enough where most sisters don't have much in common and don't grow up really all that close. But it was different for us. My father never had any sons and being the competitive son of a bitch that he is, Anna and I grew up competing at all different levels. It was kind of a weird relationship.
We were competing in so many different aspects that there were times that I think we loved each other but really didn't like each other. Let me know if this gets a little too psycho-babble for you, but I've spent a lot of time and money figuring this whole thing out."

"No," I said, "keep going. By the way, you have any objection to taking the ferry over to Bainbridge?" Testing, testing. 1-2-3 testing.

"No," she said, looking at me again, wide-eyed, with the entire universe opening up in her blue eyes. "Why would I?"

"No reason," I said. "Anyway, so you and your sister were the two sons your father never had."

"Something like that. Anyway, as we got older that kind of smoothed out a little bit and we got closer. But we still competed. I think the ultimate prize was my father's affection, but that's another story for another day. The competition was mostly physical. You know, sports of all kinds. Team sports, outdoor sports. You name it and we could find a way to make a competition out of it.

"As we got older, we got competitive with everybody. It turned out to be a real pain in the ass when you're dating and trying to have a somewhat normal relationship with some really nice guy and you're faster and stronger than he is. Apparently, guys don't deal with that real well. Anyway, my competitiveness took me through college then into the Marine Corps. Anna's took her through MIT. Turns out she was some kind of genius with computers. I hate to admit it even now, but she was a whole lot smarter than me."

Meanwhile we were coming into downtown Seattle and I started looking for an exit that would take me to Alaskan Way and the ferry terminal. I would have loved to have gone and picked up my own car but I thought that it was still a little premature.

"While I was in the Marine Corps," she said, "I signed up for a special unit and got some pretty intense physical training including weapons training and martial arts. When I got out, I was recruited by the Secret Service and spent eight years protecting the wife of the Vice-President."

I was beginning to understand how some of those guys she was talking about must have felt when they started finding out this stuff about her. Certain parts of my body were becoming noticeably smaller.

"So you're in the Secret Service?"

"No, I'm not. Not any more. I'm pretty professional or, at least, I like to think I am. But I'm also human. I was completely devoted to the Vice-President's wife and to that administration. But when this current President took office…let's just say I was afraid my conscience would get in the way of my job. There was an awful lot that I just didn't approve of. I mean, I know we weren't supposed to be political, but I was close enough to the situation to see what was happening and why it was happening and it really bothered my sense of loyalty to my country."

"So you quit?"

"Well, I resigned and decided to take a vacation after eight years of constant stress. I traveled a little, laid on the beach for a month, and just generally let it all drain out of the tips of my fingers."

"That sounds like a great ending to this story. In fact, if I was writing this story, that would be the end. Why do I get the feeling there's more?"

"Late one afternoon I was sitting in a little bar near the beach having a beer and starting to think a little bit about what I might do next when this guy comes in and sits down at the bar next to me. The bar was pretty quiet. There were a couple of people out on the deck and the bartender was busy getting things ready for the 5:00 rush and I was sitting alone. He started talking to me. You know, just small talk. Nothing unusual.

"Somehow we get talking about what I'm doing there and what am I going to do when I leave the island. I'm still relaxed, just chatting with some stranger that seems pretty nice and pretty easy to talk to."

"Didn't your mother ever tell you not to talk to strangers?" She paused for a second and looked at me. She must have thought better about telling me what I child I was – I've seen that look before – because she went on as if I hadn't said anything.

"I asked him what he did for a living and he gives me some general answer like 'I work in security', which could mean anything from a bank guard to Blackwater. But at that point I didn't much care. I was enjoying myself and I wasn't much interested in swapping war stories. Besides, in those little beach towns, people will say almost anything if they think they can get laid."

"Then he asks me about how I would feel going back to work for the government. Now I'm on my second beer and thinking this guy's pretty cute and let's see where this goes. So, not really thinking about it one way or the other, I tell him I wouldn't mind if it was the right job."

"What did he say to that?"

"He didn't say anything at first and took a long pull on his beer and glanced around the bar at nothing in particular. Then he looks at the label on the bottle as if he's reading it or something and, without looking at me, says 'I might have the right job for you'. R-i-i-n-n-n-g! Wake up call. In about a second and a half all the old training kicked in. I realized that this was no chance meeting and, as nice as he was and as cute as he was, this was no pick-up. At least not in the traditional sense. My mellow mood disappeared and all my systems were up and running.

"But I didn't say anything or show anything. He took a hit on his beer and kept looking at the label. I took a sip of my beer and said to him as casually as I could: 'What's that supposed to mean?' And he says: 'I might have a job for you that involves keeping government employees honest. And I'm not talking about stealing stamps or pencils on the taxpayers dime'.

" 'Go ahead'," I said. So he proceeds to tell me there's a small group of people that answers to someone pretty high up in the government and their job is to essentially investigate and deal with serious abuses of power – using the office for what you might term 'unpure motives'. Kind of a Constitutional SWAT team. Some intelligence gathering, some field work. Their identities and the identity of the person they work for is a closely guarded secret."

"Apparently you thought this guy was for real. What did you say to him?"

"I told him I might be interested. He said: 'Fine. Take your time with your sabbatical. When you get back to Washington, we'll be in touch.' There was no doubt in my mind they would know when I was back in Washington and how to contact me.

"Anyway, I can't give you too much more detail, but that was almost seven years ago and I'm still with them. As far as most people are concerned, including most of my family, I went to work for a private security firm."

I pulled off of Alaskan Way and onto the ferry dock. There was still a steady drizzle. I pulled into line and waited – waited for the line to move and waited for Danielle Noble to tell me why she wanted me to meet her at the airport.

Chapter 17

The line began to move and I noticed there was a whole hell of a lot less security than there was earlier today No mirrors. Only one dog that I could see. No trunks being opened. My guess was they had lowered the MARSEC Level.

We pulled up onto the outside ramp of the ferry and drove almost all the way forward. I got out and moved around to the rail. Danielle got out and stood next to me.

"So," I said, "that's all very interesting. But I'm still not sure what any of this has to do with me outside of the fact that I'm investigating Anna's death. I mean, as far as I know you've never seen me, so it can't be because I'm devilishly handsome."

She leaned her elbows on the rail and stared out at Seattle skyline that had started disappearing into the mist. After a short pause, she reached up and hooked her right thumb around a small but sturdy looking silver chain around her neck. As she ran her thumb up under the chain and pulled it our from under her coat, there appeared a small bronze colored object connected to the chain through a small loop on one corner of it. At first I thought it was some kind of cigarette lighter because of its shape. It kind of looked like a small, expensive BIC. I know, I know. A cigarette lighter on a silver chain around a woman's neck? All I'm saying is that's what I first thought.

"Do you know what this is?" she asked.

"A cigarette lighter?" I said.

She laughed. "No, it's not a cigarette lighter. A cigarette lighter?"

"It's ok to humiliate me," I said, "as long as you respect me in the morning."

She smiled and shook her head slowly from side to side. The smile slowly disappeared.
"It's a flash drive," she said. "Anna sent it to my house. Do you know what a flash drive is?"

"Of course I do," I replied, perhaps a little too quickly. She just stared at me with her thumb still under the chain and the flash drive dangling from the chain.

"Ok," I said, "so I don't know what a flash drive is. But I'm sure I've heard about it."

"It's an external memory device for a computer. You can download files onto it then take this little beauty with you. It plugs into a USB port on your computer so you can upload the files back into your computer or any other computer, for that matter."

My eyes must have looked like they were glazing over or something because she said to me: "You do know what a USB port is." It was a statement but it was really a question.

"Yes," I said. "I actually do know what a USB port is, but thank you for asking."

Ok, now I was starting to get interested. "What's in it?" I

asked.

"You mean what's on it."

"In it, on it – tomato, tomahto."

"I plugged it into my computer…."

"Into your USB port." She ignored me the way you do when Granny farts at the dinner table.

"…and at first I thought there wasn't much of anything on it. It looked like just a bunch of Justice Department stuff to do with budgets. But I figured there must be some reason Anna sent it to me so I'd better hang onto it until I could talk to her and find out why she sent it to me. The thought actually crossed my mind that maybe she found somebody fooling around with the taxpayers money or something like that.

"Then somewhere in the middle as I was scrolling through the files on this little beauty, I came to a file I couldn't open. I got a little curious and tried a couple of tricks I know but I still couldn't open it. So now it became more of a challenge than anything else. I wanted to know what was in this file – not because I particularly cared what was in it, I just couldn't give up on it.

"So I took it to this guy I know who can break into just about anything electronic. He struggled with it for almost two hours, which is absolutely unheard of for him. After about a half hour of swearing and table banging, he got real quiet. All I could hear was the keys on his keyboard. I don't think he even realized I was in the room, he was so focused and determined.

"Finally, I heard him say 'Yeesss'. I was almost dozing off and I snapped awake. I walked over to his computer and said to him 'What did you find?'. He said 'There's good news and bad news', but I had already looked at the screen and knew what the bad news was: The file was encoded so you couldn't read it. It was a series of letters, numbers and symbols all run together line after line. Somebody went to an awful lot of trouble to keep people from reading this particular file.

"He said it kind of looked a little bit like 'machine language' which is the way computers read programming instructions. People can't necessarily read it, but the computer can. But he also said it didn't really look like any machine language he had ever seen. He said he thought it was some type of encryption, kind of like a code, but very sophisticated.

"I could have called Anna, but I didn't want her to think I'd been snooping, since she hadn't told me she was sending it or told me to look at it when I got it, and I didn't particularly want her to know the kinds of resources I have. Besides, at that point I thought she was coming out to DC on Saturday anyway, so I'd just wait until she got there."

"So have you figured out what this file has in it?"

"No, I haven't. But the way it was sent to me – you know, the timing and all, I can't help thinking it may have something to do with Anna's death. Anyway, I wanted to talk to you to see what you've found out and see if maybe there's a connection."

I'm not sure if it's my line of work or just some personality defect, but I don't fully trust too many people, especially people I've only known as long as I'd known Danielle Noble. Something was missing from this story. It was only a guess, but I was thinking maybe she did know what was on that file but wasn't going to share it with me until she found out how much I knew about this whole business. I have to think that in her line of work, whatever that might be, she probably didn't fully trust too many people either, especially people she'd only known as long as she'd known me, regardless of what her father might have said about trusting me. If he really said it. I wonder if dentists or insurance men are this paranoid.

I decided to sidestep the 'see what you've found out' question that wasn't really a question but really was a question. At least for now. I thought I'd try the old answer-a- question-with-a-question trick.

"Do you know a guy by the name of Jeff Feinberg?"

She dropped the BIC lighter back down inside her blouse. Just for a fleeting instant I went down there with it. Easy John, stay focused. She leaned her arms on the rail and looked sideways at me and said: "I know he's a friend of my father's. I think I might have met him at my Dad's house once. Why?"

Did you know most people's eyes move up to their left just before they lie to you? Or is it down? Anyway, her eyes didn't move.

"No reason in particular. His name came up when I was talking to your father. Your father said he had spoken to Anna on Thursday night and she asked him how she could get in touch with this guy."

"Why do I get the feeling you and I are doing the waltz together but not really touching?"

"I'm not sure why you get that feeling, Ms. Noble. All I know is I'm trying to solve a murder - actually, two murders – and I haven't eaten since very early this morning. On top of the fact it's Saturday night and I was hoping to spend a little time with my son instead of playing taxi driver. So excuse me if I'm a little grumpy."

She stared at me for a couple of seconds and it wasn't that 'portal to the universe' stare. I stared back.

Then she smiled and said: "Look, it's obviously been a long day for both of us and I haven't eaten much today either. We're almost to the dock. Why don't we stop in the village and get something to eat?"

I was way past hungry but, all in all, it didn't sound like such a bad idea. "Ok," I said, "but I insist on paying for my own dinner. I don't want you to think you can just buy me a meal then get into my pants."

She laughed and as the ferry touched the dock she rocked towards me and I could smell her hair. "Come on," she said, "we'd better get in the car."

 I had to remind myself this was still very much a murder investigation and something else that was feeling a little more sinister than your ordinary everyday garden variety murder.

Chapter 18

The cars rolled off the boat, onto the dock and up the access road away from the water front. Keeping in mind I didn't have Little Miss Garmin with me, I asked Danielle where she'd like to go.

"Let's go to the San Carlos Café," she said. "I haven't been there in ages. Go up here and make a right on Madison. You'll see it up about a block on the right."

Although it was a Saturday night, it was still a little early for the dinner crowd and, after all, this was Bainbridge Island. People move here for a variety of reasons, but the bustling night life apparently isn't one of them. I pulled up in front of a little cottage-looking restaurant with a warm yellow glow coming from inside.

The inside of the restaurant was fairly plain with a lot of dark wood grain showing and white tablecloths. I always keep my hand on my wallet when I see white linen tablecloths. There were a couple of what I call Indian blankets hanging on the wall and some terra cotta pottery, mostly filled with cactus looking plants of one kind or another. Just enough stuff so you knew you weren't in a pizza joint.

A young man with a hint of some type of Hispanic accent came over and told us we could sit anywhere we liked and our waitress would be over momentarily. After the day I'd had, I chose a table toward the back of the restaurant where I could see the door and sit facing it. I said I was tired not stupid.

"This ok?" I asked.

"Yes, this is fine," she said and we both sat down.

Our waitress came over and asked if she could get us something to drink.

"My name's Caroline. And before you ask," she smiled, "it has nothing to do with Neil Diamond or the Boston Red Sox."

"Well, Caroline," Danielle said, "I'll have a margarita. You really should have one, John. The make the best margaritas here. Or at least they used to."

I've always found that memories of good drinks are usually more to do with where you were or who you were with when you had them as opposed to how good they really were. Like the Painkillers at the Soggy Dollar Bar on Jost van Dyke. My guess is there were some kind of fond memories attached to this place for Danielle. On the other hand, maybe they just made a really good margarita here.

On the other other hand, however, I tend to be more of a beer drinker. "Thanks, but I'll have a Corona," I said.

See, now, there's the perfect example of what I'm talking about. Bottom line is: Corona is panther piss. But I've had a few Coronas in some pretty cool places with some pretty cool people and sometimes sipping on a Corona somehow makes me feel good. After the day I'd had, I needed something to remind me of warm places and warm people.

"So, John," she said, "you know a little bit about me. Tell me something about you.
I mean something other than you hate not knowing something and becoming obsessed with finding out."

"Hmm," I said. "Pretty good."

"Not really," she said. "I mean, a 50-something homicide detective. Has to be something other than the great pay and the banker's hours."

"Yeah, I guess so. I never really thought about it, to tell you the truth. You know, things happen to you during your life and sometimes you're so focused on them that you don't really think about why you do what you do for a living. It's just what you do to pay the mortgage, or the tuitions. Or the alimony and the child support."

"So you were married? Are married?"

"Was married. Have two remarkable kids."

"Right. A son...?"

"Ben."

"The son you were supposed to be spending the evening with tonight."

"Yeah. No offense, but I'm still hoping to do that."

"You said you had two kids."

"A daughter. You'd like her. She can do just about anything. Cook, scuba dive, mountain climb. Little bit of a thing. Fools people. They're constantly underestimating her. I actually think she likes it that way. She's only 24 but she's already seen more of the world than I'll ever see."

Now don't get me wrong. I was really starting to enjoy the company of a woman who actually was willing to talk about herself, and was also willing to ask stuff about me. And I think she was really interested in my answers. But I also needed to know a little more about Anna Noble.

"So tell me about your sister. Were you two close even though you were separated by three thousand miles?"

Just then, Sweet Caroline arrived with our drinks. My Corona had the obligatory lime wedge half stuffed into the top of the bottle. I pulled it out and put it on the table. "I don't know about you," I said, "but I don't want fruit anywhere near my beer. I don't want blueberry beer or any beer with a hint of anything God never intended to be in beer." I poured the beer into a nice un-frozen plain heavy glass. "Another thing: don't ever give me one of those frozen mugs you can't touch with either your hands or your lips without getting frostbite."

"God," she said, half smiling. "And I thought James Bond was a little fussy with his 'shaken, not stirred' thing!"

"See, that's the thing, since you want to know about me. I'm only fussy about the things I care about. Like beer. I'm not one of your ordinary, every day, Felix Unger types. One look around my house and you'd know that. Give me a $200.00 bottle of wine served in a plastic cup with ice cubes. I could give a shit less. But beer…gotta be just right.

"Anyway, cheers!" I tapped the rim of my Corona against the rim of her margarita. We both took a sip. "How is it?" I asked.

She closed her eyes for a second or two and I could tell she was savoring the flavor and the memory. "Just like I remembered it," she said.

"So," I said, "tell me about you and Anna. Pardon me for saying so, but you don't seem to be particularly upset."

"I'm sure it seems that way to you," she said. "I don't think the grief has really set in yet. In some ways this whole thing over the last twelve hours – God, has it only been twelve hours? – I guess it hasn't really hit me that she's gone. But let me assure you all of my systems are in high gear. I want to know who did this and why. It's all I care about right now and I'll look for answers any way and any place I can. Maybe that's my way of dealing with it. I guess I'm not much for sitting around and crying. I'm more of an action kind of person." And she looked at me with a cold stare that gave me a chill. I thought to myself: 'There's a lot of layers here. I mean a lot of layers'.

"That's the way my Dad's always been. I guess it's one of the things he taught Anna and me. Dad always said: 'Do something'. So I'm here because this is where I ought to be, but I'm also here because this is where I have to be to find out what happened to Anna."

"And I'm part of that."

"Yes, John, you are. I need your help. And, although you may not realize it yet, you're going to need mine."

116

Chapter 19

Dinner was actually pretty good. I had the mesquite smoked Texas ribs and Danielle had the grilled chicken with Santa Fe sauce. I tried a little of hers and she tried a little of mine. After not eating all day, I was beginning to feel human again. Ribs and beer. Way better than a psychiatrist or drugs for making me feel better.

I noticed among the nighttime revelers were two guys that had come in and were sitting on the other side of the restaurant. The reason I noticed them was they weren't talking to each other. They each had some kind of drink in front of them but no food ever came out. Now I've been in restaurants where you see old married couples come in, sit down, have dinner and leave and never speak to each other, not in a hostile way, but in a way that says 'After all these years, there's nothing left to say'. But these guys didn't look like an old married couple, even in this day and age.

I made a mental note of their presence, but decided not to mention it to Danielle.

After her second margarita, I learned Danielle had an off and on relationship, if you could call it that, with a guy from Seattle.

"So," I said to her when the coffee came, "career or relationship?"

"Both," she said with a smile. "I thought you'd have figured that out by now – I want it all. I don't compromise about much."

I nodded and said: "Let's get back to Anna. Did you speak to her at all this week?"

"Yes, I did. She called me Thursday evening. She said she had come across something accidentally in the course of her job and she wasn't quite sure what to do about it. She said she needed to come to DC to see some people and asked if she could stay with me while she was there. Of course I said 'yes'. She didn't say much more. She did ask me if I had gotten a FedEx envelope and I said 'yes'. She just said 'Hang onto it until I get there and put it in a safe place."

"She act like she thought she was in any danger?"

"I've been thinking back about that myself and I have to say I don't think so. If she did, she certainly didn't come right out and say it. Of course she probably wouldn't have said anything like that anyway. One of the things about the Noble sisters is we think we can handle just about anything. So even if we were faced with a dangerous situation, we tend to look at it as more of a challenge than as something to be afraid of."

"Do you have any idea of what Anna actually did for the Justice Department?"

"Anna never talked much about it to me, but I learned through some connections of my own that she was a computer forensics expert. I'm not sure exactly what or who she worked for, but as best as I could tell she went into computer systems to see if anything was there that wasn't supposed to be."

"What, exactly, does that mean?"

"Oh, yeah," she laughed, "I forgot who I was talking to."

"I'll ignore that for now."

"Let's see how I can explain this. Ok, here's an example. You do use the Internet, right?"

"I can see this is going to be brutal. Yes, jerk face, I use the Internet."

" 'Jerk face'. Very adult, Elliott. So you know you can sit at home or wherever and look up stuff. You know, go to web sites, go to Google or Yahoo then from there to web sites and so on. Did you know other people, people you don't even know, can get into your computer and see what's there? They don't even have to be sitting in front of your computer."

"Vaguely."

"And did you know they can plant stuff in your computer so they can monitor where you go and what you look at?"

"I thought there were things like anti-spy programs and firewalls that kept those things out of your computer."

"Firewalls. Wow. You know about firewalls?"

"Can we just stick to this conversation instead of playing pin the tail on the dinosaur?"

"Anyway, apparently Anna's job was looking at Justice Department computers to see if they had been broken into and to see if there were any kinds of things planted in them that would allow the bad guys to know what was going on or to see if anyone had gotten past all of the security and stolen or tried to steal any information."

"I thought all kinds of alarms went off when people tried to fool around with government computers."

"I don't know much about the details, but from what I understand, some of these guys are pretty sophisticated. I guess it's like patching a garden hose or making flu vaccine."

"What?"

"I mean, most of the protection is based on the last thing that happened. It's almost impossible to guess ahead of time what technique they're going to use. So somebody breaks in, you catch them at it, you figure out how they did it then you fix the leak.
You just don't always know where the next leak is going to be."

"Flu vaccine?"

"Oh. This year's flu vaccine is based on last year's flu. Every year the virus is a little different. That's why you can get a flu shot and still get the flu."

Caroline came over and put the bill on the table in one of those little padded book things – you know, the thing Jerry Seinfeld calls 'the story of the bill'.

I shook my head. "So, you think that little thing around your neck might hold a clue?"

"I don't know, but I'm hoping so. I didn't get a chance to

talk to a couple of people in my outfit that might have been able to break the code on that file we were talking about. I was about to do that...." She stopped.

"God," she said. "I was going to say 'I was about to do that on Saturday'. Today is Saturday. It's been a long day." She put her face in her hands and rubbed her eyes.

"Come on, John," she said. "Let's pay the bill and get going. I want to get to my Dad's house. I still have a few things to do before I can crash."

She reached into her wallet and pulled out two twenties. "Here," she said. "Will you pay the bill? I've got to stop in the ladies room." She pushed her chair away from the table, stood up and headed off toward the back of the restaurant. I put two twenties of my own with it and waved to Caroline who was starting to hustle. She came over and took the money.

"Do you need change?" she asked.

"I sure do," I said, "Maybe a Caribbean island." She looked at me for a brief instant. "Oh, no," I said. "I thought you said do I need a change. No, Caroline, I don't need change. Thanks very much."

She walked away. No Danielle in sight, so I got up and started toward the front door. I glanced over at the two guys with no food and noticed they were paying their bill and getting ready to leave. Now as I may have mentioned before, I don't really believe in coincidences, especially after the day I've had today. So my radar immediately went into action but I was careful not to make eye contact with either of them or to give them any indication I even noticed them.

I stepped outside and walked over and stood next to the rent-a-wreck. While I was deciding how I was going to get the Department to pay the Zipcar folks, the odd couple came out, didn't look at me and walked down the street away from the restaurant. I noticed they were not holding hands. Definitely suspicious behavior.

As I watched them, Danielle came outside. "Come on, let's go."

"Are you ok?" I asked.

"Fine," she said. "Just a little tired."

I helped her open her door. Now, I'm thinking to myself: 'How dumb is this? This woman could probably break you in half without breaking a sweat and you're opening her door. She should be opening my door, for crissake! She got in and as I slammed (and I mean slammed) her door shut, I heard some faintly metallic sound from the rear of the car that sounded like something had fallen off.

As I pulled out of the parking space and started to pull away, I looked in the rear view mirror and saw headlights come on and a car pull out a little way down the street behind us coincidentally from the same direction Laurel and Hardy had been walking.

"These bastards never give up," I said kind of half out loud to no one in particular.

"I'm sorry," she said. "What did you say."

"I said 'Don't look now, but I think they found us'."

Chapter 20

"Any idea who they are?" she asked me.

"Well, I'm thinking whoever they are, it can't be good. I'm pretty sure if it was anybody reasonably friendly they would have just walked up to us."

"Pull over here and pop open the trunk, will you?" she said. "I need to get something out of my bag."

I pulled over and she jumped out and moved quickly to the back of the car. She opened the trunk and I heard the zipper on her bag open then close. I also noticed the headlights behind us slowed and stopped at the last intersection before making the corner.

The trunk slammed and she opened the passenger door and slipped back into the seat. The light was only on for a second but I could see she was holding a particularly nasty looking hand-gun. "How'd you get that through security?" I asked her, as we pulled away from the curb.

"What, this?"

"No, the bag of peanuts you stole from the plane. Yes, that!"

"Oh, we have credentials similar to air marshals. By the way, just in case, are you carrying a weapon?"

"Yeah. I have this Glock I'm kind of partial to. By the way, I have no idea where I'm going."

"My guess is if these guys are going to try anything, they're going to wait until we're over on Crystal Springs Drive near my Dad's house. If I were them, I'd have a second unit over there waiting. Go around the block again and make a left on Wyatt Way."

"How do these guys know where you're going? And what the hell do you mean 'a second unit?'"

"I think once they figured out I was here in Seattle, it probably wasn't much of a guess to expect me to come here. And they don't seem to be too concerned that we know they're back there, so I'm assuming they're not going to make a move until they have help. Especially if they're the same bunch from the airport. The only question is: How much help?"

"Shit. I should have made you take a cab. Why Crystal Springs Drive?"

"Because there's two or three ways we could get over to that side of the island and they would have to cover all of them. But once we get over to Crystal Springs Drive it's the only road. Plus it's pretty well populated between here and there, but there are a few places on Crystal Springs where the woods are fairly dense on either side of the road and very few houses, most of which are on the water side and set well back from the road. So any nosy neighbors are less likely to hear a commotion, if there is one."

"Do you have any idea who these guys are and why they may be after you? Does this have anything to do with your job?"

"You know, I've been thinking about that. I mean, there's

no way to tell at this point. I make a lot of enemies, but we go to a good deal of trouble to keep people from finding out about our identities – make a left here. I suppose it's possible. But if someone wanted to kill me, there are a lot easier and less public ways to do it. I've had a couple of attempts on my life, but they were what you would think of as assassination attempts...."

My God, she was casual about this. Although, I have to say I've been shot at a few times in my career and while I wouldn't say you ever get used to it, you don't tend to dwell on it like the average citizen. The human brain can adapt to almost anything and in her line of work apparently assassination attempts are not that big a deal. I guess if you're going to work in the Secret Service and be prepared to take a bullet for someone, it changes your perspective on a lot of things.

"...long range shots where the shooter would just as soon get as far away as quickly as possible. But these guys...I don't know. They keep wanting to get up close and personal. I'm becoming really curious to find out who they are."

"Is it possible this is all about that flash drive?"

"I've considered that, too. Right now, it's probably my best guess. I think it will be easier once we know what's on it."

"Any idea how that might happen?"

"I'm working on it. Make a right up here on. I'd suggest you stay alert from this point on. I'm guessing Crystal Springs Drive, but there's a couple of lonely spots on this road, too."

I turned right and checked the rear view mirror. About a quarter of a mile back, the headlights came around the corner. I wasn't exactly a novice at this stuff either and in my limited experience there wasn't much anybody could do from a quarter of a mile back.

I'm thinking, when they beg into close the gap, get ready to get ready.

It's pretty quiet out here and there wasn't much traffic on the road. My guess was there would be even less traffic on Crystal Springs Drive. Yeah, I know. A lot of guessing going on. But that's the way it is, at least in my business and, I suspected, in Danielle's, as well. You have to make certain assumptions or guesses and act on them otherwise you're always waiting for the bad guys to move first. Not a real good idea.

Anyway, it was looking like Danielle's guess that if anything nasty was going to happen it was probably going to be on Crystal Springs Drive was a pretty good one. Then, for no good reason, it dawned on me I should probably call Ben since it looked like I wasn't going to make it over to his house tonight. Focus, Elliott, focus.

"Ok," she said, "this next intersection is Crystal Springs. You're going to make a right.

I'd take that Glock out and put it in my lap if I were you."

I did as I was told – about the right turn and about the Glock, although I was thinking maybe a left turn might make my life a little easier. Where the hell did this day go off the rails? For the second time today I thought: 'I'm too old for this shit'.

"How far to your father's house," I asked.

"About a mile and a half to two miles from here."

We didn't have long to wait. As we passed a side road on our right, headlights came on very close to the intersection and something fairly large (read: anything bigger than our Corolla) pulled out behind us and very close. I saw Danielle pick up her gun and flip off the safety. I reached down in my lap and did the same thing with the Glock.

We came into a curve to the left and as I came around the bend in the road I could see another large something, like a Suburban or an Expedition, backing out of a driveway on my left and backing straight across the road. There was a low stone wall on my left and a pretty good sized drainage ditch on my right so any thoughts I had about an end run quickly disappeared. This was a pretty well chosen spot and, although I really hadn't had any doubts to begin with, these were clearly not your average bunch of thugs. They were definitely an above-average bunch of thugs.

I started to slow down. "All right, John," Danielle said, "this is going to have to be quick.
Head straight into that SUV. When you get close, jump out, stay low and dive your ass over the wall. And keep the Glock ready."

Before I could argue or even ask a question like: 'And then what?', the passenger door flew open and Danielle rolled out and away from the car toward the ditch on the right.
In hindsight, I don't know if I really thought about it but I did what she said to do, popped the door open and rolled out onto the ground. I hit the ground pretty hard

and it was all I could do to hold onto the Glock. But adrenaline is a funny thing. It's the magic potion that gives 110 pound women the strength to lift cars off their children in car accidents and, apparently, 50-something year old detectives the strength to fall to the ground from a moving car and not break anything or, more importantly, drop anything.

That is, of course, if you don't count my left nut.

I rolled over a couple of times onto the grassy strip at the side of the road and, keeping low, took about three crouching strides and threw myself (again!) over the wall. Man, I thought, am I going to be sore tomorrow. If there is a tomorrow.

I'm pretty sure they saw me go over the wall so I didn't want to stay in one place. On the other hand, I didn't think trying to make a run for it was such a hot strategy either. Especially since I was pretty sure they were primarily after Danielle and, call it some twisted sense of chivalry, I didn't want to run off and leave her by herself. So I kept low behind the wall and moved in the direction of the car that was across the road and away from the majority of the troops.

Things were happening quickly. The bad guys were all in their vehicles when we made our move. I was able to get over the wall before they could react. But I knew that wouldn't last long. I peeked up over the wall with the Glock out in front of me just as the Corolla hit the side of the SUV. It was moving pretty good and hit the side of that big, ugly thing with an explosion of crunching metal and shattered glass. I ducked back down.

I figured if I made it over the wall ok, Danielle probably made it into the ditch ok. I also figured bodies were going to come pouring out of all three vehicles that had us pinned in and I didn't have long to wait. I couldn't be sure, but I thought I saw four guys came out of the SUV that was behind us and two more from the car that had been shadowing us from the restaurant. I didn't know how many were in the SUV that had backed out across the road, but probably at least two. Eight to two. Not good odds.

One of the first things I noticed was, except for engines running, including the valiant little Corolla now stationary with its engine revving at pretty high speed and wedged against the side of the whale that was across the road, there was very little noise. Each one of these guys were dressed in black and carrying one kind of ugly looking weapon or another. There were hand signals and guys disappearing off either side of the road. This was definitely not the gang that couldn't shoot straight. The whole thing was very military. It looked like they had split up with three guys going over the wall and the other three guys heading toward the ditch. Uh, oh, I thought, I have a bad feeling about this.

Then a couple of things happened that gave me hope. False hope, as it turned out. I could just see the passenger side door of the SUV that had just gotten hit. It swung open and two guys jumped out and headed around to the other side of the car. One went around the front and one went around the back, moving quickly but cautiously. Apparently, however, not cautiously enough. As they stepped out from the front and the back of the car, there was a popping sound followed quickly by another popping sound, and both guys went over backwards. I could see the guy closest to me and I could tell from the rag-doll position of his arms and legs he wasn't going anywhere. Ever.

I wasn't sure about the other guy, but I had a feeling if this was Danielle's work, he probably wasn't going anywhere either.

Six to two. Better than eight to two, but still not great. Especially if these guys had night vision goggles. Another popping sound followed by a shattering sound and the right front headlight of the trailing SUV went out. As that happened, another popping sound followed by another shattering sound and the left front headlight went out. It occurred to me that staying crouched behind the wall was only a short term solution. These guys knew the general direction where we had gone and were systematically sweeping down either side of the road. I had to move and move quickly. The headlights on the SUV closest to me were still on and shining in my direction. I'm not a great shot but the car was close enough to me that I popped my head up over the wall and fired twice at each headlight, somehow managing to blow them both out.

It seemed like forever, but I'm sure it was only a matter of a few seconds. The nearest shelter was the SUV across the road which, despite having a Toyota Corolla wedged against its side, was still running. I scampered a few steps in a crouch along the wall and toward the side of the SUV that was away from the action. It was pretty dark and I rolled up and over the wall and laid flat on the ground facing the direction I had come from with the Glock ready. No movement but I did hear some slight rustling of the bushes on the side of the wall from where I had just come and probably not more than ten yards away. Better keep moving, I told myself.

Keeping low, I ran to the passenger side door which was

still open and jumped in. As I was moving into the car, it registered with me that there was someone behind the wheel.

As I brought my gun up, a voice that sounded strangely familiar said: "Fasten you seatbelt!"

"Ah, shit, Danielle," I said, "I almost blew your brains out."

"Hang on," she said. The engine was still running and she dropped it into reverse, cut the wheel hard left and stepped on the gas. I think we would have made it out of there if the right rear wheel hadn't dropped down into the ditch. This beast had all wheel drive but it slowed us down enough to the point where the bad guys came busting out of either side of the road real close. I had ideas about opening fire but between the motion of the car and the fact that all of the action was out Danielle's side of the car, I couldn't get a clear shot.

It about five seconds flat, the car was surrounded by six black clad figures all pointing weapons at us. One very authoritative voice said, calmly: "Please throw your weapons out on the ground and get out very slowly."

Chapter 21

I remember thinking 'When the hell did I sign on for this?' I also remember thinking 'I'm still alive and not bleeding from anywhere'. So, although throwing down my gun didn't sound like a really good idea, under the circumstances not throwing it down sounded like a really bad idea. So, I looked at Danielle and she looked at me and I tossed it out the passenger side window and slowly got out of the car. Danielle hesitated and I could see she was trying to decide if she could somehow take all six of these guys. She must have discarded the idea, at least for now, because she dropped her gun out the window and slowly opened the door and got out.

I think I felt a little relieved, but relieved, under the circumstances was a relative thing.
We were still surrounded by six black clad, armed, somewhat hostile looking gentlemen I could only assume were not here to take us to the Holiday Inn. These guys were all wearing those black hoods you see on the evening news usually worn by people standing on either side of a hostage.

One of the figures on my side of the car motioned with his weapon for me to walk around to the other side of the car. I moved around to the driver's side and stood with my back to the car and about an arm's length away from Danielle. Although it seemed like an eternity while it was happening, this whole thing, from the time Danielle told me to ram the SUV with the Corolla couldn't have taken more than two or three minutes and, despite the fact this was a fairly isolated stretch of road, I could see the lights from a couple of houses through the trees. That, coupled with the fact, as remarkably silent as this whole thing had been, there was some noise and, of course, the unmistakable sound of metal on metal when the Corolla crashed into the SUV, made me wonder if someone had called the police and, even now, they were on their way.

The guy who had politely but firmly ordered us out of the car stepped toward Danielle and stopped right in front of her. He looked her in the eye for about two seconds then reached for the chain around her neck. I couldn't quite decide if that was the good news or the bad news since that flash drive was pretty obviously what they were searching for. And now they had found it, I couldn't imagine they were simply going to walk away and leave us standing there.

But one of the things that makes life interesting is it sometimes moves in unpredictable ways. Take that chain for example. The last time it came out of that shirt back in the restaurant, it had a little cigarette lighter-looking thing attached to it. This time? Nothing. Now you see it, now you don't. I don't know who was more surprised, them or me.

Yet another good news-bad news situation. I suppose it was good news that whatever happened to it, these guys were not going to get it quite yet. But that meant they were probably going to ratchet up the search and I couldn't see how that could possibly be anything but bad news.

I didn't have long to wait. Except for the 'get out of the car' thing, no words had been spoken by any of us. But now, the guy who had politely but firmly ordered us out of the car stepped over in front of me and put the muzzle of his gun under my chin. Looking me straight in the eye, he said: "Where is it?"

 Somehow I knew he wasn't talking to me, so I said: "I have no idea." Good stalling tactic, John.

Still quite calmly, but a little more firmly, he said: "I don't have a lot of time to waste here. So I'll ask you one more time: Where is it?"

"Trust me," I said. "If I knew where it was, I'd tell you."

Beginning to lose his patience, he said: "I might shoot your friend here just to shut him up. For the last time, what did you do with it?"

Danielle still didn't answer him. Without moving the gun barrel from under my chin, he flipped his head in Danielle's direction and two guys moved forward and began to conduct what could only be described as a very thorough body search including, I'm sorry to say, a little crotch groping. Danielle just stood there like a soldier at attention, not reacting. I tried not to look. I know on all those cop shows on television they always have a female officer do the female searches. I guess the assumption is no woman could possibly get her jollies groping another woman. Right. But this was real world and in the real world a lot of political correctness goes out the window.

Although, in all honesty, there was nothing even remotely erotic about it. I got the impression that to these guys she was just another piece of luggage to be searched.
In fact, they were so efficient and quick I couldn't help thinking if these guys were in charge of searching luggage at the airport, those lines would move a whole lot faster. If I get out of this, I'll have to call the TSA.

They stepped away from her and as they did my new best friend said to them, with a note of impatience in his voice: "Search her luggage. And her pocketbook, if she has one." He never took his eyes off of me and I was starting to get a stiff neck from having the point of a gun pushing my chin up.

They moved quickly to the Corolla, one to the trunk and one to the passenger side door, both of which had popped open in the crash. I could see out of the corner of my eye they each had small high-powered flashlights and I could hear the sound of stuff being dumped out on the ground. I didn't know what had happened to that little flash drive, if, in fact, that's what they were looking for, but somehow I didn't think they were going to find it in her luggage or her pocketbook. I could only imagine what they had in store for me if those guys came up empty.

And then, just like that, the guy standing six inches away from me with a gun under my chin disappeared and things happened fast. As he disappeared, I heard a thunking sound like a watermelon being dropped on a sidewalk and, at the same time, a gun shot very close to my head. I must have involuntarily closed my eyes at the sound of the gun going off because I remember thinking I must be dead but it was going to take few seconds for my brain to realize it. I also remember thinking: 'Where the hell did he go?'

I couldn't have had my eyes closed for more than three seconds. During that short time I heard sounds that only after I opened them was I able to process. Apparently I wasn't dead, or even wounded, for that matter, and there were a few more guys around us than there were before I closed my eyes. I saw about eight or ten new figures that weren't there a few seconds ago.

The guy who had been standing in front of me with the gun under my chin was now laying on the ground on his side to my right maybe five or six feet away. He was in kind of a ragdoll position and the side of his head that should have been on the ground seemed to be missing. He was still clutching that ugly weapon that had been tucked up under my chin but he wasn't moving.

The guy who had been looking through the trunk of the Corolla was likewise lying on the ground in a rather awkward position and also not moving. I couldn't see the one who had been searching the interior of the Corolla looking for Danielle's pocketbook, but there were two new figures where he had been standing on the far side of the Corolla, each holding some kind of stubby automatic looking weapon across their chests.

When the command had been given to search the Corolla, there were six guys surrounding us including Igor barking orders and threatening to blow my head off which, by the way, I felt was a very real possibility.

Now there were some new players on the stage. These new guys were also dressed in black but were dressed more like what in my experience looked like a SWAT team. More military, I guess, if you know what I mean. They weren't wearing those black hoods but their faces were black nonetheless. They moved swiftly and with a sense of urgency.

With the three dead guys I could see, that only left three other bad guys. The one who had been standing a little way off but in front of Danielle and me and pointing a gun at us was down on the ground and one of the new guys (Way too many guys running around in black evening clothes) was tying his hands behind his back with a plastic strap while another one kept his weapon aimed at him.

As I was assimilating the fact that I was not dead and trying to take in this sudden turn of events, four more SWAT guys came around to our side of the SUV with the other two bad guys with their hands behind their heads. As they came around, the bad guys were pushed roughly to the ground and their hands were bound with the same white plastic straps. I have to say the whole thing from start to finish couldn't have taken more than fifteen seconds. When I say it was quick, it was quick.

Just then I could hear a siren off in the distance. My guess is somebody had called the cops. The others heard it, too, and one of the new guys who seemed to be in charge looked briefly over his shoulder back down the road and said, urgently: "Come on. This way." and turned away from us as the whole group broke into a trot, including the three bad guys with their hands bound. We headed around the back end of the SUV and into the darkness away from the approaching siren, which now sounded like more than one siren.

It was pretty dark but, based on the condition of my lungs, I'd say we jogged about two hundred yards back down the road when we came to two black kind of UPS-looking trucks. And when I say black, I mean black. Not shiny black - dull, flat, no reflection black – kind of like stealth bombers on four wheels. If a bunch of people hadn't been in front of me, I'd have run right into the back of the first one. Can you imagine the eulogy? "John Elliott. Killed in the line of duty – he ran into the back of a truck." They have a whole bunch of plaques on the wall in the lobby at headquarters for guys who have died in the line of duty. Somehow I didn't think they'd have put one up for me. I mean, can you imagine some guy bringing his kid into the lobby and pointing at my plaque and saying: "And see that one? That's the jerk who died when he ran full speed into the back of a truck."

Anyway, one more narrow miss in a life filled with narrow misses. We all piled into the trucks and pulled away. I noticed that not only were these suckers hard to see, they were quiet. I mean, no noise. Not a sound. I had the feeling these things were not powered by any kind of engine I knew anything about.

The inside, as far as I could tell, was fairly traditional – two seats up front for the driver and one passenger, and seating along either side of the rear for the troops and, in this case, the prisoners. I ended up sitting next to Danielle. I could smell her more than I could see her, but smell her in a good way. I don't know if it was her hair or her perfume or her deodorant or some other delicious concoction that she had smeared somewhere on her body, or, more than likely, some delightful mix of all of them, but I had first noticed it when we got into the car at the airport then again when we were sitting at the restaurant about a hundred years ago. And, believe it or not, when she was standing next to me while that bozo threatened to blow my head off. It was light but distinctive. You couldn't smell it all the time, but every once in a while it would just float on the air. Get ahold of your self, John. I can just imagine some shrink saying to me some day: "So, John, why do think you can only have sex with a gun under your chin?"

I turned in the direction of the scent and said, in my most seductive voice: "What the fuck just went on back there?"

I heard her draw in a breath then let it out.

"Remember back in the restaurant when I went to the ladies room just before we left the restaurant? Well, I noticed those same two guys you apparently noticed. I didn't know whether or not you saw them, but I didn't want to do anything that might alert them to the fact that I was suspicious of them. In my experience, even if you say to someone 'don't look to your left, but...' they almost instinctively do exactly that. No offense, John, but this is as close as we've come to these guys in the last couple of days and I didn't want you or anyone else to blow it. I needed to know who they were, why they were following us and what they knew. I figured the best way to do that was to let them follow us until we could grab them.

"I also figured the flash drive was the thing they were after, although I'm still not sure why it's so important. So, just to be on the safe side in case things went wrong, I took the flash drive off the chain and put it in the bottom of the trash can in the ladies room between the trash bag and the can. Then I called these guys. A couple of them went to the restaurant after we left and retrieved it. This crew has been sitting out on Crystal Springs Drive because we thought we were going to trap them. They were a little way away from us when we got hit and it took them a couple of minutes to respond.

"We've been putting a team together for the last couple of days after one of our operatives in DC began to suspect there might be an attack on the ferry system out here. These guys are stationed on the base at Bremerton. Ordinarily, we would just alert Homeland Security and let them handle it. But then it appeared perhaps not everyone in the administration was determined to keep it from happening. Anna's murder and the flash drive arriving at my door came out of the blue but seemed like more than coincidence. Especially the interest in the flash drive. None of us have connected the dots on that yet, although we're pretty sure that's why Anna was killed. We're still trying to figure it out."

"How can you do this?" I asked her. "I mean your sister was murdered less than 24 hours ago."

There was a pause. She looked away from me for a second or two and turned and looked directly at me. There was sadness in her eyes. "They tried to take me off this case," she said quietly, "but this is the only place I want to be."

"I still don't understand where I fit into all this," I said.

"You need to talk to my Dad," she said.

Just then the truck made left turn into Ed Noble's driveway.

Chapter 22

Danielle and I got out at the front door. Danielle spoke briefly to the dark figure in the passenger seat. "Let me know immediately if you get anything from these guys," she said. "I'll check in with you later."

The trucks continued around toward the back and disappeared from view. Danielle stood there for a moment just looking at the house.

There didn't appear to be any movement inside. Danielle reached over next to the door and rang the bell. I noticed a small electronic key pad next to the door, one of the visible parts of what I was beginning to figure was probably a pretty elaborate security system.

"I seem to have misplaced my keys," she said with kind of a half smile.

Ed Noble appeared from somewhere inside the house and opened the big heavy wooden front door.

"Hi, Dad," she said and stepped forward into his arms. I stepped in behind her and closed the door. They stood hugging each other for a few seconds, not saying anything. I could only see Danielle's back but Ed Noble had his eyes closed and I can only assume that Danielle did, too.

They stepped apart, looking into each other's eyes. "How are you doing?" he asked.

"I'm ok," she said quietly. "I just want the bastards that

did this." Ed Noble just smiled a little smile and nodded his head.

"Sergeant," Ed Noble said, reaching out and shaking my hand. "Good to see you again." He stepped past me and closed the front door which I noticed also had an electronic keypad on the inside. Hmmmm. Nobody in and nobody out. I hadn't noticed that the first time I was here.

"Why don't the two of you come this way?, he said. And, not waiting for a reply, he headed off down the hallway and away from the big living room or great room, or whatever the hell you call a living room in a house like this, I had been in earlier today. We passed a couple of rooms with open doors and I saw what looked like a library or a study of some sort and a room with a pool table, a big screen TV and some very comfortable-looking chairs and couches. Nothing really ostentatious, but elegant in a decidedly understated way. From the little I've seen, typical of Northwest money. They don't flash it around but you know it's there.

I happened to glance down at my watch and it suddenly dawned on me I was supposed to be at Ben's house by nine and something told me I wasn't going to make it.

"Excuse me, Ed," I said. "Do you have a phone I might use?"

"Of course, Sergeant," he said. "There's one downstairs. You're more than welcome to use it. Is it a local call?"

I must have looked a little surprised because Danielle said, in kind of a low conspiratorial whisper: "He's kidding."

We turned right and headed down a flight of carpeted stairs with recessed lighting overhead. The stairway had a set of about twelve or fifteen steps with a landing then another twelve or fifteen steps. We were going down pretty deep – not your ordinary basement. Somehow I didn't think he was taking me down to show me his workshop. At the bottom there was what appeared to be a beautiful mahogany paneled door with a shiny brass door knob or more of a door handle, I guess. Next to the door on the wall and just a little above the handle was another of those digital key pads. Only this one also had a small kind of telescope-looking thing just above the key pad. Ed Noble punched in a bunch of numbers then put his eye up to the telescope.

"See anything good"? I said.

A heavy, muffled thud came from the door and Ed Noble grasped the handle and pulled it open. As he pulled it open I could see this was no ordinary wooden door. In fact, only the part you could see from outside in the hall was wood. The entire door was about six inches thick and had three heavy metal cylinders along the edge that were retracted into the door but probably engaged the door jamb when the door was closed – kind of like a bank vault.

We walked down a long carpeted hallway. There were a couple of closed doors on either side. At the end of the hallway was another dark polished wooden door with a substantial looking brass door handle. Ed pushed a small button next to the door waited about five seconds, then there was that same heavy, muffled thud and he took hold of the door handle and opened the door inward.

We stepped into a dimly lit room with dark carpeting on the floor that I can only describe as a war room. I mean, I've never been in a war room except for a couple of CIC's in the Navy, but from what I've seen on TV or in the movies, this was pretty close. Once my eyes adjusted to the lighting, or lack of it, I could see a large wooden conference room table with about a dozen fairly comfortable looking chairs around it, a number of computer stations, all of which appeared to be manned by people with head-sets, a couple of wall mounted TV screens and some other banks of equipment that I hadn't a clue about but all seemed to have little colored lights on them, some flashing, some not. A few other people moved around the room, some standing and talking to each other and no one really looked up or seemed that interested in us. I noticed one guy standing in a group of three or four others was wearing the same black outfit the guys that rescued us were wearing minus the black stuff on his face. Well, that's not entirely true. This guy had a black face, but in his case - how can I say this?- I think he was born with it. And he was big. Really big.

"Nice rec room," I said to Ed Noble. "You must be seriously into video games." He looked back at me and smiled.

At the far end of the room, there were two doors, one of which was closed. The other one was open into what appeared to be a small office. Ed Noble headed in that direction, but before we got there he stopped next to one of the computer stations that was empty and said "You can sit here and use the phone if you like, Sergeant. When you pick it up, you won't hear a regular dial tone. You'll hear a number of electronic pulses. When they stop, you can dial out just like an ordinary phone. Take your time. We'll be in the office when you're finished."

And, without waiting for a response or any of the thousand questions I had, he and Danielle moved off in the direction of the office.

I glanced around the room tying to take this all in. What in the hell have I gotten myself into? What happened to a good old murder investigation? It occurred to me that Ed Noble had never said 'Who are you calling?' or 'Don't mention to anyone where you are' so I could only assume the phone line was monitored and there was some kind of filter or delay on the line just in case I started shooting my mouth off. When they set this place up they must have said '…and this one's for John Elliot, if he ever shows up'.

I dialed Ben's number. It rang two or three times then he answered.

"Hi, Ben. It's me."

"Oh, hi Dad. Where are you? You sound funny."

"Still working on that murder investigation," I said, resisting the temptation to say that I had apparently been abducted by aliens. I wasn't sure, but my guess is the guys monitoring this call probably didn't have much of a sense of humor. "Looks like I won't be able to make it to watch the debate with you."

"Ah, that's too bad. This election should be a run-away for the Democrats with the economy in the tank and public opinion turning against the war in Iraq. But somehow the Republicans have kept it close with the whole terrorism thing. You know: 'Who do you want in the Oval Office if the terrorists strike again?' I think there's going to be lot of Questions about their experience and threats to the security of the country and a lot of what happens on Tuesday could depend on the kind of answers we hear during the debate tonight. You know, I'm really sick and tired of this whole scare tactic thing but, unfortunately, an awful lot of people seem to be buying into it."

"Yeah, I know just what you mean. It's hard to convince people they have a better chance of being hit by an asteroid than they do of being killed by a terrorist when their gut is telling them otherwise," I said.

"I mean, we haven't seen a terrorist attack since 2001. I can't believe how much mileage the Republicans have gotten out of that. Personally, I think it was a one shot deal. I'm not sure we'll ever see another one."

"Well, Ben, let's just say that somewhere between the constant state of fear being shoved down our throats and a sense of complacency there's a rational middle ground. I wouldn't rule anything out. But, on the other hand, I wouldn't recommend a bunker mentality either."

"Yeah, I know, Dad. But did you see the article the other day on CNN about the magazine interview with one of the top Republican campaign advisors? This guy actually said that while he certainly wouldn't want a terrorist attack on this country, he thought it would really help his guy get elected!"

"I hate to say it Ben, but I think he's right. It wouldn't take much to tip the scales. Hey, listen, I have to go. I'll try to catch up with you tomorrow."

"Ok. I love you Dad. Be careful."

'Hmm', I thought. 'A little late for that advice'. "I love you, too, Ben. Say 'hi' to Abby and the cats for me."

I hung up. Now let's see what I can find out about what's going on here.

Chapter 23

I made my way toward the office at the far end of the room. Ed Noble and Danielle were just standing and chatting when I walked in but stopped and both looked at me when I came into the room.

"Everything all right, Sergeant?"

"Yes, fine, thank you," I said, "considering that not long ago I almost had my brains blown out by a bunch of ninjas over something I know nothing about, I was spirited away by another bunch of ninjas and now I find myself in what is clearly not the reservation center of the Holiday Inn."

There was a smallish polished wooden desk against the far wall with a few papers on it and hanging on the wall just top the right of it was a large, fairly detailed map of the western United States from the Canadian border down to the Mexican border It appeared to extend from a couple of hundred miles off-shore in the Pacific to just east of the Rocky Mountains. There was another of those big screen TV's hanging on the wall with just a big shiny black ebony rectangle looking back at me. With all of these big screen TV's, this place was starting to look like a high-end Best Buy.

Ed Noble walked over to the conference table, pulled out a chair, and as he sat down, he said: "Please, Sergeant, have a seat."

I sat down two or three seats away from him and Danielle sat down next to me leaving one empty chair between us. From where I was sitting, I could see out into the main room I just came through and the bathroom door, or whatever the hell it was, was more or less in front of me so I could look at Ed Noble but I could see the door just beyond his left shoulder.

"Sergeant, we're going to be talking about some things that are at a very high level of security – national security. The people you see here and a lot of people you don't see have chosen to dedicate their lives to trying to prevent unscrupulous people from hijacking our democracy. Some of these people, like Danielle, actually work in some branch of the government while others work directly for us."

I decided not to ask who "us" was just yet.

"From what we know of your background, I have personally decided – against the advice of some, I might add – to ask you to help us. Before we get too far into this, however, I need your assurance that you appreciate the nature of what we do or are trying to do and whether or not you decide to help us, you will not tell anyone anything about what you see or what you hear."

There was a pause and both Ed and Danielle looked directly into my eyes. I actually think they were getting their answer from what they saw in my eyes rather than anything I might say. I thought about what Ed Noble was saying. Part of me was curious about what was going on and part of me was trying not to think about what might happen if I said 'Thanks anyway' and tried to walk out. I mean I don't really think I was a prisoner or anything like that. I just think if I tried to tell anyone about this 'group' or what was going on in Ed Noble's basement they'd probably see to it that I'd be written off with the Area 51 people and wouldn't have much of a career in anything more than being the mochaccino specialist at Starbuck's that shouldn't be left unsupervised. Besides, you'd have to be a complete fool not to see that the present Administration in Washington was off the reservation and if these guys were legit I was feeling a little better about the country surviving until January which, at the moment, was touch and go, at least in my mind.

Anyway, I still had a murder investigation and in my experience you have to let these things take you wherever the hell they take you and this one had taken me down a very strange road. So I said: "This is the second time today somebody has asked me not to reveal information. I can only tell you what I told him. I have a murder investigation to conduct and I plan to do my job. You'll have to trust me that I will not reveal any confidences as long as it doesn't interfere with my job. So the ball's really in your court, Ed. If you trust me, I'm in. If you don't, you can call me a taxi."

There was a pause. "Well, Sergeant," he said, showing that subtle sense of humor, "you don't look like a taxi so I guess I'll just have to trust you'll appreciate the seriousness of our work."

He leaned forward with his forearms on the table, his hands clasped lightly together. He stared at them for a few seconds as if organizing his thoughts.

"The group of people you see here," he started, "are part of a larger task force that was organized and assembled shortly after 9/11. The group consists of some people previously in government and some like-minded folks who are presently in government as well as some very powerful private citizens. We recognized that one of the classic responses to terrorism in any country is the movement of the government toward the extreme right. Along with that comes a repression of individual freedoms and the suppression of any dissent, all in the name of national security. At first it all seems well-meaning and, to some, even necessary. But, by the time the general public figures out the threat from within is greater than the threat from without, it's usually too late for the average citizen to do anything about it. We recognized that classic response as it began to take shape here in this country after 9/11."

I don't know about anyone else, but I'm always a little suspicious of anybody, left or right, who thinks they know best about what's good for the American people. I kept listening, but with more than a little skepticism.

"So we've taken it upon ourselves to monitor what goes on behind the scenes in Washington and to take steps to prevent, as much as possible, the systematic dismantling of the Constitution. Some times that means putting pressure in just the right place and sometimes it means taking more direct but covert action. Hence the 'ninjas', as you described them." He looked at me and smiled: "That would be the second set of 'ninjas' not the first."

Danielle spoke up. "This has been a busy three or four weeks. As the election has been getting closer, both in time and in predicted outcome, we have detected an increase in certain activities that have led us to believe the current Administration has been trying to formulate a number of strategies for influencing the outcome."

"Such as?"

"Such as," Ed went on, "planting press releases with false or misleading information from sources other than the government that tend to undermine the Democratic candidate to promoting civil unrest and demonstrations in certain foreign countries near our embassies to pressuring certain middle eastern oil producers to temporarily drop their prices and increase their supplies of crude oil in order to bring prices down at the pump here at home until the election is over. They've even gone so far as to announce a phased withdrawal of our troops from Iraq since the polls have been showing for quite some time that the American people by and large want this debacle over with."

Danielle chimed in. "Then there was the recent diplomatic contact with some of our Middle East enemies, which this Administration had sworn it would never do but was an idea the polls were showing the American people thought was a pretty good one. It's that old expression attributed to Sun-Tzu in "The Art of War": Keep you friends close but keep your enemies closer. Apparently, as true today as it was hundreds of years ago when it was supposedly written."

That's funny, I thought it was Don Corleone in "The Godfather." I need to read more.

Ed looked directly at me with an earnestness in his eyes. "We have been watching all of this with a good deal of interest. Most of what they have been doing during this election campaign has been nothing more than good old fashioned dirty politics -- really not our concern. An area where we have focused a lot of our attention is on the question of domestic terrorism. There has been a dramatic increase in our military activity in Afghanistan and there are the periodic announcements that we think we have Bin Laden cornered but, as you know, so far, no Bin Laden. And there has been a dramatic escalation in the campaign rhetoric about who's tougher on terrorism, and that old saw that, actually, the Democrats themselves invented: Who do you want in the Oval Office if the terrorists strike again? All of which one might expect given the fact the Republican candidate is a little behind in the polls but not by much and those same polls show that national security is his one strong suit.

"The obvious message to the American people has been: This Administration is tough on the terrorists and the Republican candidate is the only one who will continue these policies."

Ed looked at Danielle and then back at me. "About two weeks ago," he said, "we began to receive information that U.S. intelligence services had detected, or thought they had detected, a massive terrorist operation here in this country on the scale of a 9/11. We continued to monitor the situation but really didn't plan to take action of any kind. We knew the FBI was aware of it. We did discuss the fact that, with the approaching election, the possibility of a terrorist strike to try to influence the election was certainly a viable possibility, but we elected to simply watch from the sidelines."

"Hold on a minute," I said. "How would a terrorist strike influence the election?"

"How much do you know about how and why terrorists operate?" Ed asked.

"Not much, really," I said. "A little bit from my FBI days but, probably like the average citizen, I only really started paying attention to it after 9/11. I know, or, at least I think I know, one of the goals of terrorism is to frighten the general population to the point where it destabilizes the government either through inaction or overreaction."

"That much is true," he said. "In the case of 9/11 we got overreaction. Over and over, the President would order some Draconian measure, the ACLU would holler like hell, the Attorney General would assure the President and the country it was all strictly legal and Congress would do absolutely nothing."

"So, I'm still not clear as to how a terrorist strike would influence the election."

"That's the tricky part," Ed said. "The fact that it would influence the election is almost a given. The real question is: Influence it how? On the one hand, you have a Republican candidate who has spent the whole campaign trying to convince people the Democrat wouldn't respond forcefully enough to such an attack. With some success, I might add."

"I guess a lie is as good as the truth if you can get somebody to believe it," I said.

"Whether it's true or not is a different story, but probably irrelevant at this point. On the other hand you have a Democrat trying to convince the voters that all of this 'homeland security' has only succeeded in taking away our freedoms and reduced our standing in the world and if there were to be another attempted attack, all of the things this Administration has done would do nothing to stop it – essentially saying we're no safer now than we were on 9/10. And, oh, by the way, 9/11 happened during the current Administration, so how safe were we?"

"And with things like all of the illegal aliens pouring
across our southern border,"
Danielle added, "no real port security, little old ladies
and babies showing up on a terrorist watch list and no
real check on the cargo that gets loaded into our
airplanes, it hasn't been a particularly difficult argument
to make either."

Ed leaned slightly forward. "Our intelligence says a few
individuals within the government, including elected
officials or career professionals or, possibly, both, are
aware of the present threat but no one seems to be doing
anything about it. There are certain protocols that are
supposed to be followed when there is a suspected
terrorist threat, certain people or departments are
supposed to be notified, and so on. But, for some reason,
none of that is happening. So we became a little more
interested."

Just then, the door at the end of the room and just over
Ed Noble's left shoulder opened and a somewhat
military-looking chap of indeterminate age but probably
in his 30's, looking hard as nails, wearing a pair of chino
pants and a polo shirt, with arms the size of Hoh
Rainforest redwoods, came over and spoke briefly into
Ed Noble's left ear.

"Please tell them I'll be right there," he said.

When the Arnold Schwarzenegger look-alike had come
into the room, I was so intent on what Ed Noble was
saying, I was caught a little by surprise and didn't look
up until he was in the room and the door behind him
had closed. This time, however, when he left I was very

attentive to what or who was behind that door. As the door opened, I could see yet another lavishly but tastefully appointed room, warmly lit, with paneled walls and gold framed art works hanging on those walls, with what appeared to be a circle or, at least a grouping, of black leather easy chairs – not overly large, but clearly comfortable. Most of the chairs seemed to be occupied and I saw, or would swear I saw, the former occupant of the Oval Office whose picture I had seen upstairs on Ed Noble's mantle seated in one of those chairs and also someone who looked very much like the head of a certain very large computer company headquartered in Seattle seated next to him. Power and money. I was beginning to believe that maybe these guys were the real deal after all.

"Earlier this week, we pieced together certain information that convinced us the threat was focused here in the northwest. Other than Seattle and, possibly, the Navy base at Bremerton, there isn't much else up here. So we set up or, rather, ramped up, our operations here. Part of that is what you see around you. We also assembled a small strike force that is temporarily housed at the Bremerton Navy base – the 'ninjas' you ran into earlier." He paused.

"Would you excuse me for a moment, Sergeant?" he half-asked as he stood up. "I'll only be a moment." And with that he walked to the door at the end of the room and disappeared inside. As he opened the door and stepped into the room, I got a better look at some of the faces and there was no doubt the individuals that I thought I saw, I saw. I caught a quick glimpse of one or two other faces and didn't really recognize them, but one of them had on a military uniform with lots of ribbons on the chest.

"So let me get this straight," I said to Danielle after the door closed. "You work for your father in the family business?"

"Something like that," she said. "Only I didn't know it at the time. Apparently, before I was approached, they asked my father's permission. He said it was ok with him and I was an adult and could make my own decisions. His only condition was they not mention his involvement in any way. He didn't want my decision influenced one way or the other. It was actually only after I finished my training and briefings that I found out he was involved."

"That must have come as a shock."

"Yes and no. I mean, I had no idea he was part of all this so that much was a shock. But, knowing my Dad, and knowing how he feels about his country – that part was really no surprise."

"How about Anna? Was she part of this, as well?"

"No, she wasn't. As far as I know, Anna knew nothing about this group or that Dad and I were part of it. Anna just followed her own muse and only coincidentally ended up in what you might call a covert occupation. I knew in general what she did but she had no idea what I did."

"So, now we get back to the $64 question."

"I thought it was the $64,000 Question," she said.

"Kids," I mumbled to no one in particular. "Not until the invention of the television game show," I said. "Anyway, the question is: What am I doing here?"

As the question was coming out of my mouth, the door quietly opened and Ed Noble stepped back into the room. I tried to sneak another peek, but Ed pretty much blocked my view and I thought it might be rude to lean back in my chair and try to look around him.

"I'll try to answer that, Sergeant."

"Listen, Ed, I think we're beyond the 'Sergeant' stage in this relationship," I said, gesturing around me. "I'd say we were pretty much sleeping together at this point. I know I'd be a lot more comfortable if you'd just call me John."

"All right, John," he said. "Let me answer your question this way. We are taking the position or making the assumption that whatever is going on and regardless of who's behind it, whatever 'it' is, it's meant to try to influence the outcome of the election on Tuesday. If that's the case, we now have about 48 hours to figure out what's going on and try to stop it since it appears the normal agencies that would or should try to stop it are not planning to do their job. Secondary to that mission is to try to establish just exactly who is orchestrating not the attack itself but this temporary paralysis which is of a great deal of interest to us."

"So far this is all very interesting, but I'm not really sure what it has to do with my murder investigation."

"We have a lot of connections," Danielle said, "but there are still some gaps in our intelligence gathering. We can't know everything about everything – partially because it would be a monumental task and partially because the more people we involve, the more of a chance we take of revealing our existence to the wrong people and thereby destroy our effectiveness."

I was beginning to see where this was going. And not feeling all that comfortable about it. Maybe these people were the real deal, but this was moving a little too quickly to suit me. What ever happened to the 'getting to know you' phase? How about buying me dinner and taking me to a movie first?

"So, to put it in layman's terms," she went on, "we occasionally employ sub-contractors. People we think we can trust that may have access to information not readily available to us, at least on short notice. You are one of those people. We're hoping because of your investigation of Anna's murder and your established information gathering network – you do have an information gathering network, John?" She looked at me as if expecting confirmation. I just stared back. "Anyway," she continued, "We are hoping if you come across or have already come across any information that would be helpful, you would pass it onto us."

"Just like that," I said looking first at one then at the other. I leaned back in the chair, looked at the ceiling for a second or two then back at them. "Before I answer that," I said, "I'm still not clear on why any terrorist would want to launch an attack now. I mean, it seems to me if the Democrat is perceived as being, shall we say, more laissaiz faire about his response to an attack and he's leading in the polls, why not just sit back and wait? If there's an attack now, there are all kinds of nasty possibilities, none of which could possibly be good for a terrorist or any of their Middle Eastern sponsors."

Ed stood up and walked to the far end of the room. "Terrorists tend to look at things a little differently than that. They don't necessarily want someone who is soft on them. They see the curtailing of freedoms going on in this country as a result of 9/11 and they see that as a good thing for them. They don't care about the war in Iraq or Afghanistan. They simply see that as part of the same front. They know they can't bring this country down from without, so their only hope is to bring it down from within – systematically destroy everything that makes us what we are as a country. The best way for them to do that is try to get someone elected who will continue to erode our Constitution in the name of national security. Right now, to them at least, it appears the best way to get that to happen is to scare the crap out of people right before they are scheduled to vote.

"We also have reason to believe," Danielle said, "that if an attack took place within, say, 48 hours of the election, this government might move to suspend elections and try to claim some type of emergency powers on an indefinite basis. If you think this Administration over-reacted to 9/11, as the saying goes: 'You ain't seen nothin' yet'."

Ok, so now my head was about to explode. What I wouldn't give for a good old fashioned mob killing right now. You know: we hate you, you hate us, 'bang!', you're dead, pick up a few suspects, squeeze 'em 'til one of them cracks, make an arrest and move on. Ah, the good old days.

"And," Ed said, "just to make things a little more complicated, as if we needed that, there are people who support the Democrat who also think a terrorist attack right before the election would cement it for their guy by being able to say to the voters: 'See, all this security doesn't amount to a hill of beans. While you wait for hours in line at the airport and have to take your shoes off to get on an airplane, these guys can strike wherever they want, whenever they want. This Administration has taken away your freedoms and given you nothing but smoke and mirrors in return.'

"So what we seem to have is a confluence of events where everybody actually wants this attack to take place. Well, maybe not everybody, but I think you get my point."

"And somehow you think I can help you."

"I don't know, John. But, if we're right, we don't have much time and you give us an extra dimension we didn't have before."

So now Ed and Danielle were looking squarely into my eyes. Again. I hate it when people do that. It generally means they're sincere which then requires me to be sincere. I'm not really much of a team player and this team was definitely outside my comfort zone. My gut was saying 'John, get as far away from these people as possible'. But my head (there I go thinking again) was sending me a different message. Besides, the fact Anna Noble had been murdered less than 24 hours ago and both Ed and Danielle were still up to their eyeballs in this thing gave them a certain credibility in my eyes.

As I was having this fascinating conversation with myself, the door opened again and Ah-nold came in. He went straight over to Ed and whispered in his ear. Ed Noble immediately stood up and said: "Danielle, I think you'd better come with me."

As he and Danielle headed for the door, he turned to me and said: "John, while you're thinking over your answer, we have some work to do. I believe they've finally decoded that file on the flash drive."

Chapter 24

As I was being driven back to the ferry from Ed Noble's house, I kept going over in my mind what had happened after Ed and Danielle left the room. I never did see them again. Ah-nold came back into the room a short time later and said: "Mr. Noble has asked me to give you a ride back to the ferry."

"What, I don't even get a 'good-bye'?"

"I'm afraid they're a little busy right now, Sergeant."

"Don't they want an answer to their question?"

"I wouldn't know," he said. "Mr. Noble simply asked me to offer you a ride or I could call you a taxi if you like."

"No thanks," I said. "We've already tried that line. It wasn't all that funny the first time."

I opted for the ride to the ferry and as we drove past the spot where the earlier ambush had taken place, the road was open and there were a couple of local police cruisers parked on the side of the road behind a tow truck. Lots of flashing lights. I resisted the urge to duck down in the seat.

The Corolla was no where to be seen, so I could only assume they had already taken it somewhere and it was only a matter of time before they traced it back to the rental company and, eventually, to me. I wasn't looking forward to trying to explain to Pistol Pete what I was doing out here and who all those dead guys in black outfits were.

We rode the rest of the way in silence. As we came down the road toward the ferry terminal, he pulled over so I could walk to the terminal building. I opened the door and said "Thanks for the ride."

As I got out and shut the door, Ah-nold rolled down the power window next to me. He said: "Sergeant. Ed Noble asked me to give you this." He held out his hand and in it was what looked like a cell phone.

"Thanks," I said, "but I have spare at home."

"I think you should take this one," he said. "It looks like an ordinary cell phone but it isn't. It doesn't use ordinary cell phone towers. You can use it like a regular cell phone, but no one can listen in or trace it. If you need us just press 7 on the speed dial. You'll either be connected to Mr. Noble or someone who can help you. Have a pleasant evening, Sergeant." I took the phone and, with that, he rolled up the window, did a three point turn and disappeared back up the road.

I stood there for a minute, hands in my beat-up trench coat pockets and watched as the red tail lights receded into the darkness. The lights disappeared and I just stood there watching the dark, empty road. I was tired and starting to feel stiff and sore. I had been in bar fights and walked away feeling better than this. I knew I had to make my way to the ferry but, somehow, I couldn't seem to make my feet move. I think part of it was from complete physical and mental exhaustion and part of it was because I knew at some level that as long as I didn't move, I didn't have to think about what to do next.

I looked at my watch and saw it was approaching 9:00. I turned and looked at the ferry that was now taking on cars and passengers. There have been a few times in my life when I've been involved in some pretty outrageous things and have looked at ordinary people going about their daily lives blissfully (or maybe not so blissfully) oblivious to the wheels turning behind the scenes and think: 'If they only knew'. This was one of those times.

I stuffed my hands deeper into my coat pockets and felt the cell phone. I pulled it out and stared at it for a few seconds before stuffing it back in my pocket. I thought seriously about chucking it into the water but the moment passed. In case there was any doubt about the reality of the last four hours, the cell phone confirmed I hadn't hallucinated the whole thing. That would have been too easy, I guess. I headed for the terminal.

The ferry pulled away from the pier about thirty seconds after I went aboard. It was still cool and damp but Seattle cool and damp, which is different than New England cool and damp. In New England the cool and the damp chills you to the bone. Here, it makes you turn up your collar but it doesn't drive you inside. I sat on one of the long benches on the top deck of the "Tacoma," crossed my leg, and watched as the Bainbridge waterfront slipped by.

I tried to focus on what I should be doing next. But, try as I might, it just wasn't happening. I think I may have even dozed off for a minute or two. My head dropped down on my chest and I snapped awake. Ok, John, you need some sleep. It's only a guess, but I suppose half of the Seattle PD is looking for me right now and I'm in no mood to deal with them. On the assumption they've made the wreck of the rental car, if I were Pete, I'd have somebody watching the ferries coming back from Bainbridge or at least circulate my picture to the State Patrol guys on the pier in Seattle in case one of them catches a glimpse of me.

I took out the cell phone and dialed Ben's number.

"Hi, Ben."

"Dad. Say, where are you anyway? Are you ok? A couple of guys from the Department were just here wanting to know if I've seen you."

"What did you tell them?"

"Not much, because I don't know much. I told them I talked to you on the phone a while ago and you said you were working."

"Who came by? Did you know them?"

"Actually, no. I didn't know them and, now that you mention it, they never said who they were. I don't think they even showed me any kind of ID either. They just said they were from the Seattle PD and they were trying to find you – they thought you might be in some trouble. Are you sure everything's ok?"

"Yeah, everything's fine."

So much for getting Ben to give me a ride. If they went to his door looking for me, they'll keep an eye on his place in case I show up. Probably do the same with a handful of other people like Marianne and Al. And they probably have a few phone taps in place, too. Shit. But, I guess I'm not too surprised. Sooner or later I'll have to deal with them, just not tonight. That is, if they're even from the Department. After what's gone on today, they could be from any one of a number of places.

"Sorry you missed the debate, Dad."

"Listen, Ben, I just wanted to check in and let you know I'm ok. I'm going to try to grab some sleep. I'll try to catch up with you tomorrow, ok?"

"Sure, Dad. Let me know if you need anything. I love you."

"Yeah, I love you, too, Ben." I hung up.

I thought for a minute then dialed Harry's number. With the exception of Marianne, I don't think anyone in the Department knows about my friendship with Harry. I mean, it's just never come up. I'm the new guy (still), I'm kind of a loner and I'm also kind of a jerk, so the people I work with tend to stick to business and otherwise don't try to engage me in conversation. The few that have tried have walked away shaking their heads. I heard the engines of the ferry slow down and I knew we were getting close to the pier.

Harry answered the phone. "Harry, it's me."

"What's up, John?"

"I'm just coming over from Bainbridge on the ferry and I need a ride and maybe a place to catch a little sleep. Can you help me out?" One of the things I liked about Harry was he never pried. If you said something it just took it

for what it was. He wasn't all 'kumbaya'.
I guess he figured if you wanted to talk about something you'd be sure to let him know.

"Yeah. Actually, this might work out for both of us. Look, I'm still at the office and I can see the ferry from here. Where do you want me to meet you?"

I thought for a minute. "How about picking me up in front of the Mariner's team store at Safeco?"

"You got it. See you in about ten minutes."

I made my way along the line of cars until I saw a kind of generic-looking white van with the name of some fence company painted on the back of it. People were all pretty much in their cars waiting for the signal to roll off. I came along side of the van and the driver, black guy about the size of an NFL linebacker, was sitting behind the wheel smoking a cigarette. I tapped on his window trying not to scare the pants off of him. He rolled the window down and I said: "Hey, man, I hate to bother you but can I ask you favor?"

This guy looked at me, looked at my clothes and said: "What kind of favor?"

I said: "My wife was supposed to pick me up but she just called me and she's working late. She works over at the team store at Safeco and I was wondering if you could give me a lift over there?"

"She works for the Mariners? Shit, man, you need all the help you can get. Climb in."
I guess it didn't occur to him that it was 9:30 on a Saturday night in November, but it was the best I could

come up with on short notice. Fortunately, this guy wasn't a moon-lighting rocket scientist. Anyway, it worked.

I went around to the passenger side and as soon as I got in the cars started to move. As we rolled onto the pier, I saw a couple of State Patrol guys on either side of the ramp. One guy was talking to a Seattle PD uniform. On the walkway overhead and to my right I could see at least one State trooper watching the passengers as they walked off.

The guys watching the cars roll off really didn't seem to be paying all that much attention. The two guys talking to each other weren't even looking into the cars as we drove by and the other guy seemed to be more interested in keeping traffic moving as he waved us off the boat. I suspect they had orders to look for me but either they really didn't expect to see me or they had no interest in trying to nail a fellow officer. Probably the latter. In any event, we got through without incident. A couple of traffic lights and a couple of turns later, the van pulled up across the street from the Mariner's team store, I thanked the guy, and jumped out.

The street was pretty much deserted. As I crossed over, I saw Harry's car come around the corner from Alaskan Way, come under the Viaduct, make a right turn onto 1st Avenue and slow down. I turned back, crossed in front of his car, opened the passenger side door and dropped into the seat.

"Holy shit," Harry said. "You look terrible. What the hell happened to you?"

"I was kidnapped by aliens."

"I guess." There was a brief pause. "Listen," he said. "I'm not going home. I'm actually going back to the office. You know that thing we talked about this morning?"

"Yeah…," I said.

"Well, you know me. I just couldn't let it go. I mean, the whole thing just didn't smell right. I've been working on a few things today and I've come up with a couple of new wrinkles."

My head felt like it was going to explode. On the one hand, I knew what he meant about not being able to let it go. On the other hand, I really needed to get some sleep or I wasn't going to be much good to anybody.

"That's great, Harry," I said. "But I need to get a little sleep."

"We have a couple of bunk rooms," he said. "You wanna' crash there?"

"That would be fine," I said. "As long as it's quiet."

We drove in silence for a couple of blocks. "Ok," I said. "What kind of wrinkles?"

Harry looked at me and grinned. He looked back at the road. "I called a friend of mine up in Vancouver in the Canadian Coast Guard. You remember I told you our guys spotted those two semi-submersibles up in the San Juan's?"

"Yeah, Harry. It's not the kind of thing you forget."

"Well, I called this guy and shot the shit for a little bit about drug trafficking and just casually asked him if they had begun seeing any of those things up his way. He says: 'Funny you should mention that. We were doing a fly-over along the coast a few days ago and our guys reported spotting what looked like semi-submersibles in a little cove down close to your border. We haven't seen those up here before so these guys weren't really sure what they were looking at. They radioed it in and we dispatched a cutter to get a closer look.' So I asked him: 'What did you find'. He says: 'Nothing. By the time we got there whatever they were were gone.'

" 'Just disappeared?' I asked. 'Yup', he said. 'Just disappeared. All four of them' ."

Chapter 25

Harry's bunk room was pretty quiet. Not much going on on a Saturday night. I took off my coat and shoes and stretched out. All I could hear was the faint hum of some kind of machinery and the soft hiss of air circulating through the ceiling vents. My body was now really screaming out in pain. Harry had given me a couple of generic pain killers and I was waiting for them to kick in.

I don't think I broke anything when I jumped from the car, but I could only imagine the size of the bruises I must have under my shirt. I've had a few serious bruises in my life and my experience is unless something is broken or something is bleeding, there's not much you can do except wait for them to go away. There was really no point in looking at them – I'm sure I'll get to see them soon enough.

As I was drifting off, I ran over in my mind what Harry had told me in the car. Four of these fucking things. Even assuming we now have two of them somewhere, that means there are still two more out there.

Harry's been with the Coast Guard for almost 30 years and, like any good government servant, has developed his own informal network: guys he's done favors for over the years, guys he can trust. When you work in government long enough, you realize it's about the only way you're ever going to get anything done.

Because of the orders he got from Washington this morning about not getting involved with those two semi-submersibles, he obviously couldn't assign anybody to anything official. So he had put out the word to his cronies that if they even heard a rumor about semi-submersibles, or anything out of the ordinary, they should call him right away.

Part of what Harry was doing here at this hour was waiting – waiting for a phone to ring or something he could move on. The other thing he was doing was going over intelligence data – things like satellite imagery, recon reports – anything he could get his hands on.

On the ride over here he gave me the short version of what he was looking at. Nothing had popped up yet, but what Harry meant when he said 'This might work out for both of us' was I would get a ride and he would get a chance to ask for my help. I don't know why everybody thinks cops must have the inside line on everything going on in the city. First Danielle and the scary dudes out at Ed Noble's place and now Harry. But, I guess if I step back from it a little bit I understand that when you don't know what the hell is going on, it doesn't hurt to collect as much information as possible from where ever you can get it. And a Seattle police detective working on what appears to be a related case probably isn't a bad possibility.

And I might learn something helpful to my case, as well. Although I was beginning to get the feeling that if, in fact, all of this was related, including Anna Noble's murder, I might never find out who actually pulled the trigger.

I tried to calm my mind and relax my body. My little bit of knowledge about meditation includes some breathing techniques I've actually found useful. Don't ever tell my daughter-in-law. I'm not really very good at it – the breathing, that is – 'the voices' have a way of drowning everything else out – but I'm getting better.

Anyway, I had gotten up to "three" for about the twentieth time when I realized I wasn't counting or listening to my breath anymore. I was thinking about Marianne. Marianne. I'm a great believer that people don't change much once they reach adulthood. Oh, they might lose some weight or give up smoking or take up origami, but overall they stay – we stay – pretty much the same. And that goes for Marianne. I think we've reached a dead end. Whatever it was that kept her from letting anyone in wasn't going to go away soon. And for one reason or another, I just didn't think I had the time or the patience to deal with it. Which may be more of a commentary on me than it is on her.

One of the things I'm not good at is ending relationships. I just tend to let them drift away. It's one aspect of saying what's on my mind I haven't fully mastered yet. So I'm struggling with whether or not to have a conversation with her or just let the whole thing die a quiet death. See, the thing is, I know she'll never mention it.. We both like to ignore unpleasantness in our own way. Breathe and count, John, breathe and count. My poor brain is much too tired for this conversation.

I was in the middle of counting and drifting off when a new thought popped up. Jesus, I can't get away from myself. Something about four of these monsters and Danielle. Or Ed Noble. Or the group working out on Bainbridge. I tried to focus on the breathing but it wouldn't go away so I tried to focus on the thought. What occurred to me was perhaps this is the type of information I ought to pass onto them

I rolled out of the bunk, tried to stand up and groaned out loud. I picked up my coat, reached into the pocket and pulled out the phone Ah-nold had given me. I flipped it open and punched up the speed dial and hit '7'. A male voice said: "Hello."

'Hello'? That's the best they can do? No 'Saving the country one fascist at a time. How can we help you?' Anyway, I said: "This is John Elliott."

"One moment please." Well, at least it sounds like I got the right number.

"Hi, John." It was Danielle. "I'm sorry we didn't get a proper good-bye. Are you ok?"

"Yeah, I'm fine. Nothing a month on the beach with a couple of Coronas wouldn't cure. Listen, I have some information I recently came across I thought might be helpful. Can I safely assume you guys know about the incident up in the San Juan's on Saturday morning?"

"You mean the two 'whales'," she said.

"Yeah, the 'whales'," I said.

"Yes, we know about them."

"Well, there's a good possibility there may, in fact, be four of them."

There was a slight pause which indicated to me this may have been a bit of a surprise. "Are you sure?" she said.

"I'm as sure as I can be about anything I've seen or heard

in the last twenty-four hours."

"I don't suppose you can tell me where you got this information from?"

"In the words of the old Count Dracula joke: I think we both know the answer to that."

"That's what I thought. How reliable is this information?"

"Pretty reliable. If I were you, I'd proceed on the assumption there are four of these bad boys somewhere in the area."

"Ok, John. Thanks. We appreciate this."

"No problem. By the way, did you find out what was so important about that little gizmo that everyone seemed so interested in?"

"Yes, John. Yes, we did."

"And?" Silence. "C'mon, Danielle. This is only going to work if it's a two-way street."

"John, I think your better off not knowing what was on that 'gizmo' as you call it. Let's just say it would certainly qualify as a motive for Anna's murder."

"So let me get this straight. You have information material to my murder investigation and you think I'm better off not knowing what it is? Who the hell are you to make that determination? You know, Danielle, I get real cranky when I'm tired. More cranky than usual, in fact. It's bad enough when the bad guys withhold information or lie or any one of a thousand things they can think of to try to keep me from doing my job. But when people who are supposed to be on the same side start doing it, excuse me if I lose my patience."

"John, I know how you feel. I really do. Excuse me for saying so, but this is way out of your league. No offense, but you'll never find the people that killed my sister."

"Oh, really?" I said. "Well, we'll see about that." I hung up.

That went well.

Chapter 26

I'm not sure how, but I must have finally fallen asleep because the next thing I knew somebody was trying to wake me up.

Harry's voice came through the haze. "John?"

I rubbed my eyes and tried to remember where I was. I rolled over and put my feet on the floor. Oh, man. I hope they found the driver of the truck that hit me. As I began to focus, I saw Harry standing next to my bunk. "Hey, Harry, what are you doing here?"

"John, you're at the Coast Guard station. My office. I live here. Sort of. Listen, sorry to wake you but it's 0800 and I'm about to head home and get away from this for a little bit. I'd love to leave you here, but I can't. Sorry buddy. Can I give you a lift somewhere?"

I was quiet for a minute as I tried to organize my thoughts. "Yeah," I said. "I suppose you'd better take me home, if you don't mind. Have I missed anything?"

"Unfortunately, no. I can't understand why we haven't seen or heard anything. I guess it's a big area and even though these suckers are a hundred feet long, apparently you can make them disappear if you really put your mind to it. The other thing is even if John Q. Citizen sees anything looking like that, chances are pretty good he'll just think it's some military thing from Bremerton and go on about his business."

"Yeah, I know what you mean. When you live near a

Navy base, you expect to see submarine-looking things. No big deal. And, I guess under the circumstances you can't exactly put out a bulletin."

"C'mon. Get your shoes on. I need to get out of here for a while."

I did as I was told and limped out to Harry's car. As we drove off the base, I said to him: "You know, I keep thinking with all the surveillance technology that's around, somebody has to have some kind of satellite photos showing these things."

"Oh, I'm sure there is. But do you have any idea how many surveillance satellites the US government has up there?"

"No, not really."

"Well, I don't either and I'm not sure any one does. The last estimate I saw was somewhere around 600. You know the whole satellite thing is about as top secret as it gets –weather satellites that are watching troop movements in the Ukraine, mapping satellites that are watching nuclear facilities in China, or India or Israel or you name it. Not to mention what ever the hell they may be watching in this country. I mean, I don't like to sound paranoid but Big Brother really is watching."

"Sounds to me like just what we need. Can't we somehow narrow it down to just those satellites looking where we want to look? I mean, there has to be some way to figure that out."

"I'm sure there is. Do I think we'd even get close to it? Probably not. And I'm not sure I want anyone to know

I'm still poking around. If I start ratcheting up my search, it wouldn't take long for somebody to notice and I'd probably be looking at puffins off the coast of Maine before sunrise tomorrow."

"No risk, no reward, Harry."

"Yeah. Easy for you to say. Think about it, John. Somebody with some pretty serious clout got the entire United States Coast Guard pulled off of this thing in approximately thirty minutes. Does that sound like somebody you'd want to mess with?"

"I see your point." And, somebody that didn't seem to care too much about getting caught, shot two Seattle citizens between the eyes.

After the pounding I took last night you'd think my next stop would be my friendly travel agent. Not that I have a travel agent. But if I had one, that would be my next stop. Since I don't have one, I needed a shower and some fresh clothes and a little time to think about what I needed to do next. I suppose that would involve checking in with somebody at the Department.

And I suppose it was a better than even shot somebody was watching my house in case I showed up there. I figured it might not be a bad idea to check out the area before I just strolled up to my front door. If there are people looking for me, good guys or bad guys, I always like to know where they are before they know where I am.

I live on a houseboat on Portage Bay Road. Not the easiest place in the world to stake out. If you've never seen them or never seen "Sleepless in Seattle," the Seattle houseboats are not really houseboats like you might see in Florida or on Lake Havasu in Arizona. These are actual houses built on wooden platforms which sit on giant floating logs or something else that floats. They're all tied up to various docks but they don't go anywhere – no motors, no steering – nothing even remotely associated with boats except that they float. Come to think of it, when they re-build the Ninth Ward in New Orleans, they might consider building houses like this.

The houses are packed in pretty tight. One dock might have five or six houses tied up to it and they stretch for maybe a mile along the southern shore of Portage Bay.

Anyway, I stumbled onto this house through a friend of my son's when I first came to Seattle and I've been renting from him at a ridiculously low price in exchange for doing a little work on the place. So far, I'm clearly getting the better end of the deal. I figure it's only a matter of time before he notices I haven't done much of anything.

It's a great location. It's the last house out on the end of the dock. Across the bay is the University of Washington, affectionately known as "U Dub." And directly directly across from me is the U Dub research vessel Thomas G. Thompson, a big ol' navy-looking ship probably a couple of hundred feet long. I don't know exactly what they research, but it's pretty neat to look at from my deck.

Behind my house and up at the very top of the hill is Fuhrman Avenue. Fuhrman is kind of a main drag that runs along the southern shore of Portage Bay just up from Portage Bay Road. The land drops off pretty seriously between Fuhrman and the bay and about half way down the embankment is Portage Bay Road. By car, there's only one way in and one way out – down beside the University Bridge.

My house is at the bottom of about thirty steps that go from Portage Bay Road down to the waterfront. There are a few things about Portage Bay Road that make it difficult to stake out. The first is it's a very narrow street – really only one car wide, so you can't just pull into a parking space and sit and watch without being obvious. The second is because it's so narrow and because there are so many houseboats packed in along the waterfront, every square inch of space that isn't actually the road, is someone's private parking space and, as you can imagine, people get really touchy when some stranger pulls in and parks. And, trust me, they notice. The third is during most of the year the trees along Portage Bay Road, which are pretty good sized, are covered with thick green leaves and between trees and general bushes you really can't see much unless you're right on top of it. That whole Seattle green thing I told you about, remember?

"Harry," I said, "drop me off up on Fuhrman. I'm going to walk down."

"Sure, John. Any place in particular?"

"Just get onto Fuhrman and I'll tell you where to pull over." I've spent a little time checking out my neighborhood and I know the spots you could watch my house from
And, frankly, there aren't many.

"Pull over here, Harry. Thanks for the lift. Listen; give me one of your cards. Let me give you my new phone number. I'd appreciate it if you'd call me if anything new develops." I wrote the number to the 'bat phone' on the back of one of Harry's cards and handed it back to him.

"Be careful, John," he said, and pulled away.

I stood on the sidewalk for a couple of minutes just scanning the street and the half a dozen or so buildings I knew looked down on either my house or the parking area and stairs that led to my house. I didn't really expect to see anything and I wasn't disappointed.

I walked down Fuhrman toward the University Bridge checking in between buildings and cut down through the parking lot of a little restaurant at the corner by the bridge and backs up to Portage Bay Road. There are about six steps at the back end of the parking lot that put you down on the road and between the overgrown bushes, parked cars and little twists in the road, I was able to get pretty close to my stairs before I could really see or be seen. As I came around the back end of a van, sure enough, I saw my place was being watched. It wasn't really too hard to miss since the car was a blue Ford with the white stripe down the side a big badge on the door and a pretty good sized light fixture on the roof.

I stepped out into the road and came up from behind it. As I came alongside the driver's side the window slid down and a fairly relaxed uniformed patrolman I didn't recognize, with a half-drunk cup of Starbuck's on his console, said: "Good morning, Sergeant."

I said: "Morning, officer," as I scanned the area for anyone else that might be waiting for me. "Been waiting long?"

"Nah," he said. "Not really, Serge."

"See anything suspicious?"

"No, sir. Not unless you count those two guys in that black Ford about three houses down on the left facing this way. You should have seen them trying to park that thing."

"I don't suppose you happened to run a plate?"

"Yes, sir. As a matter of fact I did. Great thing these on-board computers. I'm actually getting pretty good with them."

"So?"

"Oh, yeah. Plate matches the vehicle and is registered to the Olympic Land Conservancy."

"Funny place for tree huggers"

"Yeah, that's what I thought."

This guy was obviously enjoying being cross-examined. "And?"

"And so I ran Olympic Land Conservancy. No such outfit that I could find."

"Gee, there's a surprise. Anything else?"

"No, sir. Except I'm not supposed to let you out of my sight. That and call the Captain when you show up and offer you a ride downtown."

"You mind if I shower and get some clean clothes?"

"No, sir, I don't. On the one hand, I don't like to disobey a direct order. On the other hand, I have a lot of respect for your badge and hope you have the same for mine. I'll wait here for you."

"You better make that call."

"I already did, Serge."

I turned and crossed the road without looking at the black Ford and headed down my steps.

At the bottom of the steps, I headed out onto the dock. On the one hand, I was actually glad to see the patrol car, although I wasn't looking forward to my meeting with the Captain. On the other hand, I was a little concerned that the guys in the Ford didn't seem to be all that concerned about the patrol car. I mean, they didn't seem to care whether or not Officer Friendly or I saw them or their car. It just made me a little uneasy is all? It was the same kind of nonchalance the guys on the surveillance video in Post Alley had shown. And, from what I could gather, the guys at Anthony Carey's place.

As I walked down the dock and got closer to my house, I noticed there was a cat sitting outside my front door. And not just any cat. Big black dude with a white bib. My cat. Which is strange, because I never let my cat out? Which means somebody other than me let him out.

Which means somebody's been in my house.

Or somebody's still in my house.

Chapter 27

I moved a bit more cautiously as I got closer to my house and when I got even with my next door neighbor I cut around behind his house and edged my way down the side on a narrow piece of decking that stuck out about ten or twelve inches from under his house. I was hoping he didn't suddenly wake up to see me sneaking past his bedroom window.

As I got to the corner of his house, I looked around cautiously to where I could see down the side of my house and across the back. My front door, where the cat was sitting, is on the dock side of the house which I couldn't see from where I was. But I do have a little storage room on the side of the house closest to me that have a door to the outside and also a door that goes into the house. Don't ask me why, but I never lock either one of them although I'm positively religious about locking my front door. I guess I kind of figure with all the junk I have in that room anybody who tries to break in that way will be crushed to death from falling debris before they can get into my house.

I stepped from my neighbor's deck onto a little side dock that runs between his houses and mine then very slowly and carefully stepped onto my own deck. Believe it or not, if things are quiet in the house and your not moving around you can feel the houseboat shift just a little when somebody steps off the dock and onto the deck. I didn't want to go out of my way to alert anybody that might be inside.

As I stepped onto the deck, I remembered that

somewhere along the line last night someone had relieved me of my gun and I had never gotten it back. Nice time to remember that. I do keep a spare in the storage room but it's not loaded. It's been there wrapped in an oily rag since I moved in and I think there's a box of cartridges some where nearby but off hand I couldn't tell you exactly where.

I didn't relish the idea of walking in unarmed after what I'd been through in the last twenty four hours. If there was somebody still in there it wasn't the cleaning lady since I don't have a cleaning lady. In fact, I used to have one but she said she wouldn't come back until I hired somebody to clean up before she got there. Do you think she was trying to tell me something?

I moved slowly and opened the shed door and slipped inside. I didn't bother to turn on the light since there's a little open space between the top of the wall and the roof of the shed that's mainly for ventilation but let's in a certain amount of light – enough to see a gun and to look for some ammo. I found the gun right about where I thought it would be but the bullets were a different story. I tried to poke around with making any noise. I finally found a box with about twenty rounds in it and loaded the weapon.

Now comes the tricky part. The shed door actually leads into my bedroom and, fortunately for me, opens into the shed. I slowly cracked it open and as I did, tried to remember if the damn hinges squeaked or not. Turns out they don't, at least for the first half inch or so which was all I needed to see if anyone was in the room. The coast appeared to be clear.

I held the gun up in front of me in my right hand and

slowly opened the door with my left. I stopped when it was about a foot open and listened for any sounds or any movement. So far, nothing. I still wasn't sure if there was anyone in there but I wasn't willing to take any chances.

I could see my bedroom door and it was open about six or eight inches. I stepped into the room, two hands on the gun still pointing it straight up in front of me, and moved to the door. As I stepped to the door I slowly peeked around the edge of it to where I could just beg into see the living room.

That's when the door hit me square in the face. All I saw was a quick blur as someone threw themselves against the door and knocked me back into the bedroom on my ass.
I think I said something smart like "Ah, fuck!" as much from the pain in my face as from getting the shit scared out of me.

My adrenaline, what little was left of it, sprang into action and as I fell backwards I rolled to one side and came up in a crouch trying to get my gun out in front of me. By the time I came up, my assailant was standing in the doorway with a gun pointed straight at me.

"Marianne," I said, almost shouting. "What the hell are you doing here?"

"Jesus, John, what the hell are you doing sneaking in through the shed?"

"I saw the cat outside and figured someone might be in here. I didn't want to walk in through the front door and get clobbered."

"Yeah, well, next time you decide to sneak in through the shed, try actually sneaking.
What the hell were you doing out there?"

"Looking for cartridges for this thing," I said, holding up the gun.

"I thought somebody was trying to break in."

"So, what are you doing here?"

"People have been looking all over for you, John. I came over here last night to wait to see if you showed up. I fell asleep on the couch."

"Where's your car?"

"Parked up on Furman."

"We're both lucky one of us isn't dead. You better let the cat in."

She moved to the front door, opened it, The cat ran in and headed straight to the kitchen and started yelling in front of the refrigerator. She closed the door. "John, there are two guys coming down the dock and I'd say from the way they're walking they're not Jehovah's Witnesses. One guy's got a gun in his hand."

"Get in the kitchen and keep that gun ready," I said. "I'd like to take these guys alive without getting either one of us killed if we can.

She went into the kitchen and I went back through the bedroom and out through the shed.
The door to the shed is on the side away from the main

dock. I felt the houseboat rock and I knew they had stepped onto the deck. I counted to three and stepped out from behind the shed with the gun held straight out in front of me, hoping they had gone down the side of the house toward the front door.

No one in sight. I moved to the corner of the house and could see in the reflection of the sliding glass door on my neighbor's houseboat directly across from mine that they were outside the front door with one of them on each side and both with guns drawn. I stepped out from behind the house with my gun pointed directly at them and said: "Seattle Police.
Drop the weapons."

I don't think I really got much further than "Seattle Pol....," when the guy on the side of the door farthest from me and more or less facing me looked in my direction and started to point his gun in my direction. As I saw the gun coming down, I let off a single shot and John Doe No.1 went flying backwards. He let off one shot which made kind of a popping sound as it came bursting out of the silencer. I don't know if it's a reflex you learn or whether some people have it and some people don't, but under the right circumstances I don't have any hesitation in pulling the trigger against another human being. The old expression: 'He who hesitates is lost' becomes 'He who hesitates is dead'. These were clearly the right circumstances.

The second guy, John Doe No. 2, grabbed the door knob and crashed inside my house.
I got about halfway from the corner of the house to the door when I heard a shot from inside. Shit! I dropped to a crouch as I got to the front door and looked in with my gun ready. I saw Marianne standing at the far end of the

living room just outside the kitchen door holding a gun in pretty much the same two-handed out-in-front position they teach at the academies. On the floor between us was John Doe no. 2. I could tell from the sounds he was making he was still alive but I couldn't tell much more. He was moving around on the floor and the blood was starting to spread.

I stood up slowly and lowered my gun. The smell of cordite filled the air. "You all right?"

"Yeah, I think so. I'm not sure about him though. I know you said you wanted to take these guys alive, but it happened so quickly. I heard the shots then heard the front door bang open so I stepped out of the kitchen with the gun ready and saw this guy coming toward me. I don't think he was expecting to find someone in here because he looked surprised even before I shot him."

"Yeah, well, let's see if we can keep him alive. There's a patrol car up at the top of the stairs. He probably already heard the shots but I'm going up there and have him call an ambulance then call this in. Keep an eye on this guy and don't take your gun off of him. He could still be dangerous."

I raced down the dock and up the stairs. Officer Friendly was still seated behind the wheel of his patrol car. "Officer," I said as I approached the car, "I need you to call for an ambulance." As I got closer, however, I realized that Officer Friendly wasn't going to be calling anyone. He was sitting half slumped over with a round hole in the middle of his forehead.

Chapter 28

There were people everywhere, some in uniform, some not. Our wounded John Doe No.2 had been taken to the hospital. John Doe No.1 was still lying where he fell. The CSIs were going over everything with a fine tooth comb. The guy Marianne shot was hit in the abdomen and the extent of his injuries wouldn't be know until they got a look at him at the hospital. He passed out before the ambulance got here and before I had a chance to ask him any questions, although even if I had I don't really think I would have gotten much information out of him. I also wasn't really surprised that when I ran through his pockets I came up empty. Empty, that is, except for his cell phone which I pocketed before the response team showed up. Yeah, I know. Tampering with evidence and all that. But sometimes I tend to have what some might call 'situational ethics'. If I think it might help solve a case and not jeopardize the outcome, I'll bend a rule here and there. I made sure Marianne didn't see me. In addition to being a CSI, she's also an ethical CSI and I didn't want to put her in an awkward position. At least that's what I told myself.

The first guy, John Doe No.1, was either dead when he hit the deck or seconds thereafter.
I had done a quick check of his pockets, as well, and came up with nothing but lint. Not even a cell phone.

I had used the cell phone Ah-nold gave me last night and called an ambulance then called headquarters. I also figured I'd better punch lucky number 7 on the speed dial but wanted to wait until I could do it alone. A quiet

Sunday morning on the waterfront quickly turned into a major crime scene. I knew it was only a matter of time before Pistol Pete showed up.

With all the activity around us, Marianne and I sat quietly on a dock box that sits on my deck just past the front door. There was yellow tape everywhere and an entire platoon of uniformed officers trying to keep people in their houses or at least on their decks. I could only imagine there was a similar scene up at the top of the stairs where I had found Officer Friendly whose real name turned out to be Bailey. Officer Sean Bailey. Another plaque on the wall in the lobby at headquarters.

"Are you ok?" I said.

"Yeah, I think so," she said.

"Have you ever shot anyone before?"

"No," she said, "no I haven't." She paused and stared down at the deck. "I hope he doesn't die." She looked up at me. "I did the right thing didn't I?"

"You sure did, honey. If you had given him half a chance we wouldn't be sitting here talking. I guarantee you he wouldn't have hesitated for one instant to pull the trigger if he had seen you before you saw him."

"John," Marianne said, "I don't understand what this is all about. Why were those guys trying to kill you? This has been a weird twenty-four hours. Does this have anything to do with Anna Noble?"

I was trying to decide how much to tell her. Or anybody else, for that matter. In the space of those 24 hours, this thing had escalated from a routine murder investigation and now at least four people were dead, not counting the ninjas, and clearly somebody thought I would be better off dead as well. And I wasn't sure who I could trust. I kept remembering what Harry had said about somebody with enough clout to get the whole US Coast Guard pulled off the San Juan Islands thing in about thirty minutes.

While I was debating that with myself, Dan Riley came down the dock toward us. Dan's one of the detectives working out of headquarters and happened to be on duty when I called in. "John," he said, "appears we may have a witness to the shooting of Officer Bailey. One of the neighbors out walking her dog. She's up top if you want to come up."

"Yeah, Dan. Thanks."

"I'll wait here, if you don't mind," Marianne said.

"You gonna be all right?" I asked.

"Yes," she said. "I'll be fine. You go ahead."

I got up off the box and headed up the dock then up the stairs to the parking lot.
As I got to the top of my stairs, a car pulled up along side of me. Uh, oh. A dark blue Ford. A voice from out of the back seat said: "Sergeant, may I speak to you for a moment?"

I turned and said: "Sure, Captain," and got into the back seat along with him.

"Would you mind telling me what the hell is going on?"

"Well...," I started to say.

"Just don't say anything," he said. Long pause for dramatic effect. "Twenty-four hours ago we have a body in an alley. Not nice, but not all that unusual. Then we have a second body up in Northgate. Again, not all that unusual, except the second victim is the roommate of the first victim. Then I get a call saying the FBI would like to 'monitor' the case since the first victim worked for them and would I, good team player that I am, mind if one of their guys hangs around with whoever is investigating these two murders. So I figure, what the heck, what can it hurt? Beside, the call didn't come from the FBI, it came from somebody who might have something to say about my career and it wasn't really a request, if you catch my drift. So I call in the investigating officer – that would be you – and give him a direct order to cooperate with an FBI field agent, guy by the name of Todd. Now my investigating officer is not even out of my sight, when he dumps the FBI and disappears off everyone's radar. How am I doing so far?"

"Just fine, sir." I thought this might be a good time for a little formality.

"Finally, we hear from the investigating officer. Is he calling just to check in and apologize for standing me and the department on our collective ears trying to figure out if he's alive or dead, or, perhaps, to update us on the progress of his investigation?"

"No, sir."

"No, he's not. He's calling into say there are three more bodies. This time they're at his house and he's shot one of them and one of my CSIs has shot the other one. One of them is definitely dead and the other one may not be far behind. And, just for good measure, one of our finest young officers has also been killed."

He stared at me. I wasn't quite sure whether I was supposed to say anything.

"John, I stuck my neck out and hired you because I thought you were bright and honest and would help out this department. I knew from day one you weren't going to play by the rules. And regardless of what you think of me or my own personal style, I'm a results oriented person. As long as you get the job done, I'll back you a hundred and ten per cent. But when there starts to be a trail of dead bodies and I'm not seeing anything but carnage, I'm starting to have my doubts.

"So I just have one question: Is any of this leading anywhere?"

"The honest answer, Captain, is: I don't know."

He nodded. "Well, with one officer shot dead and two goons trying to kill another, I would suggest you find out and find out in a hurry." He paused and looked out the window then back at me. "I got a call at home last night suggesting I take you off the case and give it to somebody else. I had the feeling it wasn't because you weren't doing the job. In fact, just the opposite. I get the feeling you're making some people uncomfortable, which interests me. Just be careful, John. Between you and me - and I have no basis for this except my gut - just because these two guys went down, I don't think that's the end of it. I'm not dumb enough to think you went off the radar just to get an afternoon off. What ever you're after, be careful."

I started to get out of the car. "Oh, by the way," the Captain said, "you wouldn't know anything about a car accident over on Bainbridge Island about 9:00 last night would you?"

"Bainbridge Island? No, sir. Why?" I said in my most disarmingly innocent voice, making eye contact while I said it.

"Because, in addition to a bunch of twisted metal, the Bainbridge Island PD found this." He handed me my Glock.

Chapter 29

As I headed back down the stairs, I heard a familiar voice behind me.

"John."

I stopped and turned. "Hey, Al."

"What the hell happened?"

I gave him the immediate details as we walked down the dock, leaving out a good chunk of last night. "Listen, Al," I said, "I need you to do something. I think these are the same two guys who shot Anna Noble and Anthony Carey. They're this one to the hospital. I know the department will place a guard outside this guy's room just because he's a suspect. But I think the danger is more from somebody coming in than from him getting out. I need you to do whatever you have to do to make sure there are two of our guys there at all times and they stay alert, even if you have to brief them yourself. These guys have to be on the look-out for strangers, and I want one of them in the room at all times when there are any hospital personnel in that room."

"I would have thought after what these two tried to do here, you'd be just as glad if they were both dead, although you didn't hear me say that."

"Yeah, well, maybe. But here's the other thing I need you to do. I need you to talk to the doctors and let them know we need to talk to this guy as soon as possible. None of this 'two or three days after he's had a chance to recover' crap, you understand? I need to talk to him right away. And I want you to stay right there and call me the minute I can talk to him, ok?"

"All right, John, but I want you to know you owe me big time. My wife's gonna be pissed when I tell her I won't be home for a while. Her mother's birthday is today and we're having a family birthday party at our house for her this afternoon."

"You mean one of the fifteen or sixteen family birthday parties you guys have every year?"

"It's not fifteen or sixteen, it's only ten," he said with a straight face. "The other six are anniversaries."

Just then, the stretcher went by and headed up the stairs with a body bag. "I've got to get going, Al. Looks like they're wrapping it up and I need to talk to the CSIs."

I turned and started to walk away. "John," he said. "I've had trouble reaching you on your phone. Is it busted or have you just stopped answering it?"

"Ah, you know those damn cell phones, Al. Never any service when you need them."

"Yeah, right. Meanwhile, what's the best way to reach you?"

It suddenly occurred to me I had more cell phones on me than a Sprint store. After all I had been through, for some strange reason, I still had the prepaid phone. And, of course, the bat phone. And the phone I pilfered from John Doe No. 2. I decided to give him the number of the prepaid.

"Keep in touch," I said.

"I will," he said and headed back up the dock.

Marianne was still sitting on the box when I got back. "How're you doing?" I asked.

"Not great," she said.

"Well, I need you back in the game. Can you do that for me?" I needed information I thought she could probably get for me, but I also thought it would be good for her to stop thinking about what had just happened and focus on something familiar. I know what goes on in your head in these situations. You think about what happened but you also start thinking about what could have happened.

She looked up at me with kind of a half smile. "Yeah, I guess so."

"Good. Do you know any of these CSIs?"

"I know all of them. Why?"

"I need you to work with them. I'm pretty sure these are the same two guys who killed Anna Noble and probably Anthony Carey. I need the crime lab to look at the slugs from both of their weapons and compare them to the ones you guys found in Post Alley and in the wall up in Northgate and see if there's a match. And I pretty much need it yesterday. Check with Dan Riley to see if he needs anything else from you then get on it, ok?"

"You know, you never answered my question. This is all

about Anna Noble, isn't it? But why are they after you?"

I just stared back at her.

"John, what is it? What's going on here?"

"Nothing for you to worry about."

"Nothing for me to worry about? Or is this you deciding what's best for me and what isn't? I just shot somebody for the first time in my life and came within, oh, I don't know, maybe a heartbeat of getting shot myself and you've decided I don't need to know why?" This was sounding all too familiar.

"Look, Marianne, you've just got to take my word for it that you're better off not knowing." Jesus, I sound like Danielle.

"Listen, John, I know you mean well. I really do. But you just don't get it. Nobody decides what's 'best' for me. I'll make that decision. Now, I want to know what's going on here."

Don't do it, John. "Ok," I said, "you're right. I think this is about Anna Noble, that's why I want you to check and see if there's a match with anything we found at either crime scene."

"But why do you think that?"

"Well, by the look of those two guys they seem to generally match the two guys we saw on the surveillance tape from Post Alley. And the single shot through Officer Bailey's forehead had a familiar look to it."

"Why do you think they came after you?"

"That's a good question." Not really a lie. "Look, you need to get going. I need that information as soon as possible if I'm going to piece this thing together."

She looked at me for a long second. I knew she was deciding how far to push this conversation and I also knew that she knew that I knew more than I was saying.

"Ok, John, I'll see what I can do."

"Oh, hey," I said. "I'd better give you a new phone number. I lost my cell somewhere and I'm using this prepaid until I can get another one." I gave her the number and she turned and went to look for Dan Riley. As I watched her go I couldn't help thinking this kind of shared trauma usually brings the people involved closer together. But, in this case, I think it just pushed us further apart. I suppose at some level I wasn't surprised or entirely disappointed. At this rate I wouldn't have to confront the unpleasant task of telling her this thing between us just wasn't going to work out. It might just die a natural death. Avoiding unpleasantness. I need to work on that. Just not now.

I walked down to the end of the dock just to get away from the commotion and clear my head. I tend to be the kind of guy who likes sit back and take stock every once in a while and this last day or so had left me very little time to do that. There were still a lot of pieces I had to put together, which is hard for me to do when people keep shooting at me.

And I needed to call Danielle. This phone I swiped from the guy who Marianne shot might have something she

202

could use and the quicker I could get it to her, I thought, probably the better.

I sat on somebody's dock box and looked out across the water, staring at the 'Tommy Thompson'. It was another gray day in Seattle and that ever-present mist was in the air. There was a fair amount of activity on the deck of the 'Thompson'. Probably getting ready to go out. Portage Bay and Lake Union were almost perfect places for small to medium sized boats like the Thompson. They were sheltered from any good sized storms that came across the Sound, but could get out to the Sound and, eventually to the Pacific, by way of the Ballard locks which connected Lake Union to open water.

As I reached into my pocket for the bat phone, I heard a voice. "Elliott."

I turned and what to my wondering eyes should appear but a guy in a suit with a very short military-style haircut and a bearing that had FBI written all over it. Great. Just what this day needed. I stood up and walked past him. "Sorry," I said, "I'm a little busy right now. Maybe we can chat later."

"Listen, Elliott," he said, turning toward me but not moving. "I just came to deliver a message."

I stopped and turned to face him. "What is it?" I said.

"Somebody wants to talk to you."

"I'll bet." I turned to walk away.

"He said to tell you his name is Jeff Feinberg."

Chapter 30

I stepped out of the shower and dried myself off. What is it with a shower? Must be the warm water. You can be having the crappiest day on the planet, but as soon as you step into the shower everything seems to go away. In addition to a shower, a shave and clean underwear helps me feel better, too. So, I shaved, put on the clean skivvies, threw on a pair of blue jeans, an old Clemson sweatshirt of mine from my son's college days, a pair of retired running shoes that were still too good to throw away, and headed for the refrigerator.

Once all the commotion quieted down on the dock, I figured I had two priorities. First, I needed to call Danielle, bring her up to date on the events of the morning and, more importantly, get that purloined (I like that word. It sounds so much better than stolen.) cell phone over to her a quickly as possible in case it could help out with whatever she was working on. Second, I needed to go and see Jeff Feinberg.

Right now I'm thinking: You've probably got the two guys who shot Anna Noble and Anthony Carey. You definitely got the two guys who shot Officer Sean Bailey. Wrap it up. Wait for the forensic report on the two weapons Marianne was working on, hand the case over to the prosecution and let it go at that.

But, see, here's the problem: I tend to take my job seriously. And because I take my job seriously I'm not particularly satisfied just because I may have gotten a couple of trigger men. I still want to know why these people were killed and, probably more importantly, who was behind this whole thing. And, oh, by the way, who is now trying to kill me?

Now, admittedly, I'm probably operating with one hand tied behind my back because Danielle has basically told me it's none of my business. But I'm thinking maybe this cell phone might give me a little leverage. Initially I thought I'd just call her up and tell her I had the phone and would she like to come and get it, thinking more about her perfume than anything else. But, the more I thought about it, the more it occurred to me that a little blackmail wouldn't hurt.

Anyway, I wolfed down a bowl of Total and went into the living room and flopped on the couch. I pulled out the bat phone and hit '7' on the speed dial. Two rings later I got Mr. Personality.

"Hello?"

"You know," I said, "you guys have to come up with something more creative than 'hello'."

"Wait one, please, Sergeant," he said, "I'll put you through to Ms. Noble." I guess it didn't take long for the word about me to get around.

"John?"

"Yeah. Hi Danielle."

"How are you doing?"

"You mean like 'how am I doing on the case'? Or do you mean 'how am I doing'?"

"Well, to tell you the truth, both. Let's start with you. How are you doing?"

"I'm doing fine, considering."

"Considering what?"

"Considering that two guys just came to my house and tried to kill me."

"Are you all right?"

"Yeah, I'm all right."

"Any idea who they were?"

"I'm not entirely sure, but they may have been the two guys who killed Anna and Anthony Carey."

"Have you been able to question them?"

"Not really. One of them is dead and the other's in serious condition. They took him to the hospital and I'm waiting to hear from my partner when and if we're going to be able to question him."

"What makes you think they were the two guys who killed Anna?"

"We'll get to that in a minute. That's part of 'how am I doing on the case'. How are you doing?" I know that sounds like a north Jersey 'How you doin'?', but it really didn't come out that way. Actually, it sounded more like some WASP from Fairfield County unsuccessfully trying to sound like north Jersey.

"I'm doing ok. A little tired, maybe. I've been up most of the night."

"Making any progress?"

"A little."

"I've got something that might be helpful."

"What is it?"

"Mmm. Not so fast," I said. "Fool me once, shame on you. Fool me twice, shame on me."

"What does that mean?" she said, with no animosity in her voice. I've had those words spoken to me so many times as the prelude to good fight that I recognize it right away. This wasn't it. I think she was so tired she had momentarily forgotten about our last 'exchange' of information where she got my info and I got the bubble, and it didn't occur to her why I was saying what I said.

"It means I have something I think you might want, but I need to get something in return."

"Like what?"

"Like what's on that flash drive."

"Oh, not that again."

"Yeah, I'm afraid so."

"I don't know if I can do that, John."

"You mean you don't know if you want to do that."

"No, I mean I don't know if I can do it. I don't make those kinds of decisions, not when it comes to something like this. I have to ask if I'd be allowed to share that with you."

"Who do you have to ask, your Dad?"

"He's one of five people who would make that kind of decision."

"Should I hang on?"

"No, I'll have to call you back. You know they're going to ask me what you've got."

"Yeah, I kind of figured that." I paused for a few seconds. "Look," I said, "how about this? You and I have got to learn to trust each other if we're going to work on this thing together. It doesn't do either of us any good if I say 'Fuck you very much' and go off on my own. So why don't we do this: you go and discuss this with your board of directors. Get permission to share the flash drive information with me. You get that authority and tell me you have it and I'll give you what I've got, then you can decide if what I have is worth the trade. I'll trust you to decide."

"That sounds fair, John. Let me call you back." She hung up. I sat there for a minute or two thinking about Danielle Noble. There was something about her and I couldn't quite get her out of my mind. I've read lots of things about what makes one person attractive to another and the bottom line is: nobody knows. On the one hand, this was a woman who could pretty much take care of herself, which is a characteristic I've always found attractive. On the other hand, she's taken the time on a couple of occasions to ask about my favorite topic: me. And in a genuine way. Not the old 'hey, how are you and I don't really care so please don't bore me with your problems' kind of inquiry we all use at one time or another. Then there's that scent she gives off. That really makes my mind wander to places it hadn't ought to go. Like where it's starting to go right now. Better get up off the couch, John.

Onto number two on my list. The guy on the dock who had given me Jeff Feinberg's contact information had looked like FBI, but somehow, I didn't think he was. There's a whole variety of government spooks and, while this guy had all the trappings, nobody had ever said Feinberg was FBI. Plus, as far as I knew, Feinberg was a friend or an acquaintance of Ed Noble and that gave him a certain status, at least in my eyes. Put that together with the fact the FBI wasn't particularly pleased with me right now and this guy had displayed no particular animosity toward me and it just didn't add up to FBI for me.

Besides, I thought Feinberg was at least a piece of the puzzle I needed to know more about. Come to think of it, I had the phone number Al had tracked down for me and had never gotten around to calling. All I had to do was remember what I did with it. I always like to do as much background information on people as I can, especially when I'm not sure what side of the fence they're on, and this was something I meant to do before I got distracted.

I went into the bathroom and opened the door to the laundry room. Well, not exactly a 'room'. More like a closet with a stackable washer and dryer. My dirty

clothes were piled on top of the washing machine and I
went through the pile looking for the shirt I had on.
I found it and felt inside the pocket. Sure enough, there
was the card with Feinberg's number on it, a little beat
up but readable. I compared it to the number the guy on
the dock had given me and it was the same.

Ah, well. Nothing like the present. I went back into the
living room and dialed the number. I don't know about
you, but for some reason I tend to walk around when I
talk on a cell phone. I pace. So I was pacing while the
phone was ringing. Two rings and a voice said:
"Feinberg."

"Feinberg? John Elliott."

"Sergeant Elliott. Thanks very much for calling me. After
the day you've had, I wonder if you would consider
meeting with me to discuss some things that may be of
mutual interest?"

"I wouldn't mind that," I said. "Only no offices or cars or
remote parking lots, if you catch my drift. Not after the
last twenty-four hours. Where are you?"

"I understand completely," he said. "I'm here in Seattle. I
arrived early this morning."

"Do you know the walkway that goes from Pike Place
Market across Western Avenue to the parking lot?"

"Yes, I do."

"Meet me at the top level next to the elevator" - I looked
at my watch - "in an hour."

"Ok," he said. "I'll see you then."

"Wait a minute," I said. "How do I know what you look like?"

"Don't worry, Sergeant," he said. "I know what you look like."

Chapter 31

I took out the prepaid and called Ben. "Hey, Ben, it's me."

"Hey, Dad. Where are you?"

"I'm at home. Listen I need a favor. Can you swing by my house and pick me up in about fifteen minutes? I need a ride downtown."

"Sure. Where's your car?"

"Long story but I left it downtown in the International District and I need to go and get it." It occurred to me my street was still blocked off and there was still a fair amount of activity and I didn't want to have to go into a lot of detail about what had happened. I said: "You know what? There's some kind of utility truck up on Portage Bay Road. I'll walk up to East Allison and you can pick me up on the corner."

"Yeah, sure Dad. That's fine. I'll be over in a few minutes."

As I was waiting, the bat phone rang. I answered it. It was Danielle.

"Ok, John," she said, "I've got permission to tell you what we found on the flash drive. Do you still want to tell me what you've got?"

"I've got a cell phone."

"What kind of a cell phone?"

"I think it's a Nokia."

"No offense, John, but I'm really tired and under a lot of stress. Unless I'm missing something here, I don't care what brand it is, do I?"

"Sorry. No, not really. Here's the short version: This morning I had a run-in with a couple of goons I think were the ones who killed your sister. One of them is dead and the other one is seriously wounded. After the smoke cleared I checked them out and they were clean except for this phone which I found on the guy who got wounded. I figured somebody at your end might be able to get into that phone and who knows what they might find."

"You're sure?"

"I'm sure of what?"

"That these are the two guys who killed my sister?"

"No, I'm not absolutely sure, but we're running a test on their weapons and trying to match them to the slug we found at the scene of Anna's murder and also the one we dug out of a wall at her apartment building where Anthony Carey was shot. Let's just say I'm pretty sure and I figured we don't have all the time in the world so maybe you ought to look at this thing."

"I think you're right, John. I need to get a hold of that phone. Where are you now?"

"I'm at home in Seattle up near the University District. I'm actually waiting for my son to pick me up and take me downtown. Why, what are you thinking?"

"I have access to a helicopter...."

"Of course you do. Unfortunately, mine's in the shop."

"...and I'm not familiar enough with Seattle to know where there might be a landing pad we can use. I need to check with our operations team and see what they recommend. I'll call you back in about five minutes or maybe less. Can you stay where you are until I call you back?"

"I looked at my watch. "Yeah, I think so."

"Ok. I'll call you right back." She hung up. I didn't even have time to say: "What about our deal?" I was hoping I hadn't been bamboozled again.

I walked up to the corner of Fuhrman and East Allison. Just as I got there, Ben pulled up. I walked around to the passenger side and got in. It had started to rain and the warmth inside the car felt good.

"I was beginning to think we were never going to see each other again," he said.

"Yeah, I know. I was beginning to feel the same way. Listen, I'm waiting for a phone call. Just sit here for a few minutes before we go anywhere."

"Sure. No problem," he said. The windshield wipers cycled every few seconds wiping away a few stray raindrops. "You missed a good debate last night."

"Really?"

"Yeah, really. Obama kept wanting to talk about the economy and McCain kept wanting to talk about national security. I mean, I understand why the Republicans don't want to talk about the economy, what with the credit crisis and all. I'm not sure it's entirely their fault, though. When things are bad, people tend to blame whoever's in power. But I think people are getting tired of the President and McCain trying to scare everybody to death. Everything's 'the war on terror'. It's like the boy who cried 'wolf'. After a while people beg into doubt whether there's a wolf at all. What do you think?"

"I think there's a wolf all right. It just might not be the wolf most people think it is." Just then my phone rang. It was the bat phone. I fished around and pulled it out of a pocket. "Hello?"

"Hi, John. Ok, do you know where Harborview Medical Center is on Ninth Avenue?"

"Yeah. I live here, remember?"

"The top floor of the parking garage is a helipad. Can you meet me there with the phone in about ten minutes?"

"Probably, depending on the traffic."

"Ok, I'm leaving now."

"How will I know which helicopter is yours?" She hung up.

"What was that all about?"

"You don't want to know. Let's go. I need you to take me to Harborview Medical."

"You feeling all right?"

"Yeah, I'm fine."

"So, anyway, the polls this morning are showing Obama with a slight advantage. I guess, barring some unforeseen disaster, it looks like he might carry it through to Tuesday. Hey, Dad, speaking of unforeseen disasters, there was an article in the PI this morning about an unconfirmed rumor of a possible terrorist attack here in Seattle. Have you heard anything about it?"

I decided not to lie, but not to give him the whole story. Actually, come to think of it, I didn't really know the whole story. "I heard something about it," I said. "Sounded like another one of those stories that surfaces every once in a while about some type of attack on the ferries. I don't know if there's any truth to it but some people are taking it seriously. I'd suggest you play it cautious and stay off the ferries for a couple of days just for the hell of it. You don't have any plans to go anywhere on the ferry do you?"

"No. Actually, I'm on my way down to Tacoma tonight and won't be back until sometime on Tuesday."

"How about Abby? She going anywhere?"

"I don't think so."

"Do me a favor. Tell her to drive around if she needs to go over to that side."

He looked at me. "You're serious, aren't you?"

"I don't know, Ben. I've just heard a couple of things over the last day or two that makes me think this one could be a little more serious than the usual government bullshit."

He looked at me for a long second and then back at the road. "Ok. If you say so."

A phone rang somewhere in my pockets. This was ridiculous. Three phones and I had to fish around to find the one that was ringing. Turns out it was the one I had lifted from Doe No. 2. I started to answer it then, in some stroke of inspirational genius, it dawned on me if someone was calling that phone, whoever was on the other end may not know exactly what took place over the last hour or so and why alert them if I didn't have to. My guess was whoever it was would figure out pretty soon that something had gone wrong, but why help them out. Besides, the call history might just give us a clue as to who might be calling and that could be valuable all by itself. I let it ring.

While it was ringing, somewhere a second phone started ringing. Now I'm not the most coordinated person in the world and if you'd ever seen me swing a golf club you'd understand what I was talking about. Two phones ringing at the same time was close to my limit of multi-tasking. Ben looked over at me.

"Are you going to answer any of them?" he asked.

The second phone was the bat phone so I figured I'd better at least look at the screen and see who it was. Harry.

"Hey, Harry, what's up?" I said as casually as I could.

"John," he said. "Where are you?"

"I'm actually in the car with Ben. We're headed downtown. What's up?"

"We might have something. Can you meet me at my office?"

"I've got a couple of things do first but, yeah, I can meet you in about an hour. Does that work for you?"

"Maybe. I can't sit on this thing. Just get here as soon as you can."

I hung up and turned to Ben: "I know I may regret saying this but I need you to step on it."

We arrived at Harborview Medical in about seven minutes flat. I told Ben to drive into the parking deck and go to the top parking level.

We went up what seemed like about ten ramps. I'm pretty good with spatial relationships, but some of these parking garages get me so turned around I'm never quite sure where I am. We finally ran out of ramps and Ben stopped the car.

"Wait here," I said.

I jumped out of the car and headed for what looked like

a stairway to the top level. A sign on the door said "Helipad - Authorized Personnel Only." There was a security booth with some kind of private rent-a-cop inside reading a newspaper and the stairway was behind a glass door next to it. The glass door to the stairway obviously had some kind of buzzer system on it so I went to the window and pulled out my shield and ID. I think the security thing is more to keep curious people off the roof and away from rotating helicopter blades than any kind of threat protection, so this guy was a little slow in responding. He got up and looked at my ID and said: "I need you to sign in." Then he started looking around, obviously looking for the sign-in book which probably got used about once a month.

"Look," I said, only half pretending to be really pissed, "this is a police emergency. Buzz this door open now or I'll have you arrested for obstruction of justice and interfering with a police officer in the performance of his duty." I'm not even sure the last one is a real crime, but it sounded like it ought to be.

He hesitated for just an instant and then reached under the counter. The door buzzed and I went flying through it and up the stairs. Out of the corner of my eye, I saw him pick up a phone.

I came out on the roof. It was lot windier up here and the rain was starting to come down a little harder. At the far end of the roof there was a red and white helicopter with lights flashing and a knot of people around a cargo door in the side of the airplane, but no sign of anything that looked like it might be Danielle.

I stood there for a minute scanning the sky over in the direction of Bainbridge Island then spotted what looked like a small military style helicopter heading in my direction. As it got closer, I could see it was definitely some type of military chopper and it was definitely headed toward this roof. It came in across the docks at a fairly low altitude and began to slow down as it got closer. It hovered just above the deck for a few seconds, turned slightly - something to do with the wind, I guess - then settled down on the middle pad.

The side door closest to me opened and a female figure in some sort of tight-fitting flight suit jumped out and headed in my direction. As she walked toward me and took her helmet off, I could see it was Danielle. And just when I thought she couldn't get any sexier. You really need to stop this, John.

"Good morning," I said. "Did you bring the coffee and the donuts?"

"Maybe some other time," she said, looking straight into my eyes and smiling. Uh, oh. Is that my over-active eighteen year old boy imagination, or was that something more than the usual brush-off? "What happened?" she asked.

"Couple of goons came aboard my houseboat just after I got home this morning. Fortunately I was a little quicker than they were." I decided not to mention Marianne.

"What were they after?"

"I think they were after me. I think it was a heavy handed attempt to try to get rid of one more person who's been sniffing around and might know something about what's going on. Ordinarily, the bad guys don't go out of their way to kill cops. But I don't think these are ordinary bad guys and I also don't think they cared one way or the other whether or not I was a cop."

"Any idea yet who they are?"

"No, not yet. The Department is running a check on both of them. Listen, not to change the subject, but what about our deal?" I handed her the phone.

"Are you sure you want to know about this?"

"After what happened this morning? Yeah, I'm sure."

She looked at me for a couple of seconds and then said: "It's a memorandum."

"What kind of memorandum?"

"A White House memorandum. From the Office of the White House Counsel."

"What does it say?"

Before she could answer me, she glanced past me over my shoulder and said: "John, I hate to do this to you, but I've got to go. Thanks for this," she said as she turned and started hurrying toward the helicopter, holding up the phone. "I'll be in touch," she yelled back over her shoulder. Before I could protest, she broke into a trot and jumped up into the chopper.

I watched her go for a fleeting second then turned to see two guys in uniform and a guy in a suit heading toward me at a brisk walk. I turned and started walking toward them just as briskly and never slowed down as I passed them, saying: "Thanks for your help, guys. Always good to know SPD has friends at Harborview." Behind me I could hear the helicopter taking off as I ducked into the stairwell and headed back down to where Ben was waiting.

Chapter 32

I jumped into the car. "Let's go,"

To which he responded: "Go where?"

I looked at my watch. About forty minutes before I was scheduled to meet with Jeff Feinberg. I still didn't have my car and I still needed to meet with Harry. Somewhere in my pockets there was a ringing sound. I was starting to get better at recognizing the difference between the bat phone and the prepaid especially since I was now down to only two phones. This was definitely the prepaid. I fished around in my pockets until I came up with it.

"Hello."

"John, it's Al. I'm at the hospital with your lone survivor. Looks like his injuries were pretty serious but the doctors think he'll survive. They've put him on painkillers but he's still awake and he seems to be fairly stable. He's apparently got some internal bleeding and they think the slug may still be in him. They're prepping him for surgery and, once they do, he'll be out for quite a while. I don't know how much you can get out of him but I thought you might like to talk to him before they put him out completely."

"Where'd they take him?"

"Harborview Medical."

"You're kidding."

"No. Why?"

"Because I'm right across the street."

"What the hell are you doing there?"

"Another long story from a week-end of long stories. What room is he in?"

Al gave me the room information and I told Ben to drop me at the Emergency entrance.
"I'm sorry to take so much of your time, Ben. I thought this would just be a quick ride down town. Can you wait for me? I mean, it's ok if you can't."

He looked at his watch. "No, Dad, I'm fine. Go ahead. I'll wait."

Ben pulled up in front of the Emergency entrance and I made my way to the room where John Doe No. 2 was being attended to by two nurse-looking people. I was gratified to see there was a uniformed cop standing outside the door and Al and another uniformed cop inside the room. As I walked in, Al turned and saw me.

"That was quick. I've asked this guy a couple of questions but I haven't gotten much of a response. I can't tell if he's that far out of it or if he's really alert and decided not to say anything."

I walked over to the bed and looked down at him.

He appeared to be about 35 or 40 years old, closely shaved hair cut more of a military style than a skin-head, biker style, clean shaven with no beard or mustache, pretty muscular – not his head - and in decent physical shape. By the looks of a couple of roundish scars, one on his shoulder and one near his waist, this was not the first time he'd been through this drill or something similar.

As I was standing there assessing the situation, a guy in green scrubs came into the room with another nurse-looking person and a pushcart with some instruments and some vials.
He walked over to the bedside and looked down at John Doe then at me.

"I'm Doctor Raman," he said, in his best doctor voice, as if I should immediately recognize his illustrious name and genuflect. "And you are….?"

"I'm Sergeant Elliot. John Elliott. Seattle Police Department. I'm investigating a homicide and, in addition to a number of other things, this man is also a suspect in my investigation. What can you tell me about his condition?"

"Not much. I'm just the anesthesiologist. I'm here to help get him ready for surgery. So if you'll excuse me…" he said, gesturing toward the door.

I looked around and saw four faces staring at me – three nurse-looking people and Dr. Raman. I looked briefly at each face. Finally, I said : "Does anyone here know Dr. Raman?"

There was silence as the nurse-looking people looked at each other then at me, not saying anything, then at Dr. Raman, who continued to stare at me with his arm outstretched.

Finally, one of the nurse-looking people said, hesitatingly and quietly: "This is Dr. Raman." Then they glanced at each other as if to say: 'Is this a trick question or is this guy nuts?'.

"I know his little name tag says 'Tarek Raman, MD'," I said, "but I want to know if any of you recognize this man as Dr. Raman? Have you ever seen him before? Have you ever worked with him before?" Dr. Raman lowered his arm and looked at the other three.

After about two full seconds of silence, Dr. Raman turned and started heading toward the door, saying: "This is preposterous! I'm calling security. I'm not putting up with this bullshit." Everyone, including me, I'm sorry to say, froze for an instant. Then he broke into a run and headed down a crowded hallway, knocking people over and scattering a variety of gurneys and other miscellaneous medical hardware.

"Al!," I said, starting to sprint, "Don't leave this guy alone and no one touches him, understand? And nobody leaves this room!" and I took off after Dr. Raman. "Come with me!," I half yelled at the cop outside the door as I broke into a run. Harborview is a real rabbit warren of hallways, corridors, dead-ends and "No Admittance" signs, especially since all of the new construction. At first I couldn't see our Dr. Raman, or whoever the hell he was, so I tried to follow the trail of mayhem that was pretty obvious. Obvious, that is, until we reached a stairway. Then it was the old 'did he go up or did he go down?'. I stopped and listened for a minute and heard female voices in a conversational tone coming down the stairs from the next floor.

"You ladies see a doctor just go by?" I yelled up the

stairs.

"No we didn't," one of them yelled back.

"Come on," I said to the cop with me and headed down the stairs. I wasn't sure, but I figured we couldn't be more than two floors above the street, and I figured this guy in his hospital greens would opt to hide in plain sight rather than go out on the street where he'd be more apt to be seen. So I went down one flight and through the door back into the hospital. It occurred to me that only people either going into or out of surgery wear those green things and this floor didn't look like anything related to surgery since nobody on the floor was wearing green. Maybe this guy wouldn't be hard to spot after all. I stopped a nurse-looking person coming toward me and said: "Have you seen a doctor in green come this way in the last few minutes?"

"As a matter of fact, I did," she said. "He asked me which way to the elevators."

"Which way to the elevators?" I said.

"That's right," she said.

Great. I'm trying to catch a runner and I get Abbott and Costello. "No," I said. "I mean which way are the elevators?"

"Oh," she said. "Down this corridor about half way on your right."

We took off at a dead run. I think I forgot to say thank-you. We got to the elevators just as the door was closing. I couldn't see who was in it, but the little arrow next to the door was still showing a green 'UP'. I thought we passed a stairway in the corridor just before we turned into the elevator alcove. I shot back into the hall and looked back in the direction we came from. About twenty feet back down the hall on the left was an EXIT sign. I ran for the door and headed back up the stairs.

I know in the movies when you see a cop in a foot chase they run for what seems like miles and never seem to be out of breath. Well, my lungs were on fire, my heart was pounding like it was going to burst out of my chest like an alien in a Sigourney Weaver movie and stairs were the last thing I needed. I barely made it to the top, ran out into the corridor and into the elevator alcove. Nothing. I stopped to catch my breath.

Then it dawned on me that we were back on the floor we started on. Oh, shit. Don't tell me this guy isn't trying to escape. Don't tell me he's doubled back to finish the job in, shall we say, a little less sophisticated way. Ah, crap. "C'mon," I said to the cop who was still with me and, I might add, panting as badly as I was, as I started to run again. "And keep your weapon handy. If you have to shoot this guy, try not to kill him."

I pulled my gun out of the holster and ran down the corridor in a direction I thought was the right way back to John Doe's room. Now people were starting to make loud, panicky noises and scattering in all directions. Two wrong turns later I came to a stretch of hallway that looked familiar. Ahead of me I could see a guy who from the back appeared to be Dr. Raman walking briskly but calmly away from me. No greens this time, just a white lab coat. From where I was there appeared to be something in his right hand and I had a feeling I knew what it was. From about forty feet away I yelled: "Seattle police! Drop the gun Raman!" as I ran toward him.

Cool bastard turned and raised his gun in my direction.
Before he could get a shot off, he flew sideways like he
had been lifted up by a giant hand, his gun hand straight
up in the air while he fired a shot that went into the
ceiling. He hit the wall to my right and crumpled down
in a pile. Al Russo came running out of the door to the
room on my left with his gun drawn followed closely by
the other uniformed cop who had stayed behind. I saw
Al step on Raman's wrist and grab the gun from his
hand. I ran up the hallway, holstering my gun.

"Somebody get a doctor over here right now!" I yelled as
I bent over and looked at Raman. His white lab coat was
now starting to develop a nasty red stain in his side
under his right arm. A crowd was forming.

Al said: "You ok, John?"

"Yeah," I said, "I'm fine. Thanks, Al."

"Yeah, well, you don't look too good."

"No," I said. "I mean thanks for saving my ass. I don't
think this bastard would have missed me at that range." I
looked down at Raman. "This guy really doesn't look too
good."

A guy in a white lab coat and a name tag came rushing
through the knot of people that was beginning to form –
mostly hospital visitors, by the looks of them.
"Everybody please move away!," he said. "I need a nurse
and a crash cart!"

Al and I stood up and backed away. "This looks like the

same guy you were chasing," he said.

"Yeah, it is. Apparently he had no intention of escaping, just drawing us away so he could come back and finish the job. Pretty motivated, I'd say."

Al said: "Looks like you caught up with him just in time. He was right outside the room when I heard you yell and looked up to see him pointing a gun in your direction. Sorry I shot him but I didn't think I had a lot of time to talk him out of it."

"How's our patient doing?" I said to Al.

"He seems to be pretty stable," Al said.

We both turned and headed back into the room where John Doe was still lying on the gurney with the IVs stuck in his arms. The three nurses who had been in the room when I took off after Raman were standing at the door looking at the mess. We pushed past them and walked up to John Doe's side. That's when I saw that John Doe was staring up at the ceiling in a most unnatural way, his mouth slightly open and eyes not blinking.

"He's stable, all right," I said.

I looked back at the door and, not really all that surprised, saw there were now only two nurses, not three, in the doorway.

Chapter 33

Fortunately for me, my gun never went off. Otherwise, I'd have been there all day answering a lot of questions about how all of a sudden people around me were dropping like flies. I mean, I know I'll have to answer a lot of those questions at some point, just not now.

I got out of the hospital as quickly as I could and found Ben parked outside the Emergency entrance. I looked at my watch. I had about ten minutes to get over to my meeting with Feinberg at Pike Place Market and I still didn't have my car and I still needed to catch up with Harry. Oh, well. First things first.

"Drop me down by Pike Place Market," I said.

"I thought I was taking you to get your car," he said.

"Yeah, well, something's come up," I said, just as a number of squad cars pulled up in front of the door.

"You wouldn't know anything about those would you?" he asked.

"C'mon," I said. "Let's go." I pulled out the bat phone and dialed Harry.

"Harry," I said when he answered, "you still at your office?"

"Yes, I am," he said. "Where are you?"

"I'm on my way over to Pike Place Market to meet a guy

who might be helpful. How long you gonna be there?"

"Not much longer. I'm headed up toward Bellingham. Guys up there found something they think I should look at, that's why I called you. How long will you be?"

"Hard to say – maybe 20 or 25 minutes. Can you pick me up at the bottom of the elevator that goes down from the top of the Pike Place Market over to the parking deck?"

"Ok, but make it quick. I'll be waiting for you."

I hung up. "Drop me off at Pike Place Market in front of the pig," I said. Ben made a couple of turns and headed north on Eighth Avenue. We pulled up under the big red sign with the clock that says "Public Market Center" that most people think of when they think of Pike Place Market. It's right at the corner of the main market building where Pike Market Fish is located – the place where they throw the fish.

I jumped out of the car, thanked Ben and told him I'd catch up with him later.
"And Ben," I said, "I meant what I said about staying off the ferries."

"Right, Dad. Watch yourself, ok?"

I slapped the side of the car and took off into the market.

Even on a Sunday in November the main building is a crowded, busy place. It's one of the reasons I picked it to meet up with Feinberg. I'm not trusting anybody these days. If I'm meeting some spook, it's in a busy public place.

The first floor is lined with fresh fruit vendors and flower sellers. I'm not sure which of them is more colorful. I'm still overcome by the basic beauty of the place.

I hurried along trying to get to the skybridge where I had promised to meet Feinberg. Now the smell of the flowers began to fill my senses along with the color. Behind the counters at work tables those little Asian women who work most of the stalls were busy cutting and arranging even more flowers to put out on display. And the frosting on the cake is the price. I mean, you can buy a world-class bouquet here for ten bucks. Ten bucks! How can they do it? I keep thinking they must be stealing the flowers. How else could they make a profit?

And the fruit's another story. Boxes and boxes of apples, oranges, peaches, grapes, bananas – you name it. As colorful in their own way as the flowers. Every one perfect, every one looking like it was hand-polished. And cheaper than you can buy them at Trader Joe's. Sorry, Joe. No offense.

I finally made it to the entrance to the skybridge and stopped. I could see the far end where the elevator comes up but there didn't appear to be anyone there. With the little I knew about Feinberg, it occurred to me he might be somewhere nearby doing the same thing I was doing – waiting for the other guy to show up. It also occurred to me that wherever he was, he probably already knew I was here. These guys never go anywhere alone and stake out everything four ways from Sunday if they think it's to their advantage. So, as the old saying goes: in for a penny, in for a pound. Or, an even older saying: Here goes nothin'.

I stepped out onto the skybridge and walked toward the

elevator. As I got to within about ten feet of the elevator, the doors opened up and about ten people got off, talking and laughing, a couple of little kids, all pushing past me and headed for the Market.

Just as the doors were closing, a hand reached out and stopped them and they retracted back into the side walls. A big bear of a guy stepped out. He was about six foot two weighing about two-thirty, a little gray around the temples, with a visible spare tire and dressed in sneakers, blue jeans and a hooded sweatshirt with the word "Clemson" in big orange letters across the front. We looked like two classmates at a 25th reunion. Go Tigers. My guess is he didn't go to Clemson any more than I did, but he was trying to make a point. Well, if he was, he succeeded. I tried not to let on that I was totally freaked out.

He looked right at me and stuck his hand out.

"Sergeant Elliott!," he said with a big smile on his face, "I'm Jeff Feinberg!," and with a firm but not bone-crushing grip he pumped my hand about a dozen times. "I almost went back down again. I didn't realize I was at the top!"

This was not at all what I was expecting. I've met a lot of spooks in my time – FBI, CIA, NSA, Army Intelligence – they all pretty much come out of the same mold. Lean, no-nonsense type guys with short haircuts and a vision of the world about as wide as their hair is short. Not that there's anything wrong with that, as Jerry Seinfeld would say, but I was just a little surprised that's all. I immediately thought about all of the 'elevator not going all the way to the top' jokes but decided to let it go for now. Once the initial surprise wore off, I was more curious than anything else.

"Call me John," I said.

He let go of my hand. Or, actually, I kind of disengaged
from the hand shake which seemed like it might go on
for a very long time.

"Ok, John," he said, still smiling. Then the smile
disappeared and he looked – not grim – grave? Kind of
like the small town preacher who's come to console you
over the death of your 97 year old grandmother.
"Terrible thing about Anna."

"All murders are terrible," I said, "especially to the
victim."

"I guess that's true," he said. "Listen, John, I won't beat
around the bush. I'm sure you've figured out by now
that this was probably no ordinary street crime."

" 'Probably'?"

"I'm trying in some small way to help some people put
the pieces together on this. But I have to tell you you're
not helping the situation any."

"And why is that, Jeff? You don't mind if I call you Jeff?"

"No, no. Jeff is fine. It's just this whole thing has, well,
implications beyond what I would call your jurisdiction,
if you don't mind my saying so. I suppose I put that
badly.
I don't mean to insult you."

"I'll let it go. Speaking of jurisdictions, just exactly what is your jurisdiction, if you don't mind my asking? I'm finding there are an awful lot of people interested in this case and it's not always obvious what that interest might be. So, what's yours, Jeff?"

He shrugged. "I have a few connections and I'm just a friend of Ed Noble's trying to help him get to the bottom of this. I don't really have a jurisdiction," he said, a little of the smile returning to his face.

"Well, ordinarily, I'd say that's a commendable thing to do, Jeff, help out an old friend. But I happen to know" ('suspect', but I didn't tell him that) "Anna called you a day or two before she was killed and, in fact was on her way to see you before she was murdered. So, old friend of the family, it seems to me you were involved in this before Anna's murder and not too long before, at that."

I stopped talking and let that sink in. Let's see where this goes.

The smile never wavered and the eyes didn't give away anything. "Yes, Anna did call me. But all she said was she had something she needed to talk to me about and she didn't feel comfortable doing it on the phone or on the internet. She asked me if I was going to be in Washington on Saturday if she flew out. I said I would be and she should call me when she got to the airport."

"And she didn't tell you or give you any hint as to what it was about?"

"None."

"Didn't you think it was a little strange, I mean, getting a call from someone you hardly knew wanting to fly in from Seattle just to chat?"

"Well, I wouldn't say I hardly knew her. I've been a friend of the family for a long time. I've known Anna since she was a little girl."

Hmm. Really. "I'm just curious: Why do you suppose she called you?"

"I don't know. Maybe she didn't know anybody else she knew she could trust."

"Trust? Trust you with what. Or about what?"

"Don't know that either. Although after talking to Ed and a few other people, they seem to think maybe she came across something in her job."

"Did you know what her job was?"

"No idea. I hadn't seen her for quite some time."

"Do you remember when, exactly, she called you?"

"You know, I was trying to remember that. I think it was Thursday evening. Late Thursday evening. I seem to recall I was on my way to bed when the call came."

"Did she seem upset in any way?"

"No, I wouldn't say so. She just said: 'This is Anna Noble, Ed Noble's daughter'. Asked me if she could come and see me and that was about it."

"I'm still puzzled as to why she would have called you. If you don't mind my asking, what exactly do you do for a living?"

"No, no, I don't mind at all. I'm a field investigator for the Agriculture Department."

They say most good lies always contain an element of truth.

"A field investigator for the Agriculture Department. What kind of fields do you investigate?"

"Ah, good one, John," he said with a big smile, the corners of his eyes wrinkling up.
"No, I'm with something called the SPPA, which most people have never heard of."

"I guess I'm one of them," I said.

"In 2005 the President formed a working group consisting of representatives from Agriculture, the Food and Drug Administration, Homeland Security and the FBI to look out for terrorist attacks on the country's food supply. SPPA stands for Strategic Partnership Program Agroterrorism. I work for Agriculture's part of that group.
We look out for any signs that anyone is trying to affect our ability to grow food."

Somehow, I didn't think this guy was out wandering around Kansas looking for wheat rust. I also thought working with a group that includes Homeland Security and the FBI might be part of that element of truth I was talking about.

"So, do you think Anna Noble may have discovered a wheat germ in her wheat germ and that's why she called you?"

"Ah, John, I like you. And because I like you, let me give you a piece of friendly advice."
The elevator came up to our level and the doors opened. Half a dozen people got off and Feinberg stepped into the empty car. He punched a button.

"These guys you're playing with have much bigger fish to fry than a Seattle police detective. If they didn't succeed this morning, they'll try again if you keep sniffing around. Only next time they'll be a little more respectful of your abilities, if you catch my drift. And here's the advice part," he said, still smiling, " Leave this thing alone. It's Sunday. Go over to your son's house and watch some football. I'm sure he and Abby and their two cats would love to see you."

The doors closed and the elevator went down.

Chapter 34

I stood there for a second or two staring at the closed doors. I wasn't quite sure what had just happened. I mean, clearly he intended to let me know he knew more than a little about me. And maybe even letting me know if he knew that stuff, others did, too. But I really couldn't tell if he was giving me a warning or giving me a threat. I wanted to play the conversation over in my mind but had to store it away for the time being since Harry was waiting for me down in the street and I wasn't sure how long he would wait. Besides, if it was a warning, I don't think I really needed it and if it was a threat I'm probably too dumb to be scared off by it.

When I got to the bottom, I stepped out of the glass-enclosed stairwell and into the fifty-seven degree drizzle. I walked out to the curb on Western Avenue, turned my collar up and tried to retract my head into my shoulders like some kind of aging tortoise. Did I mention I hate the cold? And did I mention in my world, fifty-seven degrees with drizzle and about a ten to fifteen knot breeze is my definition of cold? I couldn't help but think of the words to that Kenny Chesney song: "Oh, I wish I was there tonight, on Jost Van Dyke, sippin' on some Foxy's Firewater rum."

I looked up and down the street and was just about to pull out one of my phones and call Harry when a shiny black sedan pulled up to the curb. Now, you would think with the day I've had so far I'd be a little leery of shiny black sedans or, at least, I should be leery of shiny black sedans. But, hard as I tried otherwise, I was still back up on the top level with Jeff Feinberg and not really focused on the car. The door popped open and I jumped in. I'd like to think that at some level I saw the license plate or some identifying mark that told me it was Harry. But, truth be told, it could have been Michael Corleone and I wouldn't have noticed until it was too late.

Turns out it was Harry.

"Where the hell have you been?" Harry asked me.

"I've been getting that a lot lately."

"This is my fourth and, by the way, last, trip around the block."

"I just had an interesting encounter with some kind of spook. Basically told me I should go away and mind my own business. That whatever is going on is bigger than a Seattle PD murder investigation. I'm not sure, but I think he threatened me."

"You think he threatened you?"

"Yeah, well, it was in the form of some 'friendly advice'."

"Oh. Kind of like an offer you can't refuse?"

"Yeah, something like that. Anyway what's going on?"

"We may have found one of the semi-submersibles."

I waited for the rest of the story. Silence. "You just gonna let that hang out there?"

"Nah, I just like to hear you beg."

"Ok, Mrs. O'Connell's little boy, Harry, I'm beggin' ya: Tell me the rest of it."

"Ok, as long as you put it that way. I got a call just before I called you. One of my guys up around Whidbey Island. Seems one of his guys with the Naval Air Station up there called him and said one of their patrol planes was coming back to Ault and was making a low over-water approach and thought he saw what looked like a small submarine half sticking out of the water near the far end of the base. Even though it's Navy, Whidbey Island is primarily an air base so they don't have a lot of ships or small boats that could check out something like that. So my guy's guy is told by his superior to call the sub base over in Bangor and let them handle it."

"And?"

"And, so, my guy thought it sounded like something I might be interested in and called me. I contacted our station up in Bellingham and told them to get a boat over there A-sap. I told the guys from Bellingham this could be a homeland security matter and all contact would now go through me."

"Have you heard anything since that initial phone call?"

"No, but I'm hoping Bangor might be a little slow in responding since they would know if it was one of theirs and it's probably not. I'm counting on the fact it's a Sunday afternoon and since it doesn't appear to be any kind of emergency, they'll get up there when they get up there. That's why I didn't want to hang around too long waiting for you. Even though they may be a little slow responding, they won't wait forever. And if it's what I think it is, somebody else is going to figure that out, too, and either light a fire under Bangor or send somebody themselves."

I looked over at Harry. "What do you thinks' going on here, Harry?"

"All I know, John, is: somebody's planning a big explosion."

Whidbey Island Naval Air Station is about 90 miles from downtown Seattle. We drove in silence for a while. I could see the wheels turning in Harry's head and I was using the time to pretty much do the same thing. We buzzed along for about 20 minutes or so not talking.

"Listen," he finally said, "I haven't asked you this but what can you tell me that might help? If you don't want to tell me, that's fine. I understand. But I'm operating pretty much in the dark here. I mean, you've apparently got some folks in the intelligence community making threats or whatever so either you know something or they think you know something. How about throwing me a line here?"

"You're right, Harry. You've been pretty open with me and you deserve the same." I noticed Harry kept glancing in the rearview mirror. "Somebody back there?"

"I don't know. There's a white SUV back there like a Suburban or a Tahoe and he's been right with me ever since we got on 5. Maybe I'm just a little paranoid these days but I'm not in the high speed lane and he stays about ten or twelve car lengths back no matter how fast I go."

"How far to 20?"

He looked down at his odometer. "I don't know, maybe another 15 or 20 miles."

Just then a voice came out of his dashboard. "Captain, this is Lieutenant Mancini."

Harry reached for a microphone mounted on his dashboard. "Go ahead Mancini."

"We're at the scene, Captain."

"Good job, Mancini. Anybody else there?"

"No, sir."

"Mancini, did Captain Adams brief you?" Harry looked over at me.

"Yes, sir, he did."

"Good. Then you know we're doing a routine check for any 'hazards to navigation'." Harry looked over at me again.

"Yes, sir, I do."

"Have you seen anything in the area that might be classified as a hazard to navigation?"

"Yes, sir, Captain. We've got one possible object that appears to be an abandoned vessel and might need to be inspected more closely."

"Does it appear to be floating, Mancini, or is it aground?"

"It appears to be aground, sir."

"Do you have divers aboard?"

"Yes, sir, we do. We have two MSST team divers aboard. Captain Adams thought it might be good for the exercise if we took them along."

"Good. Put the divers in the water and check the integrity of the hull. And Mancini?"

"Yes, sir?"

"Do not board the vessel until I get there."

"Aye, aye, Captain." Harry replaced the microphone.

"That guy still back there?"

"Yeah. I'm gonna take this next exit and see what happens."

Harry put on his right blinker, drifted over into the right lane and started to slow down. "He's still with me."

"Take the exit then get right back on."

Harry coasted up the ramp, came to a full stop then crossed over to the entrance ramp back onto the highway. As he came to the bottom of the ramp he stomped on it and some kind of overdrive thing kicked in and practically snapped my neck off. "Here he comes," Harry said glancing into his mirror. Just then one of my phones rang. It was the bat phone.

"Elliott."

"John."

I recognized the voice. My heart gave a little involuntary flutter. "Hi Danielle," I said as casually as possible. "What's up?"

"John, please tell Captain O'Connell to stop playing games. He's going to get one of us killed."

Chapter 35

I told Harry to pull over into the breakdown lane. He signaled, crossed three lanes and cruised to a stop with his four-ways flashing. The white Suburban pulled up behind us.

"Harry, just give me a minute, ok?"

"Should I be concerned?"

"No. I'll fill you in later." I jumped out of the car and walked back to the SUV. The rear door opened and I got in. Danielle was in the front passenger seat and was turned facing me. One of the ninjas was driving and a second one was seated next to me. They both stared straight ahead.

"What a small world," I said. "Imagine running into you. You on vacation? I mean, you must be on vacation. What else would you be doing out here?"

"No, John, I'm not on vacation," she said with that patient tone people sometimes use around me.

"Then what the hell are you doing following me?"

"I told you, John. We don't have a lot of information and probably not a lot of time. We're just trying to gather information any way we can. Please don't take it personally."

"Just like I shouldn't take personally two guys trying to kill me? Did you know I had a meeting with Jeff

Feinberg? You do know who Jeff Feinberg is, right?"

"Yes, I know who he is. You had a meeting with him?"

"Yes, I did. Just before Harry picked me up."

"Why did you have a meeting with him?"

"Right after the incident on my houseboat this morning, some guy looking very much like the government, comes down my dock and says Feinberg wants me to call him. Gives me a phone number. I called the number and Feinberg suggested we meet."

"So what did he want to meet with you for?"

"I think just to threaten me. Or warn me. I haven't quite figured out which, although I'm pretty much convinced he's not just looking out for my best interests."

"He threatened you?"

"Well, in so many words, he did. He basically told me to back off from my investigation because whoever's behind whatever it is we're investigating doesn't really give two shits about a Seattle police detective. He also implied he was working with you or at least your father. I think he said he was just trying to help out his old friend Ed. What do you know about this guy?"

"I know that he showed up at my dad's house this morning and basically said he was here to do whatever he could to get to the bottom of Anna's murder."

"No, I mean what do you really know about him? His background, who he works for, that kind of stuff."

"Not much, really. I mean he's a friend of my dad's and I really haven't been paying too much attention to him. Why? Do you think he's involved in this somehow?"

"All I know is he's some kind of spook, that Anna was going to Washington to see him, presumably about this memorandum you found on the flash drive, and the next thing you know, she's dead. Then he shows up here just to help out his old friend Ed and essentially tells me to back off. I don't know about you, but in my business we don't believe in coincidences."

"What else do you know about him?"

"He says he works for Agriculture doing some kind of agroterrorism stuff. I'm sure he's on their payroll but I somehow have my doubts he's checking fruit flies."

"You know, I thought it was a little strange the way he showed up. As far as I know, he and my Dad were not all that close. But I figure there's probably a lot of things I don't know about my dad. And he seemed ok with it."

"Listen, I've got to get back to Harry and figure out some way to explain who the hell you are and why you're following us."

"Where are you going?"

I paused for second or two and looked away from her and out the window at nothing in particular. I still wasn't entirely comfortable with all this sharing. "Whidbey Island."

"Whidbey Island? What's up there?"

"Something washed up on the beach up there right near Ault Field at the naval Air Station and Harry thinks it might be one of those four fish he's been looking for. His guys are already there and we're going up there to take a look at it.

"Listen, do me a favor. I know I'm going to regret this. Stop following us. I don't think I can explain you to Harry without compromising your operation and Harry's way out on a professional limb here since he received a direct order to mind his own business. I don't think he'd appreciate my sharing his involvement in this investigation with a bunch of people he doesn't know. And here's the part I'm probably going to regret: I promise I'll call you and let you know what we find. I can't do any better than that."

"All right, John, I see your point. Call me as soon as you know anything. We're starting to put some pieces together at our end and I don't like what I'm seeing. We've been focusing more on the 'who' than the 'what', but I think they pretty much go together. I have a feeling that as we get closer to what's going on, it's going to get a lot more dangerous. Don't let your guard down, ok?"

"Yeah," I said. "I won't."

As I started to get out of the car, Danielle said: "And, John, that memorandum? It was a scanned memo on White House Counsel letterhead. It was sent last Wednesday to two people: the Special Agent In Charge at the Seattle office of the FBI, and the head of Customs and Border Protection in Seattle. It was encrypted and marked 'Top Secret'. It said no federal agent was to take any action concerning any known or suspected terrorist activity involving the ferry system in the Seattle area until further notice, that any reports or information regarding such terrorist activity was to be forwarded to the sender of the memo along with any information concerning state or local activity that might be in any way related and the White House would take full responsibility for the order. It also said anyone acting pursuant to the memo would be immune from criminal prosecution, state and federal, as a matter of national security."

"Who was it from?"

"Apparently the recipients knew who they were dealing with because it was unsigned."

Chapter 36

I got back in the car with Harry. As I did, the Suburban pulled past us onto the highway and disappeared.

"Come on. Let's go," I said.

We drove for about a mile when Harry glanced over at me me. "So, you gonna tell me what that was all about?"

"Yeah." I paused. I was going to say something about begging but I didn't think this was the time. "Look," I said, "let's just say you and I are not the only ones working on this thing and everybody, except me, apparently, has a reason to keep their involvement either low key or non-existent. Those folks were 'friendlies' and thought they might learn something from me. From us. I didn't tell them who you were but they already knew anyway. But they understand you're just up here checking on golf courses, if you catch my drift, and they're ok with that."

"And?"

"And what?"

"And what did you have to promise them to make them back off?"

"What makes you think I promised them anything?"

"Because I know you. And because they backed off awfully easily."

"Yeah. Well, I promised them I'd let them know what we find."

"You did what?"

"I promised I'd call them and let them know what we find."

Harry shook his head. "Do you think that was a smart idea?"

"I don't know, I really don't. Outside of you, I don't know who I can really trust. But I don't think you and I can do this alone and from what I know about them, my gut tells me they're ok. You'll just have to trust me on this one."

"Ok, I hope you know what you're doing."

"Me, too," I said.

We drove on in silence. Just after we turned onto 20 and before we got to the Deception Pass Bridge, my cell phone rang – the prepaid, not the bat phone. It was Marianne. It seemed like days ago that I had last seen her when, in reality, it was just a few hours ago.

"Hey," I said. "What's up?"

"I'm still at the crime lab. I have some results for you on the ballistics testing you asked me to follow-up on."

"Was there a match between those weapons and the ones that killed Anna and Anthony?"

"Yes, there was. You were right. The weapon we took

from the guy in the hospital was the same one that killed both Anna and Anthony. I haven't run a check yet, but my guess is it's the same one that killed Officer Bailey."

"Ok, thanks Marianne."

"Wait a minute, John, there's more."

"What do you mean 'there's more'?"

"I took the two weapons from those goons on your houseboat so the crime lab could compare the slugs coming from them to the slugs we found near Anna and near Anthony. When I took them over to the lab, the guy I gave them to asked me where I got them. I don't know if you noticed, but they were both the same. So I told him, not thinking much about it. Then he asked me if I'd ever seen one like them before. I took a good look at them and said, no, I actually never had. They kind of look like normal 45's at first glance. But when you look closely at them, they have some little bells and whistles you don't normally see on a hand gun, or any kind of gun for that matter."

"Like what?" I said.

"Well, like some type of device that totally takes the kick out when you fire them. And some type of stabilization device that takes out any sort of vibration or movement from your hand when you squeeze the trigger. Once you aim it and pull the trigger, you can fire two or three rounds and, if you want, they all land in exactly the same place. To tell you the truth, I didn't really know what I was looking at. I mean, I know firearms, but I would never have figured those things out if the lab guy hadn't shown me."

"So these guys were packing some pretty sophisticated weaponry."

"Yeah, apparently so. And here's the best part: These things are only made by an Israeli company and only for one customer."

"Let me guess. The United States government."

Chapter 37

We crossed over the bridge, or should I say bridges, at
Deception Pass and made our way down 20 to Ault Field
Road. It's the Whidbey Island Naval Air Station but the
airfield itself is Ault Field. We turned right on Ault Field
Road which runs along the south side of the base until
we came to the Charles Porter Gate. Charles Porter Gate
is primarily for commercial traffic on and off the base so
it's only open during what would be normal civilian
business hours Monday through Friday. It's the easiest
gate to get through because their used to a lot of civilian
traffic and you pretty much can't go anywhere important
through this gate anyway. I've been up here a number of
times, mainly to visit a couple of old Navy buddies that
stayed in and were stationed here when I first got to
Seattle and they always told me to come in through this
gate.

So, here we were on a Sunday (not normal civilian
working hours) and there's a phone at the gate that you
can pick up and they'll send some one to open the gate.
Yeah, I know. The Navy sends someone to open the gate?
On Sunday? But they do.

Anyway, Harry got out of the car and went to the phone,
picked it up, punched in a few numbers, said something
like "Get your ass down here", and got back in the car. It
was raining pretty hard and Harry was soaking wet
when he got back in.

"Believe it or not, this is the easy way", he said.

"Do you know exactly where your guys are?" I asked.

"Yeah. There's a little RV park down by the water called Cliffside. Just south of that is a pretty rocky stretch of beach that's literally covered with dead trees and limbs that have washed up over the years. Lot of big boulders in and out of the water. Something about that particular stretch that seems to pick up everything that's floating loose. The prevailing wind is westerly and there's kind of a confluence of currents from the Strait, Vancouver Island and the San Juans and everything seems to end up here. It's a beautiful spot but talk about hazards to navigation. And because of the way the currents flow, there are a lot of sand bars along that stretch of the coast as well. It doesn't really surprise me that if one of these things got loose and were going to turn up, it'd turn up here."

Just then a voice came out of Harry's radio. "Captain, this is Lieutenant Mancini. We have a slight problem."

Harry picked up the microphone. "What is it Lieutenant?"

"We've got a group of United States Marines in full battle gear here on the beach that want to know 'just what the hell we're doing', begging the Captain's pardon, sir."

I looked at Harry. "Great", he said, to no one in particular. He put the mike closer to his mouth. "Mancini, let me speak to whoever's in charge of that Marine unit."
There was a pause, then a voice with a distinct southern drawl: "This is Lieutenant Alvarez, sir. Who am I speaking to?"

"This is Captain Harry O'Connell, United States Coast Guard, Lieutenant. I wonder if you would do me the courtesy of standing by for about five minutes? I am at the Charles Porter Gate waiting for someone to let me in and will be at your location as soon as they open this gate."

"Yes, sir", he said, "I can do that, Captain, if you would be so kind as to order your men to stand by as well and not do anything else with this object in the water. I have orders, too, sir."

"I understand, Lieutenant. Please put Lieutenant Mancini back on the horn."

Another pause. "This is Mancini, sir."

"Mancini, I'm almost there. Just have your men stand by. If there are divers in the water leave it up to them if they want to stay in the water and wait or if they want to climb back aboard and wait there."

"Aye, aye, Captain."

Harry put the microphone back in its place. "Great", he said, banging the top of the steering wheel with the heel of his hand. "Just fucking great."

"So", I said, "we have about five minutes to come up with a really good story."

"Yeah", Harry said. "One that doesn't set off a lot of bells and whistles. Here they come now".

A small dark blue kind of SUV looking thing came down the road toward the gate. As it pulled up, the passenger side door opened and a Marine got out and went into the guard shack. The gate started to open and the marine came back out and walked over to Harry's side of the car. As Harry lowered the window, the Marine snapped off a salute which Harry returned.

"Captain O'Connell, sir. Do you have identification, sir?"

Harry fished for his wallet and pulled out what looked like some type of military i.d. The marine looked at it, looked at Harry, then handed it back to him. He looked past Harry and said to me: "May I see your identification, sir?"

I pulled out my SPD badge and i.d. and handed it to him. He looked at it, looked at me and handed it back.

"Would you follow us please?"

Without waiting for a response, the Marine went back into the guard shack, the driver did a three point turn and started back the way he had come and then stopped. Harry pulled through the gate and the gate closed behind him. The marine from the guard shack came out at a slow trot, jumped into the passenger side of the SUV and the SUV and Harry drove in to the base.

"Where are we going?" I said.

"Damned if I know. Can't be good, though. Somebody's gotten a little suspicious, is my guess. The only question is: Is it just somebody here or is it somebody higher up. You think your 'friends' had anything to do with this?"

"Nah, I really don't think so."

"Who are those people anyway, John?"

"Truth be told, Harry, I don't really know that much about them. But I can tell you that there are some pretty impressive people on the list and they fly under the radar."

"John, don't ask me why I'm about to ask you this, but does any of this have anything to do with the election on Tuesday?"

Hmm. Didn't see that one coming. "That's a strange question, Harry."

"Only if the answer is 'no'".

I looked him in the eye. "As a matter of fact, I'm pretty sure it does."

Harry was quiet. We followed the SUV through a security gate and up to a non-descript military looking office building – two stories high, some kind of white concrete exterior, no distinguishing architectural features, you know the type. Probably built during WW2 or just after, maybe early fifties at the latest. Sign next to the door just had a number on it but no indication of what was inside. The two Marines got out of the SUV and stood on the sidewalk waiting for us.

"Look, John, here's the story: It's my day off. You and I were going over to winterize my boat and get it ready to take out of the water. Just before I picked you up, I got a call from the office that the guys up in Bellingham had found a suspicious object that they thought might be related to drug trafficking and I decided to check it out. You and I were going to spend the day together anyway.

I asked you if you wanted to go for a ride and you said 'Sure, why not?'".

"You think that'll fly?"

"I don't know. You got a better idea?"

"Not really. My only suggestion is to be indignant and not give them much of anything until we get a better idea of what this is all about."

"Ok. Let's go."

Chapter 38

The inside of the building was as anonymous as the outside. In keeping with the 1950's décor, the hallways were paved with those vinyl square tiles that are supposed to look like brown marble – very bad, phony brown marble. From the light reflecting off of them you could see the swirl marks from one of those big, ugly mil spec floor buffers that are ubiquitous throughout the military. I don't know who made those things but, based on the fact that I've never been anywhere in the service that didn't have an arsenal of them, I have to guess that whoever it was must be sitting on a 200 foot yacht somewhere lighting cigars with hundred dollar bills. They have to be like the hammers or the toilet seats that cost $5000.00 apiece. If they hadn't been around for so long, I'd suspect Dick Cheney had something to do with awarding the contract.

All of our footsteps echoed down the hallway. Well, all except mine, that is. I was wearing the same blue jeans and sneakers that I put on this morning when I got out of the shower. My footsteps just squeaked.

We came to a doorway about half way down the hall on the right and the two Marines stepped to either side of the door and came to attention facing each other.

"Captain O'Connell, sir. This is Col. Hodges's office. You may go right in, sir." He snapped a salute while staring straight ahead, not at anyone or anything in particular. The Marine on the other side, who hadn't said a word, did the same thing. Harry was not in uniform and I seem to remember from my Navy days that the salute in return is only used when in uniform and when you have your hat on. No, really. Anyway, Harry didn't return the salute but walked past the Marine into a small reception area with a desk, a desk-top computer with a screen that was turned on, a bunch of papers and office-looking stuff, an empty secretarial chair, some type of radio (the talking back and forth kind not the country music kind), and a couple of those metal chairs with the vinyl covered seats and little vinyl covered pads on the arms. And, they were – you guess it – gray. The guy who made the chairs is sitting on his boat right next to the guy who made the buffers.

I was right behind Harry as we walked through the reception area to a second door, also open. The inner office was about half the size of Harry's, with pretty typical, no-nonsense décor. There was a desk made of some kind of dark wood directly in front of us with two little crossed flags in a wooden holder, one American flag and one I recognized as the Marine Corps flag and two full-sized flags behind the desk. The name plate said: "Col. Michael J. Hodges, USMC". Seated behind the desk was a Marine about 50-ish, classic Marine hair cut, a little squared off across the top, salt and pepper-ish, olive drab uniform with a chest full of ribbons, head down, writing something as we came in to the room.

He looked up and, without smiling, stood up and said: "Captain O'Connell, Sergeant Elliott. I'm Col. Hodges. Please. Have a seat." He gestured to two actual wooden chairs in front of his desk. They had little hollowed out depressions in the seat for your butt, but no padding. Col. Hodges wanted his guests to be comfortable, but not too comfortable. By the looks of Col. Hodges, I'm guessing that there have been more than a few people sitting in these chairs that weren't the least bit comfortable.

Harry and I sat down. I also remember from my stint in the Navy that Captains and Colonels are the same rank. So, although the atmosphere was, so far, if not cordial, then at least civil, there wasn't going to be any of that ridiculous pecking order shit about who outranks who.

Harry went straight to the point. "Colonel", he said, "what, exactly the hell is going on here? Why are we being escorted or detained or whatever the hell you choose to call it?"

Colonel Hodges sat down and leaned back slightly in his chair and said: "Funny, Captain, that's precisely my question.

"First of all, let's be clear Captain, that you are not being detained in any way. Both you and the Sergeant are certainly free to go and leave the base" – I caught the 'and leave the base part' and, I'm guessing, so did Harry – "at any time. I'm just trying to figure out what exactly is going on here and I thought you might be able to help, that's all.

"So, let's get this in proper perspective and see if we can get this whole thing on the right footing. First of all, I am the week-end duty officer in charge of base security. I take that responsibility seriously. Very seriously. We are the only Naval Aviation installation in the northwest and we are home to a number of carrier-based squadrons among other things. This base is a pretty high priority target for our nation's enemies. There are a few people in this world that would like to see us out of business

"My day started off pretty routinely. Sunday morning, things pretty quiet, good chance to get caught up on some paperwork. Then my phone rings. Never a good thing. It's the tower. One of their pilots has just come in for a landing and on his approach he sees off to his right something sticking out of the water. He doesn't know exactly what it is but he thinks it looks like a small submarine and it appears to be aground. Doesn't see any people around but it just looks suspicious. You know, not like an old fishing boat or anything that we normally see washed up on the beach around here.

"He lands the plane, alerts the tower which, in turn, alerts me. I decide that since it appears to be some kind of submarine and there doesn't seem to be any kind of immediate threat that perhaps we should let the guys at the sub base over in Bangor handle it. As much as the Marine Corps hates to admit it, we're all Navy, but we each have, shall we say, areas of specialty. Here at Whidbey Island we've got aviators and we've got the Corps, but, tell you the truth, I don't think we even have a boat here.

"Then a little while later I get another call. This one from a small security detail that covers the south side of the base, telling me that it appears that the Coast Guard is now poking around the submarine or whatever the hell it is. Ok, that's not all that unusual. The detail also tells me that the Coast Guard is now putting divers in the water. No red alert, but interesting.

He paused and looked at Harry. "Then it really gets interesting. I get a call from the base commanding officer. Not the XO, the CO. I'm sure, Captain, you appreciate the difference."

Which is to say 'I'm sure you, Sergeant, being just a cop and all, have no clue about'. So, what am I, chopped liver? Is this some kind of exclusive little club that I am being specifically kept out of? Never mind. Keep you mouth shut. For once.

"On a Sunday. Very unusual. I don't like getting calls from the C.O., especially on Sunday. It either means that somebody has seriously screwed up and my ass is on the line or something out of the ordinary is happening or about to happen. Either way, it means more work for me, which I don't need. Not in the environment we live in today. I already have more than enough to keep me busy.

"The C.O. says to me: "Mike, I just got a call from Washington. They seem to think you may have an object washed up on the beach that could be a matter of national security. Do you know anything about that?' So I tell him what I know which is not much of anything. Then he says to me: 'Washington also thinks that the Coast Guard may be interested in it as well. They're going to go through normal channels to deal with that but, in the meantime, you're to keep all personnel away from that area, understood?' So I ask him if that means the Coast Guard detail as well, and he says: 'Especially the Coast Guard detail'." He looked at me then at Harry and raised his eyebrows.

"Then you show up at my front door. Along with a Seattle Police detective. Which brings me back to your question which is my question: What the hell is going on here and what are you doing here on my base?"

Harry shifted in his chair and crossed his leg, kind of slouching back just a little, trying to appear casual. "I guess the short answer, Mike –can I call you Mike? – the short answer is you know more than I do. I don't know anything about a national security matter. John and I were on the way to the marina on Lake Union to close up my boat for the season when I got a call from my guys up here in Bellingham that one of our patrols spotted something that looked like a submarine washed up near the beach. See, we get regular briefings from DEA about international drug trafficking and one of the latest wrinkles is the use of what are called semi-submersibles for smuggling drugs over water, especially from one country to another. These semi-submersibles look like small submarines although, as the name implies, they don't go fully under water. My guys thought this might be one of those and since my area of responsibility includes water-borne drug trafficking, especially between the US and Canada, they called to let me know because if it was one of these things it would be the first one we've seen and could indicate a whole new wrinkle in our enforcement efforts."

Ol' Harry was just cruising along. I was fascinated. You know, I was actually beginning to believe him myself. I had no idea what a great story-teller this guy was. I had a whole new appreciation for Harry's ability to lie with a straight face.

"So John and I turned around and headed up here. If it was one of those things, I wanted to see it myself, first-hand. Based on where my guys told me they were, it seemed like the best way to get to it was to come on to the base and head down to Cliffside. I've been up here a few times and know my way around enough to get myself over there. I figured Porter gate was the best way to get there. That's about all I know, Mike."

Hodges had been listening to all of this sitting back in his swivel chair with his elbows on the arms of the chair and his fingers touching in one of those little tent things that people do with their fingers when they're listening to absolute bull-shit. I'm a detective, Harry's head of intelligence or something, and this guy's a career Marine officer in charge of security for one of the most important military installations on the west coast. We all know bull-shit when we hear it and there was no doubt in my mind that Colonel Hodges not only knew what he was getting but, short of thumb screws or water boarding, or whatever the military uses these days, also knew it was more than likely all he was going to get.

I don't think Colonel Hodges really cared about me, but I think he recognized that if the boat story was bullshit, then I was with Harry for some reason. But I also know how the military mind works, especially career officers who like their careers and are looking forward to a nice quiet retirement. They don't want anybody or anything interfering with it. So if they can do their job and avoid complications, they are more than happy to do it.

I think he also recognized that if he got a call from the C.O. who got a call from Washington, this whole thing was something more than a skirmish in the war on drugs. But, on its face, at least, the whole thing didn't appear to be any kind of threat to base security notwithstanding the Washington bullshit about national security. We all knew, and I'm assuming that included Col. Hodges, that under this current administration there were all kinds of political things cloaked as 'national security' that had nothing to do with national security. So, Col. Hodges, being an intensely loyal Marine but also a very practical one, had made a decision that little green men (or little brown men with white cloths wrapped around their heads) were not about to overrun 'his' base and was now in the process of simply covering his soon-to-be-retired ass. I could even see by his face that he was already drafting the file memo in his head.

All that being said, he'd covered his ass by questioning us and sending his detachment down to the beach to carry out a direct order. Now that that had been done, I assumed we would be on our merry way, probably with an escort, to the gate through which we had come in. Being the practical guy that I am, I also recognize when and where I have absolutely no authority, and a U.S. Navy base an hour and a half north of the Seattle city limits is definitely one of them. I started to say: "Sorry to have bothered you…" and stood up to leave, but Harry wasn't done. Ah, shit, Harry, leave it alone.

The Colonel had gotten up from his chair when I stood up but Harry didn't move. Instead he said: "Colonel, I'm probably way out of line here and I don't want to do anything that might compromise your authority or your responsibilities." Uh, oh. "If this thing, whatever it is, down on the beach really is one of these new semi-submersibles it would mean a whole new paradigm as far as our drug smuggling efforts are concerned. I understand that you have an order to keep all personnel away from the area but, as a practical matter, it appears that some of my men are already there.

"Now, I don't know what it is about this thing that could be a matter of national security", he lied. "But I'd like to get one of my guys inside this thing, even if it's just for a couple of minutes. It would really give us a lot of valuable information.
"As I said, I know it's asking a lot, but I already have divers on the scene, your men have the damn thing surrounded, so it's not going anywhere, and, who

knows, we could have gotten inside before your men arrived to secure the area, if you know what I mean. I know you have a job to do, but I do, too. I don't know what Washington's up to and, frankly, I don't really care. We don't catch a break with these guys very often and I'd like to make the most of an opportunity that seems to have dumped itself in my lap."

Col. Hodges put both hands on his desk, leaned forward and just looked at Harry for a long minute. Harry looked back. Neither of them said anything. And then, with out taking his eyes off of Harry, he barked: "Gunnery Sergeant!"

A fairly large gentleman in a khaki uniform who practically filled the doorway appeared out of nowhere. "Yes, sir, Colonel", he said, and I thought to myself : 'This is the part where we get whisked away and wake up to find ourselves in Cuba with a small rug and a Koran'. Why couldn't Harry leave well enough alone? Why did he have to try to coerce a fucking Marine colonel of all people into a breach of national security? Excuse me, alleged national security. Although I had the feeling that the 'alleged' part was putting too fine a distinction on it. Colonel Hodges didn't strike me as a guy overly concerned with subtlety.

"Do you have Lieutenant Alvarez on the radio?"

"Yes, sir, I do. He's waiting for your orders, Colonel."

"Tell Lieutenant Alvarez that two gentlemen, one of whom is a captain in the United States Coast Guard,"-the other of whom will strongly resemble chopped liver-"will be at his location in about five minutes to take command of the Coast Guard personnel and to order them to secure from the area.

"Also tell Lieutenant Alvarez that when the Captain arrives the Coast Guard will be allowed to board the vessel with one" - Harry held up two fingers – Jesus, this guy's got balls - "make that two divers to make sure that this object doesn't contain any drugs or other contraband. They are not, repeat, NOT allowed to remove anything from the vessel. That's all, Gunny."

Harry stood up. "Thanks, Colonel. We'll try to get out of your way as quickly as possible."

"No, Captain, you won't try to get out of my way. You will get out of my way. And you'd better make it quick. I don't know who's going to show up down there, but I can guarantee you it will be someone that can make my life miserable as well as yours. And, Captain, as far as I'm concerned, there was no permission from this office for you to board that vessel. As far as I'm concerned anybody goes near that thing violated a direct order, understand?"

Harry stuck out his hand. Col. Hodges made no effort to take it. Sitting down and picking up a pile of papers and a pen, he said, without looking up: "You're wasting time."

Chapter 39

"What do you think?" I said to Harry as he backed out of the parking space and headed off in the general direction of Cliffside at a fairly high rate of speed. Before he could answer the bat phone rang. "Domino's Pizza", I said.

"Hi, John, it's me."

"Hi. Nothing to report yet except that we were, shall I say, 'interviewed' by base security as soon as we came through the gate. They apparently had already been contacted here at Whidbey and told to keep everyone away from the thing on the beach."

"That didn't take long. So where are you now?"

"On our way to check out the thing on the beach."

"I won't even ask. Listen, the reason I'm calling is that we have information that a surveillance drone just took off from Fairchild Air Force Base down in Spokane. Our sources say it looked like a 'Predator'. And it was armed."

"I didn't know they had those things at Fairchild."

"Neither did we until five minutes ago. Watch yourself, ok?"

"'Watch yourself'? Was that a surveillance joke?" I said, but she had already hung up. I stuck the phone back in my pocket. I wanted to ask her if they were able to pull anything off that phone I gave her, but I guess it would have to wait.

"Didn't know they had what things at Fairchild?"

" 'Predator' surveillance drones. One just took off and I'm guessing it's headed our way. Whatever we're going to do, we better do it quick. If Big Brother isn't already watching, he will be in a few minutes. Probably best for all concerned if all it sees is your guys and us moving away."

Harry picked up speed, cruised through a couple of STOP signs and made a sharp right turn into the RV park and headed down toward the beach. He rolled over the grass as far as he could go and as close to the beach as he could go and jumped out of the car as it barely came to a stop. "C'mon", he said, "they should be just south of here"

We ran along some foot paths through the woods. I could see the beach and the water on my right through breaks in the under growth where the bushes had lost their leaves. Harry seemed to know where he was going and I tried to keep up as best I could without slipping on the moss or the wet rocks. Harry suddenly took a sharp right and disappeared into some low evergreens. When I got to the spot where he disappeared there was a smaller, partially overgrown path and I could see water at the end of it about fifty feet away. Harry was no where in sight until I got right to the end of the path which came out on a nasty stretch of beach littered with bleached out trees and branches and a few good sized boulders.

He stood there looking up the beach to his left as I came up beside him. "You're pretty agile for an old fart," he said.

"Yeah", I said. "Comes from years of running away from all kinds of scary shit."

"There they are." He nodded up the beach to his left. "Let's go across the beach. Might be a little faster to go back through the woods but I don't want to startle these Marines, if you know what I mean." He headed down the beach without waiting for an answer.

We picked our way across the rocky shoreline like a couple of middle aged mountain goats not trying to mask our approach. The Marines were spread out on the beach standing in a rough semi-circle in some kind of at-ease or at-ready position. They were all armed but I don't think anybody there actually thought they were going to shoot anyone. The effect was enough to make you a little careful, though. They were all facing a gray kind of phallic-looking object sticking out of the water at a funny angle about thirty yards out from the shore line.

Just off to the right was a medium sized Coast Guard boat with a half dozen or so Coast Guard types visible on the deck. A couple of them had rubber dive suits on and dive masks on their foreheads. The boat was a standard Coast Guard jet boat with what looked like an inflatable hull – kind of a Zodiac on steroids – with a big square ugly pilot house taking up most of the middle of the deck and all kinds of radar antennas and whip antennas sticking out of the roof. The Coast Guard has pretty much done away with conventional outboards and in-boards and replaced them all with these jet boats. These jets don't shoot out hot air like jet airplanes, they pump water out of an underwater nozzle at a pretty high rate of speed which makes the boat go at a pretty high rate of speed. And they can turn on a dime and maneuver in some pretty shallow water. Some of them have a gun mounted on the deck, like the ones that escort the ferries. This one didn't.

As Harry and I approached the Marines they came to a kind of attention with their weapons held in two hands at a forty-five degree angle across their chest. As we stepped into the circle, one of the Marines with his weapon slung across his back, stepped forward and snapped off a salute which I assume was directed at Harry and not at me.

"Captain O'Connell, sir. Lieutenant Alvarez. I understand you'll be taking command of the Coast Guard contingent, sir."

"Yes, I will, Lieutenant", Harry said. "Everything quiet here, Lieutenant?"

"Yes, sir, Captain. We had a brief talk with a couple of your men after you and I spoke and then they left the beach and headed for that vessel out there. We've been here and they've been there ever since."

"We're going to make this quick. Do you have radio contact with my men?"

"Yes, sir, I do." Another Marine standing close by handed the Lieutenant a small hand-held radio which Lieutenant Alvarez, in turn, handed to Harry.

Harry keyed the mike. "This is Captain O'Connell. Give me Lieutenant Mancini."

Slight pause. "This is Mancini, Captain."

"Mancini, we're going to make this quick. I want two divers in the water immediately. They are to go over to that object and board it. If they can get inside, they are to go inside and look around and remember as much of the interior as they can. We've had reports that sometimes these things can have explosives aboard in case they have to be sunk in a hurry." He looked at me and then back out toward the patrol boat. "So tell the divers to be especially on the lookout for anything that looks like a bomb or other kind of explosive device. We are not going to be allowed to take anything from the vessel but if you have a waterproof camera aboard, they are to photograph as much as they can of the interior. Do you have a camera?"

"Yes, sir, we do."

"Good. Get them in the water now. They must be back on board your boat in five minutes, no longer. Is that understood, Mancini?"

"Yes, sir, it is."

"Good. Now get them in the water and then come back on the radio. I'll wait."

"Yes, sir."

It was quiet on the beach except for the sound of a small surf breaking on the beach and tumbling the rocks as it went back out. As we watched, two guys in black rubber suits with masks and snorkels jumped feet first into the water. The Coast Guard boat had maintained a position about twenty-five yards from the wreck and the two rubber clad figures were climbing up on it in about thirty seconds. This thing had a small conning tower sticking up about in the middle of it as far as I could see. It kind of looked like a submarine but I guess it doesn't go all the way under water – just far enough under to make it hard to see on radar.

"Divers are in the water, sir."

"Lieutenant, I wasn't kidding about the five minutes. The minute those divers are back on board, I want you out of there at flank speed. Head straight for open water and then back to Bellingham. I'll catch up with you there."

"Aye, aye, Captain."

There must have been some kind of hatch on the conning tower because these guys scrambled up on this thing and disappeared inside. Harry kept looking up and I knew what he was looking for, but I don't think you can see those things. Or hear them, for that matter. Although that turned out to be wrong. Harry also kept looking at his watch. Five minutes was a guess and I knew he didn't want to push it. "Come on, come on", he mumbled under his breath. Harry kept looking up at the sky in a roughly southerly direction and then back to the sub. I looked down at my watch and it was about four minutes by my count. Just as my watch started into the fifth minute there was some movement on the deck and the divers re-appeared. Harry and I both looked up at the sky at the same time. We both heard it. The sound of a small aircraft engine a long way away and getting closer. The airspace around Whidbey is closed to general aviation, so we both knew what we were hearing.

At the same moment, a voice from the radio in Harry's hand said: "Alvarez, this is Colonel Hodges. Do you copy?"

Harry turned and looked at Alvarez who was already moving in his direction with his hand out. "This is Alvarez, Colonel".

"Alvarez, I have new orders for you. You are to secure from the area immediately, is that understood."

"Yes, sir. What about the Coast guard detail?"

"They're on their own. Secure your detail from that beach now, Lieutenant."

"Yes, sir!"

I didn't like the sound of that. And I could tell from the look on Harry's face that he didn't like it either. "Shit", he said. "Come on, John, let's get the hell off this beach," and he headed straight for the woods. It took me a few seconds to put it all together. By the time I did, we were into the tree line and double timing it back the way we had come. I find that in many cases my feet and my brain don't always work at the same time and I figured that the feet were more important at the moment. I heard the engine on the patrol boat develop a throaty roar and figured the divers were back on board and Sergeant Mancini was hauling ass, as ordered. We hadn't gone more that about twenty yards when there was a tremendous explosion from the beach in the direction that we had come from.
The ground shook, the day got a little brighter for a second or two and I could hear a lot of shit raining down into the trees. I'm not sure, but I think a rock or two hit me from one direction or another.

With Harry in the lead, we never stopped running until

we broke into the clearing and could see Harry's car. Harry slowed down to a brisk walk and I pulled up along side of him, trying to catch my breath. "Let's get the hell out of here", he said.

We got into the car and Harry started to pull away almost before I could shut the door.
"I sure hope they got some good pictures," he said.

Chapter 40

We left by the main gate. Getting off a military base is always easier than getting on and the quickest way off this base was right out the front door. A Marine waved us through and we headed north on 20 back the same way we came.

"What have we gotten ourselves into, Harry?"

"I don't know but we were about 30 seconds away from being a 'training accident', I can tell you that."

Harry reached for the radio and tried to raise Lt. Mancini. "Mancini, this is Captain O'Connell." After a couple of tries, Harry got a response. "Mancini, are all of your men safely on board?"

"Yes, sir, Captain, but not by much. Begging the Captain's pardon, sir, but what in the hell was that?"

"I don't know," Harry lied. "Some kind of military screw up, I think. Apparently we were in an area scheduled for some kind of live fire exercise but the word didn't get to the Marines until the last minute."

"Too close for me, sir. We've been shot at a couple of times on drug busts, but I don't think we've ever taken fire like that. Couple of my guys are going to need clean underwear, sir."

"Roger that, Lieutenant. Listen, Mancini, I want you to meet me at the Coast Guard pier in Anacortes. Where are you now?"

"Actually, Captain, we're just off the northern end of Whidbey Island about to swing north and head back up to Bellingham. We can alter course and meet you there in about five minutes."

"It may take us just a little longer than that. I want you to lay up about 200 yards off the pier until you see us arrive. I don't want you talking to anyone, is that understood?"

"Yes, sir. Understood."

Harry replaced the microphone. "Did you notice anything unusual about that whole incident back there?"

"Let's see," I said. "You mean other than taking live fire from the US Air Force or CIA or whoever the hell runs those things and almost getting my ass blown up? Or the part where the Marines get an order to save their asses and screw the Coast Guard? No, it all seemed pretty normal to me."

"No, I mean, without seeing it, I'd say that was a pretty decent sized missile probably intended to destroy that semi. But there was no secondary explosion. If that thing had Semtex aboard, I'm not sure you and I would be here having this conversation."

I really hadn't had time to digest the entire situation, but Harry was right. Although we were still operating in the dark, I was proceeding on the assumption there were probably four of these bad boys, now down to three, and they were probably all pretty much the same, since the two the Coast Guard stumbled across yesterday morning both had Semtex aboard. I was anxious to see what the pictures Harry's guys took inside that sucker might show us.

Then another thought occurred to me. I grabbed the prepaid and punched in Al's number.

"Russo."

"Al, it's me."

"Oh, sorry, John. I still don't recognize this number. Anything new?"

"Yeah, lots. But I don't have time to bring you up to date right now. I need you to do me a favor. Who's our rep on the JTTF?"

"Let's see, I think that's Billy Nardone."

"How well do you know him?"

"Pretty well. I went to his kid's First Communion a few weeks ago. Why, what do you need?"

"I need to know anything I can find out about any terrorist activity or threats in the Seattle area that may have either come across his desk or somehow he got wind of in the last two or three weeks. And I need him to keep his mouth shut about your inquiry. Do you think he can help you out?"

"I don't know, but I can try. I'm sure he'll keep his mouth shut. You still think that's where this is headed?"

"I don't know, but it sure smells like it."

"I'll call you back soon as I know anything."

"You know, John," Harry said, "I've been trying to think if I've seen anything come across my desk in the last few weeks that could be related to all this. I see a lot of shit, and I do mean shit, so sometimes it's hard to separate out the few grains of good intel from the rest of the static. Sometimes you see something and either it doesn't make any sense or it's so crazy you dismiss it as just that: crazy. We get stuff from all over, most of it from other government agencies. You can imagine what they send us. I mean they send us everything. Typical government stuff. Some midlevel civil servant at any number of different agencies wanting to be sure if the shit hits the fan nobody can say he didn't report it to somebody and, if it's got anything to do with water, that somebody is usually us."

"Yeah, I can imagine."

"And it's gotten worse since Washington instituted this 'America's Waterway Watch' program," Harry said. "It's like a Neighborhood Watch program on water. Now we get calls from anyone that has a VHF radio and a boat. A lot of people with some kind of weird sense of wanting to be Jack Bauer. Frankly, John, I don't like it. We gotta stop telling people to be afraid."

We were starting to come into the outskirts of Anacortes.

It occurred to me I had promised Danielle I'd keep her in the loop. Probably a good idea to wait until after we talked to Harry's guys on the dock.

Harry headed straight up Commercial Street, hung a

right down toward the waterfront and pulled up on the dock. Off the end of the pier was the patrol boat. They must have been keeping an eye out for Harry because they started to head in before we got out of the car.

The boat pulled alongside the pier and the crew threw each of us a line. As soon as we cleated off the line (that's boat talk for 'tied up the rope'), Harry and I jumped down onto the deck. A guy about 6'3" came out of the wheel house and snapped off a salute at Harry. Harry shook hands with him and said: "John, this is Joe Mancini. Joe, John Elliott. He's with the Seattle Police department."

Mancini looked at me as if to say: 'Seattle Police? What the hell are you doing here?', but he didn't say anything. He just stuck out a rather large sized hand and I tried to 'give him the grip' but he was too quick for me and almost crushed my fingers. "Nice to meet you, John," he said. I mumbled something and tried to keep from screaming.

"What have you got for us, Joe?" Harry said.

"Come on inside, Captain. It started to drizzle about five minutes ago. It's a little crowded but I think we can manage."

It was a little warmer inside and there were three other guys already in the cabin. One was wearing foul weather gear and a life jacket. The other two were the divers and had on rubber dry suits.

"Forbes," Mancini said to the guy in the life jacket, "hand me that camera there."

"Aye, aye, captain." Ok, so here's the thing: the guy who's in charge of the boat is always the captain, even if he's a Lieutenant. I know, it makes you hair hurt, right? It's one of the reasons I got out of the Navy. I couldn't keep my Captain captains and my Lieutenant captains straight. Anyway, Forbes handed Mancini the camera.

"These are the two divers I sent over to that semi, Captain. I haven't debriefed them. I thought you'd like to do that yourself."

"Thanks, Joe. I wonder if you and Forbes would mind stepping out side for just a minute?"

"No problem, sir. Holler if you need anything."

"Joe, why don't you leave the camera with me?"

"Aye, aye, Captain," and he handed Harry the camera which looked like some kind of ordinary little digital point-and-shoot you might find at Wal Mart. Harry looked down at the camera and started pushing buttons. While he was doing that, he said, without looking up: "Gentlemen, I need to know everything you saw from the time you boarded that vessel." Then to the guy closest to him: "What's your name, sailor?"

"Petty Officer Hill, sir."

"And yours, sailor?"

"Chief Petty Officer George, sir."

"Alright, Chief, tell me what you saw." I could see Harry was scrolling through the pictures on the little screen on the back of the camera as he was listening.

"Well, sir, not a whole lot to be honest with you. The lighting was not all that great but between the open hatch and our flashlights, we got a pretty good look around. There appeared to be three compartments, one for an engine room, one in the middle of the vessel that had bunks along either side of the hull and a steering station of some kind, and a forward compartment that was empty but I guess could be used for some type of cargo."

Harry handed the camera to Hill. "Show me the pictures of the forward compartment."

Hill took the camera and pushed a little button on the back as the two of them looked at the screen. "Right here, sir," he said, as he handed the camera back to Harry. "This is where they start. We took a few in there from a couple of different angles but there didn't seem to be a whole lot to see."

It was hard for me to see the pictures themselves but I could see that Harry punched through four or five of them. He handed the camera to me without saying anything.
"Did either of you see anything aboard that boat that looked like explosives?" I was looking through the pictures but I looked up at the two divers when Harry asked them that question.

"Explosives?" said Hill, casting a quick glance over at Chief Petty Officer George. "No, sir, nothing that looked like explosives."

"Shit," Harry said, to no one in particular. I knew what he was thinking because I was thinking the same thing. If there were no explosives aboard that meant either there never were any or, if they were there, somebody's moved them. I wasn't sure which would be worse.

Hill and George exchanged another kind of funny look. Not funny ha-ha, funny peculiar. Harry wasn't looking at them, but I was. After years of interrogating suspects, I've gotten pretty good at reading faces, and these guys obviously knew more than they were saying. It was the kind of look two conspirators exchange that says 'You tell him' ' No, you tell him'. I had a feeling it might have been because they had answered the questions truthfully but maybe hadn't been asked the right questions.

This was Harry's show and I didn't want to be pushy but I thought there might be a little more going on here. Sticking the camera in my jacket pocket, I said: "Harry, would you mind if I talked to these two guys alone for a minute?"

Harry gave me a kind of quizzical look but said "No, go ahead, John. I'll be right outside," and he opened the cabin door and stepped out onto the deck with Mancini and the other crew members.

As soon as the door closed, I turned with my back to the door and looked squarely at Hill and George. "All right, guys," I said, "let's get something straight. I'm not military and I'm not looking to get anyone's ass fried. But I know a little something about people who aren't always telling the whole story. This is a pretty small room so it's hard to keep all those little looks and body language things from not being too obvious. So let me tell you what's obvious to me. There's something you guys are not telling us. And let's think about what that might be. If this was a drug bust, I'd suspect somebody left a brick or two behind or a pack of hundred dollar bills and you guys stuffed it in your wet suits thinking 'Hey, who's ever gonna know?'. But we all know that whatever this was, it wasn't a drug bust so let's rule that out. Then I'm thinking I heard Harry say to Sergeant Mancini 'Don't touch anything inside that semi'. I can only assume Mancini passed that along to you as a direct order."

I took a step toward them. They tried to back up a little but the cabin was small and there was no place for them to go.

"So, here's my guess: One of you guys picked up something from inside that boat and it seemed to be a good idea at the time, but standing here in this little cabin next to a full Captain who gave a direct order not to touch anything, all of a sudden it doesn't seem like such a good idea after all."

They exchanged a quick glance.

"Like I said, I'm not looking to fry anybody's ass. In case you're wondering, I'm a detective with the Seattle Police Department and I could give a shit less about who gave what kind of an order to who. I'm a results kind of guy and if you guys have anything to say that might help me in my investigation, that's really all I care about."

I let that sink in for about a second and a half. "On the other hand, if it turns out you've got something you're not telling me, I have friends in high places and I hope you guys are happy on that ice breaker up in Alaska."

I looked each of them in the eye. There was the usual look at each other, look down at the deck, look out the window. I could see the wheels turning. It was finally George who spoke up.

Chapter 41

Harry thanked Lieutenant Mancini and we both headed back to the car. It was still raining and I had both hands in my jacket pockets and my head pulled down into my shoulders like a frightened tortoise. My Red Sox hat kept dry what little hair I had left but it didn't do much for the cold water dripping down my neck. And, as if to mock me, there was the voice of Kenny Chesney in my head again singing 'Oh, I wish I was there tonight, on Jost van Dyke...'. Shut up, Kenny.

As we got to the car I heard the engines on the patrol boat rev up and I glanced back to see a couple of crewmen jumping back onto the deck of the boat as it slipped away from the dock. There were a few hardy souls working on their boats, both in and out of the water. The boats, that is, not the hardy souls. Harry looked at me across the roof of the car. "Looks like we almost got our asses blown up for nothing. Sorry John."

"Oh, I wouldn't say that," I said, smiling, and pulled my left hand out of my jacket pocket holding up a little metal canister with two wires attached to it.

Harry's eyes got a little wider. "Where the fuck did you get that?"

"I'll never tell," I said, and got into the car.

Harry jumped in and slammed the door. "Those two fucking divers give you that? I'll have their asses court martialed."

"Harry, first of all: what divers? Second of all, you and I both know this is not a court case we're building. We've got to use whatever information we can, from wherever we can get it. And, from the looks of this detonator, we know there were explosives aboard that weren't there when that thing got incinerated."

I could tell from the look on his face that he was (reluctantly) in agreement.

"Listen, we can talk some more, but I need to call Danielle. It appears that that Semtex is on the move. We may not be looking for semi-submersibles anymore. Either the needles just got smaller or the haystack just got bigger. Either way, if this stuff is on the move, it's probably getting closer to its final destination. And, as they say, eventually this stuff will turn up, but you may not like it when it does."

I pulled out the bat phone and punched in the single digit phone number.

"Hello?" I just can't get used to that.

"Hi, this is Bat Man. Let me speak to Cat Woman." Harry looked at me kind of funny.

"Wait one, Sergeant." No sense of humor.

I waited one. Then I waited two. In fact, I probably waited about ten. I think this guy was trying to send me a message.

"Hi, John. Are you ok?"

"You mean, like 'I'm ok, you're ok'? Or more like 'do I

still have all my body parts' ok?"

"Well, both. But more 'do you still have all your body parts'? Although your sense of humor seems to be intact so I'm assuming most of the rest of you is. How was your day at the beach?"

"Ah, you know, the usual. Too much sun lying around waiting for some young beauty to accidentally drop her top. Body surfing with the kids. Oh, yeah, and the part where the entire frigging world blew up around my ears – other than that, nothing special."

"I knew that Predator couldn't be good news. I'm glad you're ok. I hoped we'd given you enough warning so you could get the hell out of there."

"Yeah, thanks for that. I owe you one. Or is it one more? I'm starting to lose track.
Anyway, I wanted to let you know we have reason to believe the Semtex is no longer in the semi-submersibles. Or, at least, some of it isn't. I'm speculating it was only in those things to move it into the area and wherever it is now, it's closer to its final destination. It appears somebody doesn't give a shit about who they blow up anymore. The fly swatters are getting bigger. That, and if I'm right and this has something to do with the election on Tuesday, that only leaves tonight and tomorrow for whatever is going down to go down. So I'm guessing we're getting close to an end game. Any news on your end?"

"You want the long version or the short version?"

"Between you and me, I don't think any of us has the time for the long version of anything."

"We went over the phone you gave us and pulled out the recent incoming and outgoing phone numbers. There weren't many. A couple of numbers were interesting. One was a number that connects through the White House switchboard. But not the main number. What you might call a 'back line' – you know, not the number the general public might use. There was only one call to that number. But from there it gets a little more complicated because it's a switchboard. So there's no way of knowing from that who the call was to or from. We're working on getting the White House phone data so we can try to match up the call with the time it was made and see if we can pin it down."

"What about the other number?"

"It belongs to a cell phone. From what we can tell, the cell phone is located somewhere in Seattle, or was when the calls were made. I guess not a big surprise, but there were a dozen or so calls back and forth between the two phones in a twenty-four hour period, with the last one pretty close to the time when those guys came down your dock."

"Anybody bother to check Feinberg's phone?"

"As a matter of fact, we did. No match."

"Just as a guess, how about the head of the Seattle FBI Field Office or the head of Customs and Border Protection?"

"We thought of that. Those are a little more difficult but we're working on them."

Just then, my other phone rang. I pulled it out of my jacket pocket and checked the number. "Listen, I gotta go. Keep me posted and I'll do the same."

I hung up with Danielle. "Hey, Al, what'd you find out?"

"Hey, John. Listen, I spoke to Billy Nardone. He said a lot of things have come across his desk in the last three weeks. Wanted to know if I could be a little more specific. What do you want me to tell him?"

"Tell him anything related to threats to the ferry system."

"Got it. I'll get back to you as soon as I have anything." He hung up.

Harry made his way back to the highway and headed south on 5. I checked my watch, or more accurately, I checked my stomach then my watch and both of them concurred that it was well past lunch time. "You hungry?" I asked Harry.

"Yeah, I could use a bite. I'll pull off at the next exit. I think I know a place where we can get a decent lunch." And Harry did just that.

But a Whopper and fries wasn't exactly what Harry had in mind. Knowing Harry, I should have known. Harry's the kind of guy who when he offers you a beer it's never a Bud Light, it's always some dark and mysterious brew. Harry knows the difference between an ale and a lager. He knows just by tasting it what they make it out of and how long they cook it. I've been in restaurants with Harry when all they had were the usual American light beers. Harry ordered a glass of water. He said if he was going to drink something that tasted like water he might as well drink the real thing. I mean, I know a little about the subject myself but more like the difference between a Corona and a Sam Adams or a Killian's. Harry studies food and drink. And I don't even try to converse with him about wine. Talk about making my hair hurt. Anything more than a fifteen dollar bottle of Chianti is wasted on me. But Harry? I was on his boat one time and he pulled out a bottle of wine and said it was just some stuff he keeps on the boat. He said he keeps the good stuff at home. The friggin' thing still had the price tag on it: eighty-five friggin' dollars!

Anyway, turns out this place has just about the best steaks on the planet. Harry had a bourbon and water with his steak and I had some local brew the waiter recommended
The steak was fantastic – not huge, a rich mahogany brown on the outside, the right amount of fat running through it, just a little crispy on the edges and done in the inside just the way I'd ordered it. After a couple of bites and a couple of pulls on his bourbon, Harry said: "So what are we doing here? Are we getting any closer to figuring this thing out?"

"I don't know. I do think we need to figure out a way to step up security on the ferries for the next day or two. Apparently we, or, more properly, you, can't just raise the MARSEC level. I wonder if we can pass the word to the State Patrol guys without setting off a lot of bells and whistles. I'm afraid if we do anything out in the open it's going to get countermanded then everybody's hands are tied."

"Actually, John, it turns out the State Patrol Homeland Security Division in charge of ferry and terminal security is on Pier 36 along with us. I happen to know the WSP guy in charge – guy named Charlie Parker and, no, he doesn't play any kind of musical instrument. Maybe I should try to get hold of him and see what he thinks."

"Do you think you can trust him to keep this quiet?"

"Yeah, I think so. This guy's been around for a while and he knows how to get things done. He's a results kind of guy. Let me finish this in peace then I'll give him a call."

I went back to my steak. Somehow I had a feeling I might not get to eat again for a while. I didn't know how right I was.

Chapter 42

Harry finished his steak (and his bourbon), then called
Charlie Parker. Rather than go over it with him on the
phone, Harry suggested they meet in his office. Charlie
must have said something like: 'This better be important
for you to call me up on a Sunday afternoon' because I
heard Harry say: "Yeah, it's important." We were headed
back to Seattle anyway so Harry and Charlie agreed to
meet in an hour in Harry's office. I had Harry drop me
off at headquarters. I told Harry to call me if anything
new came up at his end.

I watched him pull away and just stood there for a
minute trying to piece this whole thing together. Even
though it looked like it, it wasn't making sense to me that
our own government would be launching a terror strike
against its own people. I know these characters in
Washington are capable of almost anything but there
was a part of me that just couldn't make that leap.

I flashed my badge at the officer on duty in the lobby and
took the elevator up to the office. There wasn't a soul in
sight except for one Detective with his sleeves rolled up
and a phone stuck to the side of his head. He looked up
and saw me coming and gave me a quick wave with the
hand holding the pen he was writing furiously with, then
looked back down at the yellow legal pad on his desk
and kept scribbling.

I dropped into the chair at the desk across from him and
waited for him to finish. "Yeah, I think I got most of it.
I'll call you back if I need any more. Grazie, Billy. Say hi
to Crissy for me...Yeah, I'll try to wait until the game is

over…Yeah, you, too…Later, brother."

He hung up the phone. "Well, I got what you asked for. I haven't had time to digest it all. You want to go over it together?"

"Might as well," I said. "Your writing looks like my napkin after a spaghetti dinner and I probably couldn't read that either."

"Was there some kind of ethnic slur buried in that remark?"

"I don't think it's appropriate for an Italian to be talking about things being buried," I said.

Al just shook his head. "You know, one of these days you're gonna say something like that to the wrong Italian."

"Whatta ya got?" Why is it when I'm around Italians I start sounding like Brooklyn? Or Providence?

"In the last three weeks Billy came up with seven reports that could be linked to the ferry system."

"My God! Seven? In three weeks? Is that normal?"

"I guess so. And these are just the ones having anything to do with the ferries. Billy says most of them are just crackpots with no real chance of carrying out the threat, but they all have to be checked out. "How old is this list?"

"Billy says it comes out every Wednesday morning. I guess it's good up until Tuesday night."

Nothing after last Tuesday night. Interesting.

"So, anyway, here's what he came up with." He leaned forward and turned the pad sideways so we could both read it. It might as well have been upside down in Chinese. But I was courteous and pretended to be following along.

"I'll have two number fours and a number seven. No rice," I said. He just glanced up at me for a long second.

"Anyway," he said, pausing and looking back at the pad, "three of these were phone calls essentially saying the caller was going to bomb the ferry. Billy says they generally don't take these too seriously, although they have to check them out. They can usually trace a phone number and find the guy who made the call. Almost always some crackpot with some sort of ax to grind. He also says once in about a thousand times when the threat is closer to being real, it's usually not a call when somebody calls up and says 'I'm going to do this or that'. Apparently the real bad guys don't call up and tell you what they're going to do, they just call up and try to take credit after it happens. But the important stuff is usually some type of lead that's developed by our own guys in the field. They smell something that's not quite right and start tracking it down."

"So all these things you got from Nardone are not necessarily phone calls."

"Well, actually, five of them were phone calls. A lot of times people call because they've heard or seen something they think doesn't seem right. You can imagine the kind of shit our guys have to sift through. Some people think every middle eastern person they see is a terrorist. Billy says he'd be rich if he had a nickel for every time there was a call about some middle eastern guy with a cell phone or a video camera on one of the ferries.

So, the other two phone calls were from people who said they had seen or heard something on the ferry that convinced them there was some type of plot. Billy said both of those have since been cleared. Apparently the State patrol guys were able to check them out pretty quickly and determined it was more of the usual. Let's see…

one turned out to be two Armenian business men from Michigan and other was…hmmm, hang on, I'm trying to read my own writing…."

I just looked at him but he refused to make eye contact with me.

"Oh, the other wasn't even a middle eastern type. He was Indian. It was a Sikh with a turban and a cell phone."

I just shook my head. "What have we come to?"

"Yeah, I know what you're saying. So, that leaves us with two more contacts, both of which were field incidents. The first one was from the border crossing up in Blaine.

Three guys with Pakistani passports trying to come into the US. I guess their papers were ok but the dogs were sniffing something that may or may not have been explosives residue and one of the customs guys found a ferry schedule on the back seat of the car."

"When was that?"

"Let's see…a week ago Wednesday."

"So what happened?"

"I don't know. That's all Billy gave me on it. You want me to follow up and see if he's got anything else?"

"Yes, I do. And tell him to be careful where he checks and who he checks with. It's getting harder and harder to tell the good guys from the bad guys. How about the last one?"

Al studied his notes for a minute without comment. "You know, if you're having trouble reading that," I said, "I think the Chinese restaurant over in Pioneer Square is open. We could run over there and see if one of those guys could help you."

"What? Oh, no, no, I'm not having trouble reading it. Oh, very funny. Chinese restaurant. I get it. No, I'm trying to figure out why this one is on the list."

"What is it?"

"Apparently a guy was taken into custody last Tuesday in San Diego when he was caught taking pictures of the bridge of a research vessel with his cell phone. I don't know why this is on the list. I was just writing like crazy while Billy was giving me this stuff and I wasn't really paying much attention to what he was giving me. I can't tell if he gave me this by accident or if I didn't write something down. You want me to call him back and find out?"

You know that old expression: 'assume nothing'? When it comes to any case I'm investigating, I never assume something isn't important. You know what they say about genius? (Humor me, I'm on a roll here with tired old expressions.) That it's ten per cent inspiration and ninety per cent perspiration? Well, in police work it's more like one per cent inspiration and ninety-nine per cent perspiration. Which is to say: follow up on everything that's even remotely related. If Billy made a mistake, we'd know in one phone call." "Yeah, why don't you?"

Al picked up the phone and dialed. He leaned back in his chair and I could see he was tired. So much had happened to me in the last thirty-six hours I hadn't really thought about Al, and I wondered if he had gotten any sleep at all. Plus, Al has a wife and kids and it was the week-end and I knew he was getting pressure from his wife to get his ass home and spend some time with the family. Al's wife was American and all that, but she was brought up in an Italian family and I know she never has liked his job, mainly because of the hours. She wants him there for those awful birthday parties and Sunday afternoon dinners after mass with both sides of the family and big plates of pasta and Al's father smoking those awful little Italian cigars after dinner and all those things that make an Italian family what it is: a family.

He hunched back over his desk and swung the pad around, cradled the phone against his ear and picked up his pen. "Hey, Billy, sorry to bother you...Yeah, I know the game isn't over yet...Listen, I gotta ask you about one of the things you gave me on that list...Yeah, I'll wait." He looked up at me: "He's going into another room where he can hear himself think...Yeah, I'm here. Listen, you gave me something about a guy who was taken into custody down in San Diego. I can't figure out why that was on the list...Yeah...Right...Uh, huh...No shit…What'd they do with the guy?…Hmm…Ok. No, that's it. Thanks, Billy, I appreciate it. Sorry to take you away from the game." I pointed to the list on the pad in front of him. "Oh, wait a minute, there was one other thing on the list about those three Pakis up in Blaine? Do you know what happened to them?…Yeah, it could be…Can you find out?…The sooner the better…I know it's Sunday, but this can't wait…Let's just say it's looking like more than just a simple murder investigation…Listen, Billy, just be really careful about who you ask or where you check. We don't know who we can trust at this point and we don't want to set off any alarms… Call me back on my cell…Ok, I know I owe you big time…Oh, Christ, not your sister's kid again…Yeah, I'll talk to Prosecution. I'll see what I can do. Apologize to Crissy for me, will you?…Yeah, you, too." He hung up.

He put the pen down, took a deep breath and slowly rubbed his eyes with both hands, letting out a big sigh. "Paesans. They drive you crazy." He picked up the pad and studied it for a second or two. "Ok, here's the story as best as he can tell, because he apparently had the same reaction we did. First of all, the guy was noticed by one of the crew taking the pictures with his cell phone. When the crewman said something like: 'What are you doing?', the guy knocked him down and tried to take off, but never made it off the ship. I guess some other crew members grabbed him and they called for whatever security was nearby. Security called San Diego PD who detained the guy and while they were going through his stuff they found other pictures on his cell phone, including a couple of shots of other parts of the ship, like the engine room."

"So, I'm still not understanding why this guy is on our

list."

"Well, because he was carrying a Pakistani passport and because, one of the pictures on this guy's phone was of Pier 52 here in Seattle."

"The ferry terminal."

Chapter 43

It was quiet. Al and I sat staring at each other but not really seeing each other. We were both trying to make the connection between a research vessel in San Diego and the ferry terminal in Seattle. I wasn't making it and neither was Al.

"What did Nardone say happened to the guy?"

"He said there was one entry in the summary – it just said the guy was turned over to the FBI."

Fucking FBI. "Any information on the ship?"

"Yeah, let's see, I got it here some where… Yeah, here it is: research vessel called the Roger Revelle. Apparently belongs to Scripps Oceanography - was tied up at one of their piers."

Just then I heard a sound. I couldn't really tell where it was coming from. It sounded like a cheap music box with one of those little ballerinas rotating on the top. Like something you might give to a five year old girl for her birthday. I looked around the room. "What the hell is that?" I said.

Al just looked at me for a second then jumped up and reached for his jacket that was thrown across the back of his chair next to his desk. "Oh. My cell phone," he said, looking a little embarrassed. He reached into one of the pockets and fished out a cell phone. "My kids gave me this new phone that takes pictures and I don't even know how to change the ringer. Hello?... Hey, Billy, what'd you find out?...Ok, thanks...No, I promise...Yeah, well, I wouldn't want that to happen...Just give her a big kiss and tell her I owe her one...Yeah, you, too." He stuck the phone back in his coat. "Billy says those three guys up in Blaine? The Customs guys turned them and their vehicle over to the FBI."

Fucking FBI. Again. On the one hand, that's probably what you would do with these guys anyway. But after what was in the memo Danielle and her people had uncovered, I wasn't taking anything for granted. I pulled out the bat phone and punched 7. It rang once.

"Hello?"

"Let me speak to Danielle."

"Wait one please, Sergeant."

He put me on hold. I heard a couple of very faint beeping sounds. Then she picked up.

"Hi, John."

"Hi.. Listen, do you guys have any way of accessing FBI records?"

"Possibly. What kind of records?"

I explained to her about the incident up in Blaine and about the guy in San Diego. "I'm trying to find out what happened to those guys after the FBI took them in."

"You're assuming there is a record."

"Yeah. True." I thought about that for a few seconds.

"Anyway, can you have your people try to find out?"

"Sure. I'll get somebody right on it."

"How you doing with that White House phone record?"

"We were able to trace the call to a phone in the Vice-President's office. No indication of who might have used it. But it's a week-end and both the President and the Vice-President are out of town. We're getting the entry log to see who was in the building at the time."

"How about those other calls. Any luck pinpointing that cell phone?"

"Yes and no. We don't know yet who it belongs to but we were able to pick up its location for a while until somebody shut it off and pulled the battery out."

"What does that mean?"

"It means who ever has that phone – or had that phone - had it turned on long enough to use it, but then shut it off and pulled out the battery – or tossed it in the bay – or hit it with a hammer - so people like us couldn't find them. We had a team on the way when we lost the signal."

"Where was it?"

"It was downtown, somewhere in the general vicinity of your office."

"Or the Federal Building," I said.

"Yes," she said. "Or the Federal Building."

"Any luck tracing the number back to the owner?"

"No. It was billed to some company in the DC area with a PO Box, but no such company exists. You didn't think it would be that easy, did you?"

"No, not really, but some times it's the little things people overlook that lead you to bigger things. We need to catch a break, Danielle."

"Yes, we do, John. I don't think we have a lot of time."

"See what you can find out about those two incidents."

"I'll call you back."

I sat there for a minute thinking. I punched in some numbers.. "Hey, Harry, didn't you sail a couple of times with some guy from the UDub School of Oceanography? Had something to do with the Thompson?"

"You mean Cyril? Yeah. Why?"

"How well do you know him?"

"Cyril used to be in the Coast Guard. I did a couple of tours with him.

"What does he do now?"

"He retired out of the Coast Guard about five years ago and took a job in charge of dockside security at the Oceanography School. Why do want to know about

Cyril?"

"Apparently there was an incident down in San Diego a few days ago where a guy was arrested when he was caught taking pictures of the bridge of a research vessel at Scripps. I guess he tried to get off the ship and the crew nailed him and called the cops who, in turn, turned him over to the FBI. When the San Diego PD looked at his pictures, he had shots of the inside of the ship and he also had a least one picture of Pier 52 here in Seattle."

"No kidding."

"No kidding. I'm trying to figure out what the connection is or if there's any connection.
I thought maybe I could pick your buddy's brain to see if I could make some connection."

"You want me to call him?"

"Yeah, could you?"

"Sure. How much do you want me to tell him?"

"Why don't you just tell him you're trying to help out a friend and ask him to give me a call. And Harry?"

"Yeah?"

"Tell him he needs to call me right away."

Chapter 44

About twenty minutes later Harry called back. He had
some difficulty locating Cyril but finally tracked him
down on the pier where the Thompson was tied up over
at UDub. Harry said the Thompson was getting ready to
get underway with some type of scientific expedition
and there was a lot of activity on the dock getting the
ship loaded up and ready to go. Apparently Cyril told
Harry he'd be more than willing to help out any way he
could but he really didn't have much time for a phone
conversation. He suggested to Harry that if I wanted to
come over to the pier and follow him around he'd be
happy to talk to me.

So I jumped into one of the Department cars and headed
up toward the University District. One of these days I've
got to go pick up the other car. I took Eastlake Avenue
out toward the University. Portage Bay Road is off of
Eastlake just before you go over the bridge. So, I figured
as long as I was going right by my front door, maybe I'd
stop off and change into something a little dryer and
warmer. I'd been in and out of rain and drizzle all day,
especially up in Anacortes, and my socks were wet and
so were my pants and the collar of my shirt, not to
mention a little wet strip down the middle of my back
that ended at my jockey shorts. None of this was helping
my disposition any. I kept trying to think about why the
hell I came out here in the first place, because it sure
wasn't the weather, or did I mention that already?

My ex-wife used to say it wasn't really the weather that
was bothering me, but the weather was a safe thing for
me to complain about instead of dealing with whatever

was really bothering me. I don't think she realized how true that was when she said it. But I also think she was a little surprised when it turned out that what was really bothering me was her.

As I came up to my parking space I could see there was already a car parked there. Every once in a while some bozo comes along, maybe to visit somebody who lives down here, doesn't realize how sacred these spaces are, and just grabs the first open spot they see. Only this time this particular bozo was apparently Marianne, since it was her Mini that was parked in my space.

I parked on the side of the road as best I could and made my way down onto the dock. I made a quick scan of the area just in case lightning was about to strike twice, but I didn't see anything or anyone unusual. I was hoping after what happened this morning, someone would realize that kind of thing was only going to piss me off. I had no doubt they (whoever they were) would still try to keep me away from whatever they were up to, but I didn't think another full frontal assault was part of the plan, even though the incident with the Predator came pretty close. But I think that was more directed at the sub than it was at me. Although I'm smart enough to think they would have been somewhat delighted if I had been standing a little too close to the scene of the accident.

It appeared all of the crime scene people were gone. There were little bits of yellow tape here and there but nothing and nobody else. I knocked on the front door as I walked in and said "Hello!," more to keep from getting my ass shot off than anything else after what happened the last time somebody came through that door.

Marianne stuck her head out of the bedroom looking a

little surprised. "Hi," she said.

"What are you doing back here? I thought this would be the last place you'd want to be for a while."

"Well, actually, this is the last place I want to be. At least for now. I came by to get my things."

I walked over and dropped onto the couch. "You want to talk about this?"

"No, not really." There's a big surprise. "It's just that I need a little space between us."

"We already have a little space between us. So apparently what you need is a lot of space."

She looked at me for a long moment then turned back into the bedroom. "Would you mind getting my skis out of the shed?" End of interview.

I sat there for a minute trying to decide whether to press her on this. After a brief conversation with the three or four people that live in my head, the consensus was: No. This space thing or barrier or whatever the hell it was clearly predated me and I had no insight whatsoever into where it came from. In the beginning I was mildly curious, but it was pretty clear from day one hat was one minefield that was not going to be entered, at least not by me. Maybe by some professional someday, but definitely not by me.

I remember once, just after I got divorced, I met this really nice girl on a vacation down in St. Barth's. She was absolutely gorgeous and she really seemed to like me. I ran into her by accident a couple of times. We started spending a little time together. We could talk about anything. We liked a lot of the same things - same music, same food. She had a great sense of humor. She drank beer. She loved snorkeling and laying on the beach. What's not to like? She was me with tits. But it never seemed to go anywhere beyond that. I couldn't get her into bed no matter what I did. I mean, it was the Caribbean – the sun was warm, the rum was flowing, everybody's relaxed and happy. I tried everything – the entire repertoire. Nothing.

Then one night I was out to dinner by myself and I looked across the room and there she was, having dinner with another equally gorgeous but a little masculine-looking woman. Holding hands across the table and gazing into each others' eyes, smiling and laughing. I began to get a little suspicious. I think it was when the waiter brought them champagne and they toasted each other then kissed each other – not one of those little air kisses - that I finally figured it out.

Now the reason I'm telling you all this is because rather than accept it for what it was, I decided my mission in life was to bring her over from the dark side. Do I even need to say what an exercise in futility that was? Marianne wasn't gay, at least as far as I could tell, but this was the same kind of futile exercise. The outcome was inevitable. And, frankly, I'd learned my lesson. What's that old Irish prayer about knowing the difference between things you can change and things you can't change? This was one of those things I wasn't going to change even if I had the stamina to try, which I didn't.

"No, I don't mind," I said, getting up off the couch. I went out into the shed, fumbled around in the gloom, knocked a paint can off a shelf, swore a couple of times under my breath, and finally came up with her skis. I walked back into the house with them, through the bedroom, and set them down by the front door.

She came out of the bedroom with a canvas boat bag stuffed with odd articles of clothing that had collected over the last few months and God knows what else. "I hope you don't have my Sinatra records in there," I said.

A little smile crossed her lips. "You don't have any Sinatra records," she said. And it dawned on me I really couldn't remember seeing her smile in a long time. "I really appreciate your not making this too difficult," she said.

"Would it have made any difference in the long run?"

"If you had Sinatra records?"

"Very funny. You know what I mean," I said.

"No, I don't think so."

"And please don't say 'It's not you, it's me'."

"Ok, I won't." She moved to the door, opened it and picked up her skis. "See you at the office," she said.

I wanted to say 'Don't let the door hit you in the ass on the way out'. Even though I was ok with it being over, nobody likes to be the one to get dumped. So I guess I was a little pissed, but only for a second or two. I also had the urge to say something like 'I hope we can work this out', but I really didn't think we could and, truth be told, I wasn't feeling all that bad about it. It was time.

"I'll get the door," I said. She stepped past me without saying anything and I watched her walk up the dock and start up the stairs. "See you around," I said. I took a deep breath, let out a big sigh, shook my head, stepped back inside and closed the door.

Chapter 45

By the time I changed and was ready to head out, it was almost dark. I could see the lights on the pier across the bay where the Thompson was tied up. The pier is a little too far away for me to see any activity, even if I put my glasses on, which I very seldom do, but I could tell by the amount of light that the loading operation was probably in full swing. The rain had stopped but that doesn't mean much around here, so I threw on some foul weather gear and a watch cap over my dry jeans and a dry sweatshirt. I think the dry jockey shorts felt better than anything.

I drove over the University Bridge and headed down toward the pier where the Thompson was tied up. I parked the car in the lot next to the gate and walked up to some kind of security guy standing at the gate. I stepped out of the way to let a small van go through that said 'University of Washington School of Oceanography' on the side then showed the guy my badge. "I'm looking for Cyril Dobbs," I said, "I think he's expecting me."

"Sure," he said as he put his hand up to a microphone clipped to the chest of his jacket. "Who should I say is looking for him?"

"John Elliott, Seattle PD."

He leaned forward just a little toward the mic and said "Captain Dobbs?" Oh, great. Is everybody a friggin' captain except me?

Crackle, crackle. "Dobbs," crackle, crackle.

"Captain, John Elliott, Seattle PD is here. Says you're expecting him?"

"Elliott? Oh, yeah. Send him through. I'm right down on the dock."

"You can go ahead, sir. Captain Dobbs will be over there on the dock next to the boat. Probably down near the stern where they're loading the gear."

"Is that the front end or the back end," I said, with a straight face.

"Uh, that would be the back-end," he said, looking at me as if to say 'You're kidding, right?'.

"Thanks," I said. "I always wondered where that was. Listen, I've never met Captain Dobbs. Can you tell me what he looks like?"

He smiled. "Yes, sir, I can. You can't miss him. Big black dude, about six-four, two eighty-five."

"Thanks," I said.

I made my way down to the dock, trying to stay out of the way of what appeared to be complete chaos. There were a couple of fork lifts running back and forth, guys with dollies, an overhead crane coming off the ship and little knots of people, men and women, talking and gesturing, saying things like 'Hey, be careful with that'.

I made my way down onto the dock and toward the stern – that would be the back end.

Sure enough, he wasn't hard to miss.

"John," he said. "Nice to meet you," and he stuck out his hand. Holy shit! His hands were huge and so was the rest of him. This was not going to be good for a skinny little white guy. Ah, well. I don't want to insult the guy. Here goes nothin'. I stuck out my hand. At least I was quick enough not to let him give me 'the grip'. Let's just say I did my best not to show any pain, but I don't think I was very successful.

"Harry said you wanted to talk to me. This official business?"

"Well, not really official. For either one of us."

He broke into a broad grin. "In that case, how can I help you?"

"Last week a guy down in San Diego was found aboard a research boat called the Roger Revelle tied up at Scripps."

"Yeah, I know that boat. What about it."

"Apparently this guy was on the bridge taking pictures with his phone and when one of the crew asked him what he was doing, he took off and tried to run. The crew nailed him before he left the ship and turned him over to the San Diego PD. San Diego PD went through his phone to see what was so interesting and apparently came up with a number of pictures of the inside of the ship – things like the bridge, the engine room, some of the compartments. They also found a couple of pictures of Pier 52 here in Seattle."

"The ferry terminal?"

"Uh huh."

"So you're trying to make a connection between the Revelle and Pier 52. Anybody ask the guy?"

"I don't know," I said. "I'm not sure where he is right now."

"So this is the 'unofficial' part. You can't go asking around if anybody's seen this guy, and if anybody asks, I ain't seen you, right?"

This guy is quick. "Right."

"Well, I wish I could help you. The only thing I can tell you is the Revelle has pulled in here on occasion, usually on its way to or from the arctic. Some times they drop people or gear off and some times they pick up. I'd say she's been in here maybe four or five times since I came here. She may pull into the ferry dock, but I doubt it. Listen, John, not to interrupt your train of thought, but walk with me. They're starting to load the instruments and I have to keep a close eye on everything."

We walked away from the ship toward a flood-lit area where some large wooden crates and a number of metal containers were surrounded by a knot of men and women and were being checked by a guy with a clip board.

"What's this?" I said to Cyril.

"Different instruments for taking various types of measurements. I don't know what all they actually do, but they're usually about the last things to go on board. My job is to make sure nobody tampers with them until they're loaded aboard. Once they're on board, they're somebody else's problem."

"Who's the guy with the clip board?"

"He's the Chief Scientist for this cruise. He's responsible for everything that gets loaded on board. He checks things like the seals on every container to be sure no seals are broken or nobody's been fooling with the crates."

"So you don't necessarily know what's in these containers."

"Right. That's his job. My job is just to be sure nobody tampers with them while they're on the pier."

I looked around. "You seem to have an awful lot of security for a marine research vessel. This normal?"

"This? No, I wouldn't say normal," he said, casually. "Just normal when they're loading explosives."

I whipped around. "What?"

He laughed. "Relax, man. Not like bombs or anything. Sometimes these guys use small explosive charges for echo sounding and things like that. The federal government has strict protocols for handling any type of explosives, doesn't matter how small they are. Everything is in magazines, all sealed and wrapped up tight.

"There are explosives designated for this particular trip and as soon as they arrive, we put everything else aside and load them on board. Even with all this security, it's easier to keep an eye on them once they're on board. That plus I don't have to keep an eye on them any more." He gave me a big smile. Ah, the military mind. Hand it off to someone else as quickly as you can.

"So getting back to my man in San Diego, you can't think of any reason he'd be taking pictures of the Revelle and pictures of Pier 52."

"No, not really." Just then one of Cyril's security guys came up to him.

"'Scuse me, Captain. That truck from NOAA with the explosives just arrived at the gate."

"Ok, tell 'em I'll be right there. Get a couple of men and clear the way down to the ship. I think they're going to load those magazines onto the bow. And get the Chief Scientist. He's gonna' want to check this stuff before it gets loaded aboard." He turned to me. "Sorry to interrupt, John, but I gotta' pay attention to this stuff. Sorry I couldn't be of more help."

"Just one more question. If I wanted to find out where the Revelle is now, how would I do it?"

"Scripps has a web site just like us. We post the details of the cruises for the Thompson on our web site. I've never looked but I imagine they probably do the same for the Revelle."

'Thanks, Cyril, I appreciate your seeing me at all. Listen, here's my card. Let me write my cell phone number on the back. Give me a call in case you think of anything." He turned and walked away from me, holding my card up in his right hand and waving it back and forth then stuck it inside his jacket.

I stood and looked around for a few seconds. My phone rang. I flipped it open and started walking back to my car. "Hey, Harry, what's up?"

"You talk to Cyril?"

"Yeah, just finished up. I'm headed back to my car."

"Anything?"

"Not really. I'm still trying to make a connection between those pictures, but I keep coming up empty. Anything new at your end? You talk to your buddy Parker?"

"Yeah. He's going to put out the word quietly to step up security."

"Has he heard anything about an attack on the ferries?"

"Nothing unusual. A few phone calls from the usual collection of nut jobs. He did tell me about three Pakistanis that got picked up at the border up in Blaine sometime last week."

"Yeah, I know about those guys." I pushed button on my car key, got a couple of bird sounds from under the hood and heard the door unlock. I got in and started up the engine.
"Three guys driving an SUV that set the dogs off."

"Then you know about the ferry schedule."

"Yes, I do."

"And did you also know all three guys were carrying seamen's papers?"

Chapter 46

I rang off with Harry and immediately called Danielle. "Listen, I need those FBI records."

"I'm fine, thank you. How are you?" she said.

"Sorry. I'm fine and I'm glad you're fine. But I'd be finer if I knew what happened to those four guys that got turned over to the FBI. Got anything yet?"

"I'm not at the house. Let me call my Dad and I'll call you right back."

I sat back in the seat. The engine was warming up and some heat was starting to come out the vents. The defrosters were taking some of the steam off the windows as I watched the activity on the pier. I started thinking about Marianne and, unlike Danielle, how she wouldn't have even noticed that I didn't ask how she was. The phone rang and scared the shit out of me. I almost dropped it between the seats. It was Danielle. "Hi."

"Hi, John."

"So, how are you?"

"You're such a jerk."

"That's been said before."

"I'll bet it has. Anyway, here's what we've got. The three

guys from the border crossing were taken to the FBI office in Seattle and held for about six hours then released. We got that from a source in the Seattle office. There's also a record in the main FBI computer in DC."

"Your source tell you anything else?"

"He says as far as he can tell, nobody questioned them. They just held them in one of the interrogation rooms then let them go. Said it seemed like they were waiting for something. He says he thinks the decision to let them go wasn't made here. He thinks it was made in DC."

"He know anything about them carrying seamen's papers?"

"No, he didn't mention it. Why? What makes you think they were carrying seamen's papers?"

"I have my sources, too."

"Is that significant?"

"My having sources? Yeah, it means you're not the only one with sources. In fact, my sources are bigger than your sources."

"I'm sure they are, John, but that's not what I meant. I meant are the seamen's papers significant?"

"It could be if these guys are planning some type of attack on a ferry. It's possible they planned to somehow get aboard a ferry as crew members and plant a bomb or somehow sabotage it."

"Or hijack it."

"Or hijack it. How about the guy from San Diego?"

"That's a little more interesting. The San Diego police turned him over to the San Diego FBI office, which you already knew. But this is the interesting part: We've learned San Diego transported the guy to the Seattle FBI office. But the official FBI records show the guy was investigated then released by the San Diego FBI field office."

All roads lead to Rome, as they say. Only in this case, all roads seem to be leading to the Seattle office of the FBI.

Then, in one of those rare moments when a little door opens up in your mind and something useful pops out, I had a thought. Yeah, I know: Alert the media. "Danielle, by any chance was there anything else on that flash drive?"

"Yes, I already told you there was a bunch of budget stuff on it."

"Are you sure?"

"Yes, I'm sure. I know government budget figures when I see them."

"No, I mean are you sure they were just budget figures? Why would Anna copy down a bunch of budget numbers?"

"I don't know. Maybe they were already on the flash drive when she added that encrypted file. She investigated a lot of stuff. Maybe at some point she was looking for budget fraud."

"Or maybe they're not budget numbers at all. Maybe there's something else on that flash drive we haven't found because we weren't looking for it. Maybe we were so focused on the encrypted file it never occurred to us to look for anything else."

"I guess that's possible."

"Have your guys look at that thing again. Only this time look at everything as if it's suspicious. If there are budget numbers, cross check them against some independent source to see if they really are legitimate budget numbers. Have your code guys look at those numbers as if they were some kind of code. Look for patterns or whatever the hell else they do. And tell them to be quick about it. By the way, did you ever get anything out of those guys who ambushed us over on Bainbridge?"

"Not so far. They seem to have been hired to do a job and don't know who hired them.
Apparently the guy who stuck the gun under your chin was the guy who assembled the team."

"Another dead end. Anyway, what little we have, including your guy in DC, seems to be pointing to an attack on a ferry. And between your sister's comment about staying off the ferries 'for the next couple of days', and the fact the election is Tuesday that leaves us pretty much with tonight and tomorrow. Not a lot of time."

"I'll get them right on it. And John?"

"Yeah?"

"I don't think these guys have necessarily given up on

you. If they think you're getting close they won't hesitate."

"That reminds me, have you seen your friend Feinberg lately?"

"Yes, he's been in and out, meeting with my Dad and some of the others. Why?"

"Because I still don't trust him. I'm going to feel much better about my own personal safety if I know right where that guy is."

I pulled out of the parking lot and headed back across the bridge. I needed to go home and get something to eat.

Chapter 47

I hadn't forgotten about the somewhat cryptic phone call from the guy who said Anna Noble worked for him. He said Todd would know how to get in touch with him. All I had to do was remember what the hell I did with Todd's card that he gave me with the cell phone number on it.

I went into the bedroom. Looking around the room, I got just a little touch of nostalgia. No sign of Marianne anywhere. Separate and apart from the pros and cons of our relationship, I never realized how much I liked seeing those little signs of female occupation around the house. Not a bra or pair of panties in sight. Maybe I'll go out and buy a couple of each and just leave them lying around. The place could use a little interior decorating. Beats the hell out of lamps and pillows.

As I was looking through my dirty clothes looking for Todd's card, I thought about the comment the mystery man had made about Todd not working for him. So, then, I asked myself, why have me call Todd to get in touch with him? I didn't have an answer to that one but made a mental note to ask him.

I found the card and dialed the number Todd had given me. "Todd, this is Elliott."

"You realize you should be dead by now."

"Is that admiration or disappointment I hear in your voice?"

"What can I do for you Elliott?"

"I got a call yesterday from a guy who said you'd know how to get in touch with him."

"Yes."

"Tell him I'd like to meet with him."

"Ok."

"Only no Federal Buildings or anything cute like that. Tell him I'll meet him in the bar at Duke's Chowder House over on Lake Union. I'll be there in twenty minutes."

"I'll do my best."

"I think we've seen your best, Todd. See if you can actually get this done." I hung up.

You'd think for a guy who likes to eat as much as I do, I might stop and do it a little more often. But, first things first. At this point, the challenge of this whole thing far outweighed my empty stomach. When I get a bone in my teeth, I just can't let it go. I figured out at some point in my life the challenge of solving a problem was far more powerful than just about anything else – sex, food, alcohol, sleep – you name it. Anybody who knows me will tell you I'm competitive about everything. I love the challenge. I don't even have to win – although winning is certainly sweet. I always tell people I don't care whether I win or lose just as long as I don't look like a jerk doing it. Besides, I can always grab a bite at Duke's.

So I threw on a sweater and a jacket, tucked my Glock

into the holster behind my back and a smaller Glock that I carry in an ankle holster just in case and trudged up the steps to my car. It was starting to get dark but I could still see around the neighborhood. I did a quick scan but everything seemed in order. Duke's isn't far from my house and I figured I'd get there before he did and pick a nice public spot.

I pulled into the parking lot at Duke's. There were a fair number of cars there. Duke's, in addition to having some of the most outstanding seafood on the planet, is also a sports bar and on Sunday nights you can usually expect a pretty good crowd watching Sunday night football. The Patriots were playing the Colts and I was looking forward to seeing Peyton Manning get his lunch handed to him. You can take the boy out of New England but you can't take New England and ten points, especially against the Colts.

I found a spot at a table close enough to the bar where I could keep an eye on the game and the door at the same time. I chose a table with a padded banquette against the wall and chairs on the other side. I sat on the side with my back against the wall in my best Mafioso style. There are a few things we can learn from those guys and when your physical safety is in some doubt, this was one of them.

Seattle has a lot of New England ex-pats (that's expatriates not ex-Patriots) and the bar was full. In true New England style, these guys had obviously been drinking since about 2:00 and the noise level was, well, noisy.

A good looking waitress named Hannah came over and asked if she could get me something to drink. Hannah was about 35, dark hair pulled back, reasonably loose fitting white shirt with a black bow-tie and black pants, not too tight, except through the hips. All in all a pleasant looking eye full. Nice smile, too. The management had clearly figured out they needed experienced help with this crowd. She knew better than to ask 'What can I get you?' or 'What would you like?' A question like 'Can I get you something to drink?' keeps the airplane in the hangar and doesn't lead to a lot of sophomoric bullshit.

"Yeah," I said. "How about some kind of local brew like amber ale or an Irish red?"

"Got just the thing," she said. "I'll be right back with it. Anything to eat?"

Ah, the magic words. "You sure know how to show a guy a good time," I said.
She smiled. "Give me a minute to look at the menu. By the way, there's going to be one more."

"No problem. I'll set another place." She turned and walked away The game was in the beginning of the second quarter and it wasn't looking good for the Pats. 7-zip, Colts.

I checked the bar looking for someone that didn't fit in just in case Mr. X had gotten there before me. After a few minutes, Hannah came with my beer and I ordered the grilled mahi mahi. She didn't even bother to write it down. "About fifteen minutes," she said. "Ok?"

"Yeah, that's fine. Thanks very much."

I sipped the beer and she was right: it was just the thing.

I'll have to ask her what it is when she brings my dinner. I started looking around to see if I could spot my date. I hate blind dates. I always get the ugly one. Half the time they don't even show up, although I had the feeling this one would.

Just as I was about to give up, figuring Todd wasn't able to get in touch with the mystery man, I noticed someone get up from the bar with a beer bottle in one hand, a glass in the other wearing a Patriots jacket. He never made eye contact with me but came in my direction. As he approached the table he stood next to it, looked at me and said: "Mind if I join you, Sergeant?"

I hesitated for a split second, trying to figure out if this was the guy I was supposed to meet, or if it was just some guy that knew me from somewhere and just decided to say hello. He had the look of someone I had arrested at one time or another.

"Todd sends his best," he said.

Chapter 48

I motioned for him to sit down but made no effort to shake his hand. I hate a hypocrite and this guy had done nothing so far to make me think he was a friend. Or, now that I think of it, a foe either. So I thought I'd just adopt a wait and see attitude and not get too friendly right off the bat.

He smiled and nodded, and slid into the chair across from me.

"I'm Michael Kelly," he said. "My friends call me Teddy. They think I look like Teddy Bruschi." He nodded up toward the TV.

"My friends call me John. They think I look like shit. You can call me Sergeant Elliott."

He smiled. "Ok, Sergeant. I can understand why you might be a little cautious, but let me start by saying I think we're on the same side."

"And what side would that be?" I asked.

"The side that's trying to figure out who killed Anna Noble and why."

"I think we've already figured out who killed Anna Noble."

"If you mean those two goons on your houseboat this morning, I think we both know they were only trigger men. I mean who caused her to die. Who ordered or suggested or planned it. You already know who pulled the trigger and, yet, you're still out poking around. I think you want to know who's behind this as much as I do."

"Ok, let's back up," I said. "Let's start with who the hell are you and what did you mean when you said Anna Noble worked for you?"

He looked at me and nodded. "Officially? Officially, I'm one of four Assistant Special Agent's in Charge in the Seattle Office of the FBI. My direct responsibility is counter-terrorism. But I have another job as well. I know you used to work for the Bureau, Sergeant. Have you ever looked at the organizational chart?"

"No, Kelly, I can't say that I ever have. I mean, it was pretty boring sometimes, but never that boring."

"Well, if you ever took the time to look at it, you'd see there's a line from the Deputy Director through an Associate Deputy Director to a whole bunch of little boxes most people never think about. And that line, by the way, does not go through any Special Agent in Charge. Really sexy stuff like 'Facilities and Logistics Services' and 'Records Management'. And way down at the bottom of that list is something called the Security Division. And if you go on the Bureau's web site and look up Security Division, you'll see a list of things they do. Way down at the bottom of that list you'll see something called 'Information Security Professionals'. That's what Anna Noble did."

"And she worked for you."

"Right."

"What, exactly, did she do for you?"

"I can't tell you 'exactly'. But I can tell you it was pretty much what it sounds like. Generally what she did was check the security levels of the Bureau's computers, especially in the field offices. And because she was often checking internal security, a lot of times the people she worked with and for didn't really know what she was doing."

"What did they think she was doing?"

"Her 'day job', or her 'cover', if you want to call it that, was essentially a research assistant. In this day and age, everything is on the computer, but there are a lot of field agents who either can't or won't take the time to learn how to use all the resources the Bureau has available. So, they'd just hand it off to Anna and a few others like her and she'd do the research then hand them the results."

"She had time for all that?"

"She was a whiz, Sergeant."

"And nobody else in your office knew what she was actually doing?"

"Not as far as I know. There's a reason the Bureau put the Security Division on a direct line to the top. Not even the SACs know who all of them are. At least for the kind of work Anna was doing. We do have folks that come into a Field Office and coordinate with the SAC and everybody pretty much knows they're there and what they are doing. But most people even within the Bureau don't know much about the existence of our unit."

"'Who watches the watchman?'"

"Excuse me?"

"I said: 'Who watches the watchman?'. It's an old expression I learned from my father.
We hire the watchman to look out for our valuables. But who watches the watchman? How do we know the watchman isn't stealing from us? So, in this case, everybody assumes the FBI is watching out for America. But who's watching the FBI? Under this Administration that's become an important question. Apparently the answer is: the FBI. No offense, Kelly, but this whole scenario doesn't give me a lot of confidence. I don't think I'm going to sleep any sounder now that I know the FBI is watching the FBI. I think I would have felt better if you told me you and Anna actually worked for Brink's Home Security."

"Well, Sergeant, you're certainly entitled to your opinion. But let me tell you we've uncovered some pretty high level breaches of security. The FBI is a big operation and we have a lot of information, and I mean a lot of information. It's a temptation to certain people. Sometimes its money, sometimes it's a grudge, either against the Bureau or the country itself and sometimes its people who think in some twisted way they're being patriotic. But the information we have is value neutral. It can be used to help us or it can be used to hurt us."

"How does Todd fit into all of this?"

"Todd is a Special Agent in the Seattle office."

"Yeah, well, I kinda figured that one out for myself."

"Todd got assigned to you by the SAC. Coincidentally, and unknown to the SAC, Todd also works in the Security Division."

"I thought you said he didn't work for you."

"He doesn't. We both work for the same boss in Washington and that's all we know about each other. We kind of watch each other's backs but I really don't know what his assignments are and he doesn't know mine. It's the old military 'need to know' thing. I'm sure you're familiar with that concept. When he got assigned to you yesterday I asked him if he'd liase with you and be my contact since he had reason to know what you were up to and where you would be. Or at least I thought he did. We underestimated you a little."

"I'll take that as a compliment. Who decided I needed to be watched? Or was that just general Bureau paranoia?"

"I don't know, although I think it was probably somebody above the SAC. Probably someone in Washington. I do know when Anna Noble turned up dead, there was quite a bit of activity at the office. It was pretty busy for a Saturday. A lot of phone calls and a lot of closed door meetings, most of which I was not invited to."

"Do you think you were intentionally left out?"

"That's a good question. On the one hand, nobody in Seattle knew she was working for me, that I know of. On the other hand a couple of people in Washington knew it but for some reason either decided not to disclose it to the SAC or maybe they did and it was decided to intentionally leave me out. I'm not sure which."

"Why would they decide to leave you out?"

He shrugged, a little too casually for my taste.

"So," I said, " even if you can't tell me what she was working on, do you think whatever it was could have been what got her killed?" I was thinking about that flash drive, but I didn't know if he knew that I knew.

"This is a funny business, Sergeant. Sometimes you find things that lead you directly to certain people and you take appropriate steps to correct the situation." Why did the phrase 'appropriate steps' make the hair on the back of my neck stand up? "And some times you find something and don't immediately recognize the significance of it."

A roar went up from the crowd at the bar. I glanced up at the screen and saw New England had just pulled ahead of the Colts. New England 12 Colts 7. Go Pats.

"And sometimes you find things certain people wish you hadn't found." That brought me back.

Just then Hannah came over and said: "That mahi mahi will be out in a few minutes." She turned to Kelley: "Can I get you anything?"

"No, thanks," he said. "I'm all set for now."

"Which do you think it was?" I said as casually as possible. Kelley was watching Hannah walk away. As she disappeared into the crowd, he looked back at me.

"What makes you think it was anything to do with her work?" he said, looking straight into my eyes. Be careful of anyone who answers a question with a question.

Now, see, here's what I'm thinking: He wants to know how much I know and probably also wants to know how many other people know what I know. I think he knows I know about the flash drive. What he doesn't know is if I know what was actually on that flash drive. Talk about making my head swim.

"I don't," I lied. "I'm trying to find out what you think."

"I have no idea," he lied back. "I'm trying to figure out why one of my best agents, and also a damn nice person, was gunned down in an alley. If was something to do with her work, I'd certainly like to know about it. I thought, after what happened this morning, since you are apparently on somebody's radar maybe you might know the answer. Somebody seems to think you know something."

"Yeah, a lot of people make that mistake. What makes you think what happened to me this morning had anything to do with this case? I make a lot of enemies in my business."

"That," he went on, seeming to ignore my question, "and the fact your activities in the last forty-eight hours would seem to indicate something more than a murder investigation."

"Listen, Kelly, I don't know what you're driving at. Besides, how would you know about my activities in the last forty-eight hours?" Careful, John, he's putting you on the defensive.

"We have some pretty sophisticated surveillance techniques, Sergeant."

"Yeah, I'm sure you do. Remind me when I get home to write out a check to the ACLU. Let's get back to Anna."

"What about her?"

"You said on the phone you had information I might find useful."

He looked at me without blinking for about ten seconds. "We think Anna might have been working either with or for the bad guys."

"And why is that, Kelly? Or is that one of those 'need to know' things?"

"We were in the process of investigating certain of her activities when she was killed.
We think she was turning over sensitive information and was killed either because she wanted more money – if she was doing it for money – or because she had turned over what they needed and had outlived her usefulness. There's even a possibility they knew we were investigating her and didn't want us to find out who she was working for."

"And why are you telling me this?"

"Because this is a very sensitive investigation and you keep getting in the way. I guess I wanted to see if I could enlist your cooperation in backing off and not beating the bushes. You're only making our job more difficult."

"Well, you're going to have to do a better job of convincing me. So far all I'm hearing is 'back off'. I keep hearing that. That could mean I'm screwing up your investigation or it could mean I'm getting close to something or someone. What makes you think Anna Noble was working for – as you put it – 'the bad guys'? And, while we're at it, which bad guys?"

He looked up at the TV screen. "They're not going to win this one. You can just feel it."
Then he looked back at me. "Ok, listen. I'll share some things with you but you have to promise if I do, you'll back off and let us do our job. Deal?"

"Kelly, do you know how many times a day I hear that or something like that? The short answer is: forget it. I don't do those kind of deals. If you trust me enough to give me the information, then you have to trust me enough to do the right thing, whatever that is. Deal or no deal?"

A smile crossed his face. Briefly. "The Bureau is admittedly a little paranoid."

"A little?"

He ignored me. "We have checks and cross-checks for almost everything. Including little warnings that go off when people access things they shouldn't be accessing. It also includes little warnings that go off when people copy things they have no reason to copy, which includes most things in the Bureau's computers. Let's just say through a series of security layers, I get information when somebody copies something. Depending on what it is or who it is either I or somebody who works for me runs it down and finds out who and why and we take appropriate steps."

There was that phrase again.

"It doesn't happen very often but usually we find that somebody is looking up personal information like the address of old an old girl friend or something not really related to national security or criminal activity. Once in a while it's a lot more serious."

"Why do I get the feeling that this was one of those times?"

"It might have been."

"'Might have been'?"

He chose to ignore the question or, rather, side-step it. "In the course of Anna's job, she would have occasion to copy files, mainly to preserve a record. I would still get an alert that a file had been copied, but I could always verify it against the work she was doing. I would routinely go over her work with her and she would provide me with whatever back-up I needed, including copies of any files that were relevant.

"Last week I was doing one of those reviews with her and there were some files, according to our systems, she had accessed and copied. But she never mentioned them or included them in any of her reports."

"When was that?"

"When was what?"

"When you met with her and went over her cases."

"Last Thursday. Why?"

"No reason, I'm just trying to establish a time frame in my own mind. I'm trying to reconstruct her actions before she was shot. Always helps me understand things a little better. How do you know it was her who accessed these files?" I said.

"It's a little complicated, but the easiest way to answer your question is to tell you that in order to get into our computers at any level you have to have certain passwords. We can tell from the password who's getting into what."

"Did you ask her about them?"

"No, I never got the chance."

"Wouldn't Anna have known that sooner or later you would find out she had copied these files?"

"Yes, she would have."

"Why didn't you confront her as soon as you found out?" I asked.

"First of all, I don't always get these access reports right away. Second, I don't always look at them right away, or if I do, it's just to scan them then wait to go over them with my agents. Anna, by the way, isn't - or wasn't - my only agent. And third, even after I met with Anna and she didn't mention these files, I needed to do a little groundwork on my own before I confronted her. I mean, think about it Sergeant. She was one of my best people. I wasn't about to accuse or even imply anything until I had a little more information."

Or maybe, just maybe, you wanted to be sure you weren't implicated in any way before the shit hit the fan.

Chapter 49

At first I thought I was having some type of heart attack. My heart felt like it was beating about 200 beats a minute. Then I realized I had set my cell phone on vibrate and put it in my shirt pocket. Only a few people had the number and they were all important. Without letting onto Kelly that my phone was ringing, I got up and told him I needed to visit the head. "Want to join me?" I asked him. He gave me a funny look and just put both hands up in front of him and shook his head 'no'. Works every time.

I made my way through the crowd to the Men's Room which, with this crowd, should have had a revolving door on it. I don't know why some of these guys didn't just put their money on the bar then bring the beer in here and pour it down the toilet. It would have saved a lot of time.

It was too noisy and too crowded for me to take a phone call so I found a little alcove just down the hall and slid into it. I checked my voicemail but didn't have any messages, so I checked my 'Missed calls' and there was one from Harry. I hit the 'Talk' button and the phone dialed his number. I don't know about anybody else, but I don't remember anybody's phone number any more. I've gotten really lazy with all the bells and whistles on these cell phones. I actually don't even know my son's number. I just look him up on my 'Contacts' list and hit 'Talk'.

"O'Connell."

"Harry, it's me. What's up?"

"Where are you, John?"

"Over at Duke's on Lake Union. Why? You got something?"

"Yeah, maybe. I'll pick you up in five minutes."

"Don't come here, Harry. Meet me over at the parking lot for the Kenmore Air Terminal over on Westlake. The lot right next to the dock. And make it ten." Looks like I'm not going to eat. Again.

"You got it." He hung up.

I made my way back to the table where Kelly was watching the game. I slid back into my seat and folded my hands in front of me on the still empty table.

"Let me ask you one more question," I said. I get that from my old lawyer days. It always means at least another half hour of questioning. I can remember judges leaning back in their chairs and looking up at the ceiling when some lawyer would say: 'Just one more question, you honor'. "Are you implying Anna was some sort of spy? I mean, I guess we already know she was some kind of spy but I mean some kind of double agent or somehow she was passing information from the Bureau to someone else?"

"You can draw your own conclusions."

"Do you know what was in the files she copied?"

"No, I don't," he said. I don't know why, but for some

reason I believed him. I know there have been books written on the subject, books like "Blink," but I've always trusted my first reaction to most situations. I'm not always right, I could have been dead wrong about this one. After all, Kelly didn't get to be an Assistant Special Agent in Charge without learning something about lying with a straight face. But there was something about his eyes, his facial expression, his body language, that said 'truth'. I still didn't like him and I still didn't trust him. But I believed him.

"But you knew she had copied some files."

"That's right."

"Did it occur to you to look at them to see what she had copied?"

"Of course it did. That's was part of what I was trying to do before I confronted her."

"And?"

"And when I went to look for them myself, they were gone."

"Gone?"

"Yes, gone. Deleted. Erased. Gone."

"Did you share any of this with anyone else?"

"What, that we might have a security breach? Yes, as a matter of fact, I did."

"Who did you tell?"

"My boss in Washington. That's protocol. When we discover a breach in security and can't get a plausible explanation, I report it to Washington."

"To who?"

"I'm afraid I can't tell you that, Sergeant."

"Oh, come on, Kelly. It's just us girls."

"No, it's not that I won't, it's that I can't. I don't know the identity of the person I report to."

I nodded my head. Typical cloak and dagger Bureau stuff. Most people think it's only the CIA that works that way.

"When did you report it?"

"On Thursday, right after I met with Anna."

I was really pushing the envelope here but, what the hell, all he can do is stop talking to me. Or shoot me. Come to think of it... Oh, well. Fools rush in. "And when did you go looking for those files?"

"Friday morning. I came into the office early – about 6 AM – and started searching for them."

"Did you tell anybody here in the Seattle office about any of this?"

"No, I didn't. The Seattle office doesn't know about my security assignment."

"Any possibility somebody in Washington would have alerted the SAC here in Seattle?"

"I suppose that's possible, but it would be highly unlikely. Usually what happens is that we work through the problem, figure out who's involved then if some disciplinary step is necessary, the SAC gets a call telling him what to do but not necessarily why. If it's an arrest, we generally make them away from the office. Then we change all of the access codes and passwords. People aren't stupid. Pretty much everybody in the office can figure out what happened."

I was starting to believe that this guy really didn't know what was on that flash drive. Or in those files.

I started to slide out from behind the table. "Sorry, Kelly," I said. "Some kind of intestinal thing. I'll be right back." I took about two steps and turned back to him. "Tell me something, Kelly. You're the counter-terrorism guy in your office, right? Have you heard anything lately about an attack on the ferries?"

"No, why?" he said, scowling. "Have you?"

"Just wondering," I said. "I'll be right back." Let's see what that stirs up.

I headed for the Men's Room and just kept going. By the time Kelly figured out I was gone, I'd be long gone. Besides, I was kind of hoping he'd be there long enough to get stuck with the check. Who knows? If he likes mahi mahi he might just stay and get his money's worth.

Chapter 50

I stepped out a side door, made my way across the outdoor patio which was deserted this time of year, hopped the low fence that ran around it and headed away from the parking lot and around the south end of the lake, past the marinas and over toward the Kenmore Air dock where Harry was supposed to meet me.

In the spirit of not making anything too easy for whoever might be tracking me or following me I decided to leave the car where it was. I also pulled the battery out of my prepaid cell phone. I'm not even sure that does any good any more. I have to remember to ask one of our tech guys about that. Up until this week-end I never really thought about it. Or had to.

I did a couple of surveillance checks on my way over but didn't see anything.

Taking as an article of faith that the bat phone was untraceable, at least by anyone other than Danielle's crowd, I called Harry.

"O'Connell."

"Harry, it's me. Drive over to the portico at the hotel across the street. Drive real slow around the circle and under the canopy and don't stop. I'll be waiting for you." I hung up without saying goodbye and quick stepped across the street, up the circular drive in front of the hotel and under the canopy over the entrance. I figured if they were watching me by satellite, they'd see me go under the canopy and might assume I was going into the hotel.

That, and if Harry went in one side of the canopy and out the other without stopping it might not occur to the watchers that I had jumped into the car. Like I said, I took the precautions I could take. I had no idea whether they had already made Harry's car and were watching him as well.

I waited in the front doorway of the hotel until I saw Harry's car slowly make the swing up the drive then moved closer to the pavement so he wouldn't have to slow down as I jumped in on his way by. For some reason I suddenly thought about Kelly and wondered if he decided to try the mahi mahi.

I didn't have much time to think about Kelly, or the food, for that matter. But I think I was just a little pissed that I missed dinner. Duke's seafood is usually pretty good, although I've never had their mahi mahi. Now that I think of it, it was probably mediocre – probably all dried out, overcooked. Yeah, right.

I jumped into Harry's car as he kept rolling.

"You want to tell me what that was all about?' he said. "And what the hell are you doing over here?"

"Tell me something, Harry. Am I still paranoid if people really are out to get me?"

"I don't know if this helps or not, but you were paranoid a long time before people were out to get you."

"Thank you, Harry. That was helpful."

"Anyway, what are you doing over here?"

"I was at Duke's having a conversation with a guy who says Anna Noble worked for him. Guy by the name of Kelly. Kelly says he's an Assistant Special Agent in Charge at the Seattle office. He also says he and Anna work under cover for the Bureau investigating internal security, mostly computer stuff. All very cloak and dagger."

"And?"

"Well, you know with those guys you have to pick through what they tell you, but here's the best I could determine: Anna Noble stumbled across some information buried in a computer file she wasn't supposed to find. We now know what at least some of it was. Somehow she figured out what was in it and decided she couldn't trust anybody in her office to share it with. So she also decides to not reveal it to this guy."

"Any idea when she might have found it?"
"This is probably on Thursday. Sometime during the day on Thursday, Kelly is routinely going over some reports related to Anna's work and sees Anna has accessed and copied some files. No big deal apparently. But then, when he goes over the reports with her later in the day, again routinely, she never mentions it to him. Being the good little spook that he is, he says nothing to her but decides to do a little homework before he confronts her – ducks in a row, and all that shit. And he says he considered she might be some kind of foreign agent."

"So what did he do?"

"Being a dedicated public servant, he reports what he knows up the chain of command. Only, in this case, his chain of command doesn't go through the local Special

Agent in Charge, it goes directly to somebody in Washington."

"Do we know who?"

"He says he doesn't know. Some kind of blind cut-out or something. Anyway, so he goes home Thursday night, or wherever these guys go at night, and by Friday morning decides to try to go into the files himself to see what was so interesting. When he tries to locate the files, they're gone."

"Why did he wait until Friday?"

"Good question. I don't know the answer to that."

"What did he do when Anna turned up dead?"

"Apparently he's conducting his own investigation. Or, at least, that's what he led me to believe. He says there was quite a bit of activity in the office on Saturday morning when they got the report that Anna had been murdered, but a lot of it was closed door and he wasn't invited."

"Do you believe him?"

"I believe they didn't include him. What I don't know is whether it was because they knew more about her death than he did and they weren't sharing, or if it was because they thought he might have actually had something to do with it. I mean, theoretically, they didn't even know she worked for him, so I don't know if there would have been any reason to include him in the first place. See, you can't ever tell with these guys. They see conspiracy under every rock, so they're always whispering in the corner and deciding who to tell and who not to tell. Sometimes it's a wonder anything gets done. Most of these guys need to take a lesson from J. Edgar and slip into a party dress and relax every once in a while."

"So, what have you got that's so urgent?"

"This whole thing has really got me worried, John, both from a Coast Guard standpoint and from a plain old US citizen standpoint. I think something big is about to happen but I'm not seeing the usual responses. I've seen more activity or just plain interest in things that have a lot less going for them."

"No shit, Sherlock. What's your point?"

"My point is I'm starting not to trust my usual channels, at least not the official ones. It started right after they started playing with the MARSEC levels yesterday morning. I just didn't like the way it was done. It didn't make any sense to me. So, as you know, I decided to go outside my official channels and do a little snooping on my own. One of the guys I got in touch with is my buddy in the Canadian Coast Guard. They have a little different mission statement than we do, but this guy has his ear to the ground just the same."

"This the same guy who told you about the four semi-submersibles?"

"Yeah, same guy. We've done some joint exercises together, sat in a couple of seminars, and are pretty much on the same page when it comes to sharing information.

"So I called him and asked him if he had heard anything recently about a possible attack on our ferry system. He says: 'You're kidding, right?'. I said: 'No. Why would I be kidding?' He says: 'You really don't know anything about it?' 'About what?' I said. Then he tells me.

"About a week ago the Mounties broke up a terrorist ring – or a suspected terrorist ring, anyhow - in Vancouver. For a reason I've yet to figure out, some of these guys think it's easier to come in through Canada then try to slip across the border instead of coming directly into the US. Maybe they're right. Maybe the Canadians need to tighten up their security.

"Anyway, their source tells the Mounties that these guys are planning an attack on the Seattle ferry system. They arrested three guys all carrying Pakistani passports and US merchant marine documentation. Apparently there were others involved but these three were the only ones they managed to catch. The Mounties interrogated these three guys for a couple of days but they're not talking, say they're just here looking for work aboard any kind of freighter.

"While all this is going on, the Mounties call the FBI in Seattle. I guess because of the target, they figured they'd better let our guys in on it. I don't know for sure, but that's probably the drill in situations like this. My guess is we do the same thing if we catch somebody down here talking about blowing up some Canadian shit.

"My guy doesn't know if the FBI took part in the interrogation or not. My guess is, knowing the little bit I do about both outfits, the answer is probably 'no'."

"So what happened to those three guys?"

"Well, according to Paul…Ah, shit. Now I have to kill

you."

"Funny."

"According to unnamed but reliable sources, the Mounties turned the three guys over to the guys from the Seattle FBI office."

"Wait a minute. Are these the same three guys that got stopped trying to cross at Blaine?"

"I don't think so."

"Why not?"

"Because the FBI and the three terrorists – excuse me, suspected terrorists – were escorted by the Mounties to the small private jet the FBI guys arrived in where they all apparently flew back to the US."

"So that means if my math is right, so far we have at least seven guys in the last week, week and a half, that appear to be interested in blowing the shit out of something, probably a ferry, right?"

"Right."

"And they all end up in the hands of the FBI here in Seattle. And there's not a word about any of this through regular channels."

"Right again."

"And if our 'unnamed but reliable sources' are to be believed, there are more of these guys out there that just didn't get caught." I stared straight ahead, not really seeing anything, trying, once again, to piece this together. The pieces were slowly starting to fit and I didn't like the picture that was starting to develop. I pulled out the bat phone and hit 7.

"Hello?"

"Give me Danielle."

A couple of faint bleeps later, she came on the line. "Hi, John."

"Hi Danielle. How're you doing?"

There was a slight delay and even though I couldn't see her, I could sense a slight smile crossing her face. "Tired but ok, John. How are you doing?"

"Hungry as hell, but otherwise ok. Listen, we need to talk and I think we'd be better off doing it face to face. Can we meet somewhere?"

"Uh, sure. Where are you now?"

I hadn't really been paying all that much attention. I looked out the windshield and out the side window. "Looks like we're on Alaskan Way headed south."

"Are you alone?"

"No. I'm with my friend from earlier today."

I heard her turn away from the phone and say something. She must have been telling someone that Harry was with me.

"John, we don't have time to fool around. Do you trust this guy?"

"With my life."

Her voice got a little faint again as she turned from the phone. I heard her say: "They're on Alaskan Way headed south...yeah, ok." She got louder again: "John? Stay on Alaskan Way until you get to Marginal Way. Do you know where the Red Barn is at Boeing Field?"

"Yeah."

"Ok. Bear left on Marginal Way until you come to the Red Barn and the museum. There's a gate to the field just south of it. We're going to meet you there. But don't stop there. Drive past the Barn all the way to the end of the field then do a U turn at the Boeing Access Road and come back to the museum building from the other direction. The gate is on your right just before the museum. We just want to make sure nobody's following you."

"Got it."

"Look for a black Suburban. Flash your lights and follow him." She hung up.

"I suppose that was your friends from earlier today. You're still not going to tell me who they are, are you?"

"They can tell you as much or as little as they like. You're about to meet them."

Chapter 51

I gave Harry the directions Danielle had given to me. He turned left off of Alaskan Way and onto Marginal Way and past the Red Barn and the Museum of Flight. We got to the intersection of Marginal Way and the Boeing Access Road and, it turns out, it's a pretty good place to check a tail. If anyone was following us, it would have been pretty obvious. There was nobody behind us and the one or two cars that were behind us before, just kept going straight when we took the left on Boeing.

I could see the main museum building coming up on our right. "Take a right at the Tomcat," I said to Harry, sounding like some kind of airplane geek. Truth be told, the only reason I knew it was a Tomcat was because I've seen "Top Gun" about a dozen times. It's probably the only plane I know. That and the Concorde.

Harry slowed down and turned right. Up ahead was a black Suburban with no lights parked on the side of the road facing away from us. Harry flashed his high beams twice quickly and the Suburban turned on his lights and pulled away. We fell in behind him. At the end of the access road was a cyclone fence with a big double gate. The right side of the gate rolled back as the Suburban approached it and cruised on through. Harry followed right on his tail. I caught a glimpse of a black-clad figure with some kind of automatic weapon over his shoulder closing the gate as we went through.

As soon as we were clear of the gate, the brake lights on the Suburban lit up and Harry almost ran into him. The figure from the gate jogged up to the driver's side of

Harry's car, tapped twice on his window and gestured for Harry to roll down his window. He was wearing a black balaclava and all I could see were his eyes. He shined a small flashlight on my face and Harry's face, did a quick scan of the back seat and said: "Follow us please, sir. Lights off." The fact they were making a visual check to be sure that we were who we were supposed to be led me to conclude that not only did they know what I looked like but, apparently, what Harry looked like. Scary shit. I turned back in my seat and jumped about a mile. There were two more black-clad figures standing right next to my door with automatic weapons pointed right at us. Not taking any chances. They shouldered their weapons and all three of them piled into the back of the Suburban.

We pulled away and drove a short distance on some kind of access road that ran parallel to the runway. We took a right turn and started to drive toward the runway when the brake lights on the Suburban went on.

We sat there for a moment not moving. I looked to my right and saw a set of landing lights headed in our general direction. About thirty seconds later, a small jet of some kind roared past us and landed. We started moving again and drove across the runway and headed up the far side of the field where there are a whole series of small buildings, mostly hangars of one sort or another. We pulled up in front of one that was completely dark and as we did, a door opened and we all drove into a dark interior. The Suburban switched on his headlights and I could see the building was pretty much empty except for a couple of small private planes, which I still refer to as Piper Cubs (I told you the Tomcat was the only plane I know.) and one small executive jet.

The doors on the Suburban opened and a total of five black clad figures got out. One of them approached Harry and me and I could tell from his voice it was the same guy who had given us the once over with the flash light. "Follow us, please," he said and turned and headed toward the far corner of the building, two figures in front of us and three behind us. I could hear my footsteps and Harry's but nothing else.

The thought crossed my mind that Harry hadn't said a word in about five minutes, but I could see he was taking it all in.

The lights on the Suburban went dark and now all we could see was a small hand-held flashlight shining on the floor in front of the lead man. The lights on the Suburban had been so bright in the dark hangar that my eyes had trouble adjusting. I almost fell head first down a small flight of cement steps that lead into a basement. We went down a dozen or so steps and through a steel door with a crash bar. The sound of the door opening echoed through the hangar. On the other side of the door was a short hallway with a dim red light. The flashlight went off and we walked to a second door. The lead guy mumbled something into a little microphone like pilots wear, attached to an ear piece.

The door buzzed then opened and we all stepped through and into a room with red lighting. I remember from my Navy days most interior lighting, especially at night, was red. I don't quite understand the mechanism but supposedly your eyes can adjust better to the darkness outside when you've been in red lighting than it can with ordinary lights.

I'm guessing the room was about twenty by thirty, ceilings about ten feet. Looking up I'd guess we were under the hangar floor. The ceiling looked like reinforced concrete. There wasn't much in the room unless you count the twenty or so black figures sitting, standing or lying around the room. One of them came toward us as the door hissed closed behind us.

"Hi, John."

"Hi, Danielle. This is Harry."

She stuck out her hand and so did Harry. "Nice to meet you, Harry."

"Nice place you've got here," I said. "Where'd you find it, on Craig's List under 'Bunkers, unfurnished'?"

"Craig's List?" she said. "This is the guy who thought a flash drive was a cigarette lighter and you know about Craig's List?"

"A cigarette lighter?" Harry said. "You're joking, right?"

"Anyway," I said, ignoring Harry, "what are you doing here?"

"We've set up three deployment areas," she said. "One here, one up in Edmonds and one over on Bainbridge. One of our board members suggested we use this space for the Seattle location. Apparently, there are things that go on here at Boeing that require secure spaces and spaces that are not obvious to the general public. He made a couple of phone calls and found out this one was available. It's reinforced concrete and pretty much blast proof for most conventional explosives, so it seemed like a good choice. That and its proximity to Seattle by air."

"Deployment areas?"

"Yes. I'll tell you about it in a minute. First tell me what you've got."

So I told her about my conversation with Kelly, especially the part about Anna and the copied files. She just listened and didn't interrupt me. Then I told her what Harry had told me from his friend up in Vancouver, except I didn't mention 'Paul'. Or Harry, for that matter. I didn't see any point in it. I figured by now she either trusts me or doesn't and I don't add anything to my credibility by dragging in anybody else by name. Besides, she's no dummy. I'm sure she figured out at least some of this had come from Harry.
But sometimes in the information game, deniability is extremely important and it wasn't up to me to compromise Harry in any way I didn't have to. It was bad enough he was here.

"So this guy Kelly knew about Anna and her copying those files and whoever he reports to in Washington also knew she had copied them."

"Right. And by Friday morning, according to Kelly, the files had been deleted and, once again according to Kelly, not by him."

"Do you believe him?"

"Yes, I think I do." She seemed to be mulling over what I had just told her. "So," I said, "what have you found out? Any luck with the rest of that flash drive?"

"As a matter of fact, yes," she said. "Your hunch was right. The budget stuff wasn't budget stuff. Our code section broke it out. That's why we're here. And in Edmonds and over on Bainbridge. It was a second memo marked 'Top Secret' that referred to a confirmed terrorist plan to launch an attack on the 'Seattle ferries' – that's what it said – 'the Seattle ferries' on the morning of November 3rd. It wasn't specific as to location or method. Or exact time. We decided to put three response teams in position and locate them strategically to be ready for most contingencies. We're still working on trying to get more information but we're figuring Monday morning rush hour is a good bet. Our feeling was if these guys were going to attack the ferry system, they'd be looking for maximum impact just like 9/11. So we're guessing Seattle or something close to Seattle as opposed to something, say, up in Anacortes."

"Why don't you just shut down the ferry system on Monday?"

"It's not that simple. First of all, our group operates under the radar. We can't 'shut it down' on our own. We have to go to someone who has the authority to do that. So all of a sudden we show up at, say, the Washington State Patrol, and they say: 'Who the hell are you? And how do you know there's going to be an attack on the ferries?' Probably followed shortly thereafter by: 'You're under arrest'. If we tell them who we are, a whole lot of other things start to unravel and years of building up this group go straight to hell in a very short time. Second, even if they might believe, say, you, for example, how do you explain to them that none of the other agencies, like the FBI, appear to know anything about it? And third, do you have any idea how much disruption would be caused if the ferry system shut down during rush hour on a Monday morning? Would you want to be the one to say 'shut it down'? On a tip from some crackpot?"

"Hey, I'm not just any crackpot. But I see your point."

"So we're set up with a reaction force in three strategic locations and hope we can catch a break."

"If something does break, how do you get there?"

"We have two helicopters at each location."

"I didn't see any helicopters upstairs."

"That's because they're not in this building."

Harry, who had been quiet up to this point, said: "Any idea who that memo was to or from?"

The 'to' is easy. It went to the same two people the White House memo went to: The Special Agent in Charge at the Seattle FBI office and the head of the Homeland Security Office here in Seattle."

"Was that memo also on White House stationery?" Harry asked.

"No. The second memo was from Homeland Security. Unsigned, but the 'From' line said 'Office of Intelligence and Analysis'."

"So," Harry continued, "it sounds like at least two people on this end were not all that comfortable with this whole scenario and wanted something in their files to cover their asses." Nothing like a government employee to cut right to the heart of the bullshit. If anybody knows anything about covering their ass, it's a career military type. No offense, Harry.

"I don't suppose that one was signed either," I said.

She smiled and shook her head. "No, John, it wasn't. You didn't think it would be that easy did you?"

I shrugged. "You never know. But, no, I really didn't think so. Listen, Danielle, not that Harry and I aren't interested in the 'who' of all of this, because we are. But, at the moment, we're more interested in the 'what, where and when' than we are in the 'who'. We'll leave that up to you. Anybody think about dragging the SAC or the local Homeland Security chief and waterboarding them?"

"I assume you're joking."

"Well, maybe about the waterboarding part, but not the part about dragging in the two people who seem to have the most knowledge about this since their names were on the memos."

"Outside of the obvious that we probably can't just kidnap the Special Agent in Charge of the Seattle FBI office, or the local head of Homeland Security either, they may not know any more than we do, at least about the attack. It appears from those two memos the plan is in motion and they're just being told to stay out of the way."

I wasn't quite ready to buy that they didn't know anything about the attack. "Was there anything in the second memo that might even give us a hint about the specifics of this attack?"

"That's really why I wanted to talk to you face to face. The short answer to your question is: no. And we're running out of time and ideas. We need to make something happen. The members of the board have been kicking this thing around for almost twenty-four hours straight. Initially, we were focusing on the FBI here in Seattle and in DC because they seemed to be the most visible presence. And, I guess, because my sister found what she found in their office, we more or less assumed what we were looking for might be there. But there are a couple of members of the board who think maybe we should be focusing more on the Homeland Security people."

"Let me get this straight. You people think Homeland Security might be behind an attack on the ferry system? Are you kidding?"

"Not 'behind it' in the sense that they're planning this thing. But we think there's a strong possibility they may know more of the details than anybody in the FBI. At least the FBI here in Seattle."

"So, why do you need to talk to me face to face?"

"We think maybe you can make something happen."

Chapter 52

Harry and I drove away from Boeing Field in silence. We got escorted off the field pretty much the same way we came in. Harry hadn't said anything since we left the hangar but I knew the wheels were turning.

"Well," he said, finally, "that might explain how we got pulled off the semisubmersibles so quickly."

"How's that?" I said.

"Homeland Security being up to their eyeballs in this. We work for Homeland Security."

"Who's we?"

"Us. The Coast Guard. The United States Coast Guard is part of the Department of Homeland Security."

It got quiet again. I was mulling over what we discussed with Danielle. On the one hand, I didn't relish the idea of poking the beast in the eye with a stick, but on the other hand I had to agree unless we did something and did it quickly, we were all going to be standing around with our collective fingers up our collective butts watching a big cloud of smoke and a lot of other nasty stuff I really didn't want to contemplate. And on the other other hand, how much worse could it get? (Be careful when you say that, John.)

I suppose I could have just walked away and said 'Sorry, this really isn't what I signed on for', but I was still a little pissed that these guys, whoever they are, had the balls to come after me at home. And, as much as I hate to admit it, I was feeling some sense of personal responsibility. I mean, out side of my job, which does have a certain amount of public responsibility attached to it and which, by the way, I get paid for, not to mention the fact that I chose it, it didn't choose me, I've always been one of these people who are quick to say 'they should do something about that', whoever 'they' are. Well, as it turns out, with apologies to Pogo, this time 'they' is me.

I asked Harry to drop me back at Duke's so I could pick up the company car. I was starting to leave a trail of abandoned vehicles not to mention I was also running out of people to mooch rides from, so I figured I'd better collect this one and see how long I could hang onto it.

Harry pulled into Duke's parking lot and my car or, really, the taxpayers' car, was still there. I suppose they put some kind of locator on it somewhere but at the moment it didn't seem quite so important. I actually didn't care if they knew exactly where I was. The only caveat was if they were still determined to slow me down, I'd better not let my guard down. Considering how hungry and tired I was, that would be no easy task. Ordinarily, if I was going to tackle what I was about to tackle, I would have chosen to get a good meal and catch a little sleep. But now it was late Sunday evening and all signs were pointing to a big day on Monday. Food and sleep would have to wait a while.

And, oh, by the way, I was starting to ache all over from that little fiasco over on Bainbridge Island. When I took that shower this afternoon, I noticed a number of purple spots on my body that weren't birthmarks. Or tattoos. And I think my left rotator cuff took a direct hit when I rolled out of that moving car. My physical therapist will be pleased. Maybe she'll be able to afford that cruise after all.

I got into the car and started it up. So far so good – no explosions. Always a good thing. I headed downtown, pulled out the bat phone and dialed Al's number. This phone really does look like an ordinary cell phone, right down to the clock on the screen when you flip it open. As I was dialing it registered with me that it was starting to get pretty late and Al was probably already in bed.

The phone rang about six times and I was about to leave a message when a sleepy voice said: "Yeah?"

"Al, it's me."

"Ah, shit, John, this better be good."

"Are you kidding? I'm calling you at eleven o'clock on a Sunday night and you think there's some way this could be good?"

"What's up, John?"

"I need you to meet me at the office."

"Now??"

"No, Tuesday morning. Yes, now. I hate to do this to you Al but it's important."

"All right, John. Give me about thirty minutes. And I just might have my wife call you so you can explain to her why I took this job. You know, before you were my partner, people in Seattle only got killed on week days between nine and five. You don't suppose there's any connection?"

"Thanks, Al. See you downtown."

The streets were pretty much empty and I made good
time getting back to the office.
The fact there seemed to be less interest in me was
making me a little concerned. The only conclusion I
could draw was whatever was going to happen was so
far along they figured there wasn't much I could do at
this point to interfere with it.

I took the elevator up to the office and stepped out onto
an almost empty floor. There were one or two guys
walking around with papers in their hand, but other than
that it was quiet. They both looked up when they heard
the elevator doors open, I gave them a wave and they
gave me a half-hearted wave back and went back to
whatever they were doing. I made my way to my desk,
logged onto my computer and went into my address
book. I actually know a lot more about computers than I
let on. I find if I pretend to be totally stupid about the
whole thing, people tend to leave me alone about it and
don't bug me with useless emails, Facebook pages,
Twitter messages and all of that mostly time wasting
shit.

I pulled up a private number for Pistol Pete. I knew he
wasn't going to be pleased to hear from me at this hour,
but he was going to be a lot less pleased if he didn't hear
from me, because he was certainly going to hear from
somebody before this night was over. I picked up the
desk phone and dialed out. The phone on the other end
rang three times.

"Gilbert."

"Captain, John Elliott."

"What is it Elliott?"

I explained to him what I was about to do but in general terms that would make anybody listening think maybe I had more than I actually did. People are amazing. They're much more likely to admit something if they think you already know it. So, if they were listening in on this conversation, I wanted them to think we already knew what was about to go down, which was partially true. Which reminds me of another rule to live by: If you're going to lie, be sure it contains some element of truth. I knew enough about what might happen to make me dangerous, to myself and to others. I also knew enough about what might happen to tell a credible lie.

As I expected, Pete went slightly off the rails. You really don't want to be the guy calling your boss to tell him his entire career is either on its way to the stratosphere or smeared all over a brick wall with yellow tape around it, but you're not sure which. After he calmed down a little, he said: "You better tell me exactly what you know, Elliott. I'm not signing off on anything without a lot more detail."

Now I subscribe to the old adage that it's easier to ask for forgiveness than it is to ask for permission, but I think that applies more to things like cheating on your wife or taking money from a collection plate. In this case I didn't think there was enough forgiveness in the universe if I screwed this up, despite what the Catholic church might think, and I'm not even Catholic. So I went through the whole scenario including the stuff we did know and conveniently leaving out the stuff we didn't know. I decided to include things we were guessing at under the heading of 'Things We Know'. I told Pete there was four hundred pounds of Semtex aimed right at the Seattle ferry system and it was scheduled to go off sometime during rush hour on Monday morning. I told him Anna Noble had accidentally stumbled onto evidence the FBI and the Department of Homeland Security were aware of a terrorist plan to blow up a ferry or two but for reasons unknown had chosen to stand by and let it happen. And I told him we had evidence that directly linked the FBI and Homeland Security to the murder of Anna Noble, Anthony Carey and Officer Sean Bailey.

I was really warming to my topic when Pete said: "Where are you now Elliott? Are you at the office?"

"Yes, sir," I said. As I said before, civility goes a long way with Pete. It's kind of like the Mafia rule that you can do almost anything you want to a fellow goombah as long as you show him respect. My ex-wife always said I made the worst analogies and I don't mean to compare Pete with the Mafia, but it's the best example I can think of.

"I'm coming in. Don't do anything until I get there. Understood?"

"Yes, sir, Captain."

"And Elliott?"

"Yes, sir?"

"Cut the 'yes, sir' crap. I know you're just trying to kiss my ass to get what you want.
It's either a good idea or a bad idea and your kissing my ass isn't going to change that. I'll see you in thirty

minutes."

"Yes, sir," I said. He hung up without saying good-bye.

Chapter 53

Al showed up first. He was a bit groggy and a bit more cranky. He came stumbling
across the floor from the elevator and dropped into his chair across from me.

"Thanks for coming in, Al."

There was a slight hesitation and I could tell there was a part of him that wanted to tell me how he really felt about being dragged out of bed at this hour - on a Sunday night – but Al's a pro. Al is also not a whiner. We each have a sense of when it's ok to bitch and moan and when it isn't. Al correctly sensed this wasn't the time.

"Ok, John. What's up?"

"Pete's on his way in so let me fill you before he gets here."

"Pete's on his way in? On a Sunday night? This must really be good. I can't wait to hear this one."

I ran through the facts as best as I could and decided to level with Al on the things that were speculation. He agreed with me that while the 'who' was a big question, the 'where' and the 'when' were much more important at the moment. About the only thing I didn't level with him on was the involvement of Danielle and her group. I didn't think it was necessary or my job to blow their cover. But Al's no dummy either.

"How do you know about this flash drive?" he asked me.

"One of Anna's family gave it to me. Apparently she sent it to them for safekeeping. After they found out she was killed, they thought it might be important. Turned out it was."

"And how did you find out what was on it?"

"I gave it to a friend that knows how to break into this stuff."

He nodded his head as if to say: 'I know you're not giving me the whole story, but I'm not going to press you on it'.

"So," he said, " you think there's going to be a terrorist attack on the ferry system tomorrow morning around rush hour and you think the FBI and Homeland Security knows about it and have decided to stand aside and let it happen."

"Yeah, that's pretty much it."

He stared at me for a few seconds, but I could tell he wasn't seeing me. The wheels were turning and he was putting together what I had just told him with what he already knew.
"You know, John, I hate to say this, but what you're telling me actually makes some sense. It would certainly tie some things together. So what are we doing here on a Sunday night?"

Just then I heard the elevator doors open, heard a few footsteps coming from the hallway and saw Pete Gilbert came striding down the hall. He headed straight for his office past our cubicles without looking in our direction. We watched him through his window as he flipped on his lights, walked behind his desk and absently rearranged a couple of pieces of paper. Then he looked through the window, motioned for us to come into his office and sat down heavily in his chair and swiveled slowly from side to side waiting for us.

"Evening, Captain," Al and I said more or less simultaneously and under our breath as we walked in.

"Sit," he said. We sat.

"Elliott, what you told me on the phone gets crazier the more I think about it. If somebody hadn't killed Officer Bailey and tried to kill you and Officer Robinson earlier today, I wouldn't even be here and I'd be thinking about recommending you for medical leave to have your head examined. I'm sure you realize the implications of what you're saying."

"Yes, I do, Captain. And I don't mind taking the fall if I'm wrong."

"Apparently you don't mind us taking the fall either. Big of you, Elliott." He looked at Al. "How much of this do you know about, Russo?"

"Most of it, Captain, since I've been working with John on this most of the week-end. Some of the details he just filled me in on. I have to say that as crazy as it sounds, a lot of it fits together."

He looked back at me. "What did you mean about Anna Noble stumbling on evidence the FBI and Homeland Security know about this supposed attack?"

I explained to him what I had learned about Anna Noble's real job with Justice. "Apparently she was doing some routine searching when she came across some encrypted information that turned out to be two memos addressed to the FBI's Special Agent-in-Charge here in Seattle and also to the Seattle Director of Customs and Border Protection.

"And?"

"And, one of the memos was from Washington. It was marked 'Top Secret' and confirmed that Homeland Security was aware of a planned attack on the Seattle ferries on the morning of November 3rd."

"Anything more specific than that?"

"No, sir, just 'Seattle ferries' and 'the morning of November 3rd'."

"What about the second one?"

"That one apparently came from a little higher up the food chain. It was a memo on White House stationery – actually, the Office of the White House Counsel - that instructed the people on the local level to essentially back off from any action to interfere with the upcoming attack and Washington would take full responsibility for dealing with the problem. It also said the SAC and the Director of CPB here in Seattle or any other federal agent would be immune from any legal liability for failure to take any action based upon matters of national security."

He looked at both of us. "Does anybody else know about this besides the three of us?"

"Officially?"

"Officially, unofficially, I don't give a crap, Elliott. It's a simple question."

"Officially, no. But unofficially the State Patrol down on the docks have been given a heads up to keep an eye out for suspicious activity or any signs of explosives coming anywhere near the ferries. And the Coast Guard is aware of the situation."

"The State Patrol. And the Coast Guard. What about the Army, the Navy and the fucking Marines? Jesus, Elliott, you have been busy."

I decided that, not counting the rhetorical question about the status of our nation's armed forces, since there was no actual question anywhere in there, I might just keep my mouth shut.

"All right, let's talk about the nuts and bolts of this. You do realize you have to have some kind probable cause to do what you're proposing."

"Yes, I do, Captain."

"And you also realize, while I appreciate you giving me a heads up on this, this decision is yours and yours alone. I know I'm going to take some heat for this – I take that back – I'm going to take a shit load of heat for this because you work for me, but my position is that, while I stand behind my men, you made the decision on your own. I did not authorize you or order you to carry this out. That goes for you, too, Russo. I know you guys are partners, but you have to decide if you want to risk it all." He looked straight at me. "I'm sure Elliott will understand if you get up and go home and go back to bed." To his credit, Al didn't move. Or maybe he just dozed off and didn't hear what Pete just said.

There was a moment of silence, which, I suppose, was appropriate given the fact that three guys were about to drink the Kool-Aid and possibly commit professional suicide.

"Ok," Pete said. "What have you got for probable cause? You do have probable cause, I assume. Or do we all have to just accept this on faith?"

"Let's start with the murder weapon," I said. "The Crime Lab tells me the gun that killed Anna Noble, Anthony Carey and Sean Bailey was a special type of hand gun manufactured under strict security for the US government. Next, we've linked one of the weapons taken from the two guys on my houseboat to all three killings. Third, Al tells me our guys have identified both shooters from the houseboat. Even though they weren't carrying any identification, their prints were on file as former government employees."

"I hesitate to ask this," Pete said, "but what did they do for the government?"

"They both worked for Customs and Border Protection," Al said. "One guy was a former Border Patrol Agent and the other one worked in the Intelligence and Operations section at CBP."

"I was afraid you were going to say that. Do we know anything else about these two? Did either of them have a rap sheet?"

"Not that we were able to find. Of course, if they were working for who we think they were working for, it would be easy enough to make something like that disappear."

"So, you think because these two worked at one time for CBP, that's the direction we should head in."

"That and the fact I know these FBI guys, or guys like them," I said. "Not that they're not capable of almost anything, but of the two, I think Customs and Border Protection are more likely to go off the reservation than the FBI. It's a different mind set. The Border Protection guys are for the most part out in the middle of friggin' nowhere with their asses on the line playing a dangerous game with guys who don't really give a rat's ass about rules. They're more like combat soldiers. You know, 'it's them or me' and they're aren't always a lot of rules out where these guys operate. I think they're more likely to make up their own rules as they go along, which seems to be what's been happening here for the last forty-eight hours."

"So, anyway," I said, "I know it's a toss up between Customs and Border Protection and the FBI, but my instinct tells me the choice should be Customs and Border Protection. I think, in some sense, the FBI is along for the ride. The memo from the White House Counsel was addressed to both the FBI SAC and the Seattle Field Office Director of Customs and Border Protection. So they both know about the other. And in order to keep a lid on this, whoever is pulling the strings needs both of them to cooperate. Maybe it makes a stronger sell if they both know about each other. Makes it less likely one of them is going to get hung out to dry if this thing goes south. My guess is initially most of this was verbal. But at some point one of the two, or possibly both, thought it would be a good idea to have an insurance policy - a written insurance policy – with two insureds. And, if I had to guess, the FBI was the one who originally came up with the idea because they weren't too excited about all this to begin with."

It was quiet. Pete was staring straight ahead and the silence, as they say, was deafening.

Just then, the silence was broken by a long rumbling explosion way off in the distance. Actually, it wasn't an explosion after all. It was my stomach. It rumbled for about four very long seconds.

"You feeling all right, Elliott?"

"Uh, yeah, Captain. Just a little hungry, that's all."

"Well, why don't you eat?"

"Long story, Captain."

"Mmm," he said. Then he said: "Just so we're all clear on this. We've had five killings since yesterday morning...."

"Six," I said.

"Six?!"

"Six counting Dr. Raman, or whoever the hell he was, at the hospital this afternoon."

"Six killings since yesterday morning. So these guys are

serious and are not above using whatever means are available to make sure nothing or nobody interferes with whatever is going on. And they don't seem to have any reservations about shooting police officers. They're either totally nuts or they have reason to believe they're immune. Or both. Either way, they're dangerous. They've already killed Officer Bailey and tried to get Elliott once, so you both need to be especially careful. I want you both together on this and take whatever back-up you need from the uniformed division. If what you're telling me is even half true, this thing is too big to let a couple of local cops get in the way. By the way, Russo, speaking of the shooting at the hospital, I'm assuming you turned in that weapon to the investigating team."

"Yes, sir, I did."

"Do you have a replacement?"

"Yes, sir, I do."

"And a back-up weapon?"

Al pulled up his right pant leg about six or eight inches revealing a small ankle holster with what looked like a Heckler and Koch P7.

"Good. What about you, Elliott?"

"All set," I said.

"Elliott," he said, "Let's get back to these memos for a minute, because they are obviously critical to this whole mess. The first memo about the attack, do we know where that came from?"

"It was unsigned but it said it came from Homeland Security. Office of Intelligence Analysis."

"Homeland Security again," he said, almost to himself. Looking back at Al and I, he said: "So, one more thing that would link this to Homeland Security. Any indication Homeland Security or the FBI or any other domestic agency has anything to do with the planning or carrying out of this attack?"

"Not as far as I can tell," I said. "I don't see any signs anybody here is making this happen. It just appears they're going out of their way to make sure nobody stops it from happening."

He was quiet for a minute. "All right, then. I'm going to sit tight here and wait for this thing to develop.. For obvious reasons I'd rather not be here on a Sunday night – strike that, Monday morning. Somebody might think I actually knew something about this before it happened. Besides, I'm sure I'll be getting a phone call or two before the night's over. It's not every day that two of my officers arrest the Regional Director of Customs and Border Protection on six counts of conspiracy to commit murder."

Chapter 54

Al called the Watch Commander and had him send over two of his uniformed officers. He didn't mention exactly what we were about to do, only that we were going to make a nighttime arrest and, although we didn't expect any trouble, we just wanted to be prepared.

Seattle is a twenty-four hour a day, seven day a week department, as you might expect in a city of six or seven hundred thousand people, and there are generally at least one or two people on duty in every department all day, every day. I called down to the Data Center and they gave me the home address of the Seattle Field Office Director of Customs and Border Protection.

Armed with that information, Al and I and the two patrolmen, each in their own patrol cars, headed out to Queen Anne. Queen Anne is a section of Seattle just north of downtown and is probably what you would describe as 'up-scale'. It's not as expensive or exclusive as, say, Magnolia, but there's some pretty nice real estate out there nonetheless. Not exactly the place you might expect to find a suspected felon, let alone one with six murders under his belt. More the kind of place you might expect to find a suspected felon with six vodka martinis under his belt. I'm sure there were plenty of potential felons out here, just a better class of felons. Mostly the ones the SEC hasn't caught up with yet.

At this hour of the night, Queen Anne is your typical quiet residential neighborhood. Al was driving because of the two of us, he was less likely to get lost. Eventually, we pulled onto a street that had more than the usual six feet of space between the houses that you see in most of Seattle and stopped in front of a brick front Federalist-type house. I'm no architectural expert, so it could have been Greek Revival. Or Neo-Classical. Or just a brick house. God, am I hungry. And tired.

"This is it," he said. We both sat there, not moving.

"Ok," I said. "Let's do this." Al and I got out and stood on the sidewalk. The air was cold and damp and I turned my collar up. The cold air actually felt good and woke me up a little. The two patrolmen got out and walked up to us.

"Ok," I said. "I want you guys to turn on your roof lights and stand next to your cars where you can be seen. I want to send a message when this guy opens his front door. Come on, Al. Let's go."

For most of the felons I've arrested in the middle of the night, you usually want two or three guys, preferably with shotguns and a good pair of running shoes, staked out behind the house. I didn't think this was going to be that kind of bust.

We walked up three or four steps onto a short brick walk way then up two more steps to the front door. The front of the house must have had a motion sensor because as we walked up the brick walk way, flood lights came on on either corner of the house.

I pushed the button next to the door and heard a chime from somewhere inside the house.
I counted to ten and leaned on it one more time just in case the occupants thought they were dreaming that

some idiot was at their front door at this ungodly hour.

I rang the bell again and this time, through one of the frosted glass panes beside the door I could see a light come on in what appeared to be a stairway from the upstairs to the front hall. I watched as a shadow moved down the stairs and came to the front door. The Data Center had also provided me with a copy of the Director's photograph from his DMV record and when the door opened I was pretty sure it wasn't the same guy, mainly because this guy was a woman.

She looked between Al and me and I can only assume she was trying to figure out why two men were at her front door with two police cars in the street in front of her house.

"Is everything all right?" she said.

"Sorry to bother you, ma'am. Are you Mrs. Callahan?" I said.

"Yes," she said, pulling her bathrobe up around her neck.

"I'm Sergeant Elliott and this is Detective Russo. We're from the Seattle Police Department. We'd like to speak with your husband."

"My husband isn't here, Sergeant. What is this about?" she said with a note of trepidation in her voice. There was no aggression in her tone, just a slight tinge of fear, which, I suppose, is what you'd expect if two cops came to your door in the middle of the night.

Sticking to my rule about not letting the interviewee

control the conversation, I said: "It's important that we speak with him. Can you tell me where he is?"

"I believe he's at his office. At least, that's what he told me." I must have looked at her funny or maybe she realized how ridiculous that sounded. You know, 'Oh, I had no idea my husband was shacking up with his intern. I just thought he was a hard worker. He works a lot of nights and week-ends', because she followed that up by saying: "It's not unusual for him to be at his office at odd hours, especially when there's an exercise."

"An exercise?"

"Yes. I'm not sure I'm supposed to say anything but George told me the government is running some kind of anti-terrorism exercise this week-end. He's been at his office most of the last two days. He came home briefly this afternoon for some clean clothes, but other than that, I haven't seen him since Friday."

"Did he say when he'd be home?" Al asked.

"He said he expected the exercise to be over on Monday," she said, shifting her glance over to Al, "and he'd be home after that." She looked back at me. "Can you please tell me what this is about?" she asked, seeming to regain her composure somewhat and starting to sound just a little bit indignant.

"Yes, ma'am. We're trying to arrest your husband for having six people murdered. We were really hoping to take him away in cuffs with his bathrobe pulled up over his head." No, I didn't actually say that. What I said was: "Nothing you need to be concerned about Mrs. Callahan. Just police business. We'll catch up with him on

Monday." I knew as soon as she closed the door she was going to be on the phone to her husband, but there wasn't much I could do about that. With cell phones you can't even cut the telephone wires. Believe me, the thought crossed my mind. But I hoped if I down-played it, she might do the same thing. My guess was, though, as soon as she told George that a very nice policeman named Elliott had come calling at 1:00AM all the alarm bells would go off. Double the guards, Elliott. God, what I wouldn't give for a donut right now.

"I'll tell him you were looking for him," she said.

"No need to bother him, Mrs. Callahan, it isn't that important. I'm sure he's got a lot on his mind right now." That's no lie.

"No bother at all, Sergeant," she said. "Besides, I'm sure that if the Seattle Police Department sent two detectives and two patrol cars, this isn't about an unpaid parking ticket. Good night, Sergeant." She closed the door.

Al and I both stood looking at the door for a second or two then turned to face each other. "What now, boss?" Al said.

The only thing worse (or, maybe, stupider, if there is such a word) than poking the beast in the eye with a stick is crawling into his cave and then poking him in the eye with a stick. But it looked like that was what I was about to do.

"Let's head downtown," I said.

We both turned around and headed back to the car. I walked over to the two patrolmen who had taken a few steps toward us as we came down the walk. I said: "I think we'll still need you. We're going to 1000 Second Avenue."

"Lights and sirens?"

I know these guys love to drive fast with the lights and sirens and watch people scramble to get out of the way. That, and the fact that it's pretty boring on patrol at 2:00AM. But I said: "No, not this time. Sorry guys." They both nodded and went to their cars.

I climbed in on the passenger side with Al and said: "Downtown, driver. And step on it." Al just smiled, shook his head and pulled slowly away from the curb.

Chapter 55

On the way downtown I thought about calling Danielle to let her know how things were progressing, or not progressing, depending on your definition of progress. As I was thinking about it, the bat phone rang.

"Domino's," I said.

"Very funny," she said. "Is that all you think about is eating?"

"Baby, you have no idea," I said. "I was just thinking about calling you."

"Interesting segue," she said. "Any news?"

"Well, we haven't caught up with Callahan yet, but his wife said he's been working all week-end. He told her there's a big security exercise underway and he can't leave his office. We're on our way there now."

I could hear her turn away from the phone and say something to someone else. All I caught was "1000 Second Avenue" then to me: "Big security exercise, huh?"

"Yeah, sounds like the beginning of a huge cover-up. 'Oh, they told us in Washington this was just an exercise. We didn't know anything'. Anything new on your end?"

"I've spoken with my Dad a couple of times. They got a hold of those White House phone logs and have it narrowed down to two people. We've sent a couple of our people from the DC area out to question them. One of them is a Deputy Counsel which is actually a mid-level position, but the other is Deputy Counsel to the Vice-President, not quite so mid-level."

"You don't really think you're going to get anything out of them do you?"

"You might be surprised. We sometimes know things about people that make them more receptive to talking to us. And, of course, there's always drugs. Waterboarding is so 90's. And slow."

"See, I can't tell if you're serious or not."

"Probably better for everybody if we keep it that way."

"Yeah, you're right. Listen, I'll call you after we talk with ol' George."

"Ok, I'll be here."

"Anything new?" Al asked.

"They've got a line on a couple of people in DC that might know something about all of this, but nothing definite so far."

"You know, John, I'm really bothered by all of this. I can almost understand some terrorist like Bin Laden wanting to disrupt our elections by pulling some shit the day before. But I can't understand what's going on with our own government

"I know what you're saying, Al. I'm not a conspiracy freak because most of the time the explanation is just plain government fuck-up. But this whole thing has me wondering, too. Although, to tell you the truth, I've been so focused on the 'how' and the 'when' that I haven't given much thought to the 'why'. I'd better call Pete and let him know what's going on." I pulled out the bat phone and dialed the office number.

"I don't like this, Elliott, he said after I explained what was going on. "This was supposed to be a clean arrest. Now you're going to try to pull this stunt in his office? This just smells like trouble. Keep me posted." He hung up without even saying good-bye. My feeling were definitely hurt.

The rest of the ride was quiet, Al and I both mulling this whole thing over. That, and the fact that it was almost 2:00 AM. I don't know about Al, but I was dog tired and, did I mention, hungry? I did know we were running out of time and I was hoping this ploy with the CBP people was going to stir something up in time for us to do something about it.

We pulled up in front of 1000 Second Avenue and the two patrol cars pulled up behind us. Al and I got out and walked back to the first patrol car. The driver rolled down his window and looked up at us. "You guys stay here until we come out. If we're not out in thirty minutes, get Captain Gilbert on the radio and tell him where you are and we haven't come out. He'll let you know what he wants you to do."

"Ok, Sergeant," he said, and rolled up his window.

"All right, Al, let's try this again. Somehow I don't think this is going to be easy."

"Yeah? What was your first clue, Sherlock?"

1000 Second Avenue is a pretty big office building. It has a wide variety of businesses in it and a few government offices, as well. Because people are coming and going at all hours of the day and night, the front door is always open and there is a guard or security guy at a desk in the lobby. He looked up from a small tv screen that did not appear to be a security camera. I suppose he was a little surprised to see anyone at 2:00 in the morning. He stood up and faced us as we walked up to his desk.

"Can I help you gentlemen?"

Al and I both pulled out our badges. "Seattle police," I said. "What floor is Customs and Border Protection?"

"Twenty-second floor," he said. "Take the elevator on your left." I started to walk away.

"Must be something big, huh?" he said.

I stopped and turned. "Why do you say that?"

"Because there's already six or seven guys up there. Not your usual Sunday night around here."

I looked at Al and he looked at me. We turned and walked toward the elevator. The door was open, we stepped inside and I pushed '22'. The doors closed and we started up. "Well," Al said, staring straight ahead, "you said it wasn't going to be easy."

"Yeah. You know what they say."

"No, what do 'they' say?"

"If it was easy, anybody could do it."

"Somehow, I always thought they were talking about hitting a ninety mile an hour fastball, which is starting to look easier than this by the minute,"

The elevator dinged, stopped and the doors opened. We stepped out into a hallway area. In front of us, on the wall, was plain sign about eighteen inches square that said "Customs and Border Protection." To our right on the wall at the end of a very small lobby was a sign about the same size that said "Department of Homeland Security." The hallway itself was the shape of an 'H' with the elevators on the cross-arm. There was no directory or anything else to tell you where to go. Clearly, Homeland Security had their own security in mind first. 'We're here to serve the public – we just don't want to be bothered by them'. Why did I have the feeling unseen eyes were watching me? If this day had taught me anything it was to be a little more paranoid than I already was. Great. Just what I needed.

Just because it seemed the right way to go, we walked to the end of the elevator banks toward the DHS sign and looked left and right down two equally short hallways, each with a single plain brown wooden door. The one on the right had a little metal box on the wall next to it. Now I was beginning to feel like a rat in a Skinner Box. I couldn't wait to see what my reward was going to be. Hopefully, something to eat, although I doubted it.

Al pushed a little button on the box. The door next to us buzzed like a high-class apartment building. Somehow, don't ask me why, I expected something a little more high tech from the Department of Homeland Security.

Although, now that I think of it, these are the same people who are keeping us safe from terrorism by not letting little old ladies take more than three ounces of shampoo on an airplane.

Directly in front of us was a security check point similar to the ones you might see at any airport these days. A standard metal detector, a standard x-ray machine for handbags, briefcases, back packs and a standard bored looking security guard sitting on a stool.
He stood up as we came through the door. Al and I both took out our badges and held them up.

"Which way to George Callahan's office?" I said.

Without answering me, he turned partially and picked up the handset from a phone on a table behind him and pushed a couple of buttons. Looking back at us, he waited for someone to answer.

Some one (guess who) must have answered because he said: "Yes, sir. They're here."
He paused. "Yes, sir." He hung up the phone. "Down this hallway," he said, pointing past the metal detector. "When you get to the end, make a left and take it all the way to the end. The Director's waiting for you."

Al and I went around the check point and headed down the hall. "'The Director's waiting for you'. Great. Are you sure you want to do this, John?"

"You got a better idea?"

"Yeah, but it would take too long to process the paperwork."

"Come on. We've been in worse situations than this. I think."

"At least nobody's shooting at us. Yet."

We rounded the corner in the hall and at the far end could see an open door. Standing outside the door in the hallway was a guy in a uniform, presumably Customs and Border Protection. He was also carrying some type of hand gun on his right hip and he had his thumbs hooked on his belt. As we got closer, I said: "We have a 2 AM appointment with the Director?"

He said, without smiling: "You're late. Go right in. He's expecting you"

The conference room door was open. Three men stood at the far end of the room talking. Two were in casual clothes and one was wearing the same uniform as the guy in the hallway, also carrying a sidearm. As we stepped into the room, they stopped talking. I recognized the guy in the middle as Callahan from the id photo the Data section had given me.

Callahan smiled and said: "Ah, Sergeant Elliott and Detective Russo. Nice to meet you both. Would you two gentlemen excuse us?" he said to the two people he was talking to when we came in. They moved around the table past us and left the room. "Alberto," he said and the guy in the uniform stopped and looked back. "Please close the door on your way out."

"Please. Sit," he said, gesturing toward the chairs and sitting down at the head of the table.

"This is not a social call, Callahan," Al said.

"No, I'm sure it's not," he said, still smiling. "But why don't you sit anyway. I'm not going anywhere."

"I'm not so sure about that," I said.

"Oh, I am, Sergeant." He sat down in a padded leather chair at the end of the table. It was a little bigger and a little more comfortable looking than the rest of the chairs around the table. It also appeared to be a little higher than the rest of the chairs, part of an old psychological ploy to put everyone else lower than the alpha male in the room. Lawyers use the trick a lot. I know because I used to do it way back when. One of the ways to avoid that psychological disadvantage if you're being offered the low chair is to remain standing. I stood.

Well it's now or never. I took out a pair of cuffs, moved toward him and said: "George Callahan, I arresting you on six counts of conspiracy to commit murder. You have the right...."

"Hold on, Sergeant," he said, still with that air of confidence and bonhomie. He stood up and moved away from me and over toward the windows. I didn't move but Al moved back toward the door, just in case. "First of all, I know my rights. I've been in law enforcement probably as long as you have so we don't have to go through that little charade. And I have no intention of admitting any of those charges. But, more importantly, I think you know as well as I do that I have a 'get out of jail free' card, so let's not waste each other's time."

"What makes you think I'd be wasting my time?"

"Precisely because whatever evidence you think you

have isn't going to make a hill of beans worth of difference. I'm pretty sure by now you know that some people pretty high up in the federal government are not going to let you pursue this."

"You mean the same way they tried to convince me not to pursue this earlier today?"

"Not at all," he said. "I heard about that. Most unfortunate."

"Try saying that with a little more sincerity, George."

"No, just the plain fact that a couple of phone calls to the right people and I'll be home with my wife before you can say 'early retirement'."

"Well, you could be right," I said. "On the other hand, you might eventually walk, but maybe not as quickly as you think. In the meantime, the press is going to have a field day with your arrest and the reasons we arrested you. And I can imagine there might be a few Congressional committees that might have some interest in how a group of terrorists were able to sneak into Seattle under your collective noses and wreak havoc on the ferry system."

"You have been busy, haven't you, Sergeant?" he paused. "Let me ask you a question, Sergeant."

"I didn't come here to answer questions, Callahan. And, frankly, I'm tired and cranky – and hungry – and that's not a good combination. So either you're going to come with us peacefully or you're not. But one way or the other" – I held up the cuffs – "you're coming with us."

He seemed to ignore me. "Do you believe there is a real, on-going terrorist threat to this country?"

"You're the Homeland Security guy – you tell me."

"Ok. The answer is 'yes'. I see it every day in this job. I see things come across my desk that would give the average citizen diarrhea. If the people in this country knew the threats we face, they wouldn't sleep at night."

"They have enough trouble sleeping knowing you guys are in charge."

"Yes, I know the liberals and the media would like everyone to think we're trying to turn this country into a police state. But we live in a different world than we did when they wrote the Constitution. We're in a war and the primary battle ground is right here in the U.S. and all of the soldiers are no longer in uniform. On either side. Part of the problem is most people in this country don't realize they're on the front lines. I guess that's partially our fault."

"'Our fault?'"

"Yes, our fault. This government. This administration. We've tried to protect the American people and all we've gotten is a lot of criticism from people like the ACLU, the New York Times and the liberal left."

"So let me get this straight: You guys are victims? Isn't that kind of like a bank robber blaming the government because they have too many of those pesky law-things?"

"All I'm saying is we walk a fine line between protecting the public and scaring the shit out of them."

"And you don't think this President hasn't tried to use fear to justify a lot of questionable if not down right unconstitutional things like, oh, I don't know, maybe surveillance and eavesdropping on average Americans, holding prisoners at Guantanamo for years without ever charging them with anything, or torturing prisoners? Or maybe like a war in Iraq? Or maybe this attitude of 'If the President says it – or the Vice-President – it's legal'? If you're looking for sympathy, Callahan, send yourself a Hallmark card."

Al finally spoke up. "C'mon, John, Let's get this over with."

But ol' George was on a roll. "Hold on a second, Al," I said. I actually thought we were going to have to take this guy over to headquarters and sweat him a little. But now it seemed like maybe we wouldn't. I still wasn't sure how much we were going to get out of him. He was no dope and I didn't think he was really going to say anything that would implicate himself in any of those six killings. But, you never know. He was feeling somewhat bulletproof, that much I could tell. So, who knows?

"No, I don't think he's tried to use fear. I think when he's tried to level with the American people he's been accused of trying to use fear. There are a number of people both in and out of this Administration who think the American people haven't been scared enough. And there are a number of people who think Barack Obama isn't scared enough and if he were to be elected President, the country would suffer and suffer in a way that would leave every man, woman and child in America in greater danger than they are now. And there are a number of people who think maybe John McCain 'gets it'."

"Would you be one of those people, George?"

He looked at me for about two full seconds before he answered me. "As a matter of fact," he said, "I am."

"And how about the FBI? Is the Special Agent in Charge of the FBI office here in Seattle one of those people?"

He looked at me and hesitated. "No," he said, "I'm sorry to say, he's not."

"Well, that's too bad because his picture is going to be on the front page of every newspaper in America along with yours."

"Our pictures may be on the front page of every newspaper, but maybe not for the reason you think."

"So what do you think it would take to wake up the American people, George?"

"Let's put it this way, Sergeant, 9/11 certainly woke up the American people."

"And maybe a major terrorist attack right now, tomorrow, might wake people up and, perhaps, re-think voting for Obama."

"Yes."

I felt like I had just stepped through the looking glass. If I understood - and believed - what this guy was saying, he, and a number of other people like him, thought what the country needed was a good terrorist attack on the order of 9/11 to keep America from getting too comfortable. People were apparently starting to question the Bush administration tactics and putting them on the defensive. So if you were going to take away people's rights, it had to be for their own good. And, apparently, taking away people's rights was for their own good.

"So if I understand all of this," I said, "you think maybe something like, oh, I don't know, maybe something like an attack on the Seattle ferry system might actually be a good thing."

"We're speaking hypothetically here, of course, Sergeant, but that might be one way to get the American people to understand the enormity of the threat and might make them a little more understanding of the security measures we have to have in this country in order to block the terrorists and keep the country safe. People have short memories."

"And it doesn't concern you that hundreds or maybe thousands of people might die in an attack like the one you're describing."

"Of course it concerns me, Sergeant. I'm a loyal American and I don't want to see Americans killed or injured by terrorists. In fact, that's the last thing I would want. But like I said, this whole country is a battle ground and everyone is a soldier in that war. Sometimes, in a war, a few soldiers have to die for the good of all."

"Even if they don't know they're soldiers."

"I think that's the whole point, Sergeant. Do you think every Israeli citizen doesn't know they're a soldier in a shooting war? It's time for the American people to wake up and face reality. They're soldiers on the front lines of a shooting war."

"So you think this country should be more like Israel." He looked at me, closed his eyes and shrugged. "Was Anna Noble a soldier in this war?"

"Of course she was."

"And how do you explain killing our own soldiers?"

"I don't know anything about Anna Noble's death. But if Anna Noble was a traitor to the greater cause of freedom and justice, then perhaps she deserved to die."

Ok, I'd heard about enough of this bullshit. It was all I could do to keep from jumping across the table and putting out a few of his teeth. But I still didn't know any more about the details of the attack. So I let it go.

"But if Obama is as 'soft' on terrorism" as you seem to think he is," I said, "why would the terrorists want to try to influence our election and keep him from getting elected? Wouldn't his election make their job a lot easier?"

"Because terrorists don't think the way we've been taught to think. They think with every attack, our government will become more and more repressive and eventually the American people will insist the government give the terrorists what they want. Either that, or the people will get fed up with the repression and overthrow it. See, to a terrorist, it doesn't really matter. Either way, they get what they want."

"Which is?"

"That's not always easy to tell. It depends on which terrorists you're talking about. Maybe getting out of the Middle East completely. Definitely out of supporting Israel. Maybe even an opportunity to establish an Islamic States of America as a prelude to a world wide caliphate."

My head was about to explode.

"So what you're saying is the terrorists want to see a more repressive American government and you'd like to give it to them."

"No, what I'm saying is what looks like repression to the terrorists is only good common sense in response to the physical threat they pose to this country. Like the measures we've put into effect since 9/11. People grumbled about the long lines at the airport, but eventually they got used to them. If the things we have to do to protect the American people are properly explained and presented to them, they'll understand and accept it as being in their best interests They'll adapt just like they have to everything else that's had to be done. Especially if they're reminded of the horrors of the alternative."

Or else find themselves down in Guantanamo Bay without a paddle. The scary part was I think this guy actually believes this shit. The only question was: How many more were there like him?

"How do you 'explain and present' to the American people that you sat here and let an attack take place on our ferry system so they'll 'understand and accept it'?"

"Hypothetically speaking, of course, as far as the American people are concerned, Sergeant, let's say the Department of Homeland Security and the US government, through our intelligence networks, uncovered a plot by Al Qaeda to launch an attack on the Seattle ferry system. Maybe a decision was made to stand back and allow the plot to develop in order to identify as many participants as possible and to learn all we could about how this operation was planned then move in at the last minute ands shut it down. Because of the delicate nature of this operation, all government agencies might have been instructed to pass along any information they might collect in connection with the planned attack to Washington for coordination at the highest levels of the Administration but not take any direct action. Unfortunately, certain members of the Seattle police department, by their actions and interference, alerted the terrorists that the US government was onto them and they changed their plan at the last minute. Because our resources were allocated elsewhere, we were unable to stop the attack. Also, a certain member of the United States Coast Guard, in violation of a direct order, may have inadvertently contributed to the success of the attack, as well, and would be prosecuted by a military tribunal.

"So you see, Sergeant, it's not beyond the realm of possibility."

"I think we've heard about enough, Callahan. Let's go." I moved around the table towards him. "If you're not crazy, you're the closest I've come to it a long time."

"Not crazy, Sergeant, just a loyal American willing to make some hard choices. And, as it turns out, hypothetically speaking, some others in the government and in private industry don't necessarily agree with most of what I've just hypothesized might also have their own reasons for just letting this thing happen."

"I can't wait to hear this."

"Think about it for a second. Don't you think there are people who would like to prove George Bush was wrong? That if there were to be a major terrorist attack, do you think they would hesitate to say "First 9/11 and now this – all on George Bush's watch'? Or think about the amount of money that has been generated in this economy since 9/11 with all of the government and private anti-terrorism personnel? Not to mention all of the security gadgets people can buy. Anti- terrorism is big business, Sergeant. Think of the money that's been pumped into our economy all because of 9/11. There are some pretty rich and powerful people who would like to give the economy another good shot in the arm, especially when you consider the current state of that economy. People who don't particularly want to see this war on terror be completely successful. They want it to be manageable, not over. It's no different than the war on drugs. Do you have any idea how many people depend on the war on drugs to put food on their table. And I'm not talking about the drug dealers, I'm talking about the good guys. If we defeat the terrorists and legalize drugs, most of my department, along with a lot of other folks, would be out of a job. Us and people like us are too important to the economy to be allowed to go out of business. What do you think finally bailed us out of the Great Depression? World War II. That war was a boon to the American economy. These wars are no different. You know the expression 'too big to fail'? Well, the war on terrorism just like the war on drugs is too big to be too successful.

"So, you see, Sergeant, when push comes to shove, it's just you and the Sundance Kid, here. There's not going to be anyone – anyone that matters, that is – backing you up."

Maybe my problem was I was assuming these people were sane and rational. The only thing that kept bothering me was some of what he was saying was starting to make sense. I didn't like it and I certainly didn't buy into it, but I could sort of understand the logic in a perverse kind of way. Must be lack of food. And sleep.

"And, speaking of back-up…Alberto!"

A split second later, Alberto came back into the room with five or six others, all in CBP uniforms, all armed, and fanned out by the door. Nobody had guns drawn, but the implication was obvious.

"Why don't you go get a warrant, Sergeant, - if you can – then we'll see where I'm going. In the meantime…." He gestured toward the door.

I made a quick assessment of the situation. I had gotten at least some information from Callahan and I didn't think I was going get anything more than what he wanted to tell me.
I wasn't even sure he knew the exact details of the plan. My guess, however, was he known more than he was telling us? He didn't seem like the kind of guy who would get this far up to his neck in all of this without a better idea of exactly what was going on or about to go on. I do think he was told to stand by and be ready when the shit hit the fan. And I still thought he knew quite a bit

about the six killings. As much as I'm a patriot and all that, I'm still a homicide detective and finding the people behind those six murders was still my primary goal. And I was pretty sure I had found at least one of them.

I made a decision. I wasn't sure it was the right one but, under the circumstances, I didn't think I had much of a choice. "C'mon, Al," I said, "let's goes. We'll be back, Callahan."

We left the room, headed back down the hall and past the security check-point. The same CBP guy was still there. "Have a nice day, gentlemen," he said with a smirk.

As I opened the door into the hallway, I definitely thought I had stepped through the looking glass. There in front of me, just walking up to the door, was Pete Gilbert and about ten uniformed Seattle police officers.

"Thought you might be able to use some back-up, Elliott," he said.

Chapter 56

Al and I watched George Callahan through the two-way mirror in the interrogation
Room sitting at the table all by himself. We had all of the audio and video equipment up and running but the room was quiet. The decision was made to let him sit there for a while and let his imagination run wild. I don't care how cool they are on the outside, most suspects spend that quiet time thinking about all the 'what ifs' and if you leave them alone they can come up with some pretty scary scenarios all by themselves. Especially when they are as guilty as this guy was.

Turns out the two patrolmen we left down on Second Avenue outside of the CBP office, had done exactly what I told them to do. Thirty minutes had gone by; we didn't show up, so they called the Captain. He decided since it probably shouldn't take a half hour to make an arrest or, even if we didn't make an arrest, Al and I should have come back out, something had gone wrong and he'd better call up the troops. Like I said, the Captain is a no-nonsense guy and when he commits to something, he doesn't do it half way. Our coming to the door when we did was apparently pure coincidence – one of the few things that have gone our way this week-end.

Right after the cavalry arrived; we went back in, cuffed Callahan and took him away. It was actually pretty uneventful. Our guys came in and two uniformed patrolmen, one on each side, took a hold of Callahan, pushed his arms behind his back, cuffed him pretty much all in one move and manhandled him out of the room. Cuffing suspects is something these guys do in their sleep and this one was quick and clean. As Callahan was hustled out past me, I said to him: "He's ba-ack."

Alberto's guys stood on the sidelines and didn't do anything to interfere. I think there was a little indecision on their part, but our guys moved so quickly that the deed was done before Alberto or anybody else in the room could do anything stupid. But I'm sure we weren't even in the elevator when Alberto was on the phone to somebody. At least, I hope he was. That was part of the plan I had discussed with Danielle when we decided to stir things up. Through some means or other - and I really didn't want to know the details - not that anyone was going to tell me - Danielle's tech guys had set up to monitor any calls coming to or from Callahan's home. But when I told her of our change in plans she must have turned to her guys and told them to re-align their monitoring equipment to the 22nd floor of 1000 Second Avenue. According to her, it didn't matter if it was land line, cell phone or some type of radio frequency. At one point in the past day or so Danielle had told me there are something like fifteen or sixteen separate surveillance and information gathering agencies in the United States government and they – 'they' being Danielle's people – had access to at least fourteen of them. Come to think of it, she never mentioned which ones they didn't have access to. But, I guess when you've got fourteen state of the art intelligence gathering operations at your disposal, the other one or two really don't make much difference.

I had taken the opportunity to check in with Danielle before I headed back to headquarters.

"Hey, gorgeous," I said when she answered the phone, "wanna go somewhere for a drink?" No response. "Anything new?" I said.

"One phone call from the CPB office apparently right after you left. We have a full recording and a trace on the number in DC. Somebody's going to have an interesting day tomorrow...or, actually, right about now."

"Good. Couldn't happen to a nicer bunch of scumbags. Anything in the transcript that would give us any more of a clue as to the details of the attack?"

"Unfortunately, no. But we're starting to get a few names of people involved and that's a plus, at least from our standpoint."

"So we were at least moderately successful."

"We'll see. These guys are not going down without a fight."

I briefly ran through the conversation I had with Callahan before we arrested him. She was quiet and let me get through it all without saying a word.

"I had no idea the opposition was so serious," she said, in a quiet voice. "So, your impression is this is being orchestrated by people from within the government, but they may have backing from outside the government, as well."

"If not backing, then at least tacit approval. My guess is if the hammerheads who are going to try to pull off this attack ran into any technical or logistical difficulties, there were a few helping hands out there to make sure they didn't fail. "

"Unless we catch some kind of break in the next few

hours, which I doubt, this attack is going to go down and all we can do is stand-by to mop up the pieces. Listen, John, I'm going to pass this information onto my father and his group. I'll call you if we uncover something. Do the same for me, ok?"

"You're first on my speed dial."

"Thanks, John. Talk to you soon."

Callahan was still sitting there looking composed. I wasn't in any rush. I was sure the wheels were turning at some level higher than mine to get this guy sprung, but we anticipated that and weren't about to just let him walk out.

"Ok, Al. Time to take our boy over to King County jail."

"Right. I have a couple of our guys available to take care of that."

"Don't forget to make sure they understand we don't want him actually booked. We want to waltz him in where everybody can see him coming in then change direction and waltz him out as quietly as possible. Tell them to ride him around for while until one of us calls them."

Al disappeared then, a few minutes later, reappeared in the interrogation room with two uniformed patrolmen. Callahan, still cuffed and looking a little confused was stood up and marched out. Over the sound system I could hear him, not a little confused, saying: "Where are you taking me?"

I made my way back out through our office and into the

Captain's office. He was writing something and said: "Sit," without looking up. I sat. And waited.

Finally he put down the pen and sat back in his chair. "What do you think?" he said.

"I think Callahan figured we'd bring him in, he'd be here about five minutes before half the lawyers in the Justice Department would be all over this place and he'd be giving us the bird."

"Is he gone?"

"Yeah, a couple of our guys just escorted him out."

"Good. Because I just told the Chief he was taken over to King County."

"Well, that was no lie. Sounds like the opposition is marshalling their troops. That must have been some conversation with the Chief."

"It was actually pretty business like. He said: 'I understand your men may have made an arrest of a high ranking government employee'. I said: 'Yes, sir. That would be correct.' He said: 'I assume you had a good reason for doing that.' And I said: 'Yes, sir, I believe we do.' He said: 'Where is he now?' That's when I told him the high ranking government employee in question was on his way over to the county jail.

"What else did he say?"

His last words before he hung up were: 'There's a lot riding on this, Pete. Don't screw it up'.

"So he didn't lean on you release Callahan?"

"No, that was the funny thing. I thought he'd be screaming to get this guy released. I don't know why, but I got the feeling he knew a lot more about this whole thing than he let on and he wasn't at all unhappy we had arrested this guy. Does that make any sense?"

"Captain, nothing about any of this makes any sense."

Just then the phone on his desk rang. "Gilbert."

"No, you may not send them up. Tell them the prisoner has been transported to another facility and you're checking to try to find out where he's been taken." He hung up. "The eagle has landed," he said to me. "Downstairs in the lobby. They'll figure it out for themselves soon enough but no sense helping them out."

"Who'd they send?"

"Ah, I don't know. Couple of Justice Department lawyers still in their jammies." He sat back and rubbed his eyes. "When was the last time you got any sleep?" he said.

"The night before I found out my first wife was pregnant," I said.

He smiled, which is as close to laughing as Captain Pete ever comes. At least when he's on duty. "What time is it?" he said, looking at his watch.

"Oh-dark-thirty," I said.

"Not far off," he said. "Just a little before 5:00. Jesus, Elliott, part of me hopes you guys are right and part of me hopes you're wrong. Either way, this is not going to be a pretty day."

Chapter 57

I went back to my desk. I toyed with the idea of trying to get some sleep, but that didn't seem to make much sense. I can take a fifteen minute power nap in the middle of the day and recharge my batteries. But to actually sleep for an hour makes me even more unfunctional than I was before I nodded off.

I picked up the bat phone and dialed Harry. I don't know why, I just assumed he was awake. Sure enough. Second ring. "O'Connell."

"Got a minute? I'd like to bring you up to speed."

"I don't know, let me check my book." At least he still had his sense of humor.

So I told him about the events of the last few hours. The only comment he made was an occasional 'Those bastards', especially after the part where Callahan said a certain Coast Guard officer might be facing a Court Martial.

When I was finished, he asked: "Did you learn anything that would help us stop this?"

"Afraid not, Harry." Silence. "Where are you now?"

"I'm in my office. I've been here all night. I don't know what I expected to happen but I just felt like this was the place to be. Charlie Parker's here, too. He's keeping everything quiet, but the little I had to tell him has made him very nervous."

"Did he tell his guys on both sides of the Bay to be extra alert, or just the guys at the Seattle terminal?"

"No, he's got all of the terminals on high alert. I think he even brought in some off-duty personnel. I know he's got extra dogs since we pretty much think this operation will involve Semtex. Frankly, John, if they think they're going to sneak a bunch of explosives on board any one of the ferries, I think they're in for a big surprise."

"I hope you're right, Harry. I think we need to think a little outside the box, though. These creeps have known for a few days that somebody's onto them, or at least sniffing around. I don't think they're planning to just waltz onto one of the ferries with a bunch of explosives. They may be a lot of things, but I don't think stupid is one of them."

"Yeah, well maybe the guys in DC, or wherever the hell they are, aren't stupid. But didn't you once tell me something about never overestimating the intelligence of the bad guys?"

"No, I think what I actually said was: 'It never hurts to overestimate the intelligence of your adversaries'."

"I'm too tired to figure out what you just said."

"Listen, Harry, I've been thinking. I mean, how much room does four hundred pounds of Semtex take up?"

"I don't know. I mean, it's a pretty good sized chunk. Maybe the size of a trash can. You couldn't put it in a duffel bag."

"But four hundred pounds of anything is pretty heavy, right?"

"Yeah, I guess."

"I mean it's not like a small bomb that you could strap to a guy or hide in a suitcase. You have to have some way to move it around and get it to wherever you're going to blow something up, right?"

"Makes sense. Although right now everything makes sense and nothing makes sense if you know what I mean."

"Yeah, I do. Anyway, if you're going to try to blow up a ferry and you're not going to be able to get it on the ferry, how else could you get it close?"

"I don't know. Maybe drop it from an airplane?"

"Yeah, maybe."

"Or on a boat."

"Ok. Anything else?"

"Not unless somebody's invented some other form of transportation that I don't know about."

"So, since the State Patrol seems to have direct access onto the ferries covered pretty well, does it make sense that we should be focused more on other ways to get that shit close enough to do some harm?"

"What are you suggesting?"

"I don't even know what I'm suggesting except the more resources we can put in place, the better chance we have of preventing this from happening. What have you got on the water right now?"

"Our usual patrol boats."

"Which are...?"

"RBs and TPSBs – twenty-five footers. Those small boats you always see out there escorting the ferries. Similar to what we saw up in Port Angeles earlier today."

"Armament?"

"Small arms and deck mounted 50 caliber machine guns. Why, what are you thinking?"

"Just that they could probably stop a small boat but maybe not anything big." I thought for a moment. "Harry, how much do your guys on the water know about what's going on?"

"Not much. I just told them to be extra careful and report anything unusual. And to stop anything headed within five hundred feet of a ferry."

"I don't know how you feel about this, but I know military types pretty well. You can tell them all you want about being alert, but unless somebody's shooting at them, they're still pretty casual. I'm afraid by the time they figure out there may be a threat, it could be too late. These guys are not going to pull up in a boat with an Afghan flag and ask for directions."

"Yeah, I know what you mean."

"I know five hundred feet is your usual threat radius but four hundred pounds of Semtex and five hundred feet doesn't leave a lot of room for error."

"Hmm. Maybe you're right. Let me take care of that. What about airplanes? Could this be another 9/11 deal where they fly an airplane full of explosives right at the target?"

"Could be. Let me make a call. And Harry? If Charlie Parker hasn't already thought of this, you might want to suggest he start screening vehicles out on Alaskan Way before they get to the Pier. Five hundred feet on land isn't any further away than five hundred feet on water."

I hung up with Harry then pressed 7 for English. Danielle answered on the first ring.

"I see you're answering your own phone. What happened, secretary quit?"

"No, I just thought under the circumstances this might save a little time."
I told her about my conversation with Harry and about how we might anticipate something from the air. "Any thoughts on how we might try to prevent that?"

"We have two helicopters here and two each over on Bainbridge and up in Edmonds. Let me talk to the air group commander and see what he thinks about putting one of our choppers in the air right now." She hung up.

"Thanks, you have a nice day, too," I said to dead air.

Chapter 58

I must have dozed off in front of my computer because I jumped about ten feet when Al said: "John!"

"Oh, Al. Sorry. Where's our boy?"

"Still riding around. How much longer do you want them to keep this up?"

"Anybody else looking for him besides those two clowns down in the lobby a little while ago?"

"Strangely, no. I'm not sure anybody wants to stick their neck out. Looks like everybody's keeping a low profile."

"What time is it?" We both looked at our watches. "A little after 5:30." I rubbed my eyes and stretched. "Here's what I'm thinking," I said. "Bear with me for a minute - see if you agree." I sat back in my chair and tried to organize my thoughts. I needed to run this by Al because I know when you're tired a lot of things that seem like a good idea at the time turn out not to stand the scrutiny of broad daylight. I thought I had come up with a reasonable plan, but you never know for sure at 5:30 in the morning. Besides, if it didn't work out I could always say Al told me to do it.

"If you're a terrorist planning an attack on one of our ferries," I said, "you probably want the most bang for the buck, am I right? Kill as many infidels as possible before you go to cash in your free virgins coupon?"

"Makes sense."

"And if we're right about the four hundred pounds of Semtex, this operation is not designed to kill a half a dozen people."

"Ok."

"So where is the biggest concentration of ferries and ferry passengers?"

"I'd have to guess right down at Pier 52."

"And when do you suppose there is the greatest number of people at Pier 52?"

"Probably Monday morning during rush hour."

"More precisely, between 6:55 and 7:20. I checked the ferry schedule on line and it turns out that between 6:55 and 7:20 in the morning there are three ferries all loading and unloading at the downtown terminal – the Vashon Island ferry at Pier 50 and the Bremerton ferry and the Bainbridge Island ferry right next to it at pier 52."

"That's pretty amazing."

"Well, not when you think about the number of people who have to come across to go to work on a Monday morning."

"No, I mean that you looked something up on the internet."

I stared at him for a second or two. He stared back. "Anyway," I said, "I also checked on the capacity of the ferries and, depending on which ones are in service, there could be as many as five thousand people between the three of them."

"Holy shit!"

"And that doesn't count the people sitting on the pier waiting to board."

"So, where does all that take us?"

"Right now it's a guessing game. We don't know for sure when or where they're going to strike. So, we can sit here and wait until we hear an explosion or we can try to use what information we can piece together and narrow our focus."

"And hope we're right."

"And hope we're right," I said.

"So here's my thinking: These clowns are probably going to try something during rush hour – my window of opportunity says between 6:55 and 7:20 – if I can read a ferry schedule, so can they - and it's probably going to be at Pier 52. I'm hoping ol' George knows more than he's letting on. I'd like to jerk him around for another hour or so, maybe even bring him back here and hammer him a little. I don't think he's going to tell us much. I think he's feeling pretty smug right now, even in his present situation. If he does, great. If he doesn't – and I suspect he won't - put him back in a squad car and take him down to Pier 52 around quarter to seven and park him in the front row. See if that improves his memory any."

Al grinned. "That's the evil genius I've come to know and love."

"Ok, I'll take that as an approval. Get a hold of the guys who are driving him around. Tell them to bring him in. Then I want you and somebody else to double team him in the interview room. I don't give a shit what you ask him or how you threaten him. The more aggressive, the better. Make sure he understands we'll do anything we have to do to keep him from getting released until we're ready. You might even mention that even his lawyers don't know where he is, in case he's still thinking they're coming to his rescue. I'm more interested in changing his mental state than I am in what he might tell you. I'll be on the other side of the glass but I don't want him to see me until he's parked on the Pier at ground zero."

I could feel a little surge of adrenaline and a little burst of energy. But I've been there before and I knew what was happening. I'm on the edge of total exhaustion and my body is fighting to keep me awake. With no food and no sleep, I wasn't sure how much longer I could last. At least with this latest plan we were doing something instead of waiting for something to happen.

Then it hit me. I don't know why I hadn't thought of it before. I leaned forward and started rummaging through my top desk drawer, knowing that it had to be in there somewhere. Damn drawer got stuck half way out. I reached all the way to the back and could just barely get my fingers on it. I fiddled with it and finally yanked it out. There it was - half a bag of dark chocolate M&Ms. With peanuts. Better than sex. I shoved a handful in my mouth and closed my eyes. Oh. My. God.

My desk phone rang. "Elliott."

"Sergeant." I recognized the voice on the other end right

away. "This is Jeff Feinberg."

"I'm a little busy right now, Feinberg. What can I do for you?"

"I believe you have George Callahan in custody, is that correct?" This guy must have been a lawyer at one time or another. Lawyers never say 'Is that right?'. They always say 'Is that correct?'.

"Whether or not we have George Callahan or anybody else in custody is none of your business, Feinberg."

"Sergeant', he said with that same jovial tone he took with me when we met over at Pike Place. "I'm only trying to help out. Some of the folks I work with think we might have more success getting information from Mr. Callahan using some – how shall I say this? – more non-traditional methods than might be available to a public employee."

"And what folks would that be, Feinberg? The farmers over at Agriculture? You gonna spray this guy with DDT?"

I still didn't trust this guy. There were two possibilities: one, he really was working for the Bainbridge Island group and they really had decided that they wanted to speed up the process, or, two, that ultimately he was part of the group of right wing-nuts and they were trying to get George away from us using honey instead of vinegar. I had no doubt Feinberg had been in touch with the Bainbridge Island folks and probably was sitting in on all of their meetings. I just wasn't sure where his loyalties lay. I wouldn't have put it past him to convince the Bainbridge group that they really needed to get Callahan away from us.

"I just think we might get our answers a little more quickly than you, that's all."

"Well, Feinberg, ordinarily I might agree with you that if we had George Callahan in custody, a little non-traditional coercion might be just the thing. But even if we did have George Callahan in custody, I don't think my Captain or his boss, or his boss's boss, would think it was such a great idea to just hand him over to – who? How would I explain who you guys are?"

"I just think you could be wasting valuable time."

"Funny, that's what my first wife said. Turns out she was right, she just didn't realize the truth and wisdom of her words. Listen, Feinberg, speaking of wasting valuable time, that's what we're doing here. I appreciate your interest in the cause of peace and justice, I really do. But right now I need to get breakfast and plan my day." I hung up.

M&Ms in hand and a smile on my face, I made my way back to the observation room behind the interrogation room where they would be bringing Callahan. The bat phone rang.

"Yeah?"

"Good morning, Sergeant, this is the front desk. You asked for a wake-up call?"

"The only wake up call I want from you, Danielle, is a whisper in my ear."

"My goodness. You must be tired. I'll let that remark go for now."

"Sorry."

"Oh, don't apologize."

"What did you decide about the air cover?"

"We think it's a good idea to have something in the air, we're just not sure how we would operate. We don't want to be shooting down every small plane that even comes close, if you know what I mean."

"Yeah, I see what you mean. Listen, all I can say is I think it would be better to have something in the air rather than nothing. I'm not sure how it would work either, except we're already playing an awful lot by ear, what's one more thing, unless you have a better idea."

"No, I don't. Ok. We'll put half the group in the air and keep the other half here on stand-by."

"Thanks Danielle. Listen, Al and I have been talking and our best guess is if this thing is going down today, the best time from their standpoint would be at the height of the rush hour. I was going to suggest you put your guys in the air around 6:30, what do you think?"

"I think we'd like to conserve as much fuel as possible since we don't know how long we might be up there. So, 6:30 sounds good, I guess."

"Ok. And one other thing. Are you going up with them?"

"I think so, yes. Why?"

"Keep your phone on. We're working an angle to try to squeeze information out of Callahan. If I get anything I may have to get a hold of you in a hurry."

"Ok. And John?"

"Yeah?"

"I just might like to take you up on that wake-up call."
Click. Note to self: Think about that last remark. Only not now.

I could hear a commotion in the hall and I turned and looked through one-way glass. Al and Ed Reinhardt manhandled Callahan into the room and sat him down at the table. I don't know how Al got a hold of Ed Reinhardt. Ed was one of our best interrogators. I looked at my watch. It was almost 6:00. This was coming down to the wire.

Chapter 59

Ed put on quite a show. For almost twenty minutes, he threatened him, cursed him, screamed at him, whispered at him, got right in his face and sometimes just sat back and stared at him. As I suspected, he didn't get much out of him, but I could tell from Callahan's body language that he was beginning to realize this wasn't going the way he thought it would. I could see him thinking: 'Where the hell are those guys?'

At about 6:20 I flipped the switch on the intercom and spoke to Al in his earpiece.
"Ok, Al. It's almost time. Come in here for a second, will you?"

Al said to Ed: "I'll be right back." He left the interrogation room and came around the corner into the observation room.

"What I'd like you to do," I said, "is to take him down to the Pier like we discussed. Don't talk to him on the way down. If he asks where you're taking him, don't answer him. He'll figure it out on his own. When you get there, drive up to the front of the line and park wherever you can close to one of the ferries. Then just get out and walk away."

"I sure hope this works, John."

"Yeah, me too, Al."

" 'Cause right now we've got just about nothing."

"Been there before, Al." He just nodded.

He went back into the interrogation room and I headed for the parking deck, found the car and headed for Pier 52.

It took me about five minutes to get to the bottom of the hill and over to Pier 52. I showed my badge to the State Patrol officer at the gate and he waved me through. I parked off to one side, out of the way of the traffic coming onto the Pier and in a spot where I could see Al when he drove up to the front of the Pier. It was still dark and – surprise, surprise – drizzling, but there's a pretty good amount of light on the Pier and the rows where the cars queue up were filling up quickly. I didn't have to wait long.

About four or five minutes later a dark blue Crown Vic came slowly across the dock, past the lanes of cars waiting to board the ferry and pulled up at the edge of the Pier about half way between the two main landing points. A State Patrolman walked over to the car and rested his hands on the roof next to the driver's side window. I could see the window roll down and there was a brief exchange between him and Al. The window rolled up, he stepped back from the car and nodded, then turned and walked away. About ten seconds later both the driver's side door and the front passenger side door opened and Al and Ed got out, slammed the doors, and walked away back towards the exit onto Alaskan Way.

I looked at my watch. A little after 6:35. Show time.

I got out of the car and walked toward the Crown Vic. The rain was coming down a little steadier. I turned my collar up and hunched down into my jacket. Cars were streaming in on my left and filling up the numbered rows getting ready to board the two ferries. Neither ferry was at the dock yet, but as efficient as they were at getting people on and off the ferries, they were equally as efficient at being on time. I had no doubt today wouldn't be any different.

I opened the passenger side door and dropped into the front seat, closing the door. I sat and looked straight ahead and not at Callahan.

"What the fuck is going on here, Elliott?" he said. Not the same attitude he had back in his office. Good.

"Well, Callahan, outside of the fact that I ask the questions, I thought since you were so excited to let the American people know that we're all on the front lines, you might like to be on the front lines yourself. Literally."

Silence.

"The way I figure it, there's going to be a big explosion sometime soon and I think it's going to be somewhere close by. I thought that since you're such a patriot, you might like a front row seat."

"You going to sit here and watch it with me?" he said, with a little bit of a sarcastic tone?

"Me? Nah. I'll be a ways away from here when the balloon goes up. I'm what you call a fair weather patriot. I like singing the Star Spangled Banner at Fenway Park. Or watching the jets fly over Gillette Stadium before a Patriots game. Gives me chills. Brings tears to my eyes. But watching the Seattle waterfront go up in smoke and

flames? Doesn't get me excited the way I'm sure it does you. I mean you're all about how we're all soldiers in some kind of war here and dying for the cause, like the hundreds or thousands of unsuspecting people who probably won't make it to their coffee break this morning, is somehow a glorious thing. I'm surprised you're not talking about all the virgins that will be waiting for you, Callahan. You know I really admire that in you. Willing to die for what you believe in. You are willing to die for that, aren't you, Callahan?"
Quiet.

"No smart comments? I bet when you left the house – when? Yesterday? I bet you didn't think you'd be a suicide bomber today. In fact, I'll bet a half hour ago you didn't think you'd be a suicide bomber. Because that's what you are, you know. You could tell me what's going down and save your own life or you can keep your mouth shut and go up in smoke and flames. Maybe you're not actually carrying the bomb, but it amounts to the same thing." I paused to let it sink in.

"Did you ever see 'The Man of La Mancha' Callahan? One of my favorite plays. All about good in the face of evil. There's a line in that play that kind of reminds me of your current situation. It goes something like: 'Whether the stone hits the pitcher or the pitcher hits the stone, it's gonna be bad for the pitcher.' See, in that story, Callahan, in case you missed it, you're the pitcher."

"You can't get away with this, Elliott.'

"Yeah? Maybe not. The unfortunate part is that you won't be around to say 'I told you so.'"

"I'm not a suicide bomber, Elliott."

"Same difference. You could stop this - or you could have stopped it – but you chose, for whatever reason, to let it happen. The only thing you didn't count on is some sick son of a bitch homicide detective who's going to let you sit right on top of the thing when it goes off. I wonder what it will be like at the instant all that Semtex goes off. Yeah, we know about the Semtex – all four hundred pounds of it. I wonder if you'll be able to watch your arms and legs flying in different directions or feel the heat from the blast. God, I wish I had your courage, Callahan. I'll bet it will be quite an experience. Once in a lifetime. So to speak."

"Look, Elliott," he said with a note of rising desperation in his voice, "I don't know whatever it is you think I know. Yes, I know there's going to be some kind of attack today. But I don't know how, or where or when. I really don't."

"That makes two of us, Callahan." I looked out the side window toward the water. I could just see the lights from one of the ferries. "Here comes a ferry. Did I tell you my theory?
No? Well, you're not going anywhere so, what the hell. Sorry. Probably shouldn't be making any references to hell. Poor choice of words in your situation. Anyway, my theory is that in about ten or fifteen minutes there will be three ferries tied up somewhere along this pier pretty close together. Lots of people coming and going. If four hundred pounds of Semtex were to blow up in the middle of all of that, it might create something akin to 9/11. At least if I was a terrorist that's what I would be thinking. The only part I haven't worked out is how you deliver the Semtex. That's where I was hoping you might jump in, Callahan."

I turned and looked at him for the first time. He looked like shit. His hair was all messed up, his skin was white and pasty-looking, he needed a shave and there were little beads of sweat along his hair line. Come to think of it, he didn't smell particularly good either, although I hadn't really noticed it until now.

"I'm telling you, Elliott, I swear I don't know the details."

"Why is it I'm having trouble believing you, Callahan? You sounded pretty knowledgeable back in your office. I mean you really convinced me with all that 'hypothetical' shit. By the way, did I tell you I met your wife? Nice lady. Pretty good looking in a bathrobe, too. Looked like a pretty decent set of tits. I wonder who'll be fucking her after you're gone?"

I thought he was coming right through the Plexiglas between the front seat and the back seat. Fortunately, he was still cuffed behind his back. "You bastard! You fucking bastard! I don't know shit, Elliott, you asshole! Let me out of this fucking car!"

"I think you're just being modest, Callahan. I think you know exactly what's going down here. And if you think I won't leave you here to be splattered all over the landscape, think again. I think you're a criminal, Callahan, and the worst kind of criminal. You wrap yourself up in the flag then let other people die for what you believe in without giving them the choice. And here's another flash: When it comes to guys like you, I'm not all that moral. I'm really not. I'm a cynical bastard and I don't trust the politics enough to think you'll get what you deserve. As far as I'm concerned, leaving you here to self-destruct is probably the cleanest and neatest way to deal with you. So don't think I'm bluffing, because I'm not.

"So, I'm looking over there and I see one ferry getting closer to the dock and I can just about make out the lights from another one off to the left there. You're running out of time, Callahan. How badly do you want to die for this? Because in about one minute I'm going back to my car and getting the hell away from here. And when I shut the door to this car and walk away, your last chance to save your own sorry ass walks away with me."

"Elliott, I swear to God, I don't know. They never told us. They just said if we heard anything to just pass the information onto them and not do anything about it. I swear to you, Elliott, they never told us."

"Who's 'they', Callahan?"

Silence.

"See, that's what pisses me off about you Callahan. You're about to go up in smoke and you're still playing games with me. You want me to believe you don't know anything, but when I ask you a simple question we both know you know the answer to, you hesitate. I've seen your 'get out of jail free' card. It's pretty clear whoever sent it was pretty well known to you. Do you think you have some kind of bargaining position here? Because if you do, you're sadly mistaken."

I waited about five full seconds. Then he mumbled something. "What? I couldn't hear you?" Then he said it louder. I didn't recognize the name but I was sure Danielle or somebody in her outfit would. All very interesting, but not the information I really wanted at the moment.

"See," I said, "That wasn't all that hard, was it? Now just tell me how they plan to do it."

"I don't know, Elliott, I swear to God, I don't know. Listen, Elliott, this thing is much bigger than you think. I don't even really know how big it is."

"You don't know what I think, Callahan."

"I'm telling you, I don't know anything. Some people I know asked me if I'd be on board with this and I agreed. All I know is my department is supposed to stand by and be ready for something big. I swear to God, Elliott, that's all I know. And I don't know anything about any of those killings or the attack on you."

"So you're just a good little soldier, is that it? Just an innocent bureaucrat taking orders?
Where have I heard that before?"

"But it's true!" he said with more than a note of desperation in his voice.

"You know enough to know that somebody in Washington is pulling the strings on this. You know enough to know that a lot of people are going overboard to try to keep Obama from being elected. In fact, you and your friends seem to know better than the rest of us what's good for America. So why is it I don't believe you when you say you don't know any of the details of this attack?"

"What do I have to say to convince you?"

"You've said enough already. Last chance, Callahan. How are they going to deliver that bomb?"

I could hear his bowels grumbling and a nasty smell was coming from the back seat. He said, quietly: "I don't know, Elliott. I really don't know."

"Too bad," I said. And opened the door, got out and slammed the door behind me. I could hear a muffled yell behind me.

"Elliott! Elliott!"

Chapter 60

I took about five steps away from the car and pulled out the bat phone. I called Danielle.
She answered on the first ring. I could hear the faint noise of what sounded like helicopter blades.

"Hi, John Anything?"

"I got you a name, but nothing on how they plan to do this."

"Where's Callahan?"

"On the Pier in the back seat of a car."

"You did your best, John."

"Yeah, but it wasn't good enough."

"Do you think he knows?"

"Part of me says yes."

"What about the other part?"

"The other part isn't sure. Where are you now?"

"We're at about fifteen hundred feet just south of the Terminal."

I was just about to say: 'See anything?' when the phone beeped to tell me there was another call coming in. I looked at the screen. "Hold on, Danielle, there's a call coming in on this phone from a number I don't recognize."

I started pushing buttons trying to switch over to the incoming call without disconnecting Danielle. After three tries I managed to disconnect both calls. Shit.

As I got to the car, the phone rang again.

"Elliott."

"Sergeant? Cyril Dobbs. Hope I didn't wake you up."

"Trust me, Cyril, you didn't wake me up." I got into my car and slammed the door.

"Say, listen, I'm sorry I wasn't able to pay more attention to you yesterday. We were a little busy and I was pretty focused on what was going on."

"Don't worry about it Cyril. I appreciate the time you gave me. Listen, I'm a little busy myself right now. So thanks for calling. You take care."

"No, no," he said. "Don't hang up. I didn't call to apologize. Well, actually, I did call to apologize. But I really called to tell you that when I woke up this morning I thought of something that might be helpful, I don't know."

"What's that, Cyril?"

"Remember you asked me about the Roger Revelle?"

"Yes."

"Well I remembered the Revelle and the Thompson are sister ships."

"What exactly does that mean?"

"It means for all intents and purposes the Revelle and the Thompson are identical."

"What?"

"Yeah. They're both built on the same set of plans. I mean there might be some little custom touches here and there, but for all intents and purposes, as they say about tits, you seen one, you seen 'em both."

"So if somebody wanted to get a good look at how the Thompson was set up without going near it, they could look around the Revelle."

"Yeah, pretty much."

"Cyril, where's the Thompson right now?"

"Well, she's supposed to be just about out of the Sound and headed north up to Alaska. Why?"

"This could be important, Cyril. Can you find out exactly where she is?"

"Hang on. I just got to the office. Let me see if I can find out."

I looked over toward the landing area and could see the first of the three ferries slowing down and making an approach. I could also see the lights from the second ferry off in the distance. I couldn't see the Vashon Island ferry from where I was standing but, like I said, these things run like clockwork so I was sure it wasn't far away. If I was right, we didn't have long to wait for whatever they were going to do or whatever we were going to do. C'mon, Cyril, c'mon.

"Elliott? This is really strange. Our radio operator says the Thompson went dark last night just after it went through the Ballard Locks. We haven't heard from them since about 1:00 this morning. I had him try to reach them on the satellite link but we're not getting any response."

"Ok, Cyril, thanks. Do me a favor. This is important. Keep trying to locate them. If you get any information about where they are, call me at this number immediately, got it?"

"That's a roger."

I hung up and dialed Danielle back.

"Hello?" she said.

"Danielle, listen to me. I think we're looking for a research vessel from UDub called the Thompson."

"What does it look like?"

"Shit, Danielle, I'm not very good at this. It's probably about 250 or 260 feet long, about 50 feet wide and it's got lots of cranes and shit like that on the deck. I mean, it looks like a research vessel. And it's painted white. My guess is if you see anything about that size anywhere near the ferries or the Pier, it's probably the Thompson. I'm also guessing the terrorists have somehow hijacked the thing and are going to use it to deliver the explosives. You better get the rest of your guys in the air and quick. I don't think we have a lot of time. I have to go. I need to call Harry."

I hung up and immediately dialed Harry. "Harry, I just got a call from Cyril. I think there's a good chance the Thompson's been hijacked..."

"You're kidding."

"...and is going to be used to deliver that Semtex. I think you better alert your guys on the water and you better let me know if they spot it so I can pass the information onto Danielle. She's got an assault team ready but first we've got to find that ship."

"I'll get right on it."

I looked at my watch. 6:55. I called Danielle. "You see anything?"

"It's hard up here. It's just starting to get daylight, but we've got a low ceiling and heavy clouds so the visibility isn't great. The lower we go, the smaller the area we can see."

"Where are you now?"

"We're stationary over the city just east of the ferry terminal trying to take in the whole area."

"I'm standing on the edge of the pier looking out over the water. I'm not seeing anything that looks like the Thompson either."

"The only big thing I see is some kind of container ship just coming out from the west side of Harbor Island over to my left. Maybe you were wrong, John."

"Yeah, maybe. But it just feels right. Can you see the ferries?"

"Yes, I can. There's one just pulling into the pier. There's a second one about five hundred yards off shore that looks like it's going to pull in next to the first one, then there's a smaller one maybe a quarter of a mile from the dock and headed this way. Wait a minute...."

"What? You see something?"

"One of our guys just spotted something over by that container ship. It looks like a mast or an antenna or something sticking up from behind it. Something that looks like it doesn't belong there. We're going to go over and take a closer look."

I leaned over on the passenger side and grabbed a pair of binoculars from the glove compartment. Jumping out of the car and holding the phone to my ear, I ran over to my left to the far corner of the pier to get an unobstructed view in the direction she was talking about. Although it was cloudy and there was no sun to be seen, the sky had brightened somewhat and the visibility was a little better. I looked over toward Harbor Island, with all of its great cranes used for loading and unloading container ships and, at first, couldn't make out a ship of any kind. But as my eyes adjusted to the light and my brain began to sort out the various objects that had all kind of blended together in that flat, two dimensional world of binoculars, I could see a massive, slow moving container ship, fully loaded, moving out into the bay.

I took the binoculars away from my eyes and as I watched, I saw two things almost simultaneously. First, I saw a small black object in the sky heading away from the pier where I was standing and in the direction of the container ship. I hadn't noticed, but it must have flown almost directly over my head. At fifteen hundred feet, you'd have thought I would have heard it go over. But I think the reason I didn't notice it go over was I really wasn't looking for it and also because it wasn't making any noise.

The second thing I saw was an even smaller black object in the sky coming in from the left from the direction of Boeing Field and also heading toward the container ship.

As I put the binoculars back up to my eyes and looked in the direction of the container ship I saw something else. There was a second ship slowly appearing stern first from behind the stern of the container ship almost as if the container ship was passing it. But I knew the minute I saw it that the container ship wasn't passing it, because the container ship wasn't that fast. The smaller ship was slowing down to let the container ship go by. It was the Thompson.

"Danielle! Danielle! Can you hear me?"

"Yes, John, I can hear you."

"That's it! Behind the container ship. That's the Thompson. It must have come out from behind Harbor Island using the container ship as a shield so we couldn't see it." As I watched, it came fully into view. Then, as it cleared the stern of the container ship, the bow came around and the Thompson was headed straight for me.

Me and Pier 52 and a couple of thousand people.

"Gotta go, John." The line went dead.

I dialed Harry. "Harry, we found it! It's coming from the west side of Harbor Island and it's headed straight for the ferry terminal. Send whatever you've got over there. I think Danielle and her people are going to try to board it from the air."

Those bastards had done their homework. I don't think any of the small Coast Guard boats that escort the ferries had any kind of armament that could stop anything the size of the Thompson. And it was an ingenious plan. Under ordinary circumstances anybody seeing the Thompson out there probably wouldn't have given it a second thought. I don't know for sure, but I have to think the Coast Guard has some kind of profile they look for in terms of the type or size of boat that might represent a threat to the ferries. And I also have to think whatever that profile is, it certainly doesn't include a research vessel from the University of Washington. In fact, I'd be willing to bet that most of those Coast Guard guys would probably have waved at her as she went by. Surpri-ise.

I could tell from the size of the bow wake that the speed of the Thompson was increasing. By the looks of it, they were almost certainly planning to drive full speed into the pier then probably detonate the Semtex. At full speed and with the weight of a ship the size of the Thompson, even without the Semtex, they could easily tear a good sized hole in the pier and end up somewhere in the middle of it, creating no small amount of death and destruction. Add to that the explosive force of four hundred pounds of Semtex and you've got one hell of a mess on your hands, certainly on the order of a 9/11 disaster.

About thirty seconds later I saw and heard three Coast Guard patrol boats crank up their engines and scream away from the pier and in the direction of the Thompson. The Thompson was about a mile away and closing fast. I started searching the skies for the black helicopters and spotted both of them, one behind the other, making a big circle off to my left and apparently sweeping around to come up from behind. I'm guessing between their blackness, their quietness and their coming in from behind the Thompson, they were hoping for an element of surprise. I'm sure whoever was aboard that ship was certainly expecting some interest from the Coast Guard at some point. What I was hoping, and was sure Danielle and her group were hoping, was they weren't expecting an airborne assault.

I knew I should probably get the hell away from this pier, but I watched with some kind of almost macabre fascination – like the old cliché about not being able to take your eyes off of a train wreck. Like most people, I suppose, in the face of some approaching disaster, my brain couldn't process the potential destruction, even my own. Either that or I'm just plain stupid - which would explain a lot of things.

As I watched, the first helicopter came over the stern of the Thompson at about twenty or thirty feet and slowed to match her speed. At the same time four figures came out of the sides and slid down ropes or cables of some kind.. Before they got to the deck of the ship, four more figures emerged and did the same thing. In about a count of five, all eight figures were on the top decks of the Thompson and the chopper peeled off to one side and began to gain altitude.

Things were happening fast. The second helicopter came on low over the stern and the same act played out. In a space of about twenty seconds, there were sixteen black figures on the top and sides of the Thompson like ants on vanilla ice cream. They spread out in groups of two and disappeared through various doors or around to the sides away from me that I couldn't see.

Then – nothing. The Thompson had closed the distance between us from when I first saw her emerge from behind that container ship to about half a mile. People on the pier were oblivious to the impending disaster and it was way too late to try to get everybody off and away from the waterfront. C'mon, Danielle, c'mon.

The Thompson was still was steaming straight at me at a pretty high rate of speed. The second ferry was just pulling into the pier and, from where I was standing, I could see the Vashon Island passenger ferry almost to the pier over to my left. If the Thompson kept coming, it was going to hit the pier right about at the time I had guessed.

Suddenly, there was a rise in the crowd noise. Some people down close to the ferries and the edge of the pier must have noticed that a pretty big boat was headed at them full speed. There was shouting and pushing as the crowd began running away from the water front and back up toward Alaskan Way.

In about a second and a half pushing and shoving turned into full-blown panic as people looked for a way off the pier and didn't seem to care who they knocked over.

I looked back out over the water. Now I could clearly see

the bridge of the Thompson high up on the superstructure, a row of good sized windows running completely across the front of it and wrapping around the sides. This thing was close. Very close.

Suddenly, there was a brilliant flash of light from inside the bridge that lit up the row of windows like a hundred flash cameras all going off at once, followed by a second flash about two or three seconds later. That was followed about three seconds later by the sound of two 'whoomps' in quick succession. Stun grenades. A good sign – I think.

Still no change in speed or direction. Better run, John. Chaos had erupted around me. But I couldn't move.

With the roar of the crowd engulfing me like an avalanche, I suddenly heard someone calling my name.

"John! John! What the fuck are you waiting for?" It was Al. He grabbed my arm and tried to pull me away. "C'mon! Let's go!"

I grabbed his hand and pushed it away. "Get the fuck out of here, Al!"

He stood there for a second. Then he shook his head, turned and jogged away.

The wind was out of the west and over the crowd noise I could begin to hear the sound of intermittent gunfire coming from the direction of the Thompson with an occasional louder thump but no light flashes this time. Some kind of grenades, probably below deck.

I moved closer to the edge of the pier. A lone figure emerged from one of the doors toward the stern deck, turned and fired a nasty looking assault weapon and ran behind a large container that was sitting on the deck. The ship was still coming straight at me. Turn, you son of a bitch, turn.

Suddenly, right side of the ship was becoming more visible. It began a slow turn toward my right and away from the pier. The entire right side of the Thompson was now visible and I could see at least two groups exchanging heavy gun fire at fairly close range. A body fell over the rail and into the water. The gun fire was loud and the staccato of automatic weapons pierced the sound of the crowd streaming off the pier.

The smaller Coast Guard boats were all around it, dwarfed by the size of the Thompson. They seemed to be firing at the Thompson, the rattle of the 50mm canons clearly could be heard and the muzzle flashes easily seen.

In the midst of all the noise and activity here on the pier, I spotted four or five of the good guys made their way up to the bow of the Thompson. I could make out two black bodies lying on the deck. Not a good thing. Shit.

As the ship changed direction and continued off to my right, various parts of the ferries and the pier structure began to interfere with my view. Cars were coming off the first ferry that had arrived as all of this was going on and the State Patrol cops were furiously trying to get as many of them as far away from the waterfront as possible. Whistles were blowing and engines were racing.

I tried to run back to my right to a different part of the pier in hopes of getting a better view. A wall of cars and people were all going the other way. I got pushed backward a couple of times but, thank God, didn't get knocked down.

By the time I got through the line of traffic and people up to where the second ferry was vomiting people and cars, I could just barely see little glimpses of parts of the Thompson as it continued on past the second ferry and the terminal building. I could still hear gun fire and so could everyone else. There was now full blown panic on the pier. Women were screaming and grown men were knocking people down to get away. So much for women and children first.

I finally made my way up to the northern end of the pier where I had a clear view of the bay. By that time the Thompson was headed back out toward the middle of the harbor and putting some distance between it and the Seattle waterfront. I could barely see an occasional muzzle flash and I could just make out the sound of gunfire. There was white smoke coming from one of the windows on the bridge. The battle appeared to be pretty much over.

The good news was there hadn't been any large explosions. The bad news was there had been a serious fire fight on the Thompson and, as far as I knew, Danielle was right in the middle of it.

As the Thompson got smaller, I stood and watched it go. It was over. Somehow we got it right. This time. What is it they say? We have to be right every time, they only have to be right once?

Suddenly I felt very tired. My legs were feeling rubbery and I started to shake all over. The last time I shook like that was years ago when I had pneumonia and my fever began to break. I couldn't stop shaking then and I was having trouble stopping now. It's a feeling of being incredibly cold, but not from the outside.

I turned away from the water, leaned heavily on a piling, and looked around me.

I thought about why I hadn't just gotten the hell off the pier. I didn't know. Later on, the best I could come up with was that it had something to do with not wanting to run away while Danielle was putting her life on the line.

The panic on the pier had pretty much settled down into general chaos. People coming and going, mostly headed into the city to go to work or whatever was on their agendas for today, not knowing how close they had come to becoming another rallying cry in the war on terror. Something else some group of politicians could use to justify whatever the hell they wanted to justify. But not today, scaremongers, not today.

I started walking back to where I had left Callahan. I'd almost forgotten about him. I wasn't stupid enough or naïve enough to think that a whole bunch of people were going to be arrested here in Seattle or in DC or wherever the hell else they were dug in. I wasn't even sure we could make anything stick against Callahan. But I thought maybe, just maybe, some of these super patriots, whoever they turned out to be, might get some small measure of good old fashioned American justice.

I walked up to the driver's side door, put my hand on the handle, and looked around one more time. "How the hell did I ever get involved in this?" I said out loud to no one in particular. And I remembered something someone said to me years ago when I was working my way through college. I was working in an all-night bowling alley and we had a new night manager. I asked the manager one day how the new guy was doing. He said to me: "You know, the other day I caught him talking to himself. I think he's gonna be ok." I've thought about that from time to time over the years when I catch myself talking to myself and I think: 'I'm gonna be ok'.

I climbed into the car behind the wheel and turned the key to start the engine. "C'mon, Callahan," I said, without looking back, "let's go. You've got a big day ahead of you."

The State Patrol guy directing traffic off of the ferry held up his hand and stopped the line to let me in. As I pulled off the dock the smell inside the car hit me. "Jesus, Callahan," I said, looking at him in the rear view mirror, curled up in an almost fetal position, "You stink."

Chapter 61

I woke up with a start. The speaker must have been right over my seat.

"Ladies and gentlemen, this is your captain. We're on our final approach and we should be on the ground in about twenty minutes, approximately fifteen minutes ahead of schedule. The weather in St. Thomas is clear with a few afternoon clouds, temperature is eighty-five degrees with a five to ten knot breeze out of the north north-east. We hope you'll have a pleasant stay whatever your final destination. Flight attendants please prepare the cabin for landing."

I pushed up the little plastic window shade and looked down. We were over crystal clear aquamarine water. It's hard to tell how high up you are when all you can see is water, but every so often I could see a sail boat and cold tell we weren't very high. I heard the high pitched whirring sound of the flaps coming down and could feel the plane slowing.

It's a long flight from Seattle and for most of it I just read or dozed. But now that we were close, I was starting to get itchy. Even with the two hour lay-over in Atlanta, I just wanted to be out of my seat and off of this airplane.

It was hard to believe almost four months had gone by since that nightmarish week-end. On the one hand it seemed like only yesterday. On the other hand, it seemed like forever ago. Every once in a while since then I would try to remember what life was like before the first week-end in November. I know a lot of things have changed, but it's been hard to put my finger on it. I know my attitude toward my own life is different.

My reverie was interrupted by a flight attendant whose skirt was just a little too tight.
"Please put your seat back up," she said with a smile. Of course, like a good little passenger, I complied. But I'm always puzzled about the seat back thing. So here's this gigantic aluminum tube with about two hundred people literally stuffed into it like a great metal sausage, hurtling toward the ground at about – what? – two hundred miles an hour? And the only thing the flight attendants are concerned about is that three inches between the seat being back and it being in the 'full, upright position'. 'You see, sir, if the plane crashes and your seat is back, you'll die. But if your seat back is in the full, upright position, you should walk away without a scratch.' Or maybe it's because if everyone leans forward the pilot can get an extra ten miles an hour out of this sucker.

The wheels came down and the plane got a little 'mushy' as it swayed from side to side. I looked out the window again and now the water was much closer. If you've ever flown into St. Thomas, you know that landing or, actually, coming in for a landing is about as close as most of us will ever get to an act of pure faith. It's almost a religious experience.

The water gets closer and closer and there isn't a speck of land anywhere in sight, at least from my window. The faith part comes in where you have to believe that just before the wheels touch down, or hopefully before the captain says something like: 'Brace for impact', there will be something solid under them. I don't know about anybody else, but all of a sudden I'm wishing I had paid more attention back in Atlanta when the flight attendants were talking about where my life jacket was stowed and how I was suppose to blow it up.

Just as I was about to give up hope, the water turned quickly to a ribbon of rocks and beach that flashed by under the plane, then into black top as the wheels touched down and the engines reversed, pulling me and everyone else about six inches forward in our seats. Those engines can't be in reverse for more than about three seconds, but I don't care how seasoned a flyer you are, you can't help but wonder if this thing, as it shakes and shudders and those engines are roaring and hemorrhaging almost to the point of self-destructing, is ever going to stop.

But it did and rolled up to the terminal. There was instantaneous commotion in the cabin as everyone jumped up, started popping open the overhead compartments and grabbing their luggage. It's always amazing to me what some people consider a 'carry-on'.

In any event, we filed off the airplane and down the steps to the tarmac.. There's something about stepping out into that warm tropical sun, suitcase in hand, sun glasses on, heading down those rolling steps and walking across the tarmac to a plain, low one story terminal building that transports you to a different time. If you didn't look back at the 737 sitting behind you, you could almost imagine you'd just stepped off of an old DC-3 or an even older Ford Tri-Motor. Some people hear voices. I hear music. In fact, most of my life has a music sound track. And right now I could hear Al Stewart. Seattle was a million miles and a lifetime away.

The terminal building was hot and crowded. Very noisy, but a happy kind of noise. People hugging friends and relatives. And laughing. A lot of laughing. Here's another of my politically incorrect observations: Black people, especially island black people, know how to laugh. It comes from somewhere deep down. And, based on their history, you wouldn't think they have a lot to laugh about. We could all take a lesson. I've been a few places in the Caribbean and, except for those places where the cruise ships, those floating monuments to over-crowding, excess and generally bad taste, have pretty much ruined everything, including the normally good dispositions of the locals, the Caribbean people are among the nicest, friendliest people on the planet.

It took a while for my bag to come out, but you have to get used to 'island time'. If you're in a rush, this is definitely not the place for you. When my bag finally showed up on the conveyer belt, I scooped it up and headed out front to look for a cab. A young black man wearing a white shirt and navy blue pants came up to me. "Where to, mon?"

"Red Hook," I said.

"Right you are," he said. "Dat cab right over dere," and he pointed to a green van with the back hatch open and an older man loading luggage into the rear compartment.

I walked over to the van, handed the driver my bag and crawled into the middle row of seats. The windows were up, the a/c was on and I could feel myself beginning to relax, although I knew from past experience that real de-stressing for me takes a few days. I couldn't wait to taste that first drink. I didn't even care what it was, as long as it had fruit juice and rum and was cold enough to give me a brain freeze.

The cab filled up, the driver jumped in and pulled away from the terminal and I closed my eyes and listened to the conversation of the half dozen or so other people that were riding with me for the short trip to Red Hook. It was the usual excited chatter about where they were staying, what they were planning to do or what other people back home had told them they had to do. All very normal stuff. I smiled to myself and thought 'You folks have no idea how different your lives could have been.'

Red Hook is about ten minutes from Cyril King airport. There's not much there except a new ferry terminal. It's where you catch the ferry across to Cruz Bay on the island paradise of St. John. I haven't been here for a few years and, as we pulled into the drop off area, it was the first time I had seen the new terminal. It's ok, I guess. But not quite the charm or the laid back feel of the old one.

From the pier where I was standing waiting for the ferry, I could look across and see Cruz Bay and the orange roofed buildings dotting the green hills of St. John. Getting to St. John is like going through a series of air locks where each one has a little less pressure in it until you finally step out on the other side and take that first breath of something that's more than just fresh air.

The boat ride over takes about twenty minutes from dock to dock. And as I sat by the rail and gazed out across the water I thought again about that first week-end last November. For the most part, I've been avoiding thinking about it. It was what it was. At times over last four the months when I allowed myself to think about it at all, I always ended up playing out those 'what if' nightmare scenarios. Although it's probably not a good analogy – I still get myself in trouble with my analogies (some things never change) – have you ever had a close call in a car, maybe some guy comes across the yellow line when you're both doing eighty on the Interstate going in opposite directions and just at the last second he swerves a little left and you miss each other by an RCH? After your adrenaline goes down you start having daymares about how terrible it could have been? It's been kind of like that for me. Sometimes I think about how my life could have been different, if I had lived at all, and how the lives of so many other people could have been changed in an instant. I don't think you can truly appreciate the tragedy that was 9/11 unless you were actually there.

It turns out the terrorists were pretty high level and the Seattle operation was well organized. They had kidnapped and held hostage the wife of the Chief Scientist for the trip that left on the Thompson that Sunday night and coerced him into allowing two or three of their thugs to masquerade as part of the scientific party aboard the ship. The researchers were from a number of different institutions so it wasn't at all unusual that everybody didn't know each other. Three other terrorists had signed on as part of the crew, so there were six of them.

The other thing they coerced him into doing was certifying two bogus containers which actually held two hundred pounds of Semtex each. Only he didn't know it. Neither did he know this was planned to be a suicide mission. He was led to believe it was some kind of drug smuggling.

The terrorists took over the ship as soon as it cleared the Ballard Locks and locked all of the crew and scientific party on the mess deck. One crew member and two of the scientists were killed in the scuffle.

I do know that some lives were changed. After we cleaned him up and got him some clean underwear, George Callahan was arraigned and formally charged with six counts of accessory to murder. He was represented by a private attorney from Virginia who was well known back east for defending some high level political figures on various felonies, most of which you could classify as white collar crime, but had included some not-so-white collar crimes, as well. Most of his clients had never gone to trial and his main claim to fame seemed to be he was somehow able to negotiate plea bargain deals extremely favorable to his clients. For some reason, it didn't seem to be his trial skills that led to his success. One could only speculate as to where his real skill lay.

In any event, Callahan was released on one million dollars bail with surety, on the condition that he 'keep the peace and be of good behavior' and show up in court whenever he was supposed to. He never returned to his office - or to court, for that matter - and his deputy ran the department during his absence. About the middle of February, a deal was entered into whereby Callahan agreed to a detailed, no-holds barred interview with the new federal prosecutor who had been recently appointed to the position by the Obama administration. Callahan resigned from Customs and Border Protection and agreed to forego his federal pension. In exchange, the State of Washington agreed to dismiss all charges "for lack of evidence."

The Special Agent in Charge of the Seattle office of the FBI handed in his resignation to the Obama administration and it was accepted. It appeared, from what was learned from Callahan, that he really wasn't a player and had simply gone along with the two memos Anna Noble had stumbled across. His seemed to be more a sin of omission rather than one of commission, but I always found it hard to understand why he just went along with something that just smelled rotten. But then again my experience with the FBI had taught me that not all Special Agents in Charge are model citizens just out to protect and defend. Sometimes they have just a touch of political motivation in an effort to advance their careers that causes them to go along to get along, if you know what I mean. I think it's the difference between amoral and immoral, if you're into making such distinctions, but I could be wrong.

There was also a flurry of resignations right after the election and before the swearing in of the new President on January 20th. It was hard to tell which ones were legitimate, which ones were pro forma and which ones were influenced by outside pressures. Let's just say there were an unusual number of resignations in the Department of Justice and the Department of Homeland Security among some upper level people that one would not have ordinarily expected to hand in resignations just because there was a change in administrations.

Captain Harry O'Connell was transferred to DC. I think in civilian terms it's what's know as being 'kicked upstairs'. Harry didn't say too much about it other than he wasn't all that disappointed. He has a daughter living in Virginia that he was anxious to see more of and now he'd have the chance. And he could still get to sail. I think from what I could piece together the Coast Guard didn't quite know what to do about Harry. There was no evidence he had disobeyed a direct order but, on the other hand, it was equally evident he had been quite busy that November week-end. I think there were certain superior officers that tacitly approved of Harry's, shall we say, initiative? Anyway, his new job was still in homeland security but more policymaking than operational. All in all, not a bad fit for Harry.

In an interesting sidelight, shortly after the inauguration, the Chief resigned his position with the Seattle Police Department and was appointed to a fairly high level position in the new Administration. I have absolutely nothing to base this on – gee, John, what else is new? – but that could go a little way towards explaining his cautiously supportive response to our arrest of George Callahan. I thought about the Captain's remark about how he felt as if the Chief knew more about what was going on than one might think. If there is one thing I've learned from this whole experience, it's that whenever it comes to power and influence, Machiavelli only scratched the surface. There are alliances and power relationships in this country the average person couldn't dream of. And the people who appear to be in charge aren't always the people running the show.

We never did find out who the hit men who killed Anna Noble and a few other people, not to mention their abortive attempt on me, really worked for. Not too long ago Seymour Hersh did an article for the New Yorker about a group called the Joint Special Operations Command and his allegations about their connection to Vice-President Cheney. I'm not saying there's any connection here, but it points up the fact or the possibility, at least, that there are probably groups of individuals who carry out special operations for our government, or people in our government, that we probably don't want to know about and probably never will. As a cop, I hate loose ends. But I've learned to live with them. Especially after this.

Speaking of not knowing things, I never did find out which side of the fence Jeff Feinberg was on. I never saw him again after that one time at Pike Place Market and never spoke to him after that last phone conversation about Callahan. I suggested to Ed Noble that somebody keep a close eye on him. Ed was non-committal.

The ferry began to slow down as we came into the harbor at Cruz Bay. Off to my right on the hillside I could see a new condominium project that looked like it was almost finished. The times, as Dylan said, they are a changin'. I guess you can't stop progress and change even comes to a little piece of paradise like St. John.

But a few things still looked the same. Wharfside Village was still right here on the beach just as you get off the ferry and the High Tide beach bar was still right where it always was with that million dollar view of the beach, the harbor and St. Thomas. Now I could almost taste that first drink. I slung my old yellow duffel over my shoulder, picked up my suitcase and walked down the dock, past the little coral colored passenger terminal building. Just at the end of the dock where a few open air taxis were waiting, I stepped off the low wall to my right and headed the fifty feet across the beach to High Tide. It was about four in the afternoon and the sun was just starting to get lower in the sky over St. Thomas. It was still a little early for the afternoon crowd and I had my pick of the seats at the bar.

I dropped my gear on the tile floor and swung myself up onto a stool. The air was deliciously warm and the paddle fans overhead spun lazily creating just enough of a light breeze to carry the moisture off of my skin. The bartender was down at the far end of the bar pouring out some kind of frozen concoction for a young couple looking tan and randy.

I looked down the beach and out on the harbor and knew that coming here was the right decision. I could already feel that feeling I described where the stress begins to ebb away.

It had been a rough few months for me. After that weekend, and especially after I had left Callahan in the car, I began to really think about what my life had become, what I had become. And, frankly, I didn't like what I saw. I stayed with the Department for a while, but my heart wasn't in the job anymore. For the first time that I can remember, I started to think about my age and silencing that voice that kept wanting me to be 'conventional', whatever the hell that means. And I began thinking about my own mortality – not in a morbid, depressing kind of way, but just that, as much as we'd all like to think so, it doesn't go on forever. And if you're going to do it – whatever 'it' is – you'd better get on with it. I don't think the Department was all that unhappy with my decision. I'm pretty sure Pete Gilbert was relieved.

And then there was Danielle. It turns out that during the assault on the Thompson she had been shot twice and fell from one of the upper decks down to a lower deck, breaking her pelvis and her right hip, plus assorted other internal injuries. She was taken to Harborview Medical and, except when I was on duty or home sleeping, I lived there for almost a month until she was finally released. They put her on full paid medical leave and she went to live with her parents out on Bainbridge Island and start a long period of rehabilitation. After that, I didn't see her every day, but I saw her often enough. After about another two months of physical therapy, she and her parents decided she could get by on her own and needed a change of scenery. So they sent her to stay at a little warm weather vacation cottage that has been in the family for years. We corresponded, mostly by email, with an occasional cell phone call and she seemed to be doing quite well. She had a housekeeper to help out with stuff around the house and she swam nearly every day but still needed crutches to get around anything longer than from the couch to the kitchen or the bathroom.

As for me, I decided it was about time to live the dream. I quit the Department and spent a few weeks clearing up some odds and ends and made my travel arrangements to come here. My son let me store what few personal belongings I had at his house, and he and I went skiing for a week up at Whistler. Spending some time alone with him was one of the things at the top of my 'to do' list. During that whole period, I talked to my daughter a few times on the phone in whatever exotic places she found herself and exchanged emails with her and she was quite supportive of my decision. In fact, I'd go so far as to say that she encouraged it. I went on Air Gorilla and bought a cheap ticket down here and here I am, just a ferry ride away from Jost Van Dyke and some Foxy's Firewater Rum, about as close to paradise as you can get.

Just then a voice behind me said: "Hey, sailor, buy a girl a drink?"

I smiled and turned. "Sure," I said. "Just set those crutches down and hop up on this stool. What's your name cutie?"

Acknowledgement

No one writes in a complete vacuum and there are always people to thank. Of course, the problem is that you're likely to miss someone. So, with apologies to anyone I may have missed, I'd like to thank a few folks and offer them (and the ones I have inadvertently omitted) my undying gratitude. So, in no particular order...

I would like to thank first, last and always, my wife, Karen without whose unwavering love, support and encouragement this, my first novel, would never have been written.

Many thanks to Mark Jamieson and members of the Homicide Unit of the Seattle Police Department who helped immensely with police procedures. Some liberties have been taken for story telling value and any variation from actual procedures is strictly my own and due to no fault of theirs.

Thanks, also, to friends and family who reviewed various versions of the manuscript and offered their suggestions. Not an easy task but one which I truly appreciate.

And thanks to those who have purchased this book. You have only encouraged me to write more!

Don Gregory

CPSIA information can be obtained at www.ICGtesting.com
Printed in the USA
LVOW102249120612

285785LV00013BA/24/P